THE SWORD OF FATE

DENNIS WHEATLEY

DENNIS WHEATLEY

THE SWORD OF FATE

Frontispiece Portrait by
MARK GERSON

Original Illustrations by
PETER WHITEMAN

Distributed by
HERON BOOKS

*Published by arrangement with
Hutchinson and Co. (Publishers) Ltd.*

© *Brook-Richleau Ltd.*
© *1973, Illustrations, Edito-Service S.A., Geneva*

For

W. P. WATT

My good friend of many years'
standing, who advised me wisely
upon many things and who suggested the main theme of this
book

CONTENTS

CHAPTER I

AN ENGLISHMAN IN EXILE

AFTER all those hours of desperate seeking, after all those days of heart-breaking disappointment and nights of tortured longing, I had found her. Daphnis was lying there, sound asleep on a pile of rugs in a corner of the cellar. All my grim forebodings had been baseless, she was alive and well. Not a hair of her lovely head had been harmed. The light of an old beaten copper oil-lamp, which stood upon a rough table, was enough to show the tender, healthy flush of her cheeks and the gentle rise and fall of the coverings under which she lay.

The cellar was fairly large and had evidently been used as a storeroom. From the ceiling there hung a number of fat, home-made sausages, which bulged in places to the thickness of the muscle in a boxer's arm, and near them dangled some big bunches of dried herbs. One corner of the room was piled high with logs; in another there were some earthenware crocks and a child's rocking-horse, carved out of wood and hand-painted which, from its battered state, looked as though it had served the children of several generations in some peasant family. The third corner had evidently been cleared to make room for the pile of goat-skins upon which Daphnis was sleeping, and the fourth was occupied by the old worn stone stairway upon which I was standing. It was the only entrance to the cellar and the only light in daytime evidently came from a grille which was set high up, in a shaft cut in the thick stone wall. There was no heating and it was very cold.

I tiptoed down the stairs and across the room. A thick soft wrap of white angora wool was drawn up below Daphnis' chin. It was early yet and she was in the first deep sleep of night. An empty glass stood on the floor near the head of her rough couch. It had a faint white film in it, showing that it had contained milk, and the slightly sour smell mingled with the pungent spicy odour of the herbs and sausages.

The relief I felt at having found her now submerged all thought of time and place and danger. I knelt down beside her. At first it was difficult to realize that I was actually gazing once again at that dear familiar face, with the short straight nose and the little birthmark on the upper lip which had always played such

1

havoc with my senses. In these last weeks I had dreamed of them so often, only to wake to bitter disillusion, but the dark lashes which curled upon her cheeks and the firm, full-lipped mouth were real. I knew that time was precious, yet I wanted to prolong that unique moment of utter relief and happiness before I woke her and we began to plan how we might get away through the battle zone to the safety of the Allied lines.

I had few fears about getting her back through the battle zone. There must be many goat-tracks over the mountains as yet unguarded by the Germans, which we could take to if I had to abandon my car, and we could count upon the Greek peasants to aid us. Although it was most unlikely that anyone would discover until the morning that she had escaped and we had the whole night in front of us, the important information that she must have obtained while at the German G.H.Q. demanded that we should put as great a distance as possible between Ventsa and ourselves before dawn.

It was just as I put out my hand to touch her dark hair that a slight sound behind me made me turn my head. For a moment I remained utterly still; it was as though I had suddenly been gripped by a painless but acute paralysis. My muscles were numbed by the same horror and fear that one might experience on bending to smell a bunch of sweet-scented flowers and suddenly seeing coiled among their leaves a deadly snake, within a few inches of one's eyes and just about to strike.

Von Hentzen was standing framed in the arched doorway at the top of the stone steps and a big German Service automatic was gripped firmly in his hand.

He was now wearing a *feldgrau* Brigadier's uniform. It hardly showed against the grey stone walls, but his heavy-jowled face and high-domed head stood out white and livid.

Utterly unexpected and ill-timed for us as his sudden appearance was, it was not that which filled me with such indescribable dread. It was the fact that he seemed entirely oblivious of my presence. He was staring straight past my head at the sleeping girl. His gun was pointed not at me but at *her*, and from every line of his powerful bulky form there radiated cold, horrible purpose.

Next second the pistol spurted flame; the whole cellar seemed to rock with the deafening thunder of its repeated explosions. Before I could draw my gun or spring up and charge the stairs, the bullets thudded into the pile of rugs where Daphnis lay sleeping.

2

She half sat up, her mouth open, her eyes staring. Her hands fluttered helplessly.

But it is useless now to dwell upon that terrible moment. If I am to tell the story of my great love and of those fateful days in Egypt and Greece, I must begin at the beginning.

.   .   .   .   .

When the war broke I was at Splitz on the Dalmatian coast. All through the long hot August days I had enjoyed the bathing among the holiday crowd mainly composed of foreigners. For over two years past I had avoided English people of my own class for very excellent reasons.

During those years there had been so many war scares that by the time the real crisis came one's apprehensions had been blunted. It seemed almost certain that the French would urge us to give way, as they did at Munich, or that Hitler's bluff would be called at last and that he would climb down. Of course, there had been quite an exodus of the panicky ones during that last fateful week, but, to most of us, even on the Sunday morning when we learned that the time limit for the ultimatum was up and that Britain was once again at war with Germany, the whole thing seemed unreal.

Those who remained, mostly Central Europeans, gathered to drink their usual *Vermouth-Cassis* or *Amer-Picon* in the smart French bars that morning and it was only in the afternoon that they began to pack for a hurried return to their own countries lest these too should be drawn into a swift spreading of the conflagration.

Léonie lunched with me in my private suite at the hotel. She was a blonde and bewitching Dane, tall, blue-eyed, slender, and one of the most graceful swimmers that I have ever known. The strong sunshine of the Adriatic had bronzed her fair skin until she now looked like a golden goddess as, with easy strokes, she sped or twisted through the water. Naturally, Léonie assumed that inoffensive little Denmark was beyond all danger of being involved in the war, so she had decided to stay on, but, seeing that I was only twenty-six, she took it for granted that I should be going home to volunteer at once and I did not attempt to disillusion her. She had made my stay at Splitz a very happy one, so our farewells after luncheon were long and tender.

Léonie had been a delightful companion for those idle summer days, but when, for the last time, the doors of my suite closed behind her, she left nothing in my heart or in my rooms but a friendly memory and a lingering breath of intriguing perfume. As I felt sure the feeling, or rather lack of depth in it, was mutual, I had nothing to reproach myself with, and, going back into the bedroom, I lay down again to face the bleak uninviting future.

Yet, was it bleak and uninviting? For most people, definitely yes. The world had gone mad again and it might be years before it recovered. In the meantime, the lives of countless thousands of men and women would be prematurely ended in an abrupt and ghastly manner, while countless millions more would suffer every kind of hardship and privation quite unnecessarily and without any gain to show for it afterwards.

Even as I lay there, the Nazis might be preparing their air armada for its first devastating attack on London. At Munich Hitler had threatened Chamberlain that he would send over a hundred bombers an hour for twenty-four hours in succession. By morning two-thirds of the British capital might be in ashes, with half a million people slain or maimed. That was the way that most of us visualized large-scale air raids before they actually happened.

In any case, for the great majority, the war would mean the breaking-up of homes, the halting of careers, the ruin of businesses and the sacrifice of all personal ambitions. But what had I to lose?

It was over two years now since I had severed all connection with my family and the friends of my youth. I had a comfortable fortune, inherited from my father, which was skilfully dispersed in investments mainly in the Americas. I had no business, profession or occupation which could be smashed by the war and no home of my own which the war could wreck. In fact, except for a few weeks of hectic excitement the previous winter, during which I wrote the fore-runner to this journal, calling it *The Quest of Julian Day*, I had lived utterly without purpose ever since I left the Diplomatic Service.

Those days were still near enough for me to remember clearly how glorious I thought it would be to wake up every morning with no tiresome telegrams to decipher, no dreary routine reports to compile and no boring elderly people upon whom I was expected to dance attendance. But I soon found that nothing can be so wearisome as idleness or so desperately depressing as the thought that there's no one to give a tinker's cuss if you stay in

4

bed for the rest of your life, provided that you pay your hotel bill regularly each week.

Here, then, seemed to be the very escape from myself for which I had been longing. Instinctively, from the moment I had learned that the war was definitely on, I felt the natural urge to volunteer, but what I had not realized was that to me it might prove a real blessing in giving my life new usefulness and direction.

The only question was where and how should I get into the Forces? Owing to my peculiar position I still did not fancy the idea of going home, where I should certainly run into many of my old friends, and if I applied for a commission there was the horrid possibility that, at some stage of the formalities, those ghosts of my past might rise again to shame me.

It was then that I suddenly got the idea of going to Egypt. The previous winter, during my quest for Cambyses' treasure, I had come into contact with that great English police chief, Essex Pasha. He was one of the few people who knew the whole truth about the grisly skeleton that lay locked in my cupboard, yet I felt confident that he would smooth the way for me into one of the Services without my having to answer too many questions.

In the course of my self-imposed exile I had got to know the Balkans and the Near East fairly well, so I needed no travel expert to tell me that, apart from the airways which would be impossible at such a time, the quickest route to Egypt was by train through Sarajevo and the old Serbian city of Uskub, or Skoplje as they now call it, down to Salonika and by ship from there across to Port Said. I managed to catch the evening train and six days later I was in Cairo.

Essex Pasha received me very kindly, and after a short talk it was decided that I should be attached to the Arab Bureau. But please don't get the idea that I was booked for all sorts of exciting Secret Service work just because you happen to know that Lawrence of Arabia was attached to the Arab Bureau in the last Great War. I was recommended solely on the fact that, in addition to several European languages, I speak fairly fluent Arabic, and it was reasonably certain that later on a considerable number of interpreters would be required for attaching to troop formations.

It was abominably hot and dusty in Cairo, so I was glad enough, a few days later, to be posted to Ismalia on the Suez Canal, where I was to lend a hand in organizing new levies of Arabs which were being recruited as extra police to patrol the

5

canal banks as a precaution against attempts at sabotage. Everything was very rough and ready in those early days, so I carried out such orders as I could get and for the rest exercised my common sense, working for the best part of eighteen hours a day until we got things into some sort of order.

Later on, my position was regularized. The Major under whom I had been working gave me a decent chit; I did an abbreviated two months' course in Cairo and emerged from it at the end of January, 1940, with a commission as a full-blown second lieutenant of the Interpreter Corps.

By that time the first Australian and New Zealand units were arriving in Egypt for advance training before being despatched to France and I was attached to a New Zealand battalion. They were grand fellows and my duties were absurdly light, consisting almost entirely of arbitrating in an occasional dispute where an Arab farmer claimed that his crops or property had been damaged by the troops, and assisting the military police in keeping under control the swarm of beggars and hawkers that were always endeavouring to get into the camp.

As we were stationed no great distance from Cairo, I was able to go in and dine at the Semiramis or Shepheard's or Jimmy's whenever I felt like going gay and, for the purpose, in a patriotic effort to economize petrol, I bought a motor-bike—a form of transport that I found both novel and exciting.

Early in April, my first leave came along. Cairo was getting pretty hot again, so I decided to take it in Alexandria, and instead of going by train I thought it would be fun to use my new toy for the journey. Having strapped a suit-case on to the back of the bike, I set off in the cool of the morning and was there easily in time to lunch at the Cecil.

As I had stayed in Alex before, I already knew something of that extraordinarily cosmopolitan city. King Farouk has a palace and most of the wealthy Egyptians have summer places there, but it is not really an Egyptian town at all. The bulk of the population is either Greek or Italian, although, of course, there is a good sprinkling of English, French and Levantine Jews, with the inevitable multitudes of Arabs forming the poorer classes.

When approached from the land Alexandria is not much to write home about, as it appears to consist of a long straggling line of mud-walled houses and tumbledown shacks inhabited by swarms of dirty fly-blown people ranging in colour from lemon yellow to the darkest ebony; but from the sea Alex presents a very different picture as the eye takes in its thirteen miles of fine buildings, spread out along a whole series of great bays. The fact remains, however, that Alexandria is really a fine façade with an unrivalled water-front, but little depth and few buildings of importance behind it, so, to get from place to place along the seemingly endless front, considerable distances have to be covered and I found that my motor-bike saved me quite a lot in taxi fares.

During the first week of my leave we had the excitement of the war at last breaking out in earnest with Hitler's sudden invasion of Norway; but that made little difference to life in Egypt. I got to know quite a number of Anglo-Egyptians at the English Club, of which all British officers had been made honorary members, and among them a nice family called Wishart. The father was, I think, something to do with the railways; anyhow, it was on the eighth day of my leave that the two girls, Barbara and Dorothy, asked me to go out to their home at Ramleh for tea and tennis. Ramleh is the fine suburb at the extreme eastern end of Alexandria in which most of the English live, and with my flannels in a small bag, I set off on my motor-bike.

I had hardly covered a third of the distance and was still passing through the Park Lane of Alexandria, where the very rich Greeks live, when an Arab in a rickety Ford, just in front of me, ignoring all the rules of highway procedure, swerved right across the road. In trying to avoid him my front wheel ran over a patch of grease. The bike skidded violently. The front wheel twisted, the handle-bars were jerked out of my grip and I found myself sailing through the air over them, head foremost, straight for the nearest lamp-post.

I don't actually remember hitting it or anything else at all until I came to. I was lying in a large cool room on a comfortable sofa; a wet ice-cold compress was bound tightly about my head and as I opened my eyes Daphnis was bending over me. Her lovely face was within six inches of mine, and as our eyes met, in that very first glance, I knew that, if only I had the courage and resolution to win her, here was the one woman who would prove the crown and glory of my life.

CHAPTER II

THE VOICE IN THE NIGHT

I'VE had quite a lot of love affairs; to be honest, more than my fair share. Perhaps the gods gave me certain qualities which are attractive to women as a sort of compensation for the evil that they did me when they sabotaged my career in the Diplomatic at its very beginning and made me an outcast with no profession and no home. The very fact of my enforced idleness during the two years before the war had led me into all sorts of amorous adventures in half a dozen European countries and in the Near East as well.

I don't want to sound a prig, but it isn't good for a young man's morals to have no background, nothing to do except to amuse himself and plenty of money to do it with. Mind you, I'm not suggesting for one moment that I regret those locust years. Each of my affairs taught me something, not only about women but about their nationalities and a score of other things of which I should know little except for them. All the same, this constant seeking of forgetfulness in the company of good-looking girls, to which I had more or less been driven by my loneliness, had certainly tended to make me rather blasé.

That blaséness evaporated utterly the very instant that I set eyes on Daphnis. She was not just another potential mistress, like Léonie or Anita or Oonas, and to be honest I doubt if she would have won the prize in a beauty contest embodying all the young women that I had kissed since leaving England for the last time. Yet there was something breath-taking and compelling about her which stirred me more deeply than anything I had felt since my very first calf-love.

What it was I couldn't say. The curling ends of her dark hair hung forward a little over her shoulders as she leaned above me and her large, brown eyes, faintly flecked with tiny bits of gold, smiled down on me, while her lips parted and showed two rows of small, white even teeth. Her mouth had a little birthmark on the upper lip that just demanded to be kissed. But it wasn't her hair, or her eyes, or her mouth, or the set of her head on her shoulders, or the warm olive hue of her skin. God knows what it was but before she spoke I knew that it was a case of love at first sight—a thing in which I had flatly refused to believe until then.

"You're feeling better, yes?" the vision spoke, and in English,

8

guessing that, of course, to be my native tongue from the uniform that I was wearing.

"Yes," I muttered a little vaguely. "I think so; what happened?" And I raised a hand towards the wet bandages under which I had suddenly become conscious that I had the grandfather of all headaches.

With a quick gesture she caught my hand in her small soft one and pressed it down again, as she shook her head.

"No, no! You must not do that. Your head pains you, I expect, but that is natural. Luckily for you it proved harder than the iron lamp-post."

"Of course," I smiled. "That fool of an Arab cut right across in front of me, and in trying to avoid him the bike skidded. How long have I been out?"

"Out?" she repeated with a puzzled lift of the delicately arched eyebrows set wide above her eyes.

"Unconscious."

"Ten minutes—no, more than that. I was looking out of the window when the accident occurred and I called to them to carry you in here at once; but it must have taken me a quarter of an hour to bathe the wound and bandage your head."

Those were not her actual words, but just the sense of what she said. Her English was fluent but far from perfect, and she had a most entrancing accent, so it would be quite impossible for me to attempt to reproduce here the subtle charm of her voice.

I thanked her and tried to sit up but she pushed me back and told me that I must lie still until the military ambulance arrived to take me away.

In spite of the acute pain, which now seemed to be lifting and lowering the top of my skull, this piece of news did not please me a little bit. I said that I didn't want to go to hospital. If I might remain where I was for a while I should be quite all right later to go back in a taxi to my hotel.

But she shook her head. While her servants had been fetching her the water and bandages with which to treat my head, she had already telephoned to the hospital, so the ambulance was on its way.

I could hardly refuse to depart in it when it turned up, and I realized then that I might not have long with this lovely person who had so suddenly been thrust into my life. If I wished to see her again, I must make the best of my time.

Her name, it transpired, was Daphnis Diamopholus, and as I had supposed, she was a Greek. Her family, as I learned later, was one of those which had been established in Alexandria for countless generations; in fact, they had come over in the days when the Greek Ptolemies, of which Cleopatra was the last, had been the reigning dynasty of Egypt; thus forming an aristocracy older by a thousand years than that of the English families whose forebears had crossed from Normandy with William the Conqueror.

Having thanked her for her ministrations and assured her that my head hardly hurt at all, although, actually, it was giving me the very devil, I asked her if she would allow me to show my appreciation of her kindness by giving her lunch next day at the Hotel Cecil.

To my surprise, her chin shot up and she gave me a haughty look accompanied by a curt refusal. Of course, it is true that we had not been formally introduced, so perhaps it did appear that I was rather rushing my fences, but I had been careful to word the invitation with almost formal politeness and I saw no reason why she should put on such a disdainful air about it.

"Whatever's the matter?" I enquired anxiously. "Have I said something that I shouldn't?"

"I regret," she replied, "if I appeared rude without cause. For the moment I had forgotten that you could hardly be expected to know our social customs. It probably sounds very old-fashioned to you, but in Alexandria Greek girls of good family never go out unchaperoned, and it is regarded as an insult for a man to suggest it."

"It's my turn to apologize." I managed to raise a smile. "But don't you find that awfully dull?"

"No," she smiled back. "I have many girl friends and er . . ." her eyes held a faint twinkle, "we see as much as we wish of men at entertainments in private houses."

"That's all very well," I said, "but I want to thank you properly for bandaging me up and everything. And I want to see you again."

"You have thanked me quite enough already for the very little that I've done," she said demurely.

"What about my calling on you here?"

"My mother would probably receive you. It is only by chance that I happen to be in alone this afternoon. But my mother does not encourage young men who are outside our own social sphere, so having accepted your thanks on my behalf she would, I am certain, have you shown out again."

"Do you mean that I wouldn't even be allowed to see you?" I exclaimed.

10

She nodded solemnly, but her eyes were mischievous.

"But, good lord alive!" I protested. "In that case, you're virtually in purdah; and even Mohammedan women are kicking over the traces about that sort of thing in these days."

Her expression changed. "It is unnecessary to be rude about the customs of my people," she said frigidly. "We find them perfectly satisfactory and my friends and I have no reason to complain. In fact, you English would have retained a much stronger hold on India and Egypt if your women had been kept more strictly and they had not lost the respect of the native populations by flaunting themselves in public, as many of them are apt to do."

Set down in writing, that may sound distinctly prudist, but I am certain that Daphnis did not mean it that way, and actually there's a lot to be said for the view she had expressed. White women, wearing the scanty clothes that have been the fashion for the last quarter of a century, have done the British Empire no good at all; and from films the coloured peoples have learnt, that they are just about as frail and sometimes as vicious as any other race, which has lowered our stock immensely.

If my head hadn't been hurting so damnably I might have thought up some plausible reply, but the loud clanging of a bell in the street cut into my laboured thoughts. A moment later a fat Egyptian butler in flowing white robes and a red fez appeared to herald in two stretcher-bearers and an R.A.M.C. corporal who had arrived with an ambulance.

Daphnis told them in a few quick words what had happened. They lifted me on to the stretcher and I only had time to say:

"Good-bye—for the moment. As soon as I'm fit, I mean to try to see you again; even if I have to have another accident on your doorstep."

She laughed then, a low delightful laugh, but she shook her head.

"You're very persistent and that's a pity, because, as you English say, we are only ships that pass in the night. But I hope that you will soon be quite recovered from your injury."

I suppose it was the excitement that she stirred in me which had braced me up during that brief conversation, but by the time I was in the ambulance and my bike had been strapped on behind I was feeling pretty grim.

At the hospital the doctor examined the wound and said that I had come off lightly, as cracking my head on a lamp-post with such force I might easily have smashed my skull. My thick black hair had saved me from worse than a cut scalp into which they

11

put four stitches, and a slight delayed concussion, but I knew by then that I should not be fit to leave hospital for some days.

They gave me a shot of something which secured me a good night's sleep, and apart from a dull ache in the head, I didn't feel too bad next morning. I wasn't allowed to read, and even if I had been I doubt if I should have bothered because my mind was entirely occupied with thoughts of Daphnis. I found that I could recall practically every word she had said, her swift changes of expression from grave to gay, and even the fascinating lilt of her voice, with its faint foreign accent and the quaint unusual way of expressing herself in English, which was such a feature of her personality.

I was absolutely determined to get to know her and the very fact that, as opposed to the young women with whom I had amused myself on my travels, she was so difficult of access made my determination all the stronger.

As a first step I got one of the nurses at the hospital to look up the number of the Diamopholi house and to order a huge bunch of stephanotis to be sent to Daphnis from the best florist in Alexandria. I purposely refrained from enclosing a note or card, as I wanted to intrigue her and I meant to keep the game up daily.

At first she might wonder who the flowers had come from, then, having ascertained that they were not from any of the young men that she knew in the Greek colony, I judged that sooner or later she would decide that they must be from me. If there were no doubt about it in the first instance she would probably brush the arrival of the flowers almost immediately from her mind, but the element of uncertainty was bound to occupy her thoughts and that was what I wanted.

I was so immersed in my speculations about her that even the news that British troops had landed in Norway hardly raised a flicker of interest in me.

On the third day I was able to get up and on the fourth I was allowed out for a short walk. On my return I found a note waiting for me. It was in a sky-blue envelope of expensive-looking paper and addressed in a heavy angular hand which did not look like that of a woman; but on opening it I saw at once that it came from Daphnis. It simply said:

Mademoiselle Daphnis Diamopholus has learned from the florist that the flowers which have been reaching her these days have come because ordered to by the Lieutenant Julian Day. Mademoiselle

12

Diamopholus makes request to Lieutenant Day that these stop please, because they make only embarrassment for her with her family.

That could hardly be considered very encouraging. Naturally, I tried to read into it that it was not Daphnis who objected to accepting the flowers, but that their daily arrival had caused her people to question her and make her write this note; putting the strange Englishman, who had temporarily and quite fortuitously known the hospitality of their house, in his proper place. However, on being firm with myself, I was forced to admit that there was no real indication of that at all. Perhaps I had blundered in sending her flowers every day and her people probably had questioned her, but there was no hint in the letter at all of thanks for the flowers or any expression of hope that I was well on the way to recovery.

After a little I sat down and wrote a note myself which read:

Mr. Julian Day regrets extremely to have caused Mademoiselle Daphnis Diamopholus the least shadow of embarrassment. He is only anxious to show his gratitude for her angelic ministrations to him in his hour of need, and within the course of the next few days he has great hopes that he will be able to find a way of doing this without offence.

I had no idea as yet what my next move was going to be, but I felt fairly confident that my note would keep the beautiful Daphnis guessing. Of course, if her affections were, as they say, 'already engaged elsewhere', there was going to be very little hope for me; but I don't believe there is a girl living who, provided she is heart-free, can keep her thoughts from a new admirer who has promised her some sort of surprise in the near future.

On the following day, having been placed on the convalescent list, I was able to take a taxi out to the scene of my accident. After driving past the Diamopholi house, I told the man to take me round to the street which lay behind it. As I had hoped, it was a quiet thoroughfare, one side of which was entirely occupied by walls at the bottoms of the gardens of the houses in Alexandria's 'millionaires' row'. I stopped the taxi and after careful checking identified the back of the Diamopholi mansion. The garden wall had a small postern door in it, but it was a good eighteen feet high, so I could see nothing of the garden except the tops of three palm trees.

I then drove back to the shopping centre of the town and spent a considerable time inspecting the stocks of half a dozen jewellers.

At last I found something to suit my purpose. It was not a valuable jewel. I knew that anything costly would certainly be sent back to me by return of post; but it had the appearance of age and unusualness, which was what mattered. The stone itself was an aquamarine, about the size of a small hazelnut. It had been cut to the shape of a heart and was edged with golden filigree which had as its design the astrological symbols of the Sun, Moon and Planets.

That night I despatched the pendant to Daphnis with another note, which ran:

Mr. Julian Day is now happy to be able to fulfil his promise. If, on the night of the next full moon, Miss Diamopholus will act as directed, she will learn a thing which can hardly fail to interest her.

She should mark out a triangle in the dust on the ground between any three palm trees; then, carrying a fair-sized bowl of fresh water and the enclosed amulet, she should enter the triangle. Placing the bowl of water on the ground, Miss Diamopholus should walk three times round it with the amulet clasped in her right hand. She should then halt, facing north, and, on the stroke of midnight, she should kneel down, pressing the amulet to her heart. She will then see, reflected on the surface of the water, the face of the man whom she is to marry.

Of course, the whole thing was the most utter hocus-pocus, but I do not think that any land in the world is so superstition-ridden as Egypt and I felt that it was a safe bet that Daphnis, being a member of a family which had lived in Egypt for hundreds of years, would be a convinced believer in the power of amulets to foretell the future.

The full moon was due two nights hence and, since she would neither come out with me nor receive me at her home, I hoped to lure her into the garden after her family had gone to bed. I had said *any* three palm trees, but I was counting on the fact that, since three palm trees stood just below the windows at the back of the house, she would hardly be able to resist trying out the experiment there.

Most of my second week of leave had been spent in hospital, and actually I was due to return to my unit on the night of the full moon; but I was not unduly perturbed by that as I felt confident that I could obtain convalescent leave as a result of my smash, and so it proved. On the sixth day after the accident

14

I was discharged and granted six days' additional furlough to recuperate before reporting back for duty.

That afternoon I visited the Arab seamen's quarter down by the docks and I did not have to pick my way far through the filth and garbage that litters those evil-smelling narrow streets before I found what I wanted—a ship's chandler. There I bought a grapnel which would have served to anchor a small boat, and a twenty-foot coil of thin rope, both of which I took back to the hotel with me, wrapped up in a piece of sacking.

I confess to a certain suppressed excitement as I sat down to dinner in the restaurant that evening; and, as I did not wish to have my thoughts distracted by casual conversation with people in the lounge afterwards, I decided to draw out the meal as long as possible. For that reason I ordered my favourite dishes, a special sweet and a bottle of champagne, then lingered over a double ration of coffee and a couple of Benedictines.

By the time I had done there was not very long to while away as I meant to walk to the back of 'millionaires' row' and to be in the Diamopholi garden before there was any chance of Daphnis coming out into it; so that I could conceal myself there and there would be no risk of her being frightened away by the noise of my coming in over the wall.

When I left the hotel I was carrying the grapnel and rope in its wrapping of sacking and over my brown shoes I had on a pair of goloshes that I had bought that afternoon. The night was fine, but the full moon was not showing to its best advantage as the sky was cloudy. I looked on that as a sign that Venus favoured my intentions, as, in brilliant moonlight, I should have stood much more risk of being spotted and taken for a burglar when I attempted to scale the high wall.

I arrived in the street behind the Diamopholi mansion at twenty past eleven. Few people were about and the silence was only disturbed by the passing of an occasional car along the main road some distance away. I tried the little door in the wall, but, as I expected, it was locked. Stepping back into the road I made quite certain that no one was approaching, then took the grapnel and rope from the sacking. Grasping the extreme end of the rope firmly, I flung the grapnel high into the air so that it sailed right over the top of the eighteen-foot wall.

It hit the brickwork on the far side with a sharp clink, but no other sound followed, so I gently hauled in on the rope until the grapnel came up and, my luck being in, hooked itself firmly at the very first trial on to the wall. I then used the rope to support the weight of the upper part of my body and swung my feet out flat against the wall, so that, going up hand over hand, I could virtually walk up it, thus preventing the old brickwork dirtying my uniform, except when I had to straddle the wall on reaching its top. Having refixed the grapnel and transferred the rope to the far side, I lowered myself into the garden and, all things considered, arrived there with remarkably little dust or dirt on my hands and clothes.

Enough moonlight was percolating through breaks in the clouds to show me the lay-out of the garden. It was little more than a large oblong sandy courtyard, with the three palm trees in the middle and a few formal beds of flowers at each side. Fortunately there were a few shrubs against the bottom wall to hide behind if necessary, and at the far end near the house I could just discern what appeared to be a small sunk garden with a fountain in its centre.

It was barely half past eleven so I thought I would investigate the place a little further before settling down in the most convenient hide-out. The back of the house was in complete darkness, so it seemed as though the family had already gone to bed. I advanced cautiously along one of the side walls until I was level with the nearest palm tree. It was then, for the first time, I suddenly became aware that I was not alone in the garden.

With alarming unexpectedness a match flared as someone near the fountain lit a cigarette and in the flame I just caught a glimpse of a man's face. He was looking my way and had his back to the house, from which he was hidden by some ornamental brickwork.

At the first spark I had gone dead still, knowing that if I remained so it was most unlikely that my outline would be distinguishable from the other shadows among which I stood; and, almost at once, I caught the sound of lowered voices. The man was not alone, and although I could not catch any distinct words, the tone in which the two people were talking told me that they were in earnest conversation.

Whoever they were, they presumably had a right there, whereas I had not, and if the moon suddenly came out they could hardly fail to catch sight of me before I should have time to get under cover. With cautious footsteps I beat a hasty retreat to the bottom of the garden, where I selected the thickest patch of bushes and sat down behind them patiently to await events.

For the best part of quarter of an hour nothing happened. I was too far off now either to see or hear anything of the two people near the fountain but at last the sound of footsteps told me that they had come out of their concealment and were approaching. The moon was now hidden completely so I could hardly see a thing, and as the footsteps grew nearer I sensed rather than saw that the man's companion was a girl.

At the postern door they halted and they could not have been standing much more than two yards from me. A key turned in the lock, then the girl's voice came quite clearly. It was Daphnis and she was speaking in Italian.

"I do hate all this subterfuge. Can't you possibly make some arrangement with Mother so that we can meet openly?"

My heart seemed to go down into my boots. Evidently she already had a lover and one in whom she was sufficiently interested to allow him to meet her clandestinely by night, so it seemed that there was little hope for me. Before I could speculate further upon this depressing revelation, the man replied, also speaking in Italian:

"But, my dear, your stepfather would never allow it. He hates me like poison. No, our meetings must continue to be in secret and it is better so; otherwise someone might become suspicious, and that would ruin everything."

I took the words in automatically, thinking little of their sense. It was their tone which riveted my entire attention. I knew that voice; I had heard it somewhere before. Where I could not think, but it had a ring about it that was quite unmistakable; a self-opinionated arrogance, tempered with a mock-politeness, and in my mind it was associated with a memory that was definitely disagreeable. Strive as I would, I could not recall the circumstances in which I had heard that voice before, but every fibre of my being cried out to me that I had reason to fear and hate its owner.

CHAPTER III

UNDER A CLOUDED MOON

THE sound of that sinister voice which stirred such vague and disquieting memories in my mind had come as such a shock to me that I was not conscious of Daphnis and the man saying good night; only that, having locked and bolted the postern door, she had turned and was walking back to the house.

As she disappeared in the shadows, I turned my face to the wall, lit a cigarette and, rising from my cramped position, stood up with the cigarette cupped carefully in my hand so that the burning end of it would not show.

I wondered if it was worth waiting now, and rather doubted it. Whether she was superstitious or not, Daphnis was hardly likely to be much intrigued by an amulet, sent her by a young man she hardly knew, when she was already deeply involved in a secret love affair. Still, there could not be much more than six or seven minutes to go till midnight, and it seemed silly not to make quite certain that I had entirely wasted my evening, before climbing back over the wall.

As I stood smoking there, I noticed that the clouds had become much more broken and that the moonlight was now filtering through sufficiently to fill the garden with a dim, uncertain light. Just as I had finished my cigarette, there came faintly on the light breeze the call to prayer of a muezzin from some distant minaret in the centre of the town. It was midnight but there was no sign of Daphnis.

I thought with regret of how I had planned to carry my ruse to its logical conclusion. During the whole of that day there had never been far from my thoughts the exciting vision of Daphnis walking round the bowl of water, then kneeling down facing the north, which was towards the house and would mean that her back was turned towards me, while I crept noiselessly up behind her and peered over her shoulder so that it should be my face which would be reflected on the moonlit surface. As bitterly disappointed as though the little scene had actually been promised to me, I was about to grasp the dangling rope when I caught sight of something whitish moving in the moonlight near the house.

Next moment I felt a terrific thrill. It was Daphnis. She had come out again, and as she approached I saw that she was wearing a loose white woollen robe over her dress, which had big full sleeves and was tightly girded at the waist.

When she reached the middle of the three palm trees she halted, but she carried no bowl of water with her and just stood there, apparently waiting for something to happen. I was in two minds whether to emerge from my hiding-place at once or to wait for a little to see what she would do when, quite unexpectedly, the question was answered for me. It was very still there in the garden, and although she spoke hardly above a whisper, I heard her say distinctly:

18

"Mr. Day, where are you?"

Feeling the most awful fool, I came out from behind the bushes and walked across to her. With a rather sheepish smile I murmured: "Good evening. How clever of you to guess that I meant to appear in person!"

"It didn't need much intelligence to see through that business of the amulet," she said slowly; "particularly as it seems that you're determined to get me into trouble."

"Oh, come!" I protested. "You know that I don't want to do that, but I simply *had* to see you again somehow."

The moon had now come out from behind the clouds. It was shining on her face, and as she stood in front of me I thought her more lovely than ever.

"You're the most beautiful thing I've ever seen," I hurried on. "I'm simply crazy about you!" And to lend force to my words I seized one of her hands and pressed it in both of mine.

In the past I had often said much the same sort of thing to other girls. Women always seem to expect it if you make love to them, but this time I was not acting and I think the earnestness of my voice must have carried conviction. She did not seek to draw away her hand and she smiled.

"You only saw me for a few minutes after you had had that awful crack on the head so you can't possibly be in love with me."

"But I am—desperately."

"That's a pity, because we live in different worlds. Nothing could come of it."

"Nonsense!" I said almost rudely. "How old are you, Daphnis?"

"Eighteen."

From her well-developed figure I should have thought that she was at least twenty, but women of Latin blood mature quickly in such countries as Egypt. At eighteen they are often married and the mother of a child.

"You're quite old enough to know your own mind and follow your own inclinations," I said. "Tradition is all very well, and I know it's the custom among the wealthy Greek families of Alex to keep themselves very much to themselves, but we're living in an age when women smoke, wear trousers and drink cocktails—in fact, they do as they darn' well please, so why shouldn't you —er—er—form a friendship with a British officer?"

"I've told you already that nothing could come of it, and I —well, I'm not certain that I want to."

19

"You knew I meant to get into this garden tonight, and you came down to meet me. If you didn't want to be friends, why did you do that?" I asked with a smile.

Her answer came without hesitation and its frankness was positively startling, "I couldn't resist the temptation to see if you really were as good-looking as I thought you the other day."

I laughed a little awkwardly: "If I were as good-looking a man as you're beautiful a girl, I'd be the handsomest fellow in the world."

It was a clumsy compliment, but for some extraordinary reason I was finding it infinitely more difficult to say the right things to this girl with whom I had fallen so genuinely in love than I ever had to women like Oonas or Deirdre, with whom I was only amusing myself. Yet, somewhat to my surprise, she took my words quite seriously, and opening her wide big eyes she said:

"Do you really believe that I am as beautiful as all that?"

I raised her little warm hand and kissed it as I murmured, "You're more lovely than the Princess out of any story from *The Arabian Nights*."

"I think we're both a little mad," she said suddenly. "I certainly should be if I believed you. As it is I'm taking a crazy risk, standing here talking to you in the full moonlight. At any moment, if any of the servants happened to wake up and look out of the window they would see me."

"Let's go into the shadow, then." I quickly took her arm and drew her along one of the side-walks to where a few steps led down to the fountain. There was a stone seat in a corner there which was out of view of the house. As we sat down on it she gently removed her arm from my clasp. Producing my cigarette-case, I offered it and she took one. After I had lit it for her she said with a sigh:

"I'd never dare to do this if Mother were at home."

"What, smoke?" I asked, perhaps a little stupidly.

She laughed. "Of course not! I often smoke and I wear trousers, and no one would stop me drinking cocktails if I wanted to. I meant sit out here with you."

"Your mother's away, then?"

"Yes. She's staying with friends in Cairo and is not due back until the day after tomorrow."

Silence fell between us and we just sat there, smoking nervously. Why, I can't think, but all my *savoir faire* seemed

20

suddenly to have deserted me. I never remember having been tongue-tied before, but I simply could not think of a single opening to resume our conversation. Everything that occurred to me seemed banal, stupid or facetious. Perhaps Daphnis had this extraordinary effect on me because she was so different from any other girl that I had ever met, but, fortunately, she did not seem to notice the frustration and mortification that I was feeling. It was she who at last broke our long silence.

"How long have you been stationed in Alexandria?"

"I'm only here on leave," I told her, "and I should have returned to my unit tonight, but owing to the crash I've now got an extra six days."

"Is your head quite all right now?"

"Yes, thanks. It was pretty painful at first, but for the last few days I've suffered no ill-effects except slight headaches."

Again that silence, so strange and so embarrassing to me, fell between us. There were a hundred things that I wanted to ask her and I knew so well that I was absolutely throwing away those golden moments when I should have been exerting myself to the utmost to entertain and interest. Yet somehow that half-serious, half-amusing chatter which usually came so glibly to my tongue when I was alone like this with a girl continued to elude me.

We could not have been sitting there much more than ten minutes, although it seemed like an hour, when she suddenly stood up and announced:

"It's getting late. I must go in."

"No, no, please don't!" I protested hastily. "I've got so much that I want to say to you."

"Really!" Her eyebrows arched and the smile which, when it appeared, seemed to light up her whole face, came again. "I was beginning to think that you were one of those strong, silent men that women novelists write about."

"I'm not," I assured her, "not in the ordinary way, at least. It's just the absolutely devastating effect that you have on me."

"Whatever do you mean?"

"Simply that, normally, I've always got masses of things to talk about, and that, for the whole of the past week, I've been simply dying to talk to you; but, now that I've got the chance, I feel as shy and tongue-tied as a boy of sixteen at his first dance."

"You know," she said, "I believe you really mean that and it's the nicest thing you could possibly have said; but I'm going in now, all the same."

For a moment I was torn between two urges: the one to make

21

her stay because I could not bear that she should rob me of her presence so soon; the other, springing from the few wits which were all that I seemed able to retain while with her, that having quite fortuitously, by my long awkward silences, created a better impression with her than I ever could have done by amusing banter and glib flattery, wisdom dictated that I should not jeopardize my gain by pressing her to remain.

She held out her hand and I kissed it, but before I released it I said swiftly, "If you insist on going now, at least promise to let me see you again."

"You must not come to the house," she said firmly. "That is impossible."

"May I come over the garden wall again at the same time tomorrow night?" I begged. "Please, please let me come. You said your mother was not coming back until the day after tomorrow, so please give me a chance tomorrow night to say all those things that I meant to say tonight."

"Very well; but there's no need to come in over the wall. Be outside the little door just before midnight and I'll let you in." With a last swift smile she turned and ran lightly up some steps towards the house.

It was not until she had disappeared that it occurred to me that she might have let me out; but as a result of her promise to see me again, I was in such a state of elation that I made my way back over the high wall with scarcely a thought about it.

As I strode along the road *en route* for my hotel, my heart was still hammering in my breast from the excitement of that queer meeting. It could hardly have been less satisfactory, regarded from the angle that I knew hardly a thing more about her than I had two hours before. But for some reason for which there did not seem to be the slightest justification I felt that more had happened in those ten or fifteen minutes that we had been together than if I had spent whole days in some other woman's company. I had told her that I found her beautiful; she had admitted to me that she found me good-looking and she had promised to let me into the garden herself on the following night. What more could any lover need to make his heart rejoice?

It was then that the thought of the other man, with whom Daphnis had been in the garden and had evidently let in by the door in the wall, came flashing back to me. It was like a hammer-blow, shattering the delicate fabric of romance that I was already so eagerly weaving about her.

Who was he? How well did she know him? The very fact that

she received him alone in secret warred horribly with the conception that I had formed of her as sheltered from all contacts with the outside world and utterly unspoiled. True, with me she had seemed frank and even ingenuous, but although I fought against it I could not prevent myself doubting if she could really be the innocent angel that she appeared.

Back in my bedroom, I turned the problem over and over in my mind. First I rated myself for my unworthy suspicions of her, then for my own stupidity in seeking to make her a spotless idol when experience had already taught me that girls are no better than men in any way, and that it is only the unwanted or half-witted among women who go through life without demonstrating at some time or other that they have feet of clay.

In my sober senses, the last thing that I really wanted was that Daphnis should turn out to be a priggish little fool; yet in my state of exultation I felt quite capable of murdering anybody who might attempt to besmirch her by as much as a breath, and the thought that she might have already been besmirched by much more than a breath was positive torture to me.

Perhaps my acute mental distress was partially accounted for by the absolute conviction that somewhere I had met the man who had been with her and that he was an evil personality. I tried again to remember where I had heard that voice before, but I could not, and although my troubled brain made capital out of an instinctive dread of this unknown man as a possible threat to Daphnis, I think I would have felt the same had his voice been quite unknown to me and full of charm.

The whole fact of the matter was that for the first time in my life I was suffering from blind, unreasoning jealousy. At last I fell into an uneasy sleep in which I dreamed that I was trying to strangle the owner of that voice, having just rescued Daphnis from him.

When I awoke I was at first under the impression that the whole of the previous night's adventure had been nothing but a dream. That may have been due to the moonlight, which had lent it a certain unreality, and from my never before having played so silent a part in any love-scene or participated in one less concrete. It was not until I had got out of bed and opened the drawer in which lay my rope and grapnel that I was fully convinced that I had actually climbed over Daphnis' wall; yet there still remained something unreal about the whole business.

It was quite impossible to reconcile the facts that she had deliberately come down to meet me, her naïve admission that she

23

thought me so good-looking, and her evident fear of being discovered talking to a strange man in her garden with the discovery that she had received another man there just before my arrival, also in secret, and one whose words had definitely given the impression that he was her accepted lover.

After a bit I began to wonder if it was the first part of the affair that I had dreamed and that there had been no other man at all. It was just conceivable that while I was sitting behind the shrubs waiting for Daphnis I had dropped off to sleep for a few moments, and that, in actual fact, she had not been down in the garden at all that night until she came down to meet me.

I tried to put the whole worrying problem out of my mind, yet all day it kept recurring to me as I waited with the utmost impatience for evening to come so that I could be with Daphnis again. Just before dinner it occurred to me that if there *were* another man, she might again be seeing him that night before she met me, so spurred on by my crazy jealousy I decided that I would go early and see.

By half past ten I was lurking in the shadows that fringed one side of the street on which the garden of Daphnis' house abutted. For an hour and a half I loitered about within sight of the postern door, but no one came to knock it and it never opened to let anyone in or out.

A little before midnight I took up my position just outside it; soon afterwards the key turned in the lock and the door was opened a fraction.

"Daphnis!" I whispered.

"Julian!" came the whisper back, and a hand was stretched out to draw me inside.

What happened exactly I have no idea, but the second the door was closed I had her in my arms. She was trembling slightly, but her arms were fastened tight about my neck, and in the moonlight I could see her smiling as she turned her face up for my kiss.

That sudden instinctive embrace was all the more surprising in that the night before I hadn't even thought of trying to kiss her. I feel quite sure that I should have ruined everything if I had. She was very young and I was quite willing to wait. As it was, I suppose that she had been thinking about me all day and waiting for this moment just as I had. In any case, those few marvellous minutes when I held her in my arms for the first time were unadulterated bliss.

Afterwards we talked—what of, I don't remember; just about

24

each other and our likes and dislikes, and silly inconsequent things which to us seemed terribly important and quite wonderful because we felt the same about them. That spontaneous embrace had certainly done something to us. We were utterly different people from those who had sat tongue-tied in that garden the night before. We were very careful not to make a noise but, as she lay in the crook of my arm on the stone bench near the fountain, we laughed a lot and talked interminably between kisses. Many, many kisses and it was nearly four o'clock in the morning before she said that she really must go in.

"How about our meeting again?" I asked anxiously. "Your mother is coming home tomorrow, or today rather, isn't she?"

"Yes," said Daphnis sadly.

"Can't I possibly call?" I suggested. "After all, I was carried into your house as the victim of an accident, and you administered first-aid. It's only common politeness to call and return thanks for such kindness in any part of the world."

"No, no!" she said hastily. "You mustn't do that. In any case, I shouldn't be allowed to see you alone."

"Not at first, perhaps. But if I get to know your mother——"

"No. I forbid you to. She became frightfully suspicious when you sent all those flowers so the meeting could only be disagreeable. I beg you not to call. You won't, Julian, will you?"

"Of course not, darling, if you're so terribly set against it, but how *am* I to see you?"

She thought for a moment, then she said: "I go riding every morning on the sands out at Stanley Bay. If you can get a mount, you could meet me there and we could have a gallop together."

"Grand. What time?"

"Eight o'clock. But I shan't go tomorrow morning, because it's so late now. I shall leave a note for my maid to tell Alcis that I'm not well."

"Who's Alcis?"

"My cousin. She has been staying with us for the last few weeks and we don't have to take a groom if we go riding together; but I'm sure that I can trust her."

I tried to hide my groan under a laugh as I said, "D'you mean that the three of us will have to remain in a party the whole time?"

"I am afraid so," she nodded her head vigorously. "You see, Alcis couldn't leave me and I couldn't leave her in case someone saw either of us riding alone. If Mother heard of it we'd get into frightful hot water for exposing ourselves to the possibility of unwelcome attentions."

This sounded fantastic on the lips of the young woman who was just reaching maturity in the year 1940, but the crumbling walls, the sun-baked paths and the fronds of the palm trees etched against the moonlit sky reminded me that I was in Egypt, the land of the dope-pedlar and the whiteslaver. In any country where the races are mixed the men naturally take every precaution to protect their women from any form of interference. One could not blame the Greek colony for the strict chaperonage that they imposed upon their attractive women.

"All right," I agreed reluctantly; "but that means it will be more than twenty-four hours before I'll be able even to see you again."

She laid a soft hand on mine. "I'm so sorry, but there's nothing that I can do—nothing. You must wait till Thursday morning and you must go now, because I'm tired; happy, but so tired."

Hand in hand we walked slowly to the bottom of the garden. I made our final embrace last as long as possible, but at length she broke away from me and pushed me through the low door into the street. I was still standing there, breathless and a little bewildered, after she had locked it, and I had lost the sound of her retreating footfalls along the sandy path.

Next morning I slept late and whiled away the rest of the day as well as I could by writing Daphnis a letter. In it I said all the absurd things that lovers always say about the object of their devotion and it rambled on for about fourteen pages, but I did not dare to post it in case, when Daphnis received it, her mother happened to be in the room, as a letter of such length would have been certain to provoke awkward questions.

I had arranged with the hall-porter about a horse and to be called early on the Thursday, so, when I arrived downstairs at half past seven, I found quite a presentable hack being held by an Arab boy ready for me. Twenty minutes later I was at Stanley Bay and it was not long before I saw two girls clad in white silk shirts and jodhpurs riding towards me, one of whom, by the outline of her dark hair and the set of her head on her shoulders, I knew at once as Daphnis.

They pulled up some fifty yards away from me, and upon Daphnis' waving her hand I rode over to join them. The cousin, Mademoiselle Alcis Diamopholus, to whom I was introduced, was a plump, round-faced girl with dull reddy-brown hair and small bright dark eyes, rather like a monkey's.

She was obviously thrilled to the marrow at being made Daphnis' confidante about her clandestine acquaintance with a

British officer, and positively bursting with curiosity about myself. I did my best to answer her questions politely, while inwardly cursing her presence, which made any chance of private conversation with Daphnis out of the question, at all events for the moment, and as the three of us rode along together the talk inevitably turned upon the war.

We had not been on the subject long before I was forced to realize that the two girls were anything but pro-British in their sympathies. I suppose I should not have been surprised, as having mixed so much with foreigners I was much more conscious than the majority of Englishmen that most of them are very far from regarding Britain as the benevolent, disinterested champion of freedom and democracy that we all like to believe her.

Great numbers of them are fully convinced that our policy is entirely inspired by selfish avarice, and that we should never go to war at all if we were not forced to protect those huge Imperial territories from which we draw our riches while keeping them half-empty and barring all less fortunate peoples out of them. Others, while admitting our integrity, have come to despise us because they consider that we have become decadent. They maintain that the ills of the world are entirely due to British weakness, incompetence and sloth. If we had given armed support to the Emperor Haile Selassie, instead of encouraging him to fight and then letting him down—if, instead of amusing ourselves with Football Pools, we had taken enough interest in the European situation to realize that Baldwin's irresponsible, deliberate and wicked refusal to face unpalatable facts that such men as Churchill, Beaverbrook and Rothermere placed publicly before him was a menace to our very lives—if we had only stood by the Czechs, etc., etc. I knew all those arguments only too well, but all the same it came as a most unpleasant surprise to me to learn that Daphnis should be anti-British.

It was not, thank God, that she was pro-Nazi, but she argued that Britain had dominated the world and made a mess of it too long. It was time that some of the other nations had a chance— Italy, for example. She considered that it was mean and hypocritical of us to grudge Italy her newly-created Empire when we had such vast territories of our own. Italy was terribly over-populated, yet worse off than practically any other nation in natural resources and arable land. She was full of praise for Mussolini and the remarkable way in which he had cleaned up Italy and lifted her from a third-class nation into the ranks of the Great Powers.

27

I agreed with her about that, as plenty of other people did before Musso did his filthy stabbing-in-the-back act, but I tried to point out that, basically, Fascism was only another name for Nazi-ism. The trouble was, though, that while Daphnis was not pro-Nazi, she certainly did not understand the full implications of National Socialism.

To her, it was just something young and new, as opposed to the doddering schoolmarmism of Britain. She said that obviously Hitler could not be such a bad man as the British painted him, otherwise he would not be so universally adored by his own people. She didn't want Britain to sustain a crushing defeat and lose everything, but she thought that the Germans were entitled to a place in the sun and that it would be a very good thing if the British and French Empires could be split up so that all the other nations of Europe could have colonies of their own.

Naturally, I took a very different view, particularly about the Germans, and I became so occupied in my denunciation of the Nazis as an unscrupulous and loathsome gang of crooks that I lost all count of time, and was badly caught out by Daphnis saying:

"Well, we must leave you now, otherwise we shall be late for breakfast."

Alcis had the decency to ride on alone for a little way, but I only had time to thrust my long letter into Daphnis' hand and beg her to suggest some way in which I could see her alone if only for a few moments.

"I don't see how I can," she murmured, "but I'll try to think of something. I could let you know if you come down to ride with us again at the same time tomorrow."

"Of course I will," I replied, and with the meagre comfort of her promise I had to be content.

You can imagine my chagrin when, on meeting the two girls again the following morning, Daphnis sadly confessed that she had failed to think of any way in which she could meet me alone without running a risk of getting into the most frightful trouble with her family. Naturally I didn't want that, but I felt I should go positively crazy if, somehow or other, I could not manage to hold her in my arms at least once more before my leave was up. It was already Friday morning and I was due back at the camp outside Cairo on the Saturday night. Four days had slipped away since I had left hospital, and I now had only two days and one night left.

I think Daphnis must have said something to Alcis, as soon

after we met our gooseberry went off for a gallop along the shore, and even after she had cantered back remained for the best part of the ride near us but out of earshot. In consequence I was at least able to talk freely to Daphnis and stress the frightfully short time that I now should be in Alex.

"I simply dare not meet you at a restaurant or a cake-shop," she insisted. "Alex is such a small place, at least the part where girls like myself could go, and my parents would be certain to hear of it. I wonder, though, if I could manage to get down to the garden at night, in spite of Mother being at home. Her room is next to mine, but she goes to bed quite early. It would mean tip-toeing past her door on going down and coming back, but if I'm awfully careful I don't think she'd hear me. I do want to see you again, Julian, and if you like I'll chance it."

That put me between the devil and the deep sea. I wanted more than anything else in the world to have that stolen meeting, but it seemed a rotten business on my part to urge her to do something which might land her in serious disgrace.

I had just made up my mind to tell her that she must not risk it when she said, with sudden decision: "That's the only thing to do, and if I'm caught I'll pretend that I'm walking in my sleep. I used to as a child and no one will be able to prove that I'm lying."

Once that was settled we had the meeting to look forward to and it put us both in a far happier frame of mind, so that for the rest of the ride both of us were full of joyous excited anticipation of the coming night.

Yet once I had left her I became restless and nervy. In vain I tried to read or amuse myself in various other ways throughout the day, but I could think of nothing except Daphnis and my all-absorbing love for her.

So far I had said nothing to her about marriage. Perhaps that was innate caution resulting from my numerous past affairs, in several of which I had had to exercise considerable skill to prevent myself being hooked by charming little gold-diggers who would have liked to establish a permanent claim on my handsome income; and I had no idea at all if Daphnis regarded me as a potential husband or not. Possibly she believed that her people would never consent to her marrying an Englishman and so had put the whole question right out of her mind. On the other hand, since she had been so jealously guarded, it was quite on the cards that, like an early-Victorian miss, she took it for granted that any man who said that he loved her and kissed her on the lips automatically wanted to marry her; but that there was no hurry

29

about going into details and that I should find a way to do so in due course.

In any case, I had definitely made up my mind that I wanted to marry her and the sooner the better. I see no point in long engagements, particularly when there is a war on, so I intended to tell her that night that there was nothing whatever to be frightened of, and that I meant to come round on the following morning to call formally on her mother and father and ask her hand in marriage before I returned to Cairo.

Had she been an English girl I might have been a little worried about my past, and the effect that its disclosure, which I could not have decently avoided, would have had upon her and my prospective parents-in-law. But I felt that I could produce the grim skeleton which I kept so carefully locked in my cupboard to Daphnis without fear when the first suitable opportunity offered, and it did not seem to me that I was bound to go into the matter at all with the parents of a girl who knew no English people, and with whom I had not the faintest intention of settling down in England to live.

Apart from that I saw no reason why a father of any nationality should consider me as an unsuitable husband for his daughter. I was young, sound in wind and limb, and had no previous encumbrances, either wives, children, or troublesome ex-mistresses. I had a comfortable fortune, carefully invested, and when my elderly uncle, the old Major-General, died, however much he might dislike me, he could not prevent me coming into the baronetcy.

With these thoughts in my mind I set off from my hotel that night, arriving outside the little door in the garden wall well before midnight, which had been the hour agreed on. As I stood there I puffed hard upon a cigarette, my nerves all keyed up with the anticipation that the next hour would prove a milestone in my life, giving again that solidity which would come from having someone besides myself to care for.

The moon was now in its last quarter and the sky was cloudy again, so that not a glimmer of moon, or even starlight, came through, and it was very dark, so dark that more than once I examined the door with my lighter to make quite certain that I was waiting outside the right one.

At last there came the sound of the turning key and a crack of greyness showed. Unable to wait a second longer, my heart thumping in my chest, I pushed the door open and stepped inside. Subconsciously I noticed a row of pale yellow squares on

30

the ground floor of the distant house, where lights were still on behind drawn curtains, but my whole attention was fixed on Daphnis, whose figure showed only a faint whitish blur on the darkness. I stretched out my arms and a moment later she was in them.

I had hardly touched her when I realized that there was something wrong. She didn't feel right. She didn't smell right. Her kiss was different and her lips were thin and hard. In a second it flashed upon me that this was not Daphnis that I was holding but some other woman, and I thrust her from me.

Out of the heavy gloom there came a stupid infuriating giggle, then Alcis' voice:

"I'm afraid you took me for Daphnis, didn't you? Are you very disappointed?"

The giggle and the voice clearly implied that she had not minded being kissed, and had purposely let me take her for Daphnis. Evidently she had been sent to let me in, but she could quite easily have stepped back instead of deliberately allowing me to take her in my arms. I was absolutely furious.

"Where—where's Daphnis?" I managed to stammer.

"She couldn't come, so she sent me to entertain you instead."

This brazen offer to act as a substitute for Daphnis was so blatant and unwelcome that I'm afraid I did not scruple about hurting Alcis' feelings as I replied curtly:

"Thanks, I don't want entertainment, and you're telling a lie when you say that she sent you for that purpose. Why couldn't she come? What's gone wrong?"

"All right, then," Alcis suddenly flared. "You shall have the truth if you prefer it. Paolo arrived unexpectedly from Cairo this afternoon, so my aunt arranged a dinner-party. The guests are still here and naturally, now Paolo has come back, Daphnis hasn't any more time to give to a stray Englishman like you."

"Who the hell's Paolo?" I demanded angrily.

In reply I got the final blow.

"He's a Secretary at the Italian Legation and he is Daphnis' fiancé."

31

CHAPTER IV

THE SINISTER MAJOR

ALCIS' explanation of Daphnis' non-appearance was so totally unexpected, the news that she was engaged to be married so shattering, that for a few moments my brain went completely blank. Without consciously parting from Alcis I found that the door had closed behind me and that I was standing in the street.

Anyone who has read the earlier part of this journal may say that it served me darn' well right, and that having dallied amorously without serious intentions in the past, Fate was evening up the balance now that I really had fallen for somebody by placing her out of my reach. Yet I can honestly declare that I have never deliberately led a girl up the garden path with the idea of just amusing myself and then throwing her over.

Of course it would not be fair to imply that Daphnis had promised to marry me while already engaged to somebody else, but she had led me up the garden path to the extent of believing that she cared for me as much as I did for her, and she had never even hinted that I had a rival who already had a definite claim upon her.

I suppose, in view of the voice that I had heard on the first night I entered the garden, I should have been prepared for something of this kind; but silly as it may seem now, in the past week I had really come to believe that I had fallen asleep for a few moments behind the bushes, and only dreamed that Daphnis had been in the garden with another man before coming down to meet me.

Now I knew quite definitely that I had not been dreaming. Alcis had said that Paolo was a Secretary at the Italian Legation, and both Daphnis and the man had spoken in Italian. Then there was her sympathy with the Italians and admiration for Mussolini's achievements—sentiments which could hardly be wondered at if she was engaged to a prominent Fascist.

Sick with rage, mortification and disappointment, I made my way slowly back to the hotel. On my arrival I ordered a bottle of brandy and a syphon to be sent up to my room with a vague idea of trying to drown my misery. Of the three emotions I think disappointment was uppermost. I wanted so frightfully the feel of Daphnis' hands and lips; the caress of her whispers and the magic of her laughter. Anyone who has really been in love will know that it is no joking matter, and that when things don't go right one can hunger for the touch of one's beloved as desperately as any dope addict ever craved for drugs.

That night I drank far more brandy than was good for me as I sat, hour after hour, engaged in a morbid inquest on what seemed the death of my one genuine love affair. I had to admit to myself that I had done my best to force myself on Daphnis, and therefore was at least partly to blame. Apparently she had been physically attracted for the moment, and as her fiancé was in Cairo had given way to the temptation to amuse herself, knowing that I should be leaving Alex at the end of the week and that if she played her cards skilfully it was most unlikely that any unpleasant complications would result. Doubtless that was why she had been so insistent that I should not call or write to her. She was evidently anxious to keep her parents entirely in the dark about me.

Only one thing remained seemingly inexplicable. If she was *openly* engaged to this fellow Paolo, which could hardly be questioned in view of the fact that her mother had thrown a dinner-party for him that night in their house, why in the world had he come secretly to see her in the garden during the previous week; and how could one account for that curious snatch of conversation I had overheard in which she had said how much she hated the subterfuge necessary to these secret meetings, and he had replied to the effect that it was quite impossible for him to see her openly as her stepfather would never permit it? Puzzle as I would, I could make no sense at all out of that part of the business, and eventually, dead tired, muzzy but not tight and maudlin with unheroic self-pity, I fell asleep.

Next morning I had a shocking head, but after my bath I felt a bit better, although still incredibly depressed. As there was no hope of seeing Daphnis again, even the sight of Alexandria had now become irksome to me, so I set off much earlier than I need have done and was back in the camp near Cairo by mid-afternoon.

Among the New Zealanders I had made some splendid friends, two particularly: Jack Benham, who was rather a serious type and a young schoolmaster from Dunedin, and Toby Spiers, a tall good-looking boy with one of those open sunny natures which win the hearts of men and women alike. I found my brother officers anything but cheerful as the only thing they had to talk of for some days was the beating that the Nazis were giving us in Norway, and it seemed that Mr. Chamberlain's remark about having missed the bus had been a bit premature.

In the days that followed I nursed a bitter grievance; yet, in spite of what I had magnified into a criminal betrayal, I could not prevent myself craving for Daphnis to an extent that at times became a positively physical ache. Then, just a fortnight after I had last seen her, Hitler went into Holland and Belgium, and as the news of the German successes trickled through in broadcasts and press, we all had something to think about in addition to our private worries.

Two days later it was decided to reinforce our outposts in the Western Desert, and the battalion to which I was attached was among those selected for the task. Periodically, for a long time past, Mussolini had been banging his little drum and this was one of his more bellicose periods, although few of us thought then that he would be fool enough to plunge Italy into war for the sake of obliging Hitler. It seemed so clear that he had everything to lose and nothing to gain. Abyssinia and the Italian East African Colonies would automatically be cut off from their homeland, so it could be only a matter of time before their garrisons were compelled to surrender. Libya lay naked in the breeze between the British in Egypt and the infinitely more powerful French Armies of Morocco, Algeria and Tunisia. We only had to squeeze and the wretched Italians, caught between two fires and cut off from succour by our Mediterranean Fleet, would be in a hopeless mess. That would be the end of the New Roman Empire. However, more, I think, with a view to reassuring the Egyptians than anything else, certain of the Australian and New Zealand troops were despatched to the Libyan border.

Mid-May was for us a period of intense activity, as the preparations for the move had to be carried out with the least possible delay, and within a few days we were converted from what had virtually been a training to a fighting unit; then there was the three-hundred-mile trek *via* Alex up to Mersa Matruh. The frontier was another hundred miles, but that was covered by outposts and flying columns of regulars. Mersa Matruh had better supplies of water than Sollum, Buq Buq or Sidi Barrani, and although it was hardly more than a large village it offered better harbour facilities, too, so for these reasons it had been selected as the main concentration point of the Imperial Forces in the Western Desert, and we were set to what then seemed the quite pointless task of strengthening its defences.

Actually, most of the work had to be done at night as one could not even lift a finger without sweating in the day-time. Sometimes the heat was so fierce that the men fainted from comparatively trifling exertions, and the temperature often went as high as 120 degrees in the shade. Owing to the extraordinary clarity of the atmosphere, however, one could see quite well for all ordinary purposes by starlight, and the moonlight was so bright that one could easily read or write letters by it.

We had ample water to drink but little to spare for other purposes, so permission was given to the men to grow beards, and we soon looked very different from the smartly-turned-out crowd that we had been in the days when we were stationed near Cairo. The sandfleas were an absolute pest, and before we had been in our new camp for a week I counted fifty-seven bites on one of my arms. Very soon we all grew to hate the very sight of the desert; but to remain there was our war for the time being, so there was nothing to be done about it.

All through those long hot days we watched with growing concern the collapse of Holland, the penetrations of France, the cutting-off of the northern French, British and Belgian Armies, the over-running of Belgium and the evacuation from Dunkirk.

It was hardly to be expected that, however bravely the Dutch fought, they would be able to stand up to the full weight of the German attack for long, and the German break-through at Sedan appeared at first to us onlookers as no more than a local disaster such as must be expected from time to time in the hazards of war. But, as we followed that extraordinary campaign and saw the Nazis thrusting through St. Quentin, Cambrai, Arras, Amiens and Abbeville, right to the coast of Boulogne and so on to Calais, we began to wonder when the French would really make a stand and bring this nightmare to an end. In the mess we could talk of little else, and it was perhaps that uneasy expectancy and anxious waiting for each fresh bulletin, day after day right through the latter half of May and early June, which, to some extent, kept my thoughts off Daphnis.

Looking back on that brief affair, which for me seemed to have ended so disastrously, I could not help admitting to myself that I had read much more into Daphnis' attitude towards me than was really justified. After all, at our first meeting I had not been conscious for more than ten minutes, on the two early-morning rides Alcis had been with us for a good part of the time, and during my first visit to the garden Daphnis and I had hardly done more than look at each other while we sat almost in silence for a quarter of an hour; so the whole affair really boiled down to that second night in the garden.

In those fleeting and now unreal hours we had exchanged

many kisses and our feelings for each other seemed to me, at least, to be beyond doubt; but that was the one and only time when Daphnis had let herself go, and that might almost be accounted for by a touch of midnight moon madness.

If I had been strong-minded I suppose I should have forced myself to put her right out of my thoughts, but instead I was lamentably weak about it, and whenever I was not occupied with routine duties or speculation as to the latest developments in the Battle for France, I tortured myself with memories of Daphnis; dwelling upon her evident complete lack of real feeling for me and the extreme unlikelihood of my ever again being able to take her in my arms with her willing consent.

Gradually my attitude changed. I began to think that there *must* be some favourable explanation for her strange conduct. The brutal shock of that last night in Alex became dulled, but the glowing picture of her beauty and her sweetness when we had been together in the moonlight remained and became more glamorous in retrospect. Slowly the resolution formed that by hook or by crook I had positively *got* to find a means of seeing her again.

For a few days I contemplated writing to her, but on consideration it did not seem to me that would do much good. It was getting on for five weeks since I had seen her, and it was utterly impossible for me to judge what sort of mood she would be in. Moreover, it was always possible that, if I wrote, I might really cause trouble for her with her parents or her fiancé.

It then occurred to me that if I wanted to marry her I was going about the business in an entirely wrong manner. That may have been because, for several years, I had been living a life of a social outcast. Otherwise I should probably have realized sooner that the most sensible line of attack was, in some way or other, to secure an introduction to her people in order that I might cultivate them socially and in due course become accepted as a friend of the family.

Owing to the exclusiveness of the wealthy Greeks in Alex I knew that getting an introduction to the Diamopholi would be no easy business, but it seemed that the old man at least must have some English friends, if only business and official acquaintances, so I sat down and wrote half a dozen letters to the various friends I had made at the English club during the first week of my leave in Alex, asking each of them if they happened to know any members of the Diamopholi family.

All the replies were disappointing except that from Barbara

36

Wishart, one of the sisters that I had been going out to Ramleh to play tennis with on the afternoon of my accident. Barbara wrote that the Diamopholi were very pro-British and that Madame had been to the house several times recently to sit on a Red Cross Committee of which Mrs. Wishart was chairman. She went on to say that if I could get down to Alex on the following Saturday, an excellent opportunity would present itself for a meeting, as a big Red Cross fête was being held on that day at which Madame Diamopholus would be present.

On the receipt of this good news I decided to ask for a week's special leave. In the ordinary way I was not due for leave again for another seven or eight weeks, but my job as interpreter put me in rather a different category from the other officers. As long as the battalion was in an inhabited area I had quite a bit of work to do in keeping smooth the relations of my unit with Egyptian officials and Arab landowners and traders, but out here in the Western Desert there was nobody for me to interpret to, and of course I had no troops directly under me, so almost my sole occupation at the moment was running the H.Q. Mess and helping the Padre to organize games and sing-songs.

I found the Colonel, a lanky New Zealander with a pleasant grin, whom we had nicknamed 'Long Willie', sitting in his office tent, employed upon the uncongenial task of making out a Report.

"Come in, Day," he called, as soon as the orderly who was on duty outside had poked his head through the flap of the tent to say that I was there. "Come in and sit down. What's the trouble?"

"No trouble at all, sir," I smiled, "but I'd be awfully grateful if you could see your way to grant me a week's special leave from the morning of June the 7th."

He drew a deep breath and sat back, mopping his perspiring forehead.

"What, fed up with the sand and the flies already?"

"No, sir, it's a case of urgent private affairs in Alex."

"I bet the urgent private affair has something to do with a young woman!" he laughed.

"Guilty!" I grinned back. "But after all there's practically nothing for me to do here."

"That's true, and we might as well be back in New Zealand for all the good we can do while the only fighting is two thousand miles away. I wish to God they'd send us to France. Perhaps they will if a new B.E.F. is despatched to help hold a line north of Paris. Now the Channel ports are gone there's a chance they might decide to draw on Egypt for reinforcements *via* Marseilles.

But if that happened we'd have to embark from Alex and you could rejoin us there."

"You don't think there's any likelihood of Musso coming in, sir, and things flaring up here?"

"Good God, no! He's much too wily an old bird to cut his own throat, and Hitler can't possibly want him to. Italy's entry into the war would close the one big leak in the blockade through which the Nazis are getting nine-tenths of their supplies."

"Can I take it that it will be all right about my leave, then?"

"Yes. Put in your application form, and I'll sign it."

Having thanked him, I went off in high humour to fill up the form, and it duly returned marked 'Granted' from Brigade two days later.

On the Friday night I was back in Alex and I took Barbara Wishart out to dine and dance at the Windsor; feeling that was the very least I could do in view of the help she was going to give me with the Diamopholi. Barbara was a tall, fair girl and she would have been quite good-looking if she had taken more care of her complexion instead of allowing it to be ruined by the Egyptian sun. However, I had never been attracted to her except on account of her rather amusing conversation, and I am sure she had no special interest in me; so there were no bones broken when over dinner she asked the reason for my interest in the Diamopholi, and I told her about Daphnis.

Of course I suppressed that part of the story which concerned our meetings in the garden for obvious reasons, merely stating that I had fallen for her badly when she had patched me up after my smash, and that I had met her out riding on the beach a few days later, which had enabled me to follow up our unofficial acquaintance. Then I asked Barbara if she had met her.

"Oh yes," she replied, "once or twice, but only on account of these charity dos in which she helps her mother. She's pretty enough, but a dull little thing."

"Dull nothing!" I protested quickly.

"God! How you do rise, Julian!" Barbara laughed. "As a matter of fact I haven't the faintest idea if she's dull or not, as I've only seen her with her mother. She looks as though butter wouldn't melt in her mouth, but probably it's a case of 'still waters'. Since she patched you up, though, why didn't you call? You should have, even out of common politeness."

"I wanted to," I said, "but she seemed to think that her people wouldn't like it."

Barbara nodded. "Yes, these rich Greeks keep very much to

their own set, and frankly I don't give much for your chances. I heard the other day that she's engaged. Sorry if that's a knock, old boy, but I thought I ought to tell you."

"I knew that already. She's hitched up to some Italian fellow in the Legation here, isn't she?"

"Yes, although I don't know how that goes with her people. You see, the old boy is terrifically pro-British. He's one of the biggest shipping men in Alex. We charter all his ships these days and he has a lot to do with our Naval authorities. As the Eyeties are pro-Hitler I shouldn't think the old chap takes a particularly good view of his prospective son-in-law."

"I see. How about the mother?"

"Oh, she's just a great fat stooge. The old man subscribes very handsomely to all the pro-British charities, so it's as a tactful compliment rather than for her usefulness that his wife is asked to sit on the committees."

The fact that the Diamopholi *père et mère* were such keen supporters of the British cause seemed to augur well for their reception of an English officer, and on the following day I could hardly contain my impatience until the time came to set out for the Red Cross fête.

It was a much bigger affair than I had visualized and was being held by special permission in the grounds of the Royal Palace. On the outbreak of war Egypt had declared her intention of carrying out all her treaty obligations, and although she had not actually declared war on Germany, the greater part of the Egyptian officials and population were taking every opportunity such as this to demonstrate their sympathy for Britain. King Farouk and Queen Farida had graciously consented to open the show, and it was certain that all official Alexandria apart from the pro-Nazi members of the Diplomatic Corps would be there.

I arrived so early that the helpers had not completed the dressing of their stalls, but that was all to the good, as Barbara was able to take me along before the crowd arrived to the flower stall, which was being run by Madame Diamopholus and two other ladies.

She handled the situation beautifully. Sailing up to a large dark woman of portly dimensions, she said:

"Oh, Mrs. Diamopholus, may I introduce Mr. Julian Day? He has kindly offered to help, and as we're full up already, Mother suggested that I should bring him over to you." Upon which, with a swift smile, she abandoned me, having not only given me the introduction that I had asked for but planted me upon Madame Diamopholus for the afternoon.

Out of the corner of my eye I had already caught sight of Daphnis. She was looking a positive dream in a very light summery frock and an enormous picture hat which set off her dark beauty to perfection, but she was standing on the other side of the stall, and I felt certain that she had not yet seen me.

Madame and I smiled politely at each other, and she murmured something about how kind it was of me to offer to help, but seemed quite at a loss to suggest anything that I could do. I had no intention of being passed on with her compliments to another stall, so I said quickly:

"I see you have some trays of buttonholes to be carried about for sale among the crowd. I'm afraid I can't carry a tray myself because I'm in uniform, but I could accompany anybody who has one and sell from it to the ladies. I've often helped my mother with bazaars at home and I know from experience that at shows like this the women will always buy much more readily from a man."

My mother had died long before I was old enough to help her at bazaars, but the mention of her was well calculated to strike the right note with Madame Diamopholus, and beaming upon me she did exactly as I had hoped she might. Daphnis was already carrying such a tray as I had mentioned. Her mother promptly called her.

When she saw me Daphnis went as white as a sheet. For a second I thought she was going to faint, but fortunately her mother hardly glanced at her before turning back to me while burbling:

"My dear, thees gentleman will 'elp you to sell from ze tray. 'E is Mr. . . ."

"Day," I supplied. "Julian Day."

She beamed again:

"Mos' kind of you to 'elp, Mr. Day. Thees ees my daughter, yes. I 'ope you make much money for ze Fund."

I did not dare to take Daphnis' arm to lead her away, but I hustled her out of earshot as quickly as I decently could, and without a word led her through the back of the refreshment marquee, where it was cool, semi-dark and there were a number of chairs. With a little gasp she plumped down on one as though her legs had been just about to give way.

"That's better," I said quietly. "Would you like a drink?"

She shook her head, so I went on:

40

"All right, then. Take it easy for a few minutes. I'm sorry if I gave you a shock."

"To see you here was the last thing I expected," she murmured.

"That's just how I felt when Alcis told me that you were engaged to be married."

"So Alcis told you. I guessed as much," she said with sudden bitterness.

"Are you implying that you had intended to keep it secret?"

She looked up suddenly, her eyes defiant.

"What has my engagement to do with you? For all I know you're engaged yourself to some girl in England. You wouldn't want to marry a Greek, and in any case my parents certainly wouldn't let me marry you, so marriages and engagements have nothing whatever to do with it, and if Alcis hadn't been a spiteful little fool she would have kept her mouth shut."

This short tirade presented an entirely new viewpoint to me. It seemed that, having decided in her own mind that there could be no question of marriage between us, Daphnis felt that fact absolved her from letting me know anything about her engagement, and in the meantime she regarded it as entirely her own affair if she cared to deceive her fiancé to the extent of entering upon a secret romance with me.

Before I could speak she went on:

"I suppose that's the reason that you didn't come back later; or was it that Alcis never gave you my message that I'd come down myself and let you in at half past one?"

"She never told me," I muttered, "but perhaps that was my fault, as I left her pretty abruptly. You—you really wanted to see me after all, then?"

"Of course I did!" she exclaimed half-petulantly, tears starting to her eyes.

"But what about Paolo?" I asked. "Where does he come in?"

"He doesn't come in—at least not as far as you're concerned."

"But, hang it all, you are engaged to him, aren't you?"

"Yes, but because one's engaged to someone it doesn't follow that one is in love with him."

At last a little light began to dawn in my bemused brain. I had been regarding this engagement all along as one would in England, where it is usual to assume in the case of young people that engaged couples are in love with each other; but in many foreign countries the old system of marriage by arrangement still goes on. Doubtless this Italian diplomat was an excellent *parti*, and Daphnis' family had fixed up the match without even

41

consulting her. With her upbringing it would be natural for her to accept such a situation and be perfectly prepared to go through with it. But she was not in love with her fiancé at all, and the inference was that she was in love with me.

"If—if you don't love him," I stammered, "do you—could you . . .?"

She began to shake her head violently. "I didn't ask you to come and make love to me, but you did and I liked you. Then you made me utterly miserable, going away like that. I hate you! I hate you!"

It was only with the exercise of the strongest control that I was able to refrain from seizing Daphnis and crushing her to me, flower-tray and all, but even in the semi-darkness of the marquee I dared not risk so much as to touch her hand unless it appeared as though it were done by accident, since people were constantly passing. The fact that she had been miserable on my account showed that she *did* love me and the happiness of knowing that was so great that, for a moment or two, I stood there absolutely tongue-tied. Suddenly she spoke again:

"You hadn't even the decency to come riding on the beach next morning so that you could say good-bye to me."

The reproach both amazed and shook me. In all those days and nights of going over the affair in my own mind it had never once occurred to me that if, instead of getting tight and sleeping late, I had gone out riding on the last morning of my leave, I could have met Daphnis and have at least obtained from her some sort of explanation about her engagement. Risking that someone who knew her might catch sight of us, I seized one of her hands for a moment and pressed it as I whispered:

"Daphnis, I've behaved like the most utter fool, but I adore you and things are going to be all right from now on."

For a moment we gazed deep into each other's eyes, and from the tenderness in hers I knew that I was forgiven. Paolo was forgotten. The only thing that mattered was that all was well between us. I knew that I must keep my head, though, and play my cards well for both our sakes, so I said:

"We mustn't stay here any longer, otherwise your mother will start to wonder what's become of us. Let's go out and sell some of your flowers. We can talk again later."

Outside in the strong sunshine the gardens of the Palace were beginning to fill rapidly with a colourful throng. Smart European women in bright silks, chiffon and lace, mostly escorted by British Naval, Army and Air Force officers, mingled with no less smartly dressed Alexandrians and Cairenes accompanied by red-fezzed Egyptian officials. As we moved among them, in intervals of selling buttonholes from Daphnis' tray, I told her how, once I had ascertained that I should be able to get an introduction to her mother through the Wisharts, I had got seven days' special leave solely in the hope of seeing her again. Then I asked what chance there was now of my being able to break into the closely-guarded family circle.

She said she thought it would be best if she told her mother now that it was I who had been carried into their house after the accident. As my face had been covered with blood, and I had hardly regained consciousness before being carted off in the ambulance, that was sufficient explanation for our having appeared not to recognize each other at once when introduced that afternoon; and a decent interval having elapsed it would be assumed that I had only turned up again through pure coincidence. After this second apparently chance meeting and now that I was sponsored by the Wisharts she did not think her Mamma's suspicions would be aroused if I hinted that I had very few friends in Alex and asked permission to call.

The afternoon passed all too quickly and during it I forced myself not to stick to Daphnis the whole time but to make myself as useful as I could to her mother and the other ladies who were running the stall. The impression I created was evidently satisfactory, as before we parted—after I had hinted that I was rather at a loss to know how best to fill in my six remaining days of leave—Madame Diamopholus herself suggested that as they were having a few people in on the Monday evening I should join them.

It was useless for me to attempt to see Daphnis out riding as Alcis had returned to Cairo several weeks previously, and Daphnis now had to ride with a groom in attendance, whom she said she dared not trust. In consequence I made up my mind to possess my soul in patience until the Monday evening, and on the Sunday morning had decided to have a good late lie in bed. However, a letter which had been brought by hand and was sent up with my breakfast-tray got me up earlier than I had intended.

It was a short note from Essex Pasha saying that he would like to see me between eleven and twelve at the Alexandria Police Offices, which he made his headquarters during the hot months of the year.

As soon as I arrived there I was shown up to a big apartment in which he was seated alone behind a desk. He was a very fine-looking man of between fifty and sixty, tall, broad-shouldered,

43

with grey hair and blue eyes. As an official of the Egyptian Government he wore a red fez, which was tilted at a rakish angle on the back of his head, and, with the scarlet gorgets of a General on the lapels of his tunic, made a bright contrast to his khaki uniform. With a friendly smile he waved me to a chair and told me to help myself to a cigarette. Without further preamble he went straight to the point.

"How well do you know the little Diamopholus girl?"

I was considerably taken aback, and I paused to light the cigarette before I answered with a laugh:

"I think Your Excellency ought to give me notice of that question."

He shook his head and the little wrinkles round his blue eyes crinkled up.

"Come, come, my boy! You were much too occupied with her yesterday even to notice me; but I caught sight of you at least half a dozen times acting as her cavalier, so you must have spent the whole afternoon with her. You may rest assured that I shouldn't dream of prying into your affairs unless I had a good reason."

"All right," I said. "In the middle of April I had a motor-bike smash and was carried into her house, where she bandaged me up. After that I saw her two or three times, mainly out riding in the early morning. Since that leave ended I haven't seen or heard from her again until yesterday. But why do you ask?"

"Because we're rather interested in her."

I frowned, for the first time feeling a little uneasiness. "Surely, sir, you're not suggesting that a girl like Daphnis is mixed up with the dope racket?"

"I've known stranger things," his strong teeth flashed in a smile, "but it's not that, and I'm concerned with even more important matters than the suppression of the dope traffic in these days. Ever since the war I've been largely responsible to the Egyptian Government for internal security in this country. However, I don't want to take up more of your time than necessary, and it's really a matter for Major Cozelli; he's the head of our Italian Intelligence Section. I'm sure you'll give him any information you can."

As he finished speaking, Essex Pasha struck a bell on his desk, and having cheerfully wished me an enjoyable leave told the negro police orderly, who appeared like an ebony jack-in-the-box, to take me along to Major Cozelli.

In a smaller office on an upper floor the Major rose from his desk to greet me. He was a hard-eyed, cadaverous, dark-skinned man who also wore the red fez of an Egyptian official. His name suggested that he was at least half-Italian, which probably accounted for his present job, but he spoke faultless English and said smoothly as I sat down:

"His Excellency tells me that you know Miss Diamopholus, Mr. Day. As you're probably aware, her family has great influence here in Alex, and it's our job to pick up all we can about influential people. These wealthy Greeks keep themselves very much to themselves, though, so it's not easy to get precise information about them. You'd be helping us a lot by giving me your impressions of this young lady and her family."

"I know very little about them," I replied with complete honesty; and having given him an account of my accident I went on: "According to Barbara Wishart the Diamopholi are one hundred per cent pro-British, but Daphnis is engaged to an Italian—a man named Paolo somebody, who is employed in the Legation here. She's eighteen—nearly nineteen—years of age, and is kept as strictly as a Victorian miss. She speaks several languages fluently and she's quite well educated."

Major Cozelli's shrewd black eyes bored into mine.

"A Victorian miss, who is kept shut away from the world, but is quite well educated, eh? Now do you really think that she has a mind of her own or that you've endowed her with one because —well, owing to your evident interest in her?"

"Probably you'll think I'm prejudiced," I smiled, "but I can assure you that she's no fool. I talked to her once for the best part of an hour on international politics, and although I didn't by any means agree with all her opinions, she seemed to have a very wide knowledge of affairs."

"And Italian sympathies?"

"Well, yes," I admitted. "Like plenty of other people who are anti-Communists, she considers that Mussolini did a good job of work in saving Italy from the Bolsheviks after the last Great War, and that he and his Fascists deserve credit for the way they've cleaned up the country."

"That may be, but they control Italy, and Britain's application of Sanctions hampered Fascist plans without thwarting them. They haven't forgiven us for that, and it not only threw them into the arms of Hitler but also enabled them to turn the Italian people against us. I'm a British subject by birth but I have many Italian connections, so I'm particularly favourably situated to judge their feelings. Mussolini gave them Imperial ambitions and their jealousy of us has been turned to hatred. There are over sixty thousand of them here in Egypt, and they're going to need a lot of looking after if Mussolini decides to take the plunge and drag Italy into the war."

"Do you really think that's likely?"

He considered a moment. "It's impossible to say. He might now that the French seem to be cracking so badly. However much we may dislike the Communists the fact remains that the Fascists are really just as bad. One lot are unwashed hoodlums who would cut your throat for fourpence, while the others are gangsters dressed up in smart new uniforms. 'Corsica, Nice, Tunisia!' has been their parrot-cry for months past, and now the true state of France's rottenness is at last being made plain to the world it's just possible that these Fascist blackguards might jump in to grab what loot they can, while everyone else has their hands full. If they do come in I'd like to know on which side your little friend, Mademoiselle Diamopholus, is going to be."

I smiled reassuringly. "I don't think you need worry. The odds are that she's only picked up these pro-Fascist ideas from her Italian fiancé, and that they're quite superficial. The marriage was, I gather, arranged, and . . . well, I think there's quite a possibility that she won't go through with it. Then, as you know, her parents are definitely pro-British."

The Major's thin-lipped mouth tightened perceptibly. "You overrate the influence of the fiancé, I think. But perhaps you were not aware that she's half-Italian herself?"

"Really!" I exclaimed. "No, I didn't know that."

He nodded. "Old Diamopholus is only her stepfather, and she took his name for some family reason."

There flashed back to me then a sentence of that conversation I had overheard on the first night that I entered the Diamopholus garden. The man had said to Daphnis, "Your *stepfather* hates me like poison." For some strange reason its implication had failed to register until that moment, but the cadaverous Major was going on:

"Diamopholus is the biggest shipping man in Alex. He works with the British Naval authorities and has a lot to do with arranging our Mediterranean convoys. Do you happen to know if Miss Diamopholus takes any interest at all in her stepfather's business?"

"I haven't the faintest idea," I smiled, "but most girls of her age find anything to do with commerce extremely boring, and in that way I shouldn't think she's an exception."

"I see. I only wondered. Well—thanks for coming in." The Major stood up, indicating that the interview was over.

That Daphnis was half-Italian was certainly new to me, but I did not consider it particularly perturbing. I was smiling still as we shook hands, then having saluted I marched towards the door.

My hand was already on the knob when Major Cozelli's voice came, seemingly casual, behind me:

"Oh, Mr. Day, duty makes some pretty heavy demands on us sometimes. If you *did* chance to discover that Mademoiselle Diamopholus was furnishing particulars about shipping to your country's enemies, you wouldn't hesitate to let us know, would you?"

Those words were like a douche of cold water down my spine. Something in the way he said them convinced me that he knew much more about Daphnis than he had disclosed. The smile had been stricken from my face as I stammered, "N-no, of course not, sir," and left the room.

CHAPTER V

CAUGHT OUT

FROM Major Cozelli's office I went straight down to the *plage*, where scores of young people were disporting themselves in the warm Mediterranean waters. The smart bathing-place at Alex consists of one of the smaller of its bays which forms almost a lagoon and has three tiers of bathing boxes built right round it, making it a natural water amphitheatre.

Now that it was mid-June the sun was very strong, so most of the members of the Forces there were having strictly to limit the time during which they exposed themselves, owing to the danger of severe sunburn; but I had done so much sun-bathing in the last few years that I was bronzed already and had little fear of getting burnt.

All the time that I swam or lounged about afterwards I thought of Daphnis and Major Cozelli's exceedingly worrying insinuations. I had never liked to ask her about the episode which

47

had taken place in her garden on the first night that I had gone into it, as I feared that to do so would have given her the impression that I had been deliberately spying on her; yet I had puzzled over it many times.

The riddle for which I could find no answer was: why should she see her fiancé in secret late at night in the garden when she could quite well have asked him at any time to the house?

Paolo had said that night something to the effect that secrecy was necessary because Daphnis' stepfather hated him so much. Perhaps, then, Daphnis and Paolo were working together for Italy. That would explain, if he were suspicious of it, old Diamopholus' dislike of Paolo and, if the engaged couple wished to exchange information, explain why they met clandestinely to do it instead of risking further trouble by doing their business more or less in the presence of the pro-British household.

Yet somehow that theory did not seem to fit. The man in the garden had definitely conveyed the impression that he was not received in the house in any circumstance, whereas Paolo quite definitely was. Perhaps, then, the man in the garden had not been Paolo after all, but some other Italian.

This theory had more sinister implications still. Having a fiancé already in Paolo, if Daphnis was running the other fellow as a beau on the side it was most unlikely, unless she was an embryo Messalina, which I did not believe for one minute, that she would have been prepared to start an affair with me. As she had, it followed that the other fellow was not a beau at all, and therefore the secret meetings between them were quite possibly in connection with some form of espionage.

True, Britain was not at war with Italy, but the Fascist Government made no secret of its partisanship for the Nazis, and it was certain that any information with regard to Allied troop movements or shipping which could be collected by the Italians outside Italy was passed straight on to Berlin.

If Daphnis had some deep-rooted feeling that her father's country was her own, one could not attach any blame to her for spying for the Italians; but if she was so engaged it meant that I was up against the most ghastly problem that any man could be called on to face. How could I betray the girl that I loved to Major Cozelli if I found her out? Yet on the other hand I could certainly not stand by with the knowledge that British lives were being lost through her operations and my cowardly hesitation to put a stop to them. It seemed for a few black hours that my wisest course would be to cut Daphnis right out; to make no further attempt to see her and do my utmost to forget her as quickly as possible.

Having seen her again in all her loveliness only the previous day made such a step ten times more difficult. I had the knowledge now that she did not love Paolo and was strongly attracted to me. The sight of her and the sound of her voice had inflamed my romantic imagination to new and almost delirious heights. After weeks of despair I had secured the right to call upon her, and was actually invited to a party at her house on the following evening. To have thrown away this magnificent new opening seemed more than I could possibly ask myself, and to attempt to forget Daphnis altogether would now be like trying to tear out my own heart.

That night a new thought suddenly came to me. There was not one iota of proof against Daphnis. All these black thoughts had been engendered solely through Major Cozelli's damnable insinuations. It was his job to be suspicious of everybody, and the fact that one of the key men in the Anglo-Egyptian Shipping Control had a half-Italian stepdaughter who was engaged to a member of the Italian Legation was more than enough to cause the counter-espionage people to wish to keep an eye upon her, but I had been given absolutely no evidence.

The odds, I now argued, with a swift revulsion of feeling, were all in favour of Daphnis' being innocent, and, I reasoned with myself, even if it turned out later that she had been passing on little bits of information to Paolo or some other Italian about her stepfather's ships, if she really cared for me she would certainly refrain from doing so in the future.

Before I fell asleep I was fully prepared to stake my reputation on Daphnis' honesty, and absolutely determined to marry her. If she became engaged to me, an Englishman, I felt certain that although she might retain Italian sympathies, she would never for one moment contemplate an act which might be harmful to the country of the man she loved.

I had been invited for six o'clock on the Monday, and when I arrived at the Diamopholi's I found a dozen people already present. Most of them were Greeks, and several were members of the family. Madame Diamopholus introduced me to her husband, the shipping magnate, a paunchy, grey-haired man, with a fattish face and quick intelligent eyes. He gave me a very friendly welcome then introduced me in turn to a British naval captain, with whom I stood talking for some time.

Daphnis had smiled at me in passing, but swiftly disengaged

49

herself, so I took my cue from her, realizing at once that if I wished to retain the goodwill of the parents, so that they would ask me to the house again, I must be very careful not to appear to be chasing their already affianced daughter.

Twenty or thirty more people flooded in, and I was introduced to a number of them. Fortunately, I knew a little Greek so I was able to join in the conversation, although I have no doubt that most of them could have conversed with me in French or English. There was apparently an unlimited supply of champagne cocktails, and the native servants in their striped silk *jibbahs* and red *tarbooshes* constantly carried round trays of sweet cakes in addition to the usual cocktail accessories.

The talk centred mainly round the desperate battle raging in France; but now that Weygand had had ample time since taking over as Generalissimo to make fresh dispositions, everyone expected to hear any day that he had performed another 'miracle of the Marne'. After all, we argued, the Boches couldn't keep up much longer the rate they were going. The master strategist was only waiting for the psychological moment, when the enemy was spent, to launch a great counter-offensive which, if really successful, might roll the whole Nazi host back in confusion.

The Greeks had no illusions about the weight of the colossal blow that Britain had sustained in the loss of all her first-line tanks, guns, equipment and vast quantities of stores at Dunkirk. An extremely bad impression had also been created by the official announcement that General Lord Gort had been recalled to report and had gone back to England on the Saturday because there was no longer remaining on the beaches a command suited to an officer of his high rank, when, in fact, many thousands of the men he had led into Belgium were still stranded there, and the last of them were not taken off until the following Tuesday. But the naval captain, who had just been flown out from home and said he knew the inside story, explained to those of us who were near him that Lord Gort had been put in an impossible position by the Cabinet.

He told us that to hearten the men Lord Gort had walked up and down the beaches without a tin hat, while they were being sprayed with machine-gun bullets by the Nazi airmen, and that when a destroyer had been sent for him he flatly refused to go home in it before the beaches were clear. Only when the Government sent a special message that by remaining he was imperilling the lives of the destroyer's crew was he induced with great difficulty by his staff to leave.

50

Opinion was most sharply divided upon the surrender of the King of the Belgians. French statesmen had publicly denounced him as a traitor, and English leader-writers of repute had called him a rat; but Churchill had asked the House of Commons to suspend judgment, and certain of the Diamopholi's friends gave it as their view that the British General Staff were entirely to blame for the Belgian collapse. They argued that at one period of the battle the British had quite obviously attempted, but lamentably failed, to close the gap and rejoin the French. In order to execute this movement it was obvious that they would have had to swing away from the Belgians on their left and leave them in the air. Either the British had attempted to rejoin the French, as had been publicly stated, or they had not; but, if they had, no one could blame the Belgians for chucking in their hand.

This argument was all very well in its way, but it did not seem to me to have the least bearing upon the point at issue. Nobody blamed the Dutch Army for having surrendered after four days' fighting, and I saw no reason why anybody should blame the Belgian Army for surrendering when they had fought very gallantly for far longer. But what had this to do with the personal act of King Leopold?

It might be argued that, as the commander of his army, he could not leave it; but all monarchs are technically commanders of their armed forces, and it is transparently clear that at certain times of crisis they have a much higher duty to their nation as a whole than to any portion of it.

The King of Norway and the Queen of Holland had already given splendid examples of that high duty. When their armed forces had been defeated by the treachery and superior strength of the enemy, these monarchs had not remained behind so that they could be forced to co-operate with Hitler and thus assist him by setting their people an example of complaisance. Instead, they had refused all dealings with the enemy and in their persons transferred the free and defiant spirits of their peoples to the country of their ally, with the intention of continuing to honour their alliance and carry on the struggle.

King Leopold was within a few hours of London. When it became necessary for his army to surrender he could quite easily have taken a ship or 'plane to England for the purpose of becoming the focal point of a continued resistance by Free Belgians all over the world. But he did nothing of the kind. He surrendered his person to the enemy.

51

To me the issue appeared to be a perfectly clear one, but whatever the rights of the Belgian surrender and the withdrawal of the British Army from the Continent, the fact remained that the French were now in an extraordinarily precarious situation and that we were no longer in any state to send them material assistance.

The blackness of the picture was relieved only by our confidence in Weygand's brilliance and the knowledge that, with Churchill now firmly established in the saddle, at long last Britain had a war leader worthy of her.

At a quarter to eight the crowd began to thin, and although I had hardly had a chance to exchange a word with Daphnis I felt that the time was rapidly approaching when decency would compel me to take my leave. From my point of view it had been a most disappointing party, but in this I judged too hastily. Old Diamopholus came up to me, still with the naval captain, the only other Britisher in the room, beside him and said:

"You will stay to dinner, I hope, Mr. Day? At these informal affairs we always expect our friends to stay on unless they already are engaged to dine somewhere else."

I accepted with alacrity, and from then on, for me at least, the whole atmosphere of the party improved enormously. There were not more than twenty people remaining, and it appeared that they were all staying on to dine. That, and perhaps the number of drinks we had had as well, lent a more intimate and carefree tone to the gathering, and when after another half-hour of steady drinking we all moved into a huge dining-room I found that Daphnis very skilfully contrived temporarily to get rid of two Greeks who had been dancing attendance on her so that she could sit beside me.

With the family, having counted heads, I found that twenty-five of us sat down to table, but from the number of servants it was obvious that the Diamopholi were used to that sort of thing, and the full six-course dinner which followed was in every way worthy of the merchant prince whose guests we were.

After dinner more than half the party collected in the lounge to play baccarat. The rich Greeks are great gamblers, and Daphnis told me that her stepfather played almost every night, going out to his friends whenever they did not have parties there. Two tables of bridge were made up in the drawing-room. I managed to escape being roped in but was resigning myself to having to spend the evening at the baccarat table, instead of talking to Daphnis, when she said in her mother's hearing:

"Are you quite sure that you wouldn't rather play than look at my stamp collection, Mr. Day?"

"No, honestly," I assured her with sudden fervour. "I'm a terribly keen philatelist—have been for years, and I can play cards any time."

"All right then," she said. "Let's go into the library. I keep them there."

I followed her from the lounge, where they were still checking out great piles of counters, into a comfortable library at the back of the house. As we entered it I made to close the door after me, but she shook her head and whispered: "Better not. If anyone comes along and finds us shut up in here it will look suspicious."

I saw the sense of that in this Victorian household, although I groaned inwardly because I wanted so desperately to kiss her, but she motioned me to a sofa along the wall immediately behind the door, and no sooner had we sat down on it than she was in my arms.

Long before I was willing for her to do so she wriggled free and whispered with a little laugh:

"Stop, now; stop! I must get out the stamps so that we can be looking at them if anyone comes in." From a cupboard below one of the big bookcases she produced two bulky volumes, but as soon as she sat down again I firmly took them from her and grasped her hands.

"Listen, Daphnis," I said. "I want to get this engagement business straight. You're not in love with this fellow Paolo, are you?"

She shook her head. "No. My mother and his arranged the marriage three months ago. He's clever and interesting. He will give me a good establishment, and I like him as a friend. But I don't love him."

"Does he love you?"

"Yes. He saw me at a dance and at once got his mother, with whom he lives here in Alex, to approach mine."

"Well, I'm afraid he's going to be unlucky," I told her firmly. "You're not going to marry him. You're going to marry me."

"But—but wouldn't you mind marrying a foreigner?" she said with a little gasp. "And I'm a member of the Greek Church, you know."

"Darling," I laughed, "I wouldn't mind if you were a Hottentot!"

"But—but I hardly know you," she murmured.

I laughed again. "You know what my kisses feel like, and although I'm not as rich as your stepfather, I've got quite enough money to keep you in every comfort. Surely that's enough?"

"But your family. They might object and it would be terrible to enter a family where one was not welcome."

"That needn't worry you. I'm an orphan. Both my parents are dead and I have no near relatives at all. I don't even want to take you away from your own family and friends. After the war we'd travel, of course, and see lots of interesting places; but I'd be quite happy to make our home in Alexandria."

"Would you—really?" her eyes were wide and bright. "Perhaps—oh, I don't know, you must give me time to think."

"You don't need time," I insisted gently. "Either you love me or you don't. If you do let me speak to your mother and stepfather tonight; then you can write to Paolo and tell him that your engagement to him is off, so that he gets it first thing in the morning."

"*Dio mio!*" she exclaimed. "I had almost forgotten, but Paolo should be here at any moment. He couldn't dine because in these days he works so late at the Legation, but he said that he would come in at ten o'clock."

"All the better," I grinned, feeling at the top of my form and ready to tackle anything. "I'm sorry for Paolo, but the sooner this thing is settled the better. When he comes you'd better have a showdown with him right away, and I'll speak to your parents immediately afterwards."

"Oh, why are you in such a hurry?" she sighed.

I kissed her lightly just behind the ear. "The main reason is because I'm nearly twenty-seven years old, and I don't want to waste another day of my life without you."

She smiled. "You couldn't take me with you to your camp in the Western Desert at the end of your week's leave, you know."

"All the more reason for us not to waste a single hour but to get engaged this very night," I countered. "Then I'll be able to spend every waking moment for the rest of my leave with you."

"What's the other reason?"

"Because I want to make you an Englishwoman as soon as possible."

For obvious reasons I could not tell her that she was on Major Cozelli's suspect list, and I felt that the one way to make quite certain that she would give up any Italian intrigues in which she might be participating was to get her to become engaged to me.

54

WHITEMAN

But that was the real motive which lay behind my decision to force the pace for all I was worth.

She considered a little, then she said:

"Marriage can't change one's love for one's own country, and I don't know if you know it but I'm half Italian."

"Yes, I know that," I said. "What of it?"

"If Britain and Italy went to war you'd expect me to hate Italy, and I could never do that."

"Of course I shouldn't," I laughed. "Britain's war with Germany is one thing. These Nazi swine are the same old Prussian bullies dressed up in new uniforms and having learnt a few even more revolting tricks, so it's natural that we should hate them. War between Britain and Italy would be quite another matter. The English and the Italians have always been good friends, and the Italians are no fonder of the Germans than we are, so if they did get dragged in through pressure exerted by Hitler, there'd be no real bitterness on either side. You and I would make the subject taboo—just ignore it."

"No, Julian," she shook her head. "We might try to but we couldn't do that. After a few months of this hateful modern war each side would have performed acts which the other would consider brutal or despicable, and we'd be bound to be affected. It would be taking an awful risk for me to marry you as long as there is any chance that war may break out between Italy and Britain."

"It won't," I declared with a confidence that I really felt. "I don't want to belittle Italy in any way, but one can't get away from facts. Italy couldn't possibly afford a war. She's only self-supporting in one of the six major commodities which are used in waging wars so she would be a liability rather than an asset to Hitler. At present Italy is the big hole in the Allied blockade. She's taking in millions of tons of surplus merchandise each month and railing it straight through to Germany. Once she went to war our Navy could put an end to that overnight and the traffic would have to start to flow back the other way. Hitler would have to help feed and support the Italians and there are forty-five millions of them. Honestly, darling, this great trumpet-blowing act that Musso is putting on now is only another big bluff."

"Perhaps you're right. I hope so! But this morning all Italian shipping was recalled to its ports, and that's a pretty serious step."

"Of course I'm right," I insisted. "Holding up his shipping

for a day or two, or even a week, may cost Mussolini a bit of money, but he can well afford it. With Britain, Germany and France at war Italy has been left without a rival for the Atlantic passenger traffic, and she's making a packet out of it. While we're all busy the Italians are cornering all the South American markets, too, and of course they're making a huge profit on every single thing they send through to Germany. If the war lasts for two years Italy will have drained Germany dry financially and conquered huge new markets for herself overseas into the bargain. From near bankrupt she will have become one of the richest countries in the world, while we've been cutting each other's throats. That's why it's absolutely inconceivable that the Italians would be such fools as to come in. Anyhow, if you won't marry me right away, we can at least get engaged."

Her eyes danced as she murmured: "Yes. I suppose we could, but it will be an awful shock for poor Paolo."

"That's settled then." I kissed her hands. "You'll break the bad news to Paolo as soon as he turns up, and while you're doing it I'll tackle your mother and stepfather."

"Oh, Julian! This is all so—so . . ."

"Sudden!" I finished for her with a laugh. "That's the classic phrase which a mid-Victorian girl would use for a situation like this."

The dimple on her cheek showed. "Do you really think that I'm so terribly old-fashioned?"

"You have no time or period. You're just the loveliest and most adorable thing in the world," I answered, staring straight into her eyes; and next moment we were locked in each other's arms again.

"Daphnis!" The exclamation of shocked surprise pierced our reeling senses, causing us to spring apart. Madame Diamopholus had come into the room unheard by us, and was staring at her daughter in anger and amazement.

I was a little breathless after that long kiss, but I came to my feet with the best grace that I could muster and said, with a solemnity due to the occasion:

"I know that I appear to have abused your hospitality shamelessly and—and that, before addressing myself to Daphnis, I should have gained the consent of your husband and yourself. But—well, I hope that you will forgive my impetuousness when I tell you that Daphnis and I love each other, and that she has just consented to become my wife."

Madame Diamopholus stood there, with her mouth half-open,

staring at me as though I had gone crazy; but I had hardly finished speaking when a newcomer violently projected himself into the midst of this good old Lyceum drama family scene. He was a thickset, olive-faced young man with black piercing eyes, and had evidently been just behind Madame Diamopholus as she entered the room, but had remained hidden from me until that moment by the open door.

"What you make 'ere wiz my fiancé?" he almost screamed. "You tella da lie and I am insult!" He thumped his chest angrily, and if looks could have killed I should have fallen stricken to the floor.

There could be no doubt at all as to who this little fire-eater was, but I said coldly:

"Am I to assume that I am adressing Signor Paolo . . .?"

"Il Cavaliere Paolo Tortino!" he roared. "And you, 'oo maka da insult! My honour is tramped. I demanda we fight."

The name Tortino had a vaguely familiar ring, and as I stared at him I felt sure that I knew his face. In his rage he had gone white to the gills, and I think he would have attacked me there and then if Daphnis had not shown remarkable aplomb and courage in so young a girl.

Instead of playing the part of a Victorian miss, to which I had likened her, and giving way to a fit of hysterics, she appeared as cool and collected as if we had been exchanging the most light-hearted pleasantries. Stepping between us, she said in Italian, which she knew that I could understand:

"Mother, it's quite true. Paolo, I'm sorry, terribly sorry, and if you hadn't surprised me we should have avoided this most unpleasant scene. I meant to tell you or write to you tonight. I should like to have parted friends, but if that's impossible it can't be helped, and in any case I absolutely forbid either of you to fight. You must release me from my engagement. I can never make you happy because I don't love you and I intend to marry Mr. Julian Day."

Her ice-cold words seemed to douse Paolo's anger, and he was now staring at me with more curiosity than hate. The feeling that we had met somewhere before grew in me, and with sudden apprehension I remembered that he was a diplomat. It was quite possible that we might have been *en poste* in the same city during the short time that I spent in His Britannic Majesty's Diplomatic Service. He spoke abruptly in Italian:

" 'Julian Day'! No—that is not your name."

My breathing quickened; my heart seemed to shrivel up

inside me. My worst forebodings were to be realized. I stood there white and speechless as he went on in a tone of such jubilant conviction that I knew it must sweep away all doubt in the minds of his hearers:

"I remember you now. Your name is Fernhurst and you were a junior attaché at the British Embassy in Brussels. You and another man named Carruthers sold your country's secrets to a gang of international espionage agents. When your treachery was discovered Carruthers at least had the decency to commit suicide, but you preferred to live on in dishonour and were expelled from the British Diplomatic Service with ignominy. Thief! Traitor! Scum! How dare you pollute with your presence any respectable house! Get out!"

For what seemed an age there was an utter silence. The Italian was glaring at me with confident fiendish triumph in his dark eyes. Madame Diamopholus had one hand pressed to her forehead. Daphnis' face was a white mask of agony and fear. She was fighting against belief, I knew, and urging me with all the power of her will to say something—to give Paolo the lie—to deny this ghastly thing of which I had been accused. But what could I say? Certainly nothing that Madame Diamopholus or Paolo Tortino would believe.

"Is—is your name Fernhurst?" Daphnis asked in a whisper.

"It was," I murmured. There could be no purpose in denying that now.

There was another awful silence. Then a calm English voice suddenly cut in, breaking the tension as swiftly as the flick of a finger would snap an overtaut violin string. It was the British naval captain, and he had just appeared in the doorway. Either he did not sense the tragedy that was being enacted there, or in view of what he had to say deliberately chose to ignore it.

"Sorry if I'm interrupting," he said in a casual tone, "but I've just received a belated message from my ship. The fool of a marine who brought it got himself lost in the town. Mussolini made a declaration at eight o'clock, our time, that Italy will enter the war against Britain tomorrow night. All British officers are ordered to return to duty immediately. I have a car here, Day, so I thought I could give you a lift back to your hotel on my way down to the harbour."

"Thank you, sir," I said, and swallowing hard I stepped past Daphnis. The captain was already out in the passage, but I was still crossing the threshold as she staggered and fell fainting into Paolo's arms.

CHAPTER VI

THE WAR IS ON IN EARNEST

I SHALL never forget the night and day that followed. For a well-proportioned blend of physical discomfort and acute mental distress I have never lived through their equal. First in darkness and later under a torrid, gruelling, merciless midsummer North African sun the endless chain of cars and lorries of which my vehicle was one stopped and started, crawled and spurted, hour after hour, along the coast road to Mersa Matruh.

We passed the old railhead at Hammam while it was still dark and reached El Imayid just before dawn. El Alamen, with its tattered palms and mud-walled houses, showed clear in the cool early-morning light, but by the time we reached El Daba we were already sweating, and after that the journey was positive unadulterated hell.

As I was not driving I had not even the job of keeping the car to its place in the steady stream of traffic to occupy my mind, and my thoughts revolved ceaselessly round that awful scene with Daphnis in which I had cut so sorry a figure.

It was largely my own fault for having kept my past concealed from her. I had meant to tell her the whole story of the tragedy which had ruined my promising career at its very outset as soon as a suitable opportunity occurred; the trouble was that I had really spent such a very little time with her, and Major Cozelli's suspicions had caused me to force the pace in a way that I should never otherwise have done.

How right he had been about the possibility of the Italians' coming in and how wrong everybody else's complacence, including my own! Perhaps he was right, too, in his guess that Daphnis was concerned in conveying information to—yes, they were now quite definitely the enemy. I closed my eyes and my heart went sick at the thought. I tried not to believe it, fought against its acceptance with all my will, yet the damnable suspicion persisted. But if I had the least shadow of a doubt about my love for her it was gone now. Whatever she was, whatever she had done, made no difference. I loved her as I had never loved anyone before or should ever love again. I knew that to the very depths of my being, now that I had lost her.

My exposure by Paolo Tortino could not have been fuller or possibly have occurred at a more decisive moment. As the long sweltering hours dragged by I tried to face up to it that my chances with Daphnis were now utterly ruined. If only I had been able to get hold of her and talk to her on the morning after the scene there might have been some hope for me; but the sudden call to return to duty had put that out of the question. I could write to her, but I had little hope that a letter reaching her days later could undo the terrible blow to her pride and belief in my decency that she had sustained.

As soon as I was back with the battalion—and could get a few moments to myself—I did write to her. In a letter I could not say very much except that, while there were things in Paolo's statement which I could not deny, I did deny absolutely that I had ever betrayed my country's secrets, and that the facts he had related were capable of a completely different explanation from the one which he had put upon them. I said that I had been meaning to tell her of this wretched affair which had caused certain people to misjudge me at the first chance that arose and begged her to have faith in me. I told her that, during the great summer heats, there was little likelihood of any major operations taking place on the Libyan border, so that, my week's special leave having been cut short, as soon as the excitement of Italy's coming into the war had died down, I thought that I would be able to get twenty-four hours in Alex to give her a full explanation. All I asked, before applying for leave, was that she should send me one line saying that she was willing to give me a hearing.

Perhaps it was stupid of me to have asked her consent and I should have strained every nerve to see her without waiting for it; but, in the mood of black pessimism which had settled on my mind like an evil fog, I felt robbed of all self-confidence and half-convinced, even before I sent the letter, that I should receive no reply to it.

Six days went by, then a letter arrived for me addressed in that same thick angular hand as the note that I had received in the hospital, and which I knew instantly to be Daphnis'. My feelings were so stirred at the very sight of the writing that I dared not trust myself to open it in the mess, where it was handed to me. Hurrying to my tent, I ripped open the envelope with shaking fingers. It had no beginning and no end, and every world of it burnt into my brain.

On the day after we first met I had the sands read for me. You came out most clear, but very plain there lay a sword between us. Already I am injured to my heart. That shall heal because it is not

60

cut too deep, but no way can the sword that Fate place there be turned aside. We are not for each other and it is hopeless for both that we make a war with Destiny. Do not attempt again to see me, please. Our paths lie different ways and this is good-bye.

Daphnis had never told me that she had consulted a fortune-teller on the day after our first meeting, and in view of his gloomy prognostications it seemed that she must have been greatly attracted to me from the very beginning, since she had gone against his warning in order to meet me in her garden; but that was little consolation now. Still half-stunned by the catastrophe which had wrecked our swiftly-blossoming love, I saw no alternative but to accept her decision; although I knew that it would be easier to forget that episode in the past which had changed the whole course of my life than to put her out of my mind.

The days and weeks that followed were sheer hell for everyone at Mersa Matruh, and our outposts which, right up to the Libyan border, provided a screen for the main army. No action took place for the simple reason that the soul-destroying heat made all movement during the daytime, and therefore any sustained military operation, utterly impossible to both sides.

If it had not been for the organized bathing parties at Mersa Matruh, God knows how the troops would have survived through those stifling weeks. The wells there are good and sufficient for the basic needs of a considerable army, but it would have been quite out of the question to provide even the scantiest fresh-water baths and sometimes we changed shirts and shorts that were sopping wet with sweat as many as four or five times a day.

Dust and flies completed with heat the triumvirate of enemies that scourged us during those ghastly summer months. It was risking acute inflammation of the eyes and temporary blindness to go anywhere without goggles as sandstorms occurred with monotonous, heart-breaking frequency. Great waves of sand would beat against the tents and the hutments, driven so fiercely that in a matter of a quarter of an hour they would scour every scrap of paint off the body of a car. While the storms lasted, one seemed to move in a pea-soup fog, and afterwards the fine grit would be found to have penetrated everywhere. Hair, nose and ears were full of it; boots, blankets and baggage were powdered inside and out, and it was impossible to protect even our food and drinks from their quota. To add to the gaiety of nations in this charming campaign, during which neither side had as yet

61

fired a shot, the sandfleas, coming from God-knows-where in myriads and swarms to this desert, which had been virtually uninhabited until the coming of the Imperial Forces, bit us and battened on us relentlessly.

To these physical discomforts was added the by no means small mental strain of wondering what in hell was going to happen in Western Europe. With longer and longer faces we listened to the broadcasts following the French withdrawals south of the Marne, south of the Seine, south of the Loire. Then the ignominious surrender which made us positively seethe with disgust and anger.

The French still had a great army in North Africa and another in Syria. They had their vast Empire, a powerful battle fleet and huge resources lying outside France itself. Why in God's name, we asked each other, hadn't they the guts to transfer their Government to Algiers and fight on with us? The Poles, Norwegians, Dutch and Belgians had all done the courageous thing in establishing Governments in London for the purpose of rallying their nationals and their resources all over the world against the common foe. With such admirable examples offered by smaller peoples why should not France, with her far vaster powers to assist in the defeat of the menace to all freedom, have done so too?

At first we were just amazed and puzzled, but gradually the true answer began to trickle through. Two-thirds of the French Army had never fired a shot. In the break-through at Sedan they had suffered practically no casualties and fled, not from the bombs of the diving aeroplanes, but from the noise they made. Scores of French regiments had thrown their arms down at the first sight of the Germans, and refused to fight.

That was the whole awful truth. It was not simply that a little caucus of venal politicians had sold France. It was that the great bulk of the French nation was absolutely rotten. The military leaders, the aristocrats and the rich industrialists were almost all openly Fascists who preferred what they considered the lesser evil of a France under Hitler to Communism, but the French masses were little better and had played every bit as large a part in the betrayal. They had been the two million French soldiers who never fired a shot, and the five million Communist-Socialist workers who thought more of politics than patriotism, and with criminal folly had followed a policy of go-slow in industry so that they could get more out of the masters instead of getting down to the job of turning out the tanks and 'planes.

Quite obviously the French treachery would have such vast

repercussions that its full effects could not possibly be measured at once. It was not only the direct threat to Britain through occupation of the French Atlantic coastline by the enemy or the loss to the Allies of France's man-power which must render the initiation of any fresh land campaign on the continent of Europe foredoomed to failure through disparity of numbers.

There was no sphere of war in which the blow would not be felt. France's merchant marine could no longer carry for the Allied cause. All the valuable minerals and other resources of her colonies would no longer be at our disposal. In the Near East we had counted upon the French Army in Syria as a solid tangible factor in strengthening the resolution of our friends the Turks to resist aggression. That prop had now been knocked away. Formerly at least six magnificent bases in the South of France, Corsica and North Africa were at the disposal of the Royal Navy, and from these the Allies could dominate the whole of the Western Mediterranean. Now there lay no place at which units of our Fleet could shelter, repair, remunition and fuel between Portsmouth and (three thousand miles distant) Alexandria; with the exception of Malta, where the harbour was now rarely free from attack by enemy aircraft, and Gib., which could be rendered untenable to shipping at any time that the Axis Powers might persuade Spain to come in on their side.

At the outbreak of the war French and Italian naval strength had been about equal. In one short week we had lost the help of one while the other had gone over to the enemy. On the maintenance of our supremacy at sea lay our one solid guarantee of eventual victory. If that went, everything went, and by the French surrender it had been brought into grave jeopardy. The Navy had had work enough before in keeping the Atlantic open; it would now have to be deprived of half its strength there to keep open our almost equally important Empire highway through the Mediterranean. Through lack of adequate protection, caused by this necessary dispersal of its forces, hundreds of our merchant ships must inevitably fall victims of Axis submarines and surface raiders. Therefore, during the coming months, the deaths of thousands of our sailors would be directly attributable to this act by the cowardly swine of Bordeaux.

In North Africa, too, the pusillanimous collapse of France had instantly changed the entire strategic situation to our peril. Had the French in Morocco, Algeria and Tunisia continued in arms, with the British in Egypt, the Allies would have had the Italians in Libya like a nut between the crackers. As soon as the heat

63

lessened, by a simultaneous advance from west and east, we could have squeezed Libya out, and with our sea supremacy cutting Marshal Graziani off from all succour from his homeland, Mussolini's Number One colony of the New Roman Empire would have been packed up in less than a month.

As it was, with the French immobilized we now had to take on the Italians alone, and they were enormously superior to us both in men and equipment. During the heat we were safe, but directly it eased we knew that we'd have to fight like hell if the Italians were not to smash their way into Egypt by sheer weight of numbers.

During those anxious days in the last half of June I thought much of Daphnis, and the only meagre consolation that I had was that, although Egypt would not declare war on Italy, she severed diplomatic relations with our new enemy. In consequence, on the 23rd the Italian Minister to Egypt left for home. Obviously his staff would be evacuated with him, so Paolo Tortino must have been compelled to leave Alex, and his presence there could no longer arouse in Daphnis memories of the way in which he had shamed me before her.

Early in July there were the actions which resulted in the destruction of certain major units of the French Fleet at Oran and Dakar; and this demonstration of Churchill's resolution cheered us all, although those of us who thought enough to analyse the news behind the headlines realized how pitifully weak we really were. In spite of the principle of resistance to aggression for which we were fighting, we had to accede to the demand of the insolent Japanese to close the Burma Road, and Rumania threw our guarantee back in our face, after having been compelled to disgorge Bessarabia, a part of her ill-gotten gains in the last World War, to Russia.

By mid-July there was already talk of the threatened invasion of Britain, and the R.A.F. began to bomb concentrations of barges in the continental harbours. Unrealized by us, the preparations for the Battle of Britain were just beginning, and the Luftwaffe was now making daily raids upon British shipping. The papers were days old when they got to us, so we had to rely for our news almost entirely on the B.B.C. broadcasts. Perhaps it's as well that we knew as little of the state of things at home as we did, since, being utterly unable to help, we should have been even more worried than we were. We knew, of course, that the B.E.F. had been compelled to leave all its arms and equipment on the beach at Dunkirk, so that there could be little hope of the new

64

output from the factories finding its way to Egypt for a long time to come, but what we did not realize was that, through going to the assistance of Belgium, Britain had thrown away practically her entire mechanized forces and that the great majority of the then "L.D.V.", who had been raised to resist invasion, had not even as much as a rifle, much less supplies of Mills grenades.

The only sign of war that we saw in the Western Desert in those days was a little sporadic air activity. Our aircraft bombed Tobruk, and the Italians raided Alexandria. Once in a while they put down a few bombs in the neighbourhood of Mersa Matruh, but there was little damage done and few casualties. The raids were not of sufficient intensity to cause us much concern, but each time I heard that Alex had been bombed I suffered the tortures of the damned for days afterwards from the thought that Daphnis might lie crushed and broken beneath a heap of ruins.

The Air Force had then not yet come into its own, and the only things we had to cheer us were Churchill and the Navy. In the last war I gathered that it was no easy matter to maintain an effective blockade although we had six out of the seven most powerful navies in the world at our disposal. Then we had the fleets of the United States, Japan, France, Russia, Italy and several smaller Powers to help us. Now the job had to be done unaided, and with the Italian as well as the German Navy against us, yet somehow our sailors appeared to be not only keeping up the blockade and maintaining the freedom of the seas throughout the entire world, but able to fight one successful action after another. Within six weeks of the opening of the war in the Mediterranean they had sunk a score of Italian submarines and destroyers and the crack cruiser *Bartolomeo Colleoni*, the fastest ship on the inland sea, in addition.

Hitler's end-of-the-month peace offensive was treated with the derision that it deserved. The fool seemed to think that because he had stamped upon three or four smaller Powers and smashed the craven French, Britain would be only too glad to come to terms, but we were not falling into that trap. We had seen him at work too often now, and had come to know that he was utterly incapable of telling the truth or keeping an honest bargain. Desperate as our position might be at the moment, we had immense potential strength in the British character and the resources of our Empire. We were in this thing now, and even in those darkest hours I don't think any of us really doubted for a moment that not only would we pull through, but that, if our politicians let us, we would deal with the Germans in such a way after this war that they wouldn't dare raise their hands against an Anglo-Saxon, or anyone else for that matter, for another century.

Early August saw an intensification of the aerial warfare over Western Europe, and the real Battle of Britain was on. Night after night, out there in the desert, with a million stars twinkling brightly above us in the purple-dark vault of the sky, we waited anxiously for the nine o'clock news (which, as our time was two hours earlier, we did not get until eleven o'clock) to hear the amazing scores achieved by our fighter pilots each day.

It wasn't until about then that I began to realize a subtle change in my attitude towards the tragic ending of my affair with Daphnis. After her letter I had considered it as closed, feeling that there was not the remotest chance that she would have any more to do with me; but that perhaps was due to the shock that I had sustained and an awful inferiority complex which I had acquired through slinking about the world during the last three years under an adopted name and always going out of my way to avoid people who might have known me in the past.

I saw now that such a policy had availed me nothing. True, I had succeeded in escaping a certain number of unpleasant incidents, but the cat had come out of the bag when least expected and in front of the one person who really mattered to me before I had had a chance to prepare her for it.

As I lay, during those sweltering afternoons, stark naked and sweating in my tent, a feeling of revolt gradually took hold of me. The damage was done now. Daphnis had heard the worst part of the affair in the worst possible circumstances. Whatever I did, therefore, she could not possibly think worse of me than she must be doing at present. Why the hell should I take it lying down and slink away with my tail between my legs? I loved her desperately; my misfortune had made me bitterly cynical, and she was the only thing in the whole world that I cared a damn about. Why shouldn't I put up a fight to try to get her back?

It was only after many days of hesitation, black bouts of despair alternating with fresh waves of the urge to act, that I at last sat down in mid-August to write her a long letter.

I told her that at the end of the month I was due for a week's leave and begged her to let me see her. I said that it was damnably unfair to judge any man unheard, and that if ever again I came across Paolo Tortino I would beat him within an inch of his life for the flat lie he had told in saying that I had betrayed my country. I then went on to tell Daphnis how absolutely, utterly and desperately I loved her, recalling the all-too-brief meetings

66

of which our love affair had consisted. Page after page was covered with my memories of how she had looked on each occasion that I had seen her, and the ever more tumultuous state of my feelings afterwards. I said that I would slave, starve, or, if need be, die for her. There was nothing, *save betray my country*, which I would not do to prove my love, and I would abide by any decision that she might make about my not writing to her again or attempting to see her in the future if only she would first give me this one chance to repudiate in detail Tortino's accusations.

For days afterwards I waited in a fever of anticipation for each mail to come in. At first I was confident that she could not possibly harden her heart sufficiently to resist my plea; but as time went on my hopes gradually dwindled until, as the date for me to go on leave drew near, I knew deep down inside myself that she was not going to write, and became once more a prey to black despair.

If it hadn't been for the acute discomfort of the heat, the dust and the flies in the Western Desert, I shouldn't have troubled to take my leave at all, but leave would at least mean seven days' escape from that hell to the almost forgotten joy of being able to bath in fresh water and the well-cooked meals which could be eaten without swallowing several ounces of the Sahara.

Having arrived in Alex I told myself that I must not behave like a weak young fool and just sit about moping and drinking the whole time but get around and force myself to take an interest in such other people as were inclined to be friendly. In consequence I 'phoned the Wisharts the next morning and Barbara asked me out there for tea and tennis.

That evening Mrs. Wishart was arranging a party she had promised to get up for a dance which was to be held in aid of the British Lifeboat Institution. It fell on the last night of my leave, and on learning this she asked me to dine with them for it; I naturally accepted.

With bathing, tennis, polo, visits to Alexandria's cinemas and one jolly session at the races the week passed more quickly than I had expected. It was quite impossible for me to be in Alexandria and not to think of Daphnis a score of times a day. As I passed the jeweller's where I had bought the amulet, or anywhere near her house, or the hospital in which I had been after my accident, memories of her crowded in upon me; but I made a stubborn stand against allowing her to monopolize my thoughts entirely, and when I went out to the Wisharts on the Wednesday evening I was quite looking forward to the dance.

I was well on time and the second man to arrive; the other being a young Air Force officer. Mrs. Wishart had not yet come downstairs, and Dorothy, Barbara's sister, was talking to the airman. As Barbara took me over to a side-table to give me a glass of sherry, she said:

"I shall expect the biggest box of chocolates in Alex from you tomorrow morning, my boy, and don't you forget to order them before you set off back to the Front."

"Of course you shall have a box of chocolates," I smiled. "I'll go into Groppi's tomorrow morning."

"That's nice of you, Julian, but you haven't asked yet what I've done to earn them."

"Asking me to this party is quite enough."

"Oh no!" she shook her head. "And I really did have to work quite hard to fix it; but, remembering your interest in her, I've got the Diamopholus girl coming for you tonight."

At that moment Daphnis was shown into the room.

CHAPTER VII

THE SKELETON IN THE CUPBOARD

I ACTUALLY felt the blood drain from my face. During the last two and a half months there had been innumerable midday heats during which I had lain, a sweating carcass, in my tent, and it had been too hot to do anything except think—think of Daphnis. There were no recreations to fill in the evenings out in the Western Desert and early to bed was the rule. On countless nights I had turned in, not yet tired enough to sleep, and lain there in the darkness only half-awake, dreaming—dreaming of Daphnis. For nearly all that time I had regarded her as irretrievably lost to me, endeavoured to force myself to accept the fact that I would never see her again, yet here she was before my eyes and to me infinitely more beautiful than my thoughts or dreams had ever painted her.

I had never before seen her in evening dress, and she was wearing a filmy crinoline frock with chains of tiny pink roses all over it so that she looked just like a Dresden china figure come to life.

I suppose I shouldn't have been so utterly taken aback to meet her at the Wisharts' house. From that last scene with her I had gone straight back to Mersa Matruh, so Barbara had no idea that there had been anything at all between us except an avowed admiration on my part, and it was just like her good nature to get her mother to include Daphnis in the party as a pleasant surprise for me.

For a second I was panic-stricken by the thought that Daphnis might think that I had planned this meeting, and if she still considered me a rogue might tell Mrs. Wishart that if I was to be in the party she must go home because, for reasons which she did not care to disclose, her mother most strongly objected to her knowing me. She might even tell the Wisharts why *she* did not wish to know me, and it was only then that I realized that neither Mrs. Wishart nor Barbara knew about my past or that I was passing under an adopted name.

My hands went cold and clammy. I momentarily contemplated flight, and I definitely wished that the floor would open and swallow me up. Barbara must have seen my evident perturbation, and, guessing something was wrong she leapt, like the good sort that she was, into the breach.

Under her make-up, and in the artificial light, it was impossible to tell if Daphnis had flushed or gone pale at the sight of me, but before we could meet absolutely face to face Barbara stepped forward and with a casual "Of course, you know Julian, don't you?" brought us both to the sherry table, but so that she remained standing between us.

As we murmured a conventional greeting our eyes met, and although she was not smiling hers were not hostile. Some of the other guests arrived almost immediately afterwards, so conversation became general, and for the moment we were spared any further embarrassment.

We were a party of ten for dinner, and I imagine that Barbara had switched the cards at the last moment, as I was right at the other end of the table from Daphnis, so escaped the ordeal of having to make meaningless conversation with her; but that was only a postponement of the crisis which I knew I now had to face, and it came at the end of dinner, when Mrs. Wishart said:

"Now, you young people had better book up any dances that you want as by the time the girls have got their wraps we shall have to be off."

It was the time-honoured formula by which a dance hostess ensures that the plainer girls in her party get a fair share of

dances before the young men arrive at the dance and start book-
ing up with the star attractions. In common politeness it was now
incumbent on each of us men to ask each girl at the table for at
least one dance, and leaving our seats we began to circulate before
the women left the room.

When I reached Daphnis I said: "I had no idea that I'd be
lucky enough to see you here. May I have a dance, or better still,
if you can spare them, two?"

"I—I promised several to men who are going in other parties,"
she said with a little catch in her voice, "so if you don't mind we'll
make it one. Would Number Four be all right for you?"

That was not particularly encouraging, but at least it was the
first fence taken without a tumble, and with a murmured "Thank
you" I turned to ask for a dance from the girl who was next along
the table.

If my very life depended upon it now I could not tell you if
my first three partners danced well or badly; if they were pretty
or plain, or even if they were dark or fair. I have no doubt at all
that I talked the usual inconsequent nonsense about the band,
the floor, the weather and the war, and I trust the poor dears
remained quite unconscious of the fact that they were dancing
with a human automaton completely incapable of registering any
facet of their personality. I simply don't remember anything more
at all until I was gliding away into the throng of dancers with
Daphnis.

We circled the floor twice in complete silence. She had lowered
her eyes as we started off, and now she kept her face resolutely
averted. Her profile was as cold as ice and for the life of me I
could not think how to open up now that I had the chance that
I had been so desperately anxious to obtain. The words would not
even form in my mind and precious moments were flying. If the
dance ended before I had broken the ice I felt quite certain now
that she would excuse herself from giving me another on the plea
that her programme was full up. Then this utterly unexpected
break which the Fates had sent me would have been entirely
thrown away.

Suddenly I felt her hand tremble on my arm and she burst out:

"Say something, can't you! Say something or else take me back
to Mrs. Wishart and get out!"

The revelation that she was as keyed up as I was lent me new
confidence and I whispered:

"Daphnis, I've so much to say but it won't be easy to say it
here. Do you mind if we sit out the rest of the dance?"

She nodded and I caught a faint sigh as though she were relieved at having escaped from the strain of dancing with me further. We went up two flights of stairs and I had an anxious time looking for somewhere where we could talk freely, until on the top floor I found a small room with a single card-table but no players and no sitters-out in it. I could only hope that we'd be able to keep it to ourselves for the next ten minutes or quarter of an hour. Abruptly I pulled one of the chairs out from the card-table and said:

"Would you sit here, please?"

As there were two comfortable armchairs in the room she looked a little surprised, so I added:

"I want to sit opposite you so that you'll be able to look me in the eyes and form a better judgment as to if I'm lying or not. I expect you think that I'm about the lowest sort of swine, but I hope to convince you that the account Tortino gave of an episode in my past was very far from being the whole truth."

She made no reply, but sat down and took out a fat Egyptian cigarette from a small gold case. As I lit it for her I went on:

"My name was not Julian Day, but it is now. I changed it legally some time back by deed poll. As a young man I did quite well at Oxford and I took a high place in the examinations for the Diplomatic Service. All my friends considered that I was on a good wicket. The trouble was that I was just a little bit too clever.

"It was when I was in my first post in Brussels that I slipped up. I ran across an elderly man there whom I had met once or twice during my time at Oxford. His name was Sean O'Kieff, and I had good reason to believe that he was a Secret Service agent working against my country. As you may know no member of the Diplomatic Corps is ever allowed to participate in espionage or counter-espionage, but I was young and enthusiastic, and I thought I would be able to bring this notorious spy to book without its transpiring that I, as a member of the staff of the British Embassy, had had any hand in it.

"To appreciate the situation fully you must understand that this man was not a small-time crook. He was very rich and he had homes in half a dozen cities, including Brussels, in which he ran a magnificent apartment with many servants. He was also an occultist with a considerable reputation, and he was one of the most entertaining raconteurs that I have ever met, so these qualities, together with ample money, enabled him to penetrate practically any social circle that he wished.

"O'Kieff appeared to take a fancy to me and gradually he

71

took me into his confidence. Even the greatest crooks seem to have that vein of conceit which goes with the criminal character. Sometimes late at night he would boast to me of the huge organization which he had built up, and I learned that it was not only concerned with selling military secrets to the highest bidder; illicit armament deals, liquor-running and dope-smuggling were also carried out by it on a world-wide scale."

Daphnis was looking straight at me now. Her eyes were inscrutable, but I had lost all sense of nervousness and continued my story without hesitation.

"Seven men controlled this huge criminal combine and every one of them had a name to conjure with which was far above the status in which the police ordinarily look for criminals. They were the real Lords of the Underworld, living in affluence and power, all unsuspected by the intellectual cream of European society into which they had been accepted on account of their wealth and dominating personalities. There was Lord Gavin Fortescue, the dwarf cripple brother of an English duke, Azrael Mozinsky, the Polish Jew multi-millionaire, a German baron, a Portuguese count, a Japanese general and a high Egyptian official named Zakri Bey.

"I found out that the Big Seven were going to meet that year in Brussels for their annual conference, and it seemed to me that it was a heaven-sent opportunity to break up the whole diabolical gang, if only I could get something on them. It was then that I committed the only real crime to which I won't deny my guilt. I got cold feet.

"Instead of going through with the job myself I went to Carruthers, who was the First Secretary of our Embassy, told him what I had been up to and asked for his help. He gave me a terrific dressing-down for monkeying with Secret Service matters at all, but he realized the immense importance of breaking up this gang, and that, as it had taken me months to worm my way into O'Kieff's confidence, it was quite impossible at the last moment to transfer the whole job to proper British agents outside the Diplomatic Service.

"More for the purpose of looking after me than anything else, I think, Carruthers agreed to meet the Big Seven and that was just the very thing that O'Kieff had been playing for. He had been on to my little game the whole time, and only encouraging me as useful bait to hook a much bigger fish.

"Carruthers and I dined with O'Kieff and Mozinsky and the rest of that unholy crew. I was given drugged wine so I passed

72

out soon after the meal, and was found in the gutter of a Brussels slum next morning. What happened to Carruthers nobody will ever know for certain, but I believe that O'Kieff hypnotized him.

"In any case, Carruthers took the whole crowd back to the British Embassy that night, and entertained them there as though they were his bosom friends. Then he led them down to the Chancellery, unlocked the safe and made them free of its contents. All the papers were put back, and it was found locked again next morning. They hadn't stolen a thing, and had actually been invited into the Embassy by one of its principal officials, so they couldn't be accused of anything; but during that midnight session those crooks had been able to possess themselves of many of Britain's most important Diplomatic secrets.

"When Carruthers woke up he remembered absolutely nothing about it; but the night porter described the men who had been in the previous night's party and testified to having seen them sitting with Carruthers round the open safe. After the showdown Carruthers walked quietly upstairs and shot himself. I was very ill for several days, and directly I was well enough I was sent home to be kicked out of the Service with ignominy. I've been a wanderer ever since. That is the truth, the whole truth and nothing but the truth, so help me God."

As I finished, Daphnis stubbed out her cigarette.

"I'm glad that we've met again tonight," she said in a low voice. "There are always two sides to every question. I had heard Paolo's; I wanted to hear yours. I wanted to know the truth—what girl wouldn't?"

"Then why in heaven's name didn't you write to me and say you'd see me?" I asked.

"Because no good could have come of our meeting. Since it's happened by chance, that's different; but I'd made up my mind that I owed it to my family and myself to avoid you as far as I possibly could in the future. "

"But why, Daphnis? Don't you believe what I've just told you?"

"What I believe makes no difference."

"It does to me. It means everything. I don't care two hoots in hell who else does or does not believe in me, but I must know that you do for my own future peace of mind."

"All right, I do believe you. I felt certain the whole time that there must be some explanation."

"Thank God!" I exclaimed, but as I spoke she stood up and said, after a second's silence:

73

"Well, I suppose we should be getting downstairs."

"Not yet," I pleaded hastily. "Tell me about Paolo. I suppose he went back to Italy with his legation? Are you still engaged to him?"

"No. There was another scene the day after you left, and he came to plead with me again just before he sailed for Italy; but I told him that, having once made up my mind I couldn't marry him, I was not going to alter it."

I had risen with her, and now, leaning forward across the table, I seized one of her hands. "Daphnis, if you're free, won't you—won't you . . .?"

"No, Julian, no," she quickly pulled her hand away. "I've already told you—it's finished."

An unworthy instinct to hurt her made me burst out: "So you're afraid of the disgrace which still attaches to me. I meant to tell you the whole sordid story before I asked you to marry me, but no suitable chance occurred. I thought that I'd paid up sufficiently for this single folly of my youth already; but apparently I was wrong. You would have sent me packing in any case, directly I told you of it and you realized that it might be unpleasant for you as my wife if once every few years we'd happened to run up against anyone that I used to know when I was in the Diplomatic."

"No. To say that is unfair and beastly. I think it was much braver of you to face the music and stick it out than to do as your friend and seek escape in suicide."

"Is it that you never really cared, then?" I asked desperately.

"It isn't that either." Her eyes were troubled, and from the way in which she suddenly clasped her hands together I could see that she was terribly distressed. Her voice came in a painful whisper. "You seem to have forgotten that Britain and Italy are now at war."

"So that's the trouble," I sighed. "Of course, I know you're half Italian, but your mother is Greek by birth, isn't she; and your stepfather's a Greek, and nearly all the friends among whom you've moved for years past here in Alexandria are Greeks; so why should you feel so strongly for Italy?"

She spread out her hands with a little helpless gesture. "Everyone thinks my love for Italy is strange, but it isn't really. I was quite young when Mother left my Italian father, and I have always idolized him. I'm an only child, you know, so I was very much alone and I had lots of time on my hands to build romances. In my daydreams it was always my tall, handsome father who turned up and rescued me unexpectedly from boring lessons and horrid governesses. The fact that I didn't even see him again until I was out of the schoolroom didn't alter that, and when I was old enough to appreciate him properly I wasn't disappointed."

She paused for a moment then rushed on: "He must have been terribly good-looking when he was younger. Whenever we've met, he's treated me as an equal instead of just a young girl who's never been anywhere or done anything very much, and he has a magnificent brain. Greece is my country and I love it dearly, but in this quarrel between Britain and Italy how can I help my heart being with my father's people? I want to shout '*Vivas!*' for every Italian victory; as I did when those splendid Blackshirts threw the British right out of their corner of Somaliland the other day."

"Oh, come!" I protested. "That wasn't much to shout about. The Italians were at least five to one against us. They had mechanized troops, whereas we hadn't a single tank in the whole of British Somaliland, and Berbera is not even fortified."

"There!" she burst out bitterly. "You see! You haven't even the grace to acknowledge a triumph when it is obtained against you. The Italian Cavalry officers are better riders than you are, as they have proved again and again at the Olympia horse shows in London, yet you English have the insolence to refer to them openly as ice-cream merchants, waiters and dagos."

"Please," I begged. " Couldn't we forget the war? We'd make a pact never even to mention it when we were together."

"How could we, Julian? That's impossible, and you must see that it is. The war shrieks at us from every hoarding. With every week that passes it is affecting life in Alexandria more seriously. Very soon it will be part and parcel of our daily lives, although, theoretically, Egypt is still supposed to be neutral."

"But if we love each other we shouldn't let the war come between us. You do love me, Daphnis, don't you?"

"I did," her voice was only a whisper, "but I made myself forget about you, and it's all over now."

"It's not. It can't be!" I insisted, taking her hand again. "You can't just love a man one day and not care if he lives or dies the next."

"I do care," she admitted suddenly, looking straight into my eyes, "but I tell you this war lies between us like a sword. It was that which the fortune-teller must have meant when he told the sands for me the day after you were carried unconscious into my home. He described you quite clearly. There could have been no mistake, and he swore to me that only ill could come to both of us if we let love have its way. Please don't make things harder for me by asking me to dance again, and—and, please, take me back to the ballroom now."

At that moment, to my dismay, four elderly people came in to occupy the table at which we were standing for a game of bridge; so I had no option but to do as she asked.

The rest of that dance was a nightmare, and it was not far off dawn before I could get away. As I walked through the silent streets the short distance back to my hotel I knew that I had persuaded Daphnis of my innocence and that she still loved me, but that nothing could remove the barrier that lay between us except the ending of the war, and I had no means of hastening that.

CHAPTER VIII

DIVIDED LOYALTIES

TWENTY-FOUR hours later I was back with the New Zealanders at Mersa Matruh. They wanted to know if I'd had a good time. I said, "Marvellous!" My special friends, Jack Benham and Toby Spiers, asked for details. It was no good making a parade of my misery so I talked vaguely of swimming and dancing, and girls. They sighed with envy and counted the days afresh until their own leave was due.

The heat was only slightly less gruelling than it had been at mid-summer and the insects were worse; but I took on every job that offered in an endeavour to keep my mind off Daphnis through sheer physical exhaustion.

The Battle of Britain continued with unabated fury. The Germans cut up Rumania, giving Hungary back her lost province of Transylvania, so that with this, the loss of Bessarabia to the Russians and the Drobuja to Bulgaria, Rumania was reduced again to the size that she had been before the 1914 war. In Bucharest there were riots against this arbitrary dismemberment which culminated in a coup by which King Carol lost his throne and had to fly the country, leaving the pro-Nazi General

Antonescu as virtual dictator. Clearly it could be only a matter of time before Hitler took over the whole country.

French Equatorial Africa, the Cameroons, Madagascar, New Caledonia and Gabon declared for General de Gaulle, but welcome as was the news that a few thousand Frenchmen here and there still understood the real meaning of the word 'honour', that was little consolation for the precarious situation in which Britain had been left by the total surrender of the main French Armies at home and the cowardly inertia displayed by the French generals in North Africa and Syria.

By mid-September the German aerial attack had moved from the ports and airfields in South-Eastern Britain on to London, and from the first reports we feared that if we ever got back there we should find nothing left of the dear old city but a vast acreage of ruins. Then gradually we became a little more cheerful as we learned of the further amazing victories of our fighter pilots, and that the Bomber Command was fighting back, hurling death and destruction down each night on the Continental ports where the Germans were said to be massing their great army of invasion.

On September 21st we were at last given other things to think about than the scanty news from home and our own individual worries. Abruptly our long months of wearisome routine under the scorching sun came to an end. News arrived that Marshal Graziani's army was on the move and that his advance striking force had crossed the border into Egypt.

At last we had the thought that we might really be going into battle with the enemy to arouse us from the torpid state into which we had fallen through weeks of filling and stacking sand-bags and trying to keep the defence works which we had constructed from being silted up by the constantly drifting sand.

We all knew that we were hopelessly outnumbered by the Italians, but all the same we were longing to have a cut at them, and the disappointment was general when, after a few days, the first excitement petered out. There had been some minor clashes up near the frontier, but no serious resistance was offered to the Italian advance and our columns were gradually withdrawn until Mersa Matruh, from outside which my own unit never received orders to move, became the last town on the road to Libya held by the British.

The men who came back from sporadic scrapping with the Eyeties reported them to be poor fighters, and it irked our fellows sadly to retreat. But we all felt that General Wavell knew what he was up to, as it was obvious that the odds against us would be considerably lessened if the Italian line of communication was first stretched as far as possible, and the Army of the Nile was able to meet the invader on its own chosen ground.

Few of us doubted that would be Mersa Matruh, as the whole area round the small white-walled town had been trenched, sand-bagged, wired, revetted and made into a defensive zone of great depth with innumerable cunningly concealed tank-traps, strong points and gun-emplacements. It seemed unlikely that the results of so much labour would be lightly sacrificed and almost certain that within the next few days a major battle would be raging there; but neither eventuality actually occurred.

Having advanced as far as Sidi Barrani, which was seventy miles west of us along the coast road, the Italians halted to con-solidate their gains, construct airfields, improve roads, and bring up the vast quantity of supplies and ammunition which they would need before they could launch their main attack on Egypt. The seventy miles between Mersa Matruh and Sidi Barrani became a No Man's Land in which mechanized patrols operated against each other from time to time, but by the end of the month it was clear that the main armies were not likely to be engaged yet, and we returned rather glumly to our previous routine.

During those days of tension General de Gaulle's expedition to Dakar had fizzled out like a damp squib. It seemed a most stupid blunder to have allowed him to go there at all unless he was prepared to fight if he encountered resistance. As it was, the British Admiral appeared to have had insufficient authority to take full command of the expedition and order the Free French Forces ashore, and although he went into the action with the obvious intention of trying to pull the chestnuts out of the fire, he was let down and left unsupported. In consequence, this miserable half-hearted affair caused a very great deal of bad blood without having achieved anything at all, and by it we sustained a still further loss of prestige. But early in October we got better news.

The United States Government declared itself ready to hand over to us fifty destroyers in exchange for the bases which they were leasing in our Atlantic possessions. God knows our over-worked Navy needed the ships badly enough, but there was much more to it than that. This epoch-making deal showed that at last the people of the United States were really awaking to the fact that, if the British Navy failed to hold the seas, sooner or later they would have to face the whole might of Hitler on their own.

It was early in October, too, that Chamberlain at last passed from office, resigning on account of ill health. The following day those younger, more vigorous men with whom he had striven in vain at Munich, Hitler and Mussolini, met on the Brenner and the whole world proceeded to speculate upon what further devilry they had arranged to undertake between them. But there were signs that Britain was getting her second wind. Many new units were now arriving in the Middle East to reinforce the Army of the Nile and, by the announcement that we intended to reopen the Burma Road, Churchill indicated pretty clearly that he meant to stand no further nonsense from the Japs.

Italy proceeded to adopt a most threatening attitude towards Greece, so it was suggested that one of the decisions reached at the Brenner was for her to attack her small neighbour. While Germany exerted pressure upon Yugoslavia, Italy strongly reinforced her garrisons in Albania. For a week there was terrific tension. The Germans forced a trade agreement on the Yugoslavs which, being interpreted, meant that the Yugoslav Government had given way and decided not to go to Greece's aid if Italy attacked her. Hitler had a meeting with Laval, then a meeting on the Franco-Spanish frontier with General Franco, then a meeting with Marshal Pétain. There were endless rumours about these comings and goings and what they portended. On October 28th Hitler met Mussolini again, this time at Florence, and on that day the Italian forces in Albania invaded Greece.

When I heard that the invasion was an accomplished fact I gave my thought free rein along a track off which for several days past I had had the greatest difficulty in heading them. This new war concerned me personally. Daphnis was half Italian and half Greek. Now that the two nations were at each other's throats to which of them would she give her loyalty? It might be that her romantic idealism of her father had secured such a strong hold on her imagination that whatever the views of her family and friends in secret, she would still remain pro-Italian. On the other hand, she was half Greek by blood and wholly Greek by adoption and upbringing, and she herself had told me that she loved Greece. Italy had attacked Greece, brutally, wantonly, and without the slightest provocation, and in view of that there seemed a good chance that Daphnis had experienced a revulsion of feeling. If so, the one thing which had seemed utterly impossible when I had last seen her over two months before had happened.

79

Without the war between Britain and Italy having come to an end, Fate had smoothed away the apparently insurmountable barrier which lay between Daphnis and myself.

The moment that I could get 'Long Willie' alone I asked him if he would grant me forty-eight hours' special leave to Alex on urgent private affairs.

"That's a matter for the Brigadier," he said, but added kindly: "Still, things look like remaining quiet here, so put in your application. I don't doubt it will go through if I recommend it."

Having thanked him I wrote off at once to Barbara Wishart to let her know that I hoped soon to be in Alex on short leave, and was most anxious to get half an hour alone with Daphnis. I had developed a regular correspondence with Barbara in which I had told her all about my ill-starred love affair, and that Daphnis would no longer go to any place willingly where she thought she would be likely to meet me; but I felt sure that Barbara would give me all the help she could.

Three days later my leave came through, and once more I took the long dusty coast road to the east. That road was very different now from when I had first seen it in the previous May. It had since been more than doubled in width, and strong concrete bridges which would bear two columns of tanks abreast had been thrown over all the nullahs. For every soldier stationed along it then there were now three or four. With great courage the decision had been taken, while the Battle of Britain was still in its early stages, and invasion a very definite menace, to despatch troops from England to reinforce the Army of the Nile.

After Italy's entry into the war the passage of the Sicilian Channel had been virtually denied to us by the enemy. That narrow bottle-neck, which connects the two great seas of the Western and Eastern Mediterranean, is less than a hundred miles across, and right in its centre lies the island of Pantellaria, which, in the years before the war, had been converted by the Italians into a military base bristling with great guns. If the French had remained with us Pantellaria and Trapani, the Italian naval station at the eastern end of Sicily, could have been neutralized by the Allied Navies operating from the great French base of Bizerta, while Axis aircraft, based on Sicily, could have been countered by Allied squadrons stationed in Tunisia. But by the shameful complaisance of the French generals in North Africa we were robbed of these measures for protecting our shipping. Every vessel which now dared the channel had not only to dodge the

Italian submarines but run the gauntlet of the dive-bombers; so although our warships still made the passage as necessity dictated, all convoys with reinforcements and supplies for our forces in Abyssinia, Egypt and Palestine had had, since the previous July, to be sent right round Africa *via* the Cape of Good Hope.

Most of us who realized what was happening could cheerfully have shot those French generals for the part they were playing in increasing Germany's chances of victory. No man can serve two masters, and the issue was plain to all. It is to be hoped that the part these men have played will not be forgotten after the war, but that they will have to answer to an Allied court-martial for their poltroonery and the lives of the countless defenders of Freedom which have been lost through it.

In spite of the many weeks' delay, which had occurred entirely owing to the above reasons, reinforcements from Britain were now pouring into Egypt, and when I reached Alexandria I found six times the amount of khaki in the streets that there had been the previous summer.

As soon as I arrived I telephoned to Barbara and she said that she would try to get Daphnis to come in for drinks that evening, although normally she did not go to cocktail parties given by members of the British Colony. Half an hour later she rang me back to say that, somewhat to her surprise, Daphnis had accepted at once and that I had better be out at Ramleh myself at six o'clock.

When I got there Barbara told me that she had asked in one or two other friends just to keep us in countenance, but that if I wanted a private session with Daphnis I could either take her out into the garden or into the small sitting-room at the back of the house.

I sank three sherries in rapid succession with Barbara and her sister Dorothy before any of the other guests arrived. The girls were most amused at my state of jitters, and I was both astonished and ashamed at the way my nerves always seemed to let me down whenever Daphnis was in the offing. I seemed to have altogether lost that calm self-assurance which had always been mine until seven months before.

The arrival of a naval lieutenant necessitated the talk becoming general, and I pulled myself together again. Soon afterwards a gunner captain and his wife arrived, and I found myself tied up in a conversation with the wife when Daphnis entered the room. To my fury the sailor pounced on her before I could make my escape, but Barbara took in the situation, rescued me from the gunner's wife, and to the sailor's dismay saddled him with her, leaving the field clear for me with Daphnis.

To my intense relief she smiled, and almost instinctively the two of us turned to walk out of the french windows on to the little terrace behind the house.

"Why were you looking so worried just now?" she asked, with an amused glance, as soon as we were out of earshot of the others.

"I was terrified that you might be furious at finding me here," I confessed.

"How silly of you!" she laughed. "If I hadn't wanted to see you I could have refused the invitation. I hardly ever visit any of our few English acquaintances in their houses, and after the way that Barbara Wishart planted you in their party for the Life-boat Institution dance I felt quite certain that she could only have asked me this evening at your instigation."

We sat down in two basket chairs beneath a gaily-striped sun umbrella. It was hardly needed now, although the sunshine was still pleasant, as it had lost most of its force with the decline of the year.

As I lit a cigarette for Daphnis I said with a beating heart, "Your coming here this evening, then, means that you really wanted to see me?"

She inhaled deeply and lowered her long curling lashes so that they veiled her eyes. "I can't forget what that old Arab fortune-teller said. He's been so uncannily right in his predictions about other people. For that reason I still feel that it's out of the question for us to think of each other seriously. But having thought it over I don't see why we shouldn't meet occasionally as friends."

Inwardly I smiled, and something of my old self-confidence came back. In admitting so much, Daphnis had as good as proclaimed her own defeat. She would not, of course, have acknowledged that to herself as yet, but in an effort to square her declared attitude with her subconscious desire, she had adopted the most ancient female gambit of all time—'Why can't we just be friends?'

"I'm glad you feel that way," I said, "because I was afraid that as long as the war between Britain and Italy continued you would regard that as an insurmountable barrier between us."

She made a little grimace. "I've thought a lot about that too, lately, and I've come to the conclusion that I was wrong. If we only meet as friends we ought to be able to ignore the war."

82

"I suppose the invasion of Greece has helped quite a lot in changing your views?" I hazarded.

"No, it's not that. I'm desperately sorry for the Greeks, of course; but it doesn't make me any the less fond of Italy and the Italians. If you were to see two of your friends fighting you would be most unhappy for them both, but it would not make you like either of them less."

"Oh, come!" I protested. "Not if one of them were a great big husky man of six foot two and the other were a small boy of, say, thirteen and without the slightest provocation the big man smashed his fist into the small boy's face? You might have liked the big man before but I'll bet you wouldn't feel much friendship for him after you'd seen him do that."

She sat forward and stared at me earnestly. "That's not fair. You don't understand. It's not the Italian people who have attacked the Greeks. They are charming, cultured, home-loving, and have no wish to make war on anybody. It is Mussolini who has done this horrible thing."

"I thought you were an admirer of Mussolini's?"

"I was, and you admitted at one time you used to admire him, too."

I nodded. "Yes. Any number of people did, but most of us saw the red light when he chose Easter Sunday to send his bombers and his Blackshirts against the helpless peasants of Albania."

"They were brigands—bandits—everybody knows that—just as were the Abyssinians. Mussolini was right to take over both countries so that law and justice might take the place of the corrupt old-fashioned Governments."

"There's quite a lot to be said for that," I agreed, "but do you really believe that the Italian people have no responsibility at all for this war, and that they were forced into it against their will by Mussolini, Ciano and Co.?"

"Yes. It was a tragedy that Marshal Balbo was killed in that air crash because he was a really great Italian, and Count Grandi, who is another, seems to have lost his influence. Ciano, Starace, Faracini, Ansaldo, and the other extremists who were probably in the pay of Germany, must have got hold of Mussolini and, of course, in these days once a war is declared the ordinary soldiers and the people have no say at all. They simply have to do as they are ordered."

"Daphnis, I adore you," I said. "But honestly that's only the superficial, not the basic, cause of the trouble. Just because we call

83

these upstart rulers 'dictators' it's the greatest mistake in the world to believe that they could continue to rule for any length of time without the consent of the mass of their countrymen.

"They can persecute small minorities without stirring up the bulk of the nation against themselves. Through their secret police they can establish a state of terror in which people become mighty careful what they say in public. They can enforce certain inconveniences and hardships upon their entire populations, but —if they are to keep their hold—for every individual that they persecute they must provide a good job, a fine uniform or a state of prosperity for at least half a dozen others. No matter what measures they take for the suppression of the Press and free speech, they cannot stop people whispering among themselves, and if they demand sacrifices from their nations they will only get them when the purpose for which they demand them is one with which the bulk of the people are in full sympathy."

"I've never thought of it that way before," she said slowly. "D'you really believe that?"

"I do," I assured her earnestly. "In Hitler the German people got the leader that they asked for, and these Nazi swine are the same flesh, blood and cold calculating brain as the brutal jack-booted Prussians of the past. Hitler hasn't thought up anything new. All he's done is to assimilate the teachings of other Germans, most of whom are dead and gone, and carry those teachings into harsh realities.

"The same applies to England. In the years of our wicked refusal to face facts we got Baldwin, in the days of our honest but ill-informed seeking to avert a second world catastrophe we had Chamberlain; but now that the nation is roused to a full sense of its responsibilities and has regained its old fighting spirit we have Churchill. That's where the Germans make such a stupid mistake. They seem to think that a Jewish capitalist clique, led by Churchill, is running this war, and that the wretched British are being forced to stand out against a peace by agreement which they would simply jump at if they only had their own way. But that isn't so at all. Churchill is England—the very heart and soul of it —and every one of us would give his eyes to have all his qualities. Yet Churchill is only where he is today because he is the most perfect vehicle through which the people of Britain can express their defiance of their enemies, their intrinsic rock-like strength and their utter confidence in complete and final victory."

"How do you explain, then," she asked, "the fact that prominent Englishmen are so often reported in the papers as saying that you are not fighting the German people—only the Nazis; and that the French are still your allies at heart and were only deceived by their 'wicked leaders'?"

I smiled. "That's the price we have to pay for being a democracy. Some of these people are irresponsible fools, others are fifth columnists in the pay of Hitler; but unless we can definitely prove that a man is a traitor he's still allowed to say what he likes. Unfortunately they do immense damage to our war effort, although most of them are only stupid old men who're afraid to face hard facts. But I want you to face them if you can. If we're to be friends it's best that I should never refer to the subject again; but now that the Italians have gone into Greece I feel it's only right that you should know what other people think about them. Can you take it, or would you rather that I dried up?"

"No, go on," she said.

"All right, then. The Italian masses are just as much responsible for the actions of their Government as any other people, otherwise the Fascist Party could not possibly have remained in power for eighteen years. Mussolini appeared as a leader offering just that programme and personality which the bulk of the Italian people were ripe to accept and endorse. He cleaned up their country and the strength of their confidence in him grew. Italy is horribly overcrowded, and since the last war emigration to the United States has been made much more difficult through the quota system. Italy had to have breathing-space somewhere. Naturally the Fascist Government did their best to develop such colonial territories as Italy already had in Libya, Italian Somaliland and Eritrea. From that it was only a step to the popular cry for the new Roman Empire. You know how the Italian people loved that idea and cheered themselves hoarse at all the Imperial caperings to which their Fascist leaders treated them. Well . . . the inevitable outcome of all that is this, so it's no good now to turn round and say that the Italian people are guiltless and that their heart is not in the war. 'Nice, Corsica, Tunis!' was their cry, and you can take it from me that they're in this war simply for anything that they can get out of it. That's the truth, Daphnis."

"Perhaps." She stared at me unhappily. "I'm sure you're right about the Germans. They always have been a race of brutes, and the French—well, everybody except the English seemed to have realized years ago that they had become hopelessly decadent. About your own people I don't know, but no one's ever accused them of lack of courage and ever since they've been getting the worst of it they seem to have taken on a new lease of life. I still

85

don't think that you're right, though, about the Italians. I'm desperately sorry for the Greeks, but I shall always love my father's people. If you want us to be friends it can only be on the understanding that we ignore the war; because as far as that is concerned we must remain enemies."

CHAPTER IX

AT THE ANCIENT TEMPLE

I SAW that it was useless to argue further. For a second I was a little frightened. The fact that she continued to be so strongly pro-Italian in spite of the attack on Greece seemed to lend support to Major Cozelli's damnable suspicions that she was actively assisting the enemy. If she was and, through continuing to know her, I found her out, I should have only myself to blame for creating a situation in which I should suffer sheer unadulterated hell.

Yet, as she sat there, so young, so clear-eyed and so utterly the antithesis of everything one connects with stealthy plotting and unscrupulous deceit, I could not believe that Cozelli was right. And, after all, that we should ignore the war was the very line that I had advocated myself when we had last met in August. It was only natural that the feelings of a lifetime could not be suddenly reversed in a single week; and it was not yet a week since the Italians had gone into Greece. Soon there were certain to be stories of their German-inspired ruthlessness, and that would bring about a change of heart in her more genuine than could any of my academic arguments. She had offered me her friendship. I felt that I should be crazy to refuse it.

"All right. Let's leave it at that," I smiled. "There are such masses of more pleasant things that I'm longing to talk to you about, and I'm only down here on forty-eight hours' leave. How and when am I to see anything of you? Can I come to the house openly or is that impossible?"

She sighed: "I'm afraid it is. You see, I never told Mother that I met you again at that dance last August, so she still believes Paolo's version of—of your misfortune. If you called I'd

86

never be allowed to see you, and Mother is not the sort of person to whom I could explain about you at just a few minutes' notice."

"How about my coming to the garden late tonight, then?" I asked, but she shook her head.

"No, that's no good either, because Alcis is staying with us again. We had a frightful row about the way she behaved that night I sent her to let you in, and she knows all about the scene with Paolo. I simply dare not trust her now, and as her room is on one side of mine and Mother's is on the other, I'd never be able to get down and back without one of them hearing me. You see, the house is very old, and at night when it's quiet every board in the passage and on the staircase creaks appallingly."

"I see," I said glumly. "But it's not much good our being friends if we're never to meet, is it? And I have to start back tomorrow evening, so we've barely twenty-four hours, and if I don't see you again in that time it'll probably be weeks before I get another chance."

"I know!" she exclaimed. "Now that Greece is at war we're all doing every possible thing we can to help. Tomorrow afternoon I've promised to roll bandages and make cotton-wool pads for wound dressings at the Headquarters for Help to the Motherland, which has just been opened in the Sidi el Mitwalli. The car will drop me there at half past two and pick me up again at five. I must go into the building, but I could slip out again, and if you were waiting in another car outside . . ."

"Splendid!" I said eagerly. "I'll be there to the minute and keep a sharp lookout for you. But I won't bring the car I hire too close to the building in case any of your friends who might be going in or out see you drive off with me."

It was Daphnis who a few minutes afterwards suggested that we ought to go inside and join the others, and reluctantly I agreed. Twenty minutes later we parted with formal smiles, and through the front window I saw her driven away by an elderly Eurasian chauffeur in a large old-fashioned pale blue Rolls.

That night I threw a party at the Cecil for Barbara, and all the friends I could persuade her to invite to it. For the first time in months I was really happy, and I wanted everybody else to be happy, too. My meeting with Daphnis had proved infinitely more successful than I had dared to hope. True, I had failed to convince her fully that the Italians were not the little heroes that she had always pictured them, and there was still just a remote possibility that Major Cozelli's suspicion that she was working for them was correct. The mystery of the man she had met in the garden and whose voice had filled me with such acute perturbation had also not been cleared up. But when a really favourable opportunity occurred I could ask her about that; and in the meantime, since she was so plainly distressed for the Greeks, it was hardly conceivable that she was acting as a secret agent for their enemies. For the moment it was enough that Daphnis could no more keep her thoughts from me than I could mine from her, to make my heart sing with joy.

After lunch next day I took up my position with the smartest hired car that I could find about a hundred and fifty yards to the north of a big building in the Sidi el Mitwalli, which had large brand new streamers draped across its frontage calling upon all Greeks in Alexandria to give every aid that they could in the defence of the sacred soil of the Hellenes.

Ten minutes after my arrival the old-fashioned pale blue Rolls drove up. Daphnis got out and went into the building, while the car drove off. She was inside for about seven minutes, then coming out again she glanced quickly up and down the street. I was standing on the pavement beside my car, and directly she caught sight of me I got into it, started the engine and drove slowly out of the main thoroughfare into a small side street, where I halted. Two minutes afterwards Daphnis, deliciously flushed and trembling with excitement, scrambled in beside me.

"Have you never cut a party like that before to do something you wouldn't like your mother to know about?" I asked, as we drove away.

"Yes," she laughed a little breathlessly. "Another girl and I used to play truant from the meetings of the Orthodox Church Working Guild sometimes last year. We managed to see three films that we'd been forbidden to go to, and each time it was a tremendous adventure. I think things will be all right today. I spoke to several people I know who are working in different rooms and each of them will probably think that I'm working with one of the others."

"You're a bold bad woman!" I mocked her, and I could have laughed aloud now at the cadaverous Major Cozelli's absurd suggestion that this adorable child-woman might possibly be an Italian spy.

I drove out through the back of the town to the open country beside Lake Mareotis. In these days it is not a lake at all but marshy ground, much of which has been reclaimed for sugar plantations and other crops. It runs for several miles, and I followed its northern edge through half a dozen straggling native villages where humped oxen, goats, chickens, native children and myriads of flies huddled together in dusty squalor, until we reached more open country in the neighbourhood of Maryut. Turning off the high road, I headed for a big grove of date palms, and driving slowly through it pulled up the car near a small ruined temple.

The little building was of the so-called decadent Ptolemaic period and only a mere two thousand years old, so it probably had no more than a couple of lines in the guide-books, and even the troops, who had now taken the place of the pre-war tourists as the sightseers of Egypt, were hardly likely to bother to visit it.

A padlocked board door had been fitted against the entrance to the shrine, as the Egyptian Government is a firm believer in not allowing visitors to Egypt to see even the least interesting of the ancient monuments without paying for it. Doubtless a local Arab guide, living somewhere near by, made a few piastres a month by being dug out once a week or so to show really keen archaeologists round the dark dank chamber by the light of a guttering candle; but the last thing that Daphnis and I were thinking of that afternoon was wall sculptures and the long-dead Pharaohs.

I collected a few things that I had brought with me in the car, and entering the open forecourt of the temple we sat down on the sun-warmed stone of a fallen monolith, the lotus flower capital of which had once helped to support the gaily-painted ceiling of the forecourt, now long since crumbled in the dust.

The things I had brought in the car were the largest box of chocolates that I had been able to buy that morning, a big packet of real *foie gras* sandwiches that I had had made up for me at the hotel, and a bottle of Louis Roederer 1928 in a pail of ice. Why I should have imagined that Daphnis would be hungry or wish to drink champagne in the middle of the afternoon, I can't think; but perhaps it was because I was debarred from entertaining her in the ordinary way to lunch or dinner, and was so anxious to give her the best of everything that money could buy.

On seeing the things she asked me if, for some reason, I had missed my lunch, but on my explaining that I'd only brought them just in case, she insisted on eating some of the sandwiches, and as it turned out the warmth in that sheltered sunbaked place made the iced champagne by no means unwelcome to both of us.

She seemed gayer and happier this afternoon than at any time that I had previously seen her, and I really began to wonder if she regarded this friendship business as a serious proposition, but

I felt sure that it could not satisfy her for long any more than it would me. We laughed a lot during the first hour that we were there, perhaps because we both felt that we had plenty of time before us; but as the afternoon wore on both of us became conscious of a gradually growing tension in which it became more and more difficult to talk about indifferent matters, until finally we fell silent.

It was very still there; not a breath of wind rippled the palm fronds which hung gracefully from the tufted tops of the tall trees beyond the wall. For a few moments I watched a lizard frisking about the cracked and battered bas-relief on the inside of the temple gateway, until it disappeared into a hole under the god Anubis' head. Then I followed the point of Daphnis' parasol, with which she was drawing pictures in the age-old dust.

As we were sitting now, countless other lovers must have sat in that self-same spot. Travelling English, German and American couples of George V, Edward VII, or Queen Victoria's times; French soldiers of Napoleon's army and British sailors from Nelson's ships, making love to some Pasha's daughter who had escaped the vigilance of her duenna for the afternoon; Mamelukes, Crusaders, early Christians, Romans, Phœnicians, and Greeks; all must have passed that way and doubtless lingered there, since the place had been abandoned by its priests and fallen into ruin. But for them time had not been such a slave-driver as it is with us. In the not far distant modern city ten thousand clocks were inexorably ticking away. I had to get Daphnis back there by five o'clock and I must leave it again to return to the Front that evening.

Very gently I laid my large hand over Daphnis' small one and stopped her drawing with the parasol, as I said: "You know, darling, I'm afraid it's impossible for us to be only friends. Men and women can be friends—my friendship with Barbara Wishart is a good instance of that—but only where nothing deeper has been touched in either of them or where both have indulged their passion for each other, and it has burnt out. Neither state applies to you and me. We've started something and we've got to see it through to its logical conclusion or else tear the whole thing out, root and branch."

She went a little pale as she replied, with a lightness which I could see was assumed:

"All right. If you don't want to be friends perhaps we'd better not see each other again. I'm over the worst effects of our affair already."

"Are you quite sure of that? Absolutely dead certain that you never want to see me again?"

"No. I do want to see you," she answered a little hoarsely, "but—but as a friend."

I was very tempted to let it go at that. It seemed, when I thought of the apparent finality of that night in August at the dance, that she had since come more than half-way to meet me; but I felt that if only I had the guts to stand out I might succeed in winning her back altogether.

"How can we be friends?" I reasoned. "It's nearly seven months now since we met. Each time I've seen you I've suffered the tortures of the damned for weeks afterwards from the longing to hold you in my arms. And for your part, however much you pretend that you don't, you still want to feel my kisses. That's true, isn't it?"

"Yes, Julian," her voice was only a whisper.

I put one arm about her shoulders and drew her unresisting towards me. While I had been speaking she had remained staring at the ground, so that the brim of her hat hid her face from me, but now she lifted it and I saw that she was crying.

Suddenly her arms were round my neck, and she was clinging to me while she sobbed as though her very heart would break.

"My sweet!" I murmured. "Please, please, I can't bear the thought that it's I who have made you cry."

"Oh, Julian!" she sobbed. "I love you—I love you so much. I think I'd die now if I could never see you again."

It was surrender, complete and utter surrender; but I felt no sense of triumph, only a breathless joy and timid hesitant wonder. How could a girl so sweet and so unspoilt really care for a cynical worthless devil like myself? Yet she had said "I love you!" and I was kissing away her warm wet tears as she repeated again and again, "Oh, Julian, I love you, I love you so!"

For what seemed a long time we clung together, murmuring little phrases until her tears were dried and the smiles came like sunshine after rain, lighting up her lovely shining eyes.

She had thrown aside her hat and her dark head was nestling on my shoulder. Under her thin dress I could feel her heart beating against my side. Raising one of her hands to my lips I kissed it and said:

"Listen, darling. We understand each other now, don't we? Nothing else matters but the fact that we love each other and that you're going to marry me."

"Yes," she murmured.

"When?" I asked.

"Whenever you like."

I caught my breath, hardly daring to believe that I had heard her whispered words aright; but she went on: "I was a fool to believe that stupid fortune-teller who said that we were not meant for each other, and that only misfortune could come from my allowing myself to fall in love with you. I've kept you waiting so long; all I want now is to make you happy."

"I must go back tonight," I said, "but as soon as I see my Colonel I can put in for special marriage leave. How about your parents, though? I don't want to come between you and them, so perhaps it would be best if I saw your stepfather before I leave this evening."

She shook her head. "I'd rather break it to them myself, if you don't mind. My wanting to get married at once will be an awful shock to them. I simply wouldn't dare suggest it if they didn't know about you already. Fortunately they both liked you when you came to the house, and of course they knew that I broke off my engagement to Paolo because of you; but—but there'll be an awful lot of explaining to do. I'm sure things will go much more smoothly if you leave it to me to choose the right moment."

"How long is it likely to be before one occurs?" I asked. "A few days, a week, or more than that? I shall be terribly anxious until I know that everything's going to be all right."

"Give me a week. I promise I won't keep you waiting longer."

"Just as you wish, angel. But in that case it'd be better if I don't apply for marriage leave until I hear from you, and I'm due for a week's leave towards the end of this month, anyway. It might be an idea to combine the two, as that would give us a much longer honeymoon."

"Oh do, Julian!" She sat up and clasped her hands. "That would be much better because it would give me time to turn round in."

"You're not in half such a hurry as I am," I teased her.

"It's not that, silly, but a girl only gets married once in her life; at least, that's the way I've always wanted it to be, and I know that it will be with you. You wouldn't grudge me a proper wedding, would you, with a lovely dress and bridesmaids, and a trousseau and everything? All those things take time to arrange, you know. Mother would want it that way, I'm certain, and it will be much easier for me to win her over if I say that we're going to get married at the end of November than if I declare that, whether

92

she likes it or not, I'm going to marry you at the end of next week."

"All right, beloved, that's settled then." I smiled and took her in my arms again.

A long shadow thrown by the old temple gateway roused us to the fact that she would be shockingly late if we did not set off back to Alex at once, and after a last kiss we hurried to the car.

On the way in I said that probably one of the stiffest fences to be faced would be her parents' fear that she was rushing into marriage with someone who could not support her. Families like the Diamopholi, to whom marriages by arrangement were almost a sacred creed, would naturally be shocked out of their senses at the idea of what in their eyes would seem a war marriage based on infatuation with a complete outsider. They would perhaps even lock Daphnis up or pack her off to South Africa or somewhere, unless at least some satisfactory settlement was put forward to lull their worst apprehensions. To get over this I suggested that I should write to Essex Pasha, who was the one person in Egypt who knew all about me, and ask him to call on Diamopholus *père*. I felt sure that he would vouch for my character, and I would also empower him to make any marriage settlement on my behalf that lay within my considerable means.

Daphnis thought that was a splendid idea, as it would at least assure her people that she was not being carried off by a penniless adventurer.

Once we were in the city I had the inspiration of driving her to the back of the big building which housed the Greek Relief Fund, so that she was able to slip into it and walk straight out to the front where we knew that her car would already be waiting for her. She had to abandon the huge box of chocolates, otherwise there would have been inconvenient questions as to where she had got them, but she took the big bow of ribbon off the box, kissed it and stuffed in my pocket to be, as she said, 'a talisman' for me during our few weeks' separation.

There was a last hurried kiss snatched in the car, then she was gone, running lightly across the pavement and into a dark entrance.

At the hotel I packed as though I were moving in a dream, and that night I took the road to the west in a haze of delirious happiness.

Immediately I reached my unit I sat down and wrote a long letter to Essex Pasha. Each day afterwards I spent every leisure moment in writing reams to my dearest one, and on the fifth day

I received a letter from her. Almost bursting with excitement I tore it open and hastily scanned the first page. Joy of joys! Everything was all right. Daphnis' mother had been difficult at first, but old Diamopholus had come to the rescue. He had had a long talk with Essex Pasha and afterwards succeeded in convincing his wife that, from the worldly point of view, I was not really a bad match for even a millionaire's stepdaughter. From that point everything had gone swimmingly. They were already discussing the wedding dress and the bridesmaids' frocks. The next step was for me to let her know the date that I could get leave.

Two days later I was able to let her have it. The Brigadier had granted me a fortnight as from November the 26th.

On the following Monday I had another letter from Daphnis. The invitations were now being printed, and all the preparations were going forward for the wedding. Once the opposition had been overcome her whole family had been wonderfully human, petting her, spoiling her, and deriving a reflected joy from her romance. She wrote that she was living now only for the moment when, in the sight of God and Man, on Wednesday, November the 27th, she would become my adoring wife. But the accursed Sword of Fate still lay between us. On November the 12th I was taken prisoner by the Italians.

CHAPTER X

IN THE HANDS OF THE ENEMY

M Y approaching marriage to Daphnis had put it completely out of my mind that a fortnight earlier, just before Italy had invaded Greece and I had applied for my forty-eight hours' special leave, I had expressed great keenness to take part in one of the raids that our forward elements occasionally made across No Man's Land. Although we had been at war with Italy for over five months, my own battalion had not yet seen an Italian except for a few prisoners who had been captured in raids and enemy airmen who bailed out at the sight of the R.A.F. It was sheer overzealousness on my part to witness some actual fighting which led to my grievous undoing.

A Coldstream captain named Archie Melrose had been dining with us at the battalion H.Q. His company was holding a chain of advance posts and it was when I complained that we seemed much more likely to die of boredom than from enemy action that he said at once:

"If you're all that anxious to have a crack at the Italians come up and spend a day or two with me, and we'll take you along on our next show."

As battalion interpreter I had no routine duties which would be seriously affected by my absence, so it was only a matter of my obtaining 'Long Willie's' formal consent, and he gave it at once. Soon after I got back from leave I was told that it had been fixed up that I should join Melrose on the early morning of November the 11th, and of course it was too late to back out then, even if I had wanted to.

Long before it was light on the Sunday my batman roused me, and as soon as I was fully awake I realized that there was no time to be lost if I was to catch the early morning supply column, which was affording me transport up to the advance unit.

When I arrived Melrose introduced me to his brother officers, who proved a very friendly crowd, and I soon settled in. The padre came up to hold a short Armistice Day service, which was rather impressive out there in the desert, and after that I was on the move most of the time, accompanying Melrose on his rounds from post to post, openly admiring the discipline and turn-out which the Guards maintained even in that desolate waste.

That evening Melrose told me that he had been ordered to send out a reconnaissance party towards the oasis of Bir Fuad, which lay about seventy miles inland along the caravan track leading from Mersa Matruh to Siwa. Most reconnaissance work was done by the light tanks of the Cavalry, but their numbers were limited, and now that the African campaigning season was upon us, the General Staff were calling for more frequent and thorough reports upon the enemy's strength and dispositions.

The party was to consist of six Bren-gun carriers under the command of a lieutenant, and it was to take off at sundown so that advantage could be taken of the darkness before the moon got up, and scouting enemy aircraft would not see the clouds of sand which the caterpillar tractors churned up whenever they went fast and far. Melrose said that here was my chance for a little fun if I cared to make one of the party.

Naturally I accepted, and after a high tea it was time for us to make our preparations. Gerald Aitken was the name of the lieutenant who had been selected, and he was a rather a quiet young man with a little dark moustache. He and I went out first to see that everything was shipshape, then Melrose inspected the party in the weird reddish light of a marvellous sunset and we set off.

From time to time we were challenged by our own outposts, but Aitken had the password and we bumped on over the hard stony ground, first through the short afterglow, then into the night. There was no visible track to guide us, and after dark Aitken directed the party by a compass bearing on the Pole Star. For most of the way the desert was quite flat, but now and again it was broken by shelf-like ridges leading down to long depressions, the beds of which were crusted with salt. These depressions were extremely tricky to cross in mechanized vehicles, so each of them held us up for a considerable time.

At about half past ten the moon got up and an hour later its pallid, unearthly light made the desert almost as bright as day. When we reached the next depression Aitken ordered a halt in the bottom of it and told me that he intended to sit tight there until the moon was within an hour of setting, as he did not want some desert patrol to spot us and get back to give warning of our approach.

All of us were wearing our greatcoats, as now that we were well into November the nights in the desert were bitterly cold, but we did not dare to light a fire for fear of giving our position away to any enemy scouts or aircraft which might be within sight of us. However, hot strong tea had been sent out with us in special containers, and very welcome it was. With it we ate some of the sandwiches we had brought in our haversacks, and whiled away the time as well as we could by swapping yarns.

It was getting on for three when we moved on again and just before dawn the order was given to halt once more in another big depression. Aitken said that if his compass bearings had been accurate we should now be about twenty miles north-west of Bir Fuad, the neighbourhood we had been ordered to reconnoitre, and after camouflaging the Bren carriers with their rag-bedecked netting we settled down to wait for daylight.

The sun rose dead behind us over Cairo, although of course between us and the city there lay three hundred miles of uninhabitable desert. It so happened that I was one of the very few people who had ever crossed that desert. In the early months of 1938 I had spent several weeks there, hunting for the treasure which had been abandoned by the lost legions of Cambyses when they foundered in that waterless wilderness, and not one of them ever got back to report the terrible fate by death from thirst which had overtaken his thirty thousand companions. Even the Arabs, who called it the 'Sea of Sand', had never crossed it, and only the invention of motor vehicles, which could travel great distances without requiring fresh supplies of water, enabled us to operate there now with any safety.

The sunrise was a miracle of flaming colour, but all of us were used to that, so we paid little attention to it and employed ourselves without delay, now that the light had come, in fulfilling the purpose of the expedition. It was essential that the carriers should be left concealed in the hollow, as otherwise they would have been spotted from a considerable distance or by any enemy 'plane that chanced to come over. But small groups of khaki figures are extraordinarily hard to pick out against a background of sand and limestone, particularly if they remain motionless, so our job was to select points of vantage and scan the desert through binoculars for any signs of movement; then if a small enemy force appeared we were to engage it in the hope of securing prisoners, but if a large force came into view we were to remain dead still, secure in the knowledge that unless it came within a quarter of a mile of us it would pass us by unnoticed.

Having detailed several parties, Aitken gave me two men and asked me to climb out of the depression towards the west, where I was to take up my position on the highest ground that I could find within a square mile of the depression's edge; then to sit tight there until further orders, or I spotted anything which justified sending one of the men back with a report.

Half an hour later the three of us found a rocky cleft upon the near slope of a valley beyond the depression where our main party had halted, and we decided that this would be a good place from which to keep watch. While the lance-corporal, who was one of my companions, chose a position for the Bren gun, I scanned the monotonous yellow-brown landscape with my field-glasses for as far as I could see, which was no great way ahead but a considerable distance to either side.

Perhaps I ought to have crossed the valley and chosen a place on the next ridge, from which I could have seen much further ahead and so had earlier warning of any enemy approaching in force; but the shallow dip was the best part of half a mile across, and to have done so would have been to exceed the distance which Aitken had laid down for the area in which I was to choose a position.

97

It was a little after ten o'clock in the morning when I caught the warning blast of a whistle on my right. One of our other pickets had evidently spotted something, and next moment I was blowing my own whistle for all I was worth. A line of medium tanks had suddenly popped up on the skyline of the ridge opposite and was now bumping its way clumsily but swiftly down into the valley straight towards us.

It was incredibly ill luck that in all that vast area a formation of tanks should come blundering right into our midst, but that was what had happened. They could not possibly pass without seeing us, and if we had broken cover we could never have run the distance back to the shelter of the depression before the tanks had either caught up with us or sent machine-gun bullets spattering through our backs.

The neighbouring picket commander had realized our desperate plight as soon as he saw the tanks, and, since the Bren-gun carriers could not possibly take on such a vastly superior enemy, blown his whistle as a warning to them to get out. The one chance for Aitken was instant retreat, as if he got away at once he would probably be able to save the bulk of his party through the superior speed of his vehicles.

As the tanks came over the crest they made the sort of target that a gunner dreams about, but unfortunately the Bren was the only gun we had and that was much too light to smash a well-armoured tank. However, there was always a chance that some of the bullets might penetrate the observation slits, and my lance-corporal was already blazing away with the Bren while the Guardsman who was with us hastily opened up the spare ammunition containers.

I could hear the bullets ring as they smacked on to the nearest tank, but it came steadily up the slope. Then one of its machine-guns began to chatter. The lance-corporal half sprang into the air, gave a single wavering cry and slumped down again, blood gushing from a ghastly wound where half a dozen of the enemy's bullets had torn open his neck.

I grabbed the Bren and loosed off with it. I'm a pretty good shot, but I think it was luck which aided my aim in the wild excitement of that moment. A spate of bullets from the Bren spattered on to the tank all round its forward observation slit. Some of them must have gone through and killed the driver as the tank suddenly lurched sideways and came to a halt.

But my triumph was short-lived. Another tank, fifty yards to my left, had now come level with us. Seeing that its companion had been crippled it swung its cannon into action. I saw the first shell burst with a blinding flash. Bits of it hissed through the air and clattered on the rock, while a big puff of evil-smelling smoke billowed out then hung, almost unmoving, in the air. The second shell must have burst within a few feet of us, but I did not see it. I only felt myself lifted bodily, then hurled back to earth. The breath was driven right out of my body; there was a sharp pain in my temple as my head hit a rock and I passed out.

How long I was unconscious I have no idea, but it would not have been for very long because the sun was still nearly overhead when I came to. Cautiously I examined myself and found that, apart from a severe bruising, I was quite all right. The Guardsman also appeared only to have been temporarily knocked out. His face was quite calm and he looked as though he was asleep, but the moment I started to shake him I realized that he was stone dead. A small fragment of shell had entered his back and gone right through his heart.

Taking every precaution against again being surprised by the enemy, I crawled back to the lip of the depression. There was no sign of the Bren-gun carriers or the tanks, so presumably Aitken had succeeded in getting away. The next thing to find out was if I were stranded alone out there, or if there were other survivors from our small isolated parties. I blew a blast upon my whistle and repeated it several times but got no answer. Then a few minutes later a head with a crop of bright ginger curls popped up over a rock and its blue-eyed owner grinned at me.

"Thought I'd better 'ave a looksee 'oo you was, sir, insteada whistling back, in case you was those Heyeties," he shouted, adding with a wave of his arm, "H'our sergeant's copped a packet, but 'e's still able to lay about 'im wiv' 'is tongue."

I followed the red-headed Guardsman across the waste until I reached a hollow in which another of our parties had been lurking. A brawny sergeant was sitting there, nursing a shattered knee-cap, and his language was something to marvel at.

While the redhead and I were dressing the wound as well as we could with our first-aid kit, two more survivors joined us. They had seen me in the distance, walking back with the redhead. One had a slight wound in the arm, but the other had escaped without a scratch.

Having consulted with the sergeant we decided our only course was to follow the tracks of our own Bren-gun carriers, since we thought there was a fair chance that, provided Aitken had escaped, as soon as he was clear of the tanks he would come back by the same route to look for any of his party that might have escaped death or capture.

After collecting all the water-bottles and iron rations from the dead and distributing them evenly among ourselves, we made a sling out of some webbing equipment which would keep the sergeant's wounded foot off the ground. We then set off with him hopping along, his arms thrown over the shoulders of two men, while I went ahead with the other slightly wounded man to act as guide and lookout.

But it proved to be our unlucky day. Instead of meeting a patrol of our own people we ran slap into the squadron of enemy tanks on its way home. We tried to hide among some loose rocks, but the country was very flat there and we were spotted almost immediately. Three tanks swerved from their course and charged right up to us. To have fought with revolvers against those steel monsters would simply have been chucking the lives of myself and my men away without such a sacrifice achieving the least useful purpose, and we'd have been dead in ten seconds if we'd attempted to run. I felt so bitter that I think I could have spat gall as those Italians swivelled their tank cannon on to us and yelled to us to put up our hands; but the only possible course was to surrender.

The hatches of the tanks were opened, a lieutenant and some men climbed out, relieved us of such weapons as we had, ran through our pockets confiscating all our papers but returning the other things, and divided us among the nearest tanks. We were then ordered to climb on their backs and hang on there, while an Italian soldier in each tank that had prisoners on it covered them with a gun for the purpose of shooting them if they tried to jump off.

Tanks are not made to cling to, and it took all our strength and skill to hang on to our precarious perches while we bumped over the desert heading almost due west. At about two o'clock in the afternoon we came to one of the big depressions, and in it I saw that the Italians had established a strong advance-post. Apart from the tank unit whose base it was, at least a company of mechanized infantry were encamped there, and the place was well defended with anti-aircraft guns.

I was taken at once to the tent of a small dark officer with flashing teeth who questioned me in poor English. Actually, had I chosen, we could have conversed fluently in Italian, but I thought it might prove an advantage to me later if none of them knew that I understood their language.

My questioner was quite a decent fellow as he made me sit

down and gave me a drink and a smoke. After a little he accepted my reiterated assurance that I was only an interpreter of Arabic who had come up to the front line the previous morning and gone out with the reconnoitring party for fun, and that, therefore, I knew nothing whatever of the British dispositions.

Having taken down these scant particulars he ordered a soldier to take me to an empty tent, where I sat with my back against the tent-pole in miserable dejection for the rest of the afternoon.

In the evening an orderly brought in an ammunition box for me to sit on and two more to form a makeshift table, then a tray upon which there was quite a passable meal.

Now that night was approaching I began to consider seriously the possibilities of escape. As far as I could judge the Italian camp was not much more than ten miles from the depression in which Aitken had halted his small force that morning. I thought I ought to be able to cover that distance in the course of the night, if only I could get away, and once I had got so far there was quite a reasonable chance of my running into one of the British patrols.

One thing was certain: if I did not make a bid for liberty while I was still at this advance post, it would be infinitely harder once I had been carted off into the interior of Libya, as I felt quite certain that I should be. It was now or never, and as darkness fell without anyone coming to handcuff me or tie me up, the despondency that I had felt in the afternoon gradually gave way to half-fearful hope.

True, I could not possibly have escaped in broad daylight, for a sentry had been posted outside the tent ever since I entered it. But I had no wild idea of endeavouring to overpower him. My prison was a perfectly ordinary round bell-tent and its skirt was held down in the usual way by being half-buried in a shallow trench. It seemed that all I had to do was to scrape the sand away with my hands, scoop out a shallow tunnel and crawl out of the back while the sentry was drowsing in front. After that it would be largely a matter of luck as to whether I got caught while picking my way between the enemy vehicles or managed to reach the desert undetected. I reckoned that my best chance would be at about three o'clock in the morning, as by then the maximum number of troops would probably be asleep; but it was decreed that I was never to make the attempt.

Shortly before midnight the sentry called to me to come out, and a non-commissioned officer marched me away to the western end of the depression where a small convoy of vehicles was waiting. They were mainly light lorries with two Fiat cars, and all of

them had huge balloon tyres, the invention of which, in comparatively recent years, has made desert travel so much safer and
easier.

Except for the badly-wounded sergeant, who had been taken
to the hospital tent on our arrival, the rest of my companions of
the morning were already seated on the floor of one of the lorries.
My guard raised no objection when I went over to the men and
had a few words with them. There was little I could say to cheer
them up, but I shared my remaining cigarettes with them and
learnt from the redheaded fellow that the sergeant was being
well-cared for.

I was then ordered over to the leading Fiat and into its back
seat, where I was joined shortly afterwards by an Italian officer.
He spoke no English and I don't think he liked us as he produced
his gun and pointed it first at me and then at the window,
indicating quite clearly that he meant to shoot me if I jumped
out, and from his unpleasant smirk I gathered that it would give
him considerable pleasure to have the chance of doing so. I didn't
like him, either, for a variety of reasons, amongst others that he
reeked of cheap scent.

It was about four o'clock in the morning and the moon was
low in the sky when we reached our destination, which, as I
learned the following day, was Fort Maddalena—a desert stronghold just over the Libyan border and about sixty miles from the
sea. It had been no more than an ancient mud-walled castle set
in an oasis of a few acres of date palms before Mussolini had
decided to become a modern Roman Emperor; but the whole
fertile area had since been surrounded by a deep ditch which
bristled with anti-tank obstacles. Beyond the ditch was a reinforced concrete wall broken here and there by round flat-topped
casemates that obviously contained powerful guns. Inside these
fortifications the whole place was now a great armed camp.

In a clearing among some palm trees a barbed-wire prisoners'
cage had been erected, with a score of long hutments inside it,
two of which were separated and fenced off from the rest as
officers' quarters. I was taken straight to one of these. Opening
the door, the guard flashed his torch for a moment upon a big
pile of blankets, indicating that I was to look after myself; then
he left me in the dark, slamming and locking the door behind him.

After fumbling round I made myself up quite a comfortable
bed from a pile of blankets, and pulling off my boots and tunic
snuggled down into them. It would obviously have been futile
to contemplate escape any further that night, knowing nothing

more of my new surroundings than I had glimpsed by the setting moon, and it was now twenty-four hours since I had slept. Almost before I knew it my anger and my dejection at my capture were overcome by fatigue and I had dropped off.

When I awoke it was broad daylight and another British officer was bending over me. He was the only other occupant of the hut, and he said he had been sound asleep when I had been brought in, so had known nothing of my presence until he had discovered me, a few minutes earlier, coiled up in the pile of blankets. As I sat up I saw that one side of the hut was occupied by rows of bunks made of wire-netting stretched across wooden frames, and that each had a palliasse already laid out on it; but evidently my guard of the night before had been too lazy or antagonistic to flash his torch on these.

My fellow-prisoner was a garrulous Irish lieutenant named Malone. He said that he had been taken prisoner three weeks before and, as it transpired, in a very similar circumstance to myself. He asked me innumerable questions about the units I had been with and how things had been going at Mersa Matruh since his capture; but as the conversation progressed it struck me that he seemed to know strangely little about the composition of the Army of the Nile and was altogether too curious.

We were given a very decent breakfast of quite drinkable coffee, brown bread, honey and dates, soon after which I was called out of the hut and taken along a path through the palm trees to a big white building. My guard shepherded me into one of a long row of offices where an officer was sitting behind a desk and it soon transpired that I was in for further questioning.

My interrogator on this occasion was a sharp-eyed grizzled man of major's rank who was evidently a trained intelligence officer. He spoke English fluently and put a great number of very shrewd questions to me, the business lasting for well over an hour.

I stonewalled most of the time, simply repeating that I was not a real soldier at all but only an officer of the Interpreter Corps who had qualified in Arabic, and that as I had been stationed in Alexandria up to a few days ago I knew nothing whatever about the numbers or dispositions of the British forces in the line. The fellow could not prove me a liar and it made things slightly less unpleasant to maintain that one simply did not know than to dig one's heels and flatly refuse to talk.

At the end of the interview he handed back the papers that had been taken from me; I was overjoyed to have them as they consisted mainly of the few letters that I had ever received from

Daphnis. Hardly an hour had passed since my capture without my thinking of her. Overwhelmed as I was by this tragic separation, which might become a torture of months or even years if I could not find a way to escape, I was even more concerned on her account than for myself. She would, I knew, be as heartbroken as I was when she heard that I had been taken, but she would have all the additional agony of having to cancel the arrangements for our wedding and live on among her family and friends as an object of their well-meant but infuriating pity.

As I was taken back to the prison I kept my eyes skinned to take in every mortal thing I could which might later aid me if I was able to make a break for liberty, but what I saw was far from encouraging. Every corner of the oasis was full of troops, and I came to the conclusion that there must be the best part of a brigade there, as well as large numbers of specialists. The place was stiff with tanks, guns, lorries, searchlights, ambulances, water-carts, and every other type of military equipment, and as the Italians carried out most of their troop movements, like ourselves, at night, it was quite certain that right round the clock there would always be considerable numbers of them awake and moving about on one duty or another.

The prospects of getting out of the cage and then away from such an active, well-populated hive seemed extremely slender, and if I did succeed in getting clear of the fortress I was now at least a hundred miles from the line of British outposts which ran south from Mersa Matruh. Without proper preparations it would, I knew, be positive madness to attempt such a journey and hazardous to make it at any time, even with a car, unless one had proper guides.

Back in the hut Malone recommenced his lighthearted but persistent questioning, and it suddenly struck me that his enquiries followed very similar lines to those of the Italian major who had just grilled me. In consequence I formed a disquieting theory about my room-mate that he might be Irish or part-Irish, but that he was not a British officer at all.

By the evening I had definitely reached the conclusion that Mr. Malone was an Irishman with Italian blood who had probably lived in Italy for a good part of his life. Just as Major Cozelli was half Italian—but almost fanatically pro-British in feeling—so Malone was, I concluded, fanatically anti-British, and he had been put in the cage only as a stool-pigeon to listen to what other prisoners said and report any plans for escape they might be making.

It was a depressing thought that my sole companion was an Italian spy, but I felt so certain that I was right that I decided that it was now useless to make any attempt to escape until they had realized the futility of keeping him locked up with me any longer.

Two days passed and I began to wonder why I was being kept there instead of being sent back to one of the Italian bases. I hardly knew whether to hope for or dread that now. It is true that in the coastal region, if I could once evade my gaolers and get an Italian uniform or an Arab *burnous*, since I spoke both languages, there would be quite a decent chance of my working my way gradually back to the British lines; but the other side of the picture was that, once I was sent to the coast, I might not be kept there for more than a few hours before being despatched to Italy, and once there all hope of getting to Egypt would be out of the question.

On the third day an officer of the Gurkhas was brought in, a nice fellow and very different from the garrulous, untrustworthy Malone, whom I could cheerfully have murdered by now. The Indian Army man's name was Bannister and we soon struck up a friendship, whiling away our time by telling each other about various places at which we had stayed during our travels and our pet theories upon how the war could be won. On numerous occasions when Malone was asleep we discussed the possibilities of escape, but Teddy Bannister agreed with me that we dared risk nothing as long as the Irishman was quartered with us.

I suppose the fact of the matter was that neither Bannister nor I was a big enough fish to warrant our being sent with a special escort to an Italian Divisional Headquarters. Anyhow, nothing was done about us and we settled down to an unbroken routine. Apart from the infuriating fact that we were refused the wherewithal and permission to write letters, we were treated quite decently. They took us out for exercise twice a day and gave us plentiful helpings of good plain food. Those optimists at home who informed a credulous public that the Italians in Libya were woefully short of supplies, and would soon be starved out by our Mediterranean blockade, were the most dangerous kind of wishful thinkers. The Italians had masses of everything and they were quite convinced that it was only a matter of weeks before they would be lording it over the defeated British in the Nile Valley.

Time hung heavily as we had nothing to do, and Bannister and I did not care to talk freely, even about things which had nothing to do with the war, while Malone was with us; but five days after my arrival at Fort Maddalena he suddenly disappeared and we never saw him again. Either we had grossly maligned him in our thoughts and for some reason known only to the Italians he had been spirited away, or, as we felt convinced, having failed to get anything out of us he had decided that the game was not worth the candle and resumed his freedom until other British officer prisoners were brought in.

It was on the day Malone vanished that while at exercise I picked up a small Italo-Greek phrase book. The guard, who was a very decent fellow, allowed me to keep it. That pleased me a lot, as it had a considerable vocabulary and the study of this enabled me to occupy myself polishing up my Greek. To prevent myself from going mad from frustration I had determined to put away from me the thought that I might be kept a prisoner for months or years, and instead cultivate the belief that any any day an opportunity for successful escape might occur, so that it would not be very long before I was able to marry Daphnis. I spoke some Greek already, but as I was marrying into a Greek family I felt that it was only a matter of politeness to study the language until I could speak it fluently, so the little phrase book was a most fortunate find.

It looked as though it was one of those issued by Mussolini to his legions to facilitate their relations with the inhabitants when they carried out the easy carefree advance down into Greece which had been planned for them. Probably it had been dropped by a specialist or airman who had been stationed in Albania a few weeks previously and since transferred to the Libyan front. So far the opportunities for Mussolini's blackguards to use such little books had been extremely limited. In the first days of the attack their mechanized columns had thrust as far as Janina, about fifty miles into Greece, but with real military genius General Papagos had trapped their far larger army in the mountains, annihilating one division and badly mauling two others.

From that point on the Greeks had taken the offensive, and in spite of the fact that they had neither the numbers nor the modern equipment of the Italians, by a series of brilliantly-directed blows they had hurled the Italians back over the Albanian border, capturing Koritsa and Pogradec, which were well inside enemy territory.

The only means that Bannister and I had of getting any news was by my straining my ears to listen to a loudspeaker that gave the Italian bulletins three or four times a day to some soldiers quartered in huts on the far side of the barbed-wire fence. Afterwards I translated such snatches as I could make out.

We had to allow for the fact that the bulletins were mainly faked up by Mussolini's propaganda chief, 'Woe! Woe!' Ansaldo, but there were certain concrete facts about the course of the war which had to be admitted sooner or later. One of these was the action at Taranto which had taken place during the night that I had made my trip out into the desert with Aitken's reconnaissance party. Rather obscure references to the action kept on coming through for several days after I reached Fort Maddalena. What exactly had occurred I could not discover, but I learned quite enough to be certain that the British Navy had once again pulled off a magnificent feat of work and either sunk or crippled several of Mussolini's capital ships while they were still lying in harbour.

From Axis accounts the Luftwaffe was still knocking hell out of England, and in the middle of the month it was declared that they had razed Coventry to the ground; while some days later Portsmouth, Plymouth and Bristol were claimed as victims.

Towards the end of November there was another British naval victory off Sardinia, although once again the Italians strove to minimize the damage they had suffered. A piece of news which pleased me almost as much was that the filthy little Corsican traitor, Chiappe, one of the most venal of the Vichy crooks, had been killed in an aircraft which got mixed up in this battle by accident. He was the French Police chief—Gestapo Boss Himmler's opposite number—and on his way to take over the Governorship of Syria, which the little swine undoubtedly meant to hand on a platter to the Germans when the time was ripe.

On December the 6th there was terrific excitement owing to the resignation of the veteran Marshal Badoglio from the position of Chief of the Italian General Staff, and this was followed the next day by the resignation of General de Vecchi, the Commander-in-Chief of the Italian forces in the Dodecanese. Badoglio had always been opposed to Mussolini and a King's man. It was he who had offered to bust the entire Fascist outfit at the time of the march on Rome if the King would allow him to order out a single division of troops; but Victor Emmanuel had not had the courage to back his general and preferred to resign to taking orders in future from a dictator.

It was Badoglio, too, who had pulled the chestnuts out of the fire in Abyssinia. Mussolini first appointed the ancient Marshal

De Bono to the Supreme Command, solely because he was one of the original Fascists; but this elderly goat was so terrified that the Abyssinians would massacre his men in a second Adowa that he hadn't the guts to advance a hundred miles in three months, although he had a numerous air force, scores of tanks and was only opposed to half-naked blackamoors. The whole campaign would have had to be postponed at enormous cost for the best part of a year through the coming of the rains if De Bono had not been sacked at the eleventh hour and replaced by the non-Fascist Badoglio, who took the Italians to Addis Ababa in a month.

The resignation of Italy's greatest soldier and numerous other high Italian officers in all three services certainly seemed to indicate that something was very wrong inside the Fascist State; so Bannister and I at least had that to cheer us.

Late on the afternoon of December the 9th, somewhat to our surprise we were ordered without warning to collect our few belongings and hurried out to a big motor coach. We had not been seated in it for more than a few minutes when about twenty British non-commissioned officers and men, including the fellows who had been captured with me, scrambled on board, and it was clear that all the prisoners were being evacuated in one body.

The Italian Intelligence major arrived and addressed us clearly in staccato English. An armoured car would be following immediately behind us during the whole of the journey that we were about to make, and we were warned that at the first sign of any funny business its machine-guns would open fire.

Having passed through the great gates of Fort Maddalena we saw that on the Libyan side of the frontier the desert roads were a very different proposition, with the one exception of the coast road which had been re-made by the British troops, from the miserable tracks, half-buried in the sand, which served for roads in Egypt. From the fort a fine broad metalled highway, with trees planted at intervals on either side of it, stretched away as far as one could see, running as straight as an arrow to the north.

As soon as we were clear of the oasis we caught the sound of distant gunfire. None of us thought very much about it at the time, although, as Bannister remarked, one of our tank patrols must have penetrated unusually far west. We both looked longingly towards the east, knowing that our fellows must be somewhere out there in that trackless yellow waste, but neither of us even contemplated slogging the driver and trying to make a bolt for it, as we knew that, with the wind in the right direction, gunfire could easily be heard thirty miles away across land which presented no natural barriers.

On that fine road it took us less than two hours to cover over sixty miles, and while there was still half an hour to go to sundown we reached Fort Capuzzo, the great desert stronghold which Mussolini had created to dominate Halfaya Pass, Sollum, and the coast road into Egypt. It was more like a town than a fort and was garrisoned by the best part of the division which had its headquarters there.

The bus drew up in a small square which appeared to be the centre of the place, and as we got out of it I was vaguely conscious of a subdued excitement in the air. Italian soldiers do not as a rule jump to obey their officers. They are docile enough but decidedly lethargic by habit; yet here officers and men were hurrying in all directions as though their business was of the utmost urgency.

Before I had a chance to try to find out the cause of this bustle and excitement my attention was caught by two Blackshirt officers who were walking swiftly across the square and about to pass within a few yards of us. The figure of the nearest of them was vaguely familiar. At that moment he glanced casually at the dejected little crowd of British prisoners among whom I stood. As his glance met mine recognition was instantaneous and mutual. Stopping dead in his tracks he swung round and glared at me. I knew then that I was in for trouble. It was Daphnis' ex-fiancé —Paolo Tortino.

CHAPTER XI

IN THE "BIG HOUSE"

"*Sapristi!*" he exclaimed. "If it's not the ex-diplomat who now calls himself Day! I have a bone to pick with you, my friend. We must have a little talk together."

He was speaking in Italian and I replied in the same language, "If you want to talk to me I can't stop you."

"You certainly cannot." He nodded his head up and down, and smiled in a self-satisfied manner. "How long have you been a prisoner?"

109

"Twenty-eight days."

His smile broadened into a grin. "That is no time at all. No wonder you still look so stiff-necked. It will be different when you have done twenty-eight months in an Italian prison." He turned to speak to the officer in charge of us and I heard him mutter: "Good. Then I will come over to see this fellow after mess."

As he stalked off we were marched away to a large white building that had heavy bars across all its windows. It was the fortress prison which was being used now both for Italian soldiers who had been sentenced by courts martial for various offences and the comparatively few British prisoners of war. The place was thoroughly up to date and had been built on American lines in which galleries of cells run one above the other and the door of each is not solid but a gate of bars through which the warder can see the prisoners the whole time.

The cells were quite roomy with two bunks in each, and I managed to get put in with Teddy Bannister. We had not been inside for five minutes when a bell clanged; all the cell gates swung open from an electrically-controlled lever having been thrown over and we were shepherded down to a big dining-hall. I don't think that there was any difference between the food served to the officers and men or the prisoners of war and the Italians, but we were segregated to different parts of the hall.

There were five other officers besides Bannister and myself, and it was from them we learned the reason for the signs of unusual activity which we had observed on entering Fort Capuzzo. The British had attacked along the whole front at dawn that morning.

The others had all been taken while on patrol before the attack had started, so they knew nothing of the details. It might be an attack in force with the objective of throwing the Italians right back to the Libyan frontier, or it might only be a powerful demonstration to cover large-scale raids designed to destroy certain of the preparations which the Italians had been making for their own projected offensive.

Naturally we were all thrilled by the news and Bannister and I agreed that the distant gunfire we had heard soon after leaving Fort Maddalena must have been part of this operation; but we did not feel that there were any grounds for hoping that the British attack would alter our own situation. Even if the Italians were driven in it was quite certain that they would remove their prisoners further to the rear before there was any chance of their being rescued, and it was doubtless because Fort Maddalena, although no further to the east than Fort Capuzzo, was in a much more exposed position that we had already been transferred to the larger fortesss.

My own delight on hearing that our people were at last slapping into the Eyeties was to some extent overshadowed by the knowledge that Paolo Tortino had announced his intention of coming to see me after dinner that evening. What exactly he could do to me I had no idea. From my own experience and that of the other captive officers that I had so far met it seemed that the Italians treated their prisoners very decently, and to date there was no act of mine which the authorities could pick on as an excuse to single me out for special hardship.

On the other hand, since he had held a post in the Italian Diplomatic Service, Tortino must be a member of the Fascist Party, and in a totalitarian State there is never any knowing what the limits of the arbitrary powers of an official of the ruling party may be. I did not think that I need fear being beaten with steel rods or rubber truncheons, as might have occurred had Tortino been an influential Nazi and myself a prisoner in Germany, but all the same I had an uncomfortable feeling that he might be able to make things extremely disagreeable for me.

As it turned out I had nothing to fear after all that night as Tortino never put in an appearance. I suppose he was prevented from doing so by some urgent duty. Instead, I met another acquaintance, and this time one whom I was frankly glad to see.

It was just before lights-out that the guards suddenly called us to attention, and a few moments later a rather portly individual, who appeared to have been poured into a spotless uniform and quite obviously was the Prison Governor, came into view, followed by several officers composing his small staff.

I recognized the fat, good-natured face under the peaked gold-braided cap immediately. It was Gonzaga, who used to be the head waiter at the Tiberius Hotel in Capri. I had spent several weeks there in the spring of 1938, and although it was now nearly three years since I had seen him he knew me at once and stopped abruptly outside my cell.

"Well, well," I said in English, knowing that he understood it perfectly. "This is a pleasant surprise. Do I congratulate or commiserate with you upon this change of occupation?"

He returned my smile and his soft brown eyes were full of humour as he replied: "Et is much easier to keep ze eye on a 'undred cell than on a 'undred tables, an' 'ere we do not lose ze

111

customer ef 'e is dissatisfi'. Also, before I bow to ze peoples; now all ze peoples bow to me!"

"Then I certainly congratulate you, Gonzaga," I said. "Or should I address you as *Comandante* in these days?"

"As you like." He shrugged good-naturedly. " 'Ave you everyzing you want?"

"Yes, thanks," I replied, "except pens and paper. At Fort Maddalena, where I've been for the last four weeks, they wouldn't give me any, and I'm very anxious to write a letter."

"I senda you in ze morning," he said, and with a friendly nod continued on his tour of inspection.

Next morning the promised writing material was brought to me, and I was able at last to write a long letter to Daphnis. In it, knowing that it would be censored, I could only tell her why she had not heard from me before; how I came to be taken prisoner, that I was well and as cheerful as could be expected, and of my undying love for her; but I covered sheets of paper, and it was a great relief to have this privilege of writing to her, which had been denied me for a month.

The day passed without incident, except for exciting rumours, which reached us from goodness-knows-where, that the British offensive was going well; and when I turned in that night Tortino had still not made his threatened visit.

On the Wednesday at about eleven o'clock I was taken out of my cell and the big cage-house, through some corridors to a roomy well-furnished office. Gonzaga was sitting there behind a bulky desk. His big head and heavy bluish jowl made him rather an impressive picture of authority. As he barked at the guards who had brought me in there was nothing of the head waiter about him, at least nothing of the head waiter that the customer usually sees; but once we were alone he smiled and waved a beringed hand towards a chair.

"Ples, Meester Day, you are at 'ome 'ere—sit down."

"Thanks very much," I said, taking the chair and a cigarette from the box he pushed towards me. "I'm afraid, though, if you mean to interrogate me I've nothing to add to the statement that I have made already."

"No, no. Zis is not interrogation," he said quickly. "I am not police spy. I aska you down because for me et is nice to see someone of ze old days an' for you—why, it maka da little change from sitting in da cell."

"If that's the case, I think it's charming of you," I laughed. "But tell me: how did you ever become a prison governor?"

"Et was ze great Balbo. 'E persuade me to leave ze Tiberius and take over ze Miramere at Derna. 'E often come zare but ze 'otel, she go broke an' I am on ze rocks. So ze Marshal 'e say: 'Don't you worry, Gonzaga. Any man 'oo runna a restaurant so good as you maka de big success in any job. I giva you good post in my Colonial administration.' One thing goes to anozer, yes, so 'ere I am."

"That was a bad business about the Marshal's death, wasn't it?" I said.

My words seemed to electrify him. His dark eyes flashed and he sat forward suddenly. "Balbo was ze greatest man in alla Italie. Ze greatest, yes, an' zose pigs, zey kill him!" He made a most unhead-waiter-like gesture with his head over the side of the desk as though about to spit.

I glanced swiftly at the door to make quite certain that it was shut, then I hazarded, "You're not exactly one hundred per cent for Mussolini, then?"

"Zat one! Bah!" he snapped his fingers. "At one time, yes, 'e was good for Italie, but zese last years 'e 'as been bad for Italie. You 'ave an English saying, no? 'Zose whom ze gods wish to destroy zey first maka dem mad.' Il Duce 'e losa 'is 'ead and ze Italian peoples zey foota da bill. But we giva politics ze go-bys; et is better zat we not talk too much. Instead, we splitta da bottle."

Getting up, he went into an inner room to return with a gold-foiled bottle of Asti Spumanti and some glasses. The wine was dead cold and had evidently just come off the ice. I abominate sweet champagne, but I am very fond of rich wines such as Tokay, Chateau Y'Quem and the great Hocks; and sparkling Asti has an aromatic flavour that is all its own, so while we talked of the old carefree days when he had been a great *hôtelier* and I had been a guest at the Tiberius in Capri, I thoroughly enjoyed my share of the bottle.

I hardly liked at first to ask for the latest news, but on my remarking that surely it was the rumble of distant gunfire which was drifting in through the partly opened window, he said at once:

"Ze British 'ave given us ze great surprise. On Monday zey go *zip* through our outposts. On Tuesday zey are outside Buq Buq. Zis morning Sidi Barrani 'as fallen."

"Good God! Do you mean that?" I exclaimed.

He hunched his shoulders and spread out his hands in a rather pathetic gesture. "We 'ave no warning an' ze British tanks zey

113

are veree fast. Ze firing you 'ear is below 'Alfaya Pass where ze British try to storm et an' retake Sollum."

"If they advance much further we'll be in the front line here," I grinned.

He shook his head. "Fort Capuzzo et is veree strong an' zere is also much good fortifications at Bardia. Now we know ze attack comes we meet et."

He evidently saw my face drop as he laughed and went on: "I guess what you are zinking. Ef you stay put 'ere Capuzzo she falls an' you are rescue. But don' fool yourself. Capuzzo will not fall. Also war prisoners we do not keep 'ere. Zey go firs' to Tobruk, zen to Italie."

He had caught the wild hope that had just flamed in my mind, but extinguished it in the same breath.

"When are we likely to be moved?" I asked.

"Veree soon—tonight, tomorrow night. I cannot tell until I getta da order."

We talked again of Capri, fine cooking and great wines, until we had finished the bottle of Asti Spumanti; then, just as he was about to summon the warder, I gave him my letter to Daphnis and asked if he would censor it personally and post it for me.

He agreed at once and I felt that, although it would have to go *via* Italy, the Balkans, Turkey and Palestine to reach Egypt, and might be among mail destroyed in a ship or 'plane by British action while crossing the Sicilian channel, there was still a reasonably good prospect of its reaching its destination in due course. After thanking Gonzaga most heartily for his kindness I was taken back to my cell.

That evening, down in the dining-hall, all the British prisoners were in a great state of elation. I had naturally passed on such news as I had received from Gonzaga, but where the others had obtained theirs I have no idea. It is always something of a mystery as to how prisoners get their information, but it is well known that important news always reaches men living in captivity pretty nearly as quickly as it does other people. Everyone knew that the British offensive, now nearing the close of its third day, had met with a most amazing success. Sidi Barrani had been cut off and surrounded before the Italians realized what was happening. Thousands of prisoners and great quantities of stores which the Italians had prepared for their advance into Egypt had fallen into our hands, and our columns were said to be pressing on for all they were worth, with the Italians fleeing before them.

Gonzaga had seemed quite confident that they would be able

to hold our thrust on the frontier, but these stories of our successes filled all of us with feverish excitement, and every one of my brother officers had the same idea as I had had that morning. If our comrades were pushing on at such a rate they might take Fort Capuzzo and rescue us before the Italians had a chance to pack us off into the interior.

Personally I was not at all sanguine about our chances, as a mighty fortress like Capuzzo would take a deal of subduing, but when Teddy Bannister and I got back to our cell that evening we discussed at great length the problem of if there was any way in which we could manage to prevent ourselves from being shifted, and we both decided to feign illness.

That was unfortunate, as when orders came through for our removal half an hour later, and we were told to get our few belongings together, it transpired that every single officer, N.C.O. and man among the British prisoners of war in Fort Capuzzo had had the same not very brilliant idea.

In vain we pleaded that the bean soup, which we had had for our evening meal, had poisoned us, held our tummies, made faces and pretended to twist about in agony. The genial Gonzaga appeared and just laughed at us, ordering his men to pull us out of our cells by the scruff of the neck when the time came if we would not march out of our own accord on receiving the order.

We had been given a quarter of an hour to prepare for our departure, and ten minutes of it had already gone when one of the head warders arrived in front of my cell and behind him I saw Paolo Tortino. The gate was unlocked and Tortino swaggered in, closing it with a clang behind him.

As he was a professional diplomat it had been rather a surprise to see him in an officer's uniform, but I soon guessed the reason. After Italy entered the war, the number of embassies and legations which Mussolini could continue to maintain abroad was considerably lessened, and it was one of the sounder tenets of his creed that a good patriot should be willing to serve his country in any capacity, so there could be no argument if he ordered a number of his surplus diplomats to become army officers, and Paolo was evidently one of the surplus diplomats who had been detailed for service with a Blackshirt formation.

For a moment he gloated in silence, then he said:

"You have heard, I suppose, that you are shortly leaving for Tobruk on your way to Italy?"

I nodded and he went on, "I was too busy to come to see you before, but when I heard that you were leaving I felt that I must

115

spare a moment to come over and give you some idea as to your future."

I shrugged, "The future of all prisoners of war is pretty much the same, so I don't think you need bother."

"But yours will be different," he said, with a malicious grin. "You see, you were at one time in the Diplomatic Service."

"What's that to do with it, since I've been out of the Service for years?" I enquired. "I certainly can't claim Diplomatic immunity."

"Oh no. You can't do that; but it makes you an especially interesting prisoner, particularly as while you were in the Diplomatic Corps you indulged in espionage. Once a spy, always a spy, you know. I wanted the satisfaction of telling you myself that I'm sending a special chit to the authorities about you to ensure that you receive individual attention."

His voice had sunk to a lower note, and it was positively dripping with honeyed malice as he finished, "I have taken steps to make certain that you will be treated as a political prisoner and handed over to the *Ovra*."

My mouth went dry, and I swallowed hard. The Fascists may not be quite as ruthless as the Nazis, but there is little to choose between either in the treatment of their political prisoners by their secret police, and the *Ovra* is the Italian equivalent of the *Gestapo*.

CHAPTER XII

A DESPERATE GAMBLE

ONE does not hear so much about the *Ovra* as about the *Gestapo*, and we are too apt to form a picture of the Italian as a lazy, pleasure-loving fellow who is content to loll about in his sunny vineyards, roll his eyes at every young woman he sees and warble 'O Sole Mio' in the moonlight.

We forget that some of the most hard-headed, dynamic and unscrupulous men in the world are also Italians—Al Capone and his gangsters, for example. The Italian secret police are staffed by just such men who prefer to wield power as servants of the Fascist State to becoming criminals. Many of them are the assassins of

116

the old Black-Hand and Camorra which Mussolini broke up, afterwards taking over its professional knifemen for his own purposes.

The instant Paolo Tortino had told me of the revenge which he had planned to take on me for breaking up his engagement with Daphnis I saw myself no longer an ordinary prisoner of war but a poor wretch in perpetual solitary confinement in some damp, dark cell on one of Mussolini's prison islands; subject without hope or reprieve to any beastliness which the agents of the *Ovra* cared to inflict upon me.

Almost at the same second a way in which I might possibly avert that fate and even turn the tables on Tortino flashed into my mind. With a last malicious smirk he had contemptuously turned his back and strode to the barred gate of the cell, where he was calling to the guard to let him out.

In two strides I was after him. He was a good two inches shorter than myself. It was easy for me to fling my left arm round his neck so that his chin came in the crook of my elbow. Jerking back his head so that he fell against me, with my right hand I wrenched open his pistol holster and pulled the pistol from it. Next moment I had dragged him away from the gate and had the muzzle of the pistol firmly pressed against his spine.

"You rat!" I snarled. "Stop struggling. Not another movement or I'll empty the whole contents of your gun into your body!"

He went dead still at once—which told me the thing that I was desperately anxious to know. From its weight I had thought that the gun was loaded, but now the fact that he made no attempt to get at the dagger in the back of his belt assured me that I had only to press the trigger and Paolo would get a bullet in his liver.

One of the guards had heard the brief struggle and came running up to find out what was going on. Immediately he saw the lieutenant pinioned against my chest he shouted: "Hi! Stop that! Let the *tenente* go this instant or it will be the worse for you!" He drew his pistol.

I swung Tortino round a little so that his body almost covered mine as I called back: "Don't shoot or you'll hit the *tenente*, and don't attempt to enter this cell. If you do I shall shoot the *tenente* myself. I've got his gun here and it's loaded."

The guard stared at me undecided for a moment, then he lowered his weapon and yelled for his superior.

Bannister had been at the inner end of the cell when, only a

117

moment before, I had leapt upon Tortino. I caught a glimpse of his face, comically round-eyed with surprise, but now he stepped swiftly forward.

"Good God, Day! What the devil are you up to? You'll get hell for attacking one of their officers."

"Leave this to me," I said abruptly.

By this time the head warder and half a dozen other guards had all come hurrying up and were eying us angrily through the bars, while they jabbered excitedly in Italian.

"Shoot him in the legs!" "No, no, be careful! You may hit the *tenente*." "Let me go in!" "Stop, I say! He has threatened to kill the officer." "He has a gun!" "The Englishman is mad!" "Open the gate and let us rush him together!"

Eventually the head warder shouted the others into silence and stormed at me, demanding that I release my prisoner, and threatening me, if I refused, with all sorts of dire punishment.

I waited until he had finished, then replied firmly: "If anyone attempts to come in I shall shoot the *tenente*. Go and fetch *Il Comandante* Gonzaga."

There was some further argument, but failing to find any way out of the impasse in which I had placed them, their chief sent one of them running to fetch the Governor. Five minutes later the ex-head waiter, now hatless, very pink in the face and far from friendly looking, came briskly along the gallery.

"So! Et ees Meester Day!" he exclaimed, and I thought his eye softened a little as he realized that I was the delinquent who had caused him to be fetched from his quarters. "What for you maka da troubles in my prison, eh? Let go ze *tenente* at once now —quick! I commands it."

"Would you please send your men away?" I said. "I want to talk to you alone."

With a swift order he despatched the guards about their routine business, then he said, in a slightly more conciliatory voice: "Come now, no more of zese nonsenses. For attacking ze officer you will getta da punishment, but eff you 'angs on to 'im you maka da business worse."

"Listen," I said. "I don't like this fellow. I don't like his face; I don't like his smell; I don't like anything about him. I only tell you that because I want you to have no doubts at all that when I say that I'll shoot him if any of your men try to come into this cell I really mean it."

"What 'ave you against 'im?" Gonzaga inquired.

"The little rat told me just before I collared him that he's sending a special chit to Italy which will ensure that directly I get there I'll be handed over to the *Ovra*."

Gonzaga gave a long sigh and shook his large head. "Zat ees bad. But why does 'e do zis bad zing to you?"

"Because I pinched his girl."

"Ah!" Gonzaga sighed again and rolled his eyes to heaven. "Ze women, zey maka da trouble everywheres—even in my nice prison! But finish! Zis cannot go on. I giva you da order—let ze *tenente* go!"

"I'm sorry," I said, "but I'm not hanging on to him just because I happen not to like him. It's because I've made up my mind that I'd rather not go to Tobruk."

"What you say? Not go to Tobruk! But zis is mutiny!"

I nodded. "I know that but I can't help it. I mean to stay here, anyhow for the next twenty-four hours, and the *tenente* is staying with me. Any attempt to get me or him out of this cell and I'll make him dead as macaroni!"

"Oh, come," the Governor's voice took on a wheedling note and even in that tense moment I felt an almost uncontrollable desire to laugh because it was so reminiscent of the tone that he used to use in the old days when trying to persuade me to have another helping of some special dish, or to gloss over some small defect in the generally perfect service of his restaurant.

"Oh, come, Meester Day. What for you maka da troubles in my nice prison? We treata you well 'ere. You 'ave no complaint. Sooner or later you 'ave to let ze *tenente* go. You cannot 'old 'im like zat for ever. What ees the difference eff you let 'im go now or zis time tomorrow?"

"A lot," I answered promptly. "By this time tomorrow the British Army may be here."

His fat face broke into a smile and he began to chuckle: "No, no; we 'ave plenty big guns in Capuzzo, plenty tank, plenty everythin'. Even if we were besiege we 'old out for one month, three month, six month—so you see you are be'aving like ze bloody fool!"

"I don't care," I said stubbornly. "I'm not going to Tobruk and the *tenente* is remaining here with me."

Gonzaga began to mop his bald brow with a large bandanna handkerchief. He was evidently at his wit's end as the chief warder came up to whisper something to him. With a muttered "*Si, si,*" he stepped back from the cell gates.

A moment later the bell rang, the main switch was operated and all the gates swung open. For a second I thought that they meant to rush me; then I heard the other prisoners being ordered out of their cells and realized that, it now being past the time at which all of us had been scheduled to leave for Tobruk, it had been decided to get the rest of them down to the yard before entering into any further arguments with me.

My neighbours had been agog with excitement ever since they had heard the guards bellowing at me, and as they ran from their cells it looked as if a general mutiny might follow. But some of the guards had fixed bayonets and others covered the prisoners with tommy-guns, so it would have been madness for our people to have raised a finger. I was relieved of a frightful responsibility when they confined their sympathy to shouts of encouragement and allowed themselves to be hustled away.

All this time Tortino had remained motionless, leaning back against me and partially supported by the crook of my left arm being round his neck and under his chin, but the sight of the open gate proved too great a temptation to him; suddenly he began to struggle wildly.

I had no scruples about dealing with the little brute, and I played the sort of trick on him to which his friends of the *Ovra* would probably have treated me every morning before breakfast. With a violent jerk of my left arm I wrenched his head almost off his neck. At the same time, twisting slightly sideways, I swung the heavy gun butt round which my fingers were clasped and brought it crashing down on top of his right kidney. He gave one strangled yelp, and after jerking about a little spasmodically, went limp as a dead fish.

"Next time it will be a bullet," I remarked conversationally, both for his benefit, if he was still in a condition to hear me, and for Gonzaga's.

Gonzaga groaned: "Zis maka et worse for you. For 'itting 'im ze court martial mus' now taka place an' zey giva you da solitary cell."

"In for a penny, in for a pound," I answered with somewhat forced cheerfulness. "Every time the little swine struggles he's got it coming to him."

"Alla right," he looked past me and addressed Bannister. "In zis foolishness you 'ave no part. Steppa out, please, to joina ze prisoner zat go to Tobruk."

Teddy shook his head. "No, thanks, I think I'd rather take a chance with Day in the hope that if we stay here we'll be rescued by our friends."

Still keeping a tight grip on Tortino, I looked quickly over my shoulder: "Don't be a fool, Teddy. Nobody's threatened to hand you over to the *Ovra*. The British advance may not get as far as this. Even if it does, it may be weeks before the fortress surrenders. I've taken on such long odds only because it means the next worse thing to a German concentration camp for me if they ever get me to Italy."

"All the more reason I should stay with you," he said firmly. "Alone you couldn't hang out for much more than twenty-four hours before you fell asleep; then they'd rush you. But with two of us we can take turns to guard our hostage."

"I starva you out!" interjected Gonzaga angrily. "No food, no drink—nozzings!"

"All right, do your damnedest," Teddy snapped with equal heat. "I'm staying."

"No, Teddy, it's grand of you to offer," I said gratefully, "but you mustn't all the same."

"I'm staying, I tell you. After all, if the Governor starves us he'll have to starve our prisoner as well, and somehow I don't think he'll let the lieutenant die of hunger or thirst."

As he spoke Teddy leaned past me and drew the little six-inch dagger that went with Paolo's Blackshirt uniform, and added: "I think I'd better take charge of this in case it proves too great a temptation to him. It will come in useful if anyone starts an invasion of our Sovereign State, hereby declared to consist of Cell 311."

"Well, since you're set on it, bless you," I exclaimed at the same moment as Gonzaga, realizing that it was useless to argue further, turned away swearing in Italian and gave a signal upon which the cell gates crashed to.

Now that we were locked in again we were able to put this prison within a prison, or the Sovereign State of Cell 311, as Teddy called it, on a slightly less emergency footing. Obviously I could not continue to hold the pistol to Paolo's spine for hours on end, and we set about deciding measures which would allow us to enjoy reasonable comfort while ensuring that there was no chance for the guards to catch us napping or Paolo to make a quick getaway.

We first made him take off his trousers, shoes and socks. Italians have an ungentlemanly habit of kicking people they dislike in a particularly tender region of the body; so in case Paolo decided to have a crack at us some time I thought it a wise precaution to ensure his being bare-footed.

The trousers we cut up with his knife into thin strips which we plaited into ropes. With some of these we tied Paolo's wrists behind his back and secured his ankles; with others we arranged a contraption which would give us warning if the gate of the cell were stealthily opened in the night. The cell had two bunks, one above the other, and as the gate swung inwards a rope tied to it, which ran over the top bunk, would slacken so that Paolo's shoes, which were attached to the other end of the rope, would fall upon the head of anyone sleeping in the lower bunk. With two more of the ropes we attached Paolo to ourselves so that, if he got within two feet of the gate during the night, we should feel the tug and be able to pull him back.

During most of our preparations several warders remained outside the cell eying us curiously, but when we had finished they went away and the whole of our tier in the Big House having been occupied by British prisoners of war was now quite silent.

Nobody brought us an evening meal, but fortunately our carafe was over half full already, and by keeping it out of Paolo's reach we hoped that he would have to plead for water long before we were reduced to giving in. We did not mean to start any altruistic nonsense about sharing with our unwilling guest. If Paolo wanted water he would have to persuade his compatriots to give it to him.

Lights were put out at the usual time, which was nine o'clock, so Bannister and I settled down in our bunks, having warned Paolo that he really would be taking his life in his hands if he tried any funny business.

Although the big lights were out, small blue lights which enabled the night warders to keep the prisoners under observation were still burning, and by the dim glow of these I watched the poor devil for a bit. He was sitting hunched up on the floor and he must have been so damnably uncomfortable that I was almost sorry for him, but I felt that one night at least of acute discomfort would do no harm at all to this cocky little Fascist blackguard.

Now that no one was moving in the great brick and steel cage, I could hear the sound of gunfire plainly, but how far away it was I had no idea. I was still wondering about that when I dropped off to sleep.

I woke with a start. It was pitch dark as the blue lights had also been put out while we were sleeping, evidently in the hope of using the Stygian blackness as cover for an attempted rescue.

It was Teddy's shout which had wakened me, and almost at the same moment I felt my right arm pulled as the rope which was attached to its wrist suddenly tightened. With all my strength

I threw myself back, jerking Paolo bodily towards me. He must have been squirming his way towards the gate of the cell, which somebody had opened with a key instead of the automatic lever.

Next second the silence was broken by a rush of feet; there came a scream from Paolo and Teddy yelled in English, "Tell them that I've got the point of his knife just over his liver and that I mean to jam it in if they come a step further."

But there was no need for me to do so. Paolo himself was pleading with his friends in Italian, which must have been tumbling from his lips at the rate of five hundred words a minute, not to come nearer. Calling upon the Mother of God and Gonzaga alternately, he begged them to have pity, otherwise these fiends of English would cut him in little pieces. Somebody out there in the darkness swore and somebody else called: "All right, *tenente*, have no fear. We will retire rather than bring you into danger."

Fearing that this might be a trap I told Teddy to keep his knife pricking Paolo while I held the gun ready to blaze off if anyone tried to rush us, but after a few moments the cell gate clanged to and the blue lights went on. For the rest of the night we suffered no further disturbance.

On the Thursday morning Gonzaga came to have another talk with us, but all his arguments and the fact that we had had neither supper nor breakfast failed to move us.

Without meals or exercise to break it that Thursday proved a long and dreary day, which was broken by only two excitements. The dull rumble of the distant guns had been there for many hours past whenever one chose to listen for it, and the comparative silence was rudely shattered soon after Gonzaga's visit by a terrific explosion.

It was followed by others and the building rocked. Evidently British bombers were somewhere high up in the heavens above us and dropping their 'eggs' on Fort Capuzzo. The raid went on for over half an hour, and from the tinkling glass on the floors below us we knew that a number of windows had been shattered.

Our other excitement only caused us to laugh, although in a way it was pretty sinister. From having said very little since his capture Paolo suddenly became loquacious. He let himself go upon just what he meant to do to Bannister and myself when we were forced to give in. It appeared that he had plenty of friends in high Fascist circles, and he swore that if it was the last thing he ever did he would see to it that our lives were made a living hell for months on end in the worst political prison that Italy could boast. Whatever the sentence which the court martial

123

passed upon us for having physically maltreated an Italian officer, he swore that we should never live to complete it.

At first it was rather amusing to listen to his blasphemous invective, but it got rather wearisome so eventually I cut him short by saying:

"Since that's your plan, Tortino, it seems there's only one thing for us to do. If we're forced to throw in our hand, rather than submit to imprisonment while leaving you alive to urge your gangster friends to kill us by inches, it would obviously be better for us to face a firing-squad for having killed you first."

After that he piped down, and we had no further trouble with him until late that night, when there was another air raid. This time the bombs fell much closer, and we could hear them whistle over the building. It was damnably unpleasant, and both Teddy and I felt pretty shaken, but Tortino lost all control and began to scream to the guards to come and shoot us and let him out.

They came along, but I told them that if there was any shooting to be done I was going to start it, and I pressed the barrel of the pistol to Tortino's sweating neck, upon which he begged them to go away again. They offered to take us down to the air-raid shelter, but we knew that to accept meant chucking up the sponge, and we were now determined to stick it out.

After midnight the bombing eased a bit, and we all began to realize that we were distinctly hungry and thirsty. The unfortunate Paolo was in an even worse state than Teddy and myself, at least as we had had two sparing drinks out of our carafe in the course of the day.

Having remained quiet for a bit, he apparently decided to try to induce the guards to give him some water. For long spells he argued with them or yelled alternate pleas and threats while they reiterated that no water was to be furnished to anybody in the cell without the Governor's order; but at last he persuaded them to go and rouse Gonzaga.

The ex-head waiter arrived, tousled, ill-tempered and clad in a flamboyant silk dressing-gown. It was quite impossible for him to ignore Paolo's pleas, and he agreed to one small cup of water being fetched to slake the lieutenant's thirst, but I wasn't going to let him get away with that.

"Oh no," I said. "Not one drop of water goes down his gullet unless the same quantity is given to Mr. Bannister and myself. From now on we shall share and share alike. If Tortino drinks we drink, and if Tortino feeds we feed. Talking of which, all three of us could do with a good hearty meal."

"Zen you canna damn' well go 'ungry!" Gonzaga snapped. "Water, yes, zat I giva so da *tenente* do not die; but food, no, I see you damn' first. For da *tenente* I am sorry, but eff you maka 'im share wiz you not one zread of vermicelli do I give." He stalked indignantly away, and after that we got a few hours' sleep.

Soon after dawn on the Friday we were roused by a fresh series of crumping detonations, and at first we thought it was another air raid; but the explosions had a different sound from bombs and seemed heavier than even the thousand-pounders, which were the largest that we were then using. Preceding each, too, there was a prolonged rumble as though a train were passing overhead, and after a few minutes I felt certain I knew what it was. Some of our capital ships must have come up the coast and were flinging shells from their big guns into Fort Capuzzo.

The bombardment lasted for over half an hour, during which we could hear the cascading roar of brick buildings as they collapsed, the whine of great shell splinters as they whizzed through the air, and the cries of the wounded Italians outside; but the prison was not hit.

The day passed uneventfully except for two more air raids, but by evening it was over forty-eight hours since any of us had had anything to eat and we were feeling absolutely ravenous.

On the Saturday our distress was added to by Gonzaga's arriving at midday with a wicked little smile on his chubby face, and two army cooks behind him carrying trays of steaming savoury-smelling food. These were put down outside the cell for our inspection, and he spent half an hour in trying to wheedle us into surrender as the price of this excellent dinner.

Paolo had to be forcibly restrained, and to us it was a sore temptation, particularly for the first ten or fifteen minutes, but as the food grew colder and the sauces began to congeal on the plates, resistance to it grew easier and we managed to survive the ordeal.

There were more air raids that day and the following night; six or seven at least, but after the fourth I lost count. It was now over three days since we had eaten, and the pangs of hunger were playing the very devil with us.

At what should have been breakfast-time on the Sunday morning, Teddy and I began to wonder how long it would be before we should have to chuck up the sponge. Heavy fighting was still going on somewhere to the east of us, but we agreed that the gunfire did not sound a mile nearer than it had the previous Monday when we had first arrived at Fort Capuzzo. We knew that, both numerically and in armoured vehicles, the Italian Army was infinitely stronger than our own, so although the British had initiated the battle and succeeded in penetrating the enemy's lines to a considerable depth, it was hardly reasonable to expect that they would be able to advance very far once the element of surprise had ceased to give them any special advantage.

We both felt ghastly, and the trouserless Paolo, with a four-days' growth of bristly stubble on his blue chin, now looked a most repulsive object. In the last twenty-four hours he had taken a very different tone, begging us hard to see reason and end this wretched farce. He swore by all his gods that if only we would let him go he would undertake to fix it that there should be no court martial, that we should continue to be treated as ordinary prisoners of war, and even receive preferential treatment on reaching Italy; but I felt dead certain that we couldn't trust the little rat so I didn't believe one word he said, and neither did Teddy.

At midday Gonzaga turned up again with more tempting dishes. Our mouths positively watered, and Paolo, straining at his bonds, knelt on the floor gibbering like an animal. The food looked more delicious than anything we had ever set our eyes on but we could not smell it as, owing to lack of sanitary accommodation and the fact that we had now been confined there for so long, the cell stank to high heaven. I think we might have given in then if it hadn't been for the fact that pride forbade us to do so spontaneously. Teddy and I owed it to ourselves to talk matters over first, and see if we could secure some sort of terms from Gonzaga before we actually confessed defeat to him.

That afternoon we did discuss it, but during the morning the guns of Fort Capuzzo had been in almost constant action and British shells of comparatively small calibre had been whining and cracking into the great desert citadel; so we felt that our troops must have advanced for another few miles at least.

We had often heard that the cravings of hunger are at their worst for the first three days, and it certainly seemed to us that the gnawing in our insides had lessened just a little since the previous night. There was no danger of our suffering from thirst, as each morning and evening the guards brought us a plentiful supply of cool refreshing well water. In consequence we determined to try to complete a week, feeling another three days to be about the maximum time that we could possibly resist Gonzaga's

126

blandishments if the old devil had fresh varieties of tempting food brought to us.

On the Saturday and Sunday he had confined himself to inflicting on us only a lunch-time temptation, but on Monday morning, after a night during which guns thundered and bombs crumped hour after hour without intermission, we found to our distress that an increased strain was to be put upon our powers of resistance. Gonzaga appeared soon after we wakened and was himself carrying a large tray which held a big coffee-pot, a basket of rolls, butter, honey and something on a hot dish under a big cover.

Instead of setting it down outside the cage he called to the warder and made him unlock by hand the gate of our cell. Then with the tray thrust out in front of him he walked right in.

"Hi! Get out!" I called in sudden alarm, grabbing up the automatic and levelling it at Paolo's head. "Halt, I say! Or I'll blow the *tenente's* brains out!"

Gonzaga halted, but his face was wreathed with smiles. "No need," he said. "Et is feenish. You win, Meester Day. Fort Capuzzo 'ave surrender. You eata da good breakfast and taka me prisoner now so zey treata me good."

For a moment we thought that it was some new trick that he was trying on us; then we realized that the guns of Fort Capuzzo were no longer in action, and that such firing as we could hear was further away to the west.

It was the 15th of December. I had been a prisoner of war for a month and five days and it was eighteen days since the date that had been fixed for my marriage to Daphnis. I felt then that had I allowed myself to be sent to Tobruk and Italy that marriage might never have taken place, but by my own determination I had won my freedom and thus ensured that the marriage upon which I had set my heart could not, after all, be long delayed.

I was so relieved and overjoyed that, having thanked Teddy Bannister a score of times for having stuck so loyally by me, I even allowed Paolo to share the magnificent omelette which was under the cover on the tray that smiling Gonzaga set before us.

CHAPTER XIII

GREAT DAY

As a matter of fact it was not really our fortitude which saved us but Gonzaga's foresight in deciding to insure himself against possible eventualities. The cheerful old villain told me afterwards that if he had pretended to be sorry for us on the second or third day, and given us food without making any conditions, he could easily have first ordered the doctor to put some drug in it. Since we had not thought of that I am quite certain that we should have eaten it and could then have been overpowered during our drug-induced sleep.

But, as he said, by the third day of the offensive Sidi Barrani had been captured, and by the fourth the British had taken twenty thousand prisoners. Reports were coming in from all sides that our tank columns were moving with incredible swiftness and turning up in the most unexpected places; so by the 13th, Fort Capuzzo having been entirely surrounded, the wily old bird had formed the conclusion that it might well be forced to capitulate under threats of further devastating bombardments from the British Mediterranean Fleet. In consequence he had privately decided that Teddy Bannister and myself had now become valuable personal hostages to him, since, provided he did not treat us unfairly, we would put in a word for him if he in turn became prisoner, and he had already made up his mind to give us that breakfast on the Monday morning whether Capuzzo had capitulated by then or not.

Unfortunately neither Teddy nor I was in a situation to do much for him by the time a crowd of lusty young Australians entered the prison, and with terrifying yells drove all its guards into a corner at the point of the bayonet. After starving for four days that rich and luscious omelette had proved too much for us. We two and Paolo were sweating with agony and rolling about with acute stomach-ache. However, when an officer came to our cell, where Gonzaga was doing his best for us, I pulled myself together sufficiently to explain that we had not been poisoned or maltreated, and that the Governor had proved a good friend. Later I wrote to Essex Pasha telling him the story of my capture and asking that the ex-head waiter should have any little amenities granted to him which might ameliorate his captivity.

Paolo, Teddy and I were carried away by the Australians to

the prison infirmary, where we spent the next two days in bed recruiting our strength after the privation which we had suffered. My first act, naturally, was to write a long letter to Daphnis, telling her all that had happened to me and that I was applying for leave immediately in order that we could celebrate our postponed wedding. My second was to make a formal application for leave on the grounds that it was now long overdue. Teddy Bannister also put in an application, although he had been on leave just before his capture, on the grounds of his imprisonment and that he was to be my best man.

The result was far from what we had expected and bitterly disappointing to myself. His leave was granted whereas my application was rejected.

An intelligence officer had taken statements from us both on the Monday afternoon, and it was through him that we had put in our applications for leave. On the Wednesday morning he came to the infirmary again to break the bad news to me personally.

"You see, Day," he said, "all you interpreters have had a darn' easy time so far during this war. But now we need every Italian-speaking officer we've got to tackle the prisoners. We're roping in thousands of the blighters every day, and even by working from dawn till dusk we can't question one in ten of them properly; so you see you can't possibly be spared. It's hard luck that being taken prisoner forced you to postpone your marriage, but the Brigadier is quite adamant about it. He says that you shall have your leave as soon as it can be managed after the situation becomes static; but as long as the offensive continues it will be useless for you to renew your application."

There could be no argument against the Brigadier's decision. I knew how disappointed Daphnis would be, but I realized that, having had such an easy time for months, now I had a chance to pull my weight it was only right that I should do so.

While we were in the sanatorium we heard the details of General Wavell's first magnificent success, and although there was a feeling that the advance could not be maintained at this headlong pace for many days longer, good news continued to come in from the front almost every hour. Sollum had fallen on the same day as Fort Capuzzo, and now that the British were on Libyan soil the whole chain of desert forts along the frontier were surrendering one after another.

A terrific battle was said to be raging at 'Hellfire' Pass where the low coastal strip which lies between the sea and the great escarpment that forms the central plateau of the Western Desert narrows to barely a mile in width. Along this flat narrow ribbon, bounded by the Mediterranean on one side and cliffs towering up sheer to five hundred feet in height on the other, the Imperial Forces were having to fight for every inch of ground in order to force the main gateway by which the all-important military road ran into Libya; but further south our mechanized units had penetrated to a much greater depth, and by the Thursday Bardia, the first considerable town over the frontier, had been surrounded.

It was on that day that I saw Paolo marched off as a prisoner on the road to Egypt, and took an affectionate leave of Teddy Bannister. I had told him all about my affair with Daphnis and he had promised to call on her and deliver another long letter from me personally.

With the Army of the Nile now operating over thousands of square miles of territory and units here one day only to be gone the next, I knew that the field post-offices could not possibly cope with the situation, and I had been considerably worried that Daphnis might not get my first letter or hear that I was a free man again perhaps for weeks, so it comforted me a lot now to know that Teddy would be seeing her within the next few days and be able to put a definite period to the anxiety which she must be feeling on my account.

Half an hour after we had parted I was on my way to join my old friends, the New Zealanders, who had taken up their positions just outside Bardia. I found them after no little difficulty in the early hours of the morning on Friday, December the 20th.

From them I learned that the first lightning assault which had broken the Italian front had been launched by regular units of the British Army, including the battalion of the Coldstream Guards with whom I had been when captured, and first-line troops of the Indian Army. These peace-time-trained shock troops had then been withdrawn and the eager volunteers from the Dominions allowed to go in for their baptism of fire; so after their first sweep forward, during which they had chivvied the enemy in a running fight, they were mad keen to get into Bardia.

The town was now completely encircled on land, and its harbour was closed by units of the British Navy, but as the first town on the Libyan side of the border, unlike Sollum on the Egyptian side, it had been systematically prepared over a number of years to resist attack.

The white-domed mosques and spindly minarets which we could see in the far distance through our field-glasses gave no

130

hint of the strength of the defences of the town, but every good site for miles around it had been surveyed long before the war by Italian staff officers, and pill-boxes with fields of crossfire built where they could be cunningly concealed by great mounds of sand. Further in, deep ditches had been dug as tank-traps and barbed wire had been set up in great quantities to render infantry advances difficult and hazardous.

When I arrived before the town our field guns were not even in range of it, but night and day our men gradually ate their way into the fringe of the defensive works, crawling over long stretches of sand at the imminent risk of their lives to lob Mills grenades into some strong-points, taking others by surprise in skilfully planned night attacks and causing others again to be hammered to pieces by the shells of our artillery.

Not a day passed without fresh prisoners being brought in, and it was my job to carry out their first interrogation before despatching them under guard to join the long stream of green-clad captives which was now wending its way into Egypt. Except for a few extra rounds of drinks, Christmas Day and New Year's Eve passed just like the others.

During the months before my own capture I had watched the experienced intelligence officers at Brigade and Division doing this work on the comparatively few Italians which we were able to bring in for questioning in those days. I had soon seen that some of these officers got much more out of the prisoners than others and that often much better results could be obtained by jollying the prisoner along or appearing sympathetic than by threats of rigorous confinement.

There was one regular captain that I had seen at work for whom I had the greatest admiration, and I tried to model myself on him. Using at first an entirely non-committal and colourless attitude towards each prisoner I attempted to sum him up psychologically, then I either thawed out to a state in which we eventually joked and smoked cigarettes together or, with violent blows of a short whip against a packing-case which served me as a table, I demanded answers to my questions with the same fierceness as any Prussian.

I soon discovered that to do such work well one needs to be something of an actor, and the first essential is to throw overboard any silly inhibitions about its not being done for a British officer to lose his temper or make a scene. I learned to work myself up into what appeared to be a frenzy of anger, often three or four times in a morning, and some of the wretched prisoners would

131

cower away from me in terror, thinking that I meant to shoot them on the spot as I stood over them with my pistol levelled. But more often I yarned pleasantly for ten minutes or a quarter of an hour about his native city with each fellow who was brought in, and, luckily, I knew Italy pretty well.

These methods were certainly successful as, either from a desire not to appear oafish when spoken to decently or from blue funk that I would have them treated as they had seen the Libyan Arabs treated at the orders of their own swinish commander, Marshal Graziani, they gave away any number of little things which helped us in planning our attacks locally and also for my reports which would later assist the high-ups at Headquarters to assess the number and disposition of the forces with which the Italians had garrisoned Libya.

The days were pleasantly warm as we had the benefit of the North African sunshine which in peace-time winters thousands of fortunate people pay the tourist agencies considerable sums to obtain; but the nights were bitter. We wore every scrap of clothing we could, including our greatcoats, yet we still shivered in our bivies until we fell asleep. Many of our fellows even preferred to go on night patrols or sentry duty in order that they could keep warm by moving about during the chill hours and sleep in comfort in the daytime.

On January the 3rd the Australians delivered a great frontal attack and made a considerable breach in the outer defences. There followed two days of most desperate fighting. The Navy shelled the town; the Air Force sent any Italian machine that appeared reeling from the skies, and bombed or machine-gunned the Italians wherever they endeavoured to concentrate their land forces; while the Army, tired, covered with dust, but in magnificent heart, strafed the Italian soldiery without cessation, chasing them from ridge to ridge until at last, on Sunday, January the 5th, Bardia surrendered.

Most of the troops reckoned then that they would get at least a few days to rest and refit before they were ordered to undertake further operations, but like the splendid soldiers they are Generals Wavell and Wilson knew that the last time to rest is during those rare precious hours when it is possible to pursue a fleeing enemy. On Monday the 6th, the advance on Tobruk was ordered. On Tuesday the 7th Tobruk aerodrome was captured, and on Wednesday the 8th, only three days after the fall of Bardia, Tobruk was entirely encircled.

However, I was not among those who executed this fine

forced march. The trickle of prisoners had, during the last days of the attack on Bardia, increased into a spate, and with the fall of the town we had taken a further 40,000, so I was detached from my battalion with a squad of men to help deal with them.

Although we worked night and day the herds of dejected-looking men in the wire cages were so great that the work of interrogation could only be carried out in the most perfunctory manner. All I could do, after glancing through their pay-book and private papers to pick up what I could of their peace-time background, was to pull out about one in twenty for ten minutes' quick grilling and one in a hundred for special questioning by Intelligence at the base, owing to his Fascist connections or some other reason that made him one of the more interesting fish in our net.

During this time I had the benefit of a roof over my head, which was a great blessing in view of the coldness of the nights. The Navy had confined its bombardments of Bardia to the fortifications and harbour works, while the R.A.F. had loosed its bombs mainly upon similar objectives or troop cantonments, so the town had not sustained as much damage as we expected, and with several other officers I occupied half the house of a wealthy Arab.

His uncle had been one of the minor chieftains whom the playful Graziani had taken up in an aeroplane and flung out to be dashed to pieces on the rocks a thousand feet below, in order to induce the Arabs to accept Fascist culture, when he had been Governor-General of Libya in the days before the more clement and far-sighted Marshal Balbo took over. In consequence our host regarded the British as the liberators of his people, and he could not do enough for us; but by the 15th we had at last sorted out and despatched the best part of the Army Corps which had been taken at Bardia, and I was ordered to rejoin my unit outside Tobruk.

It took me all day to cover the seventy miles as the one road was chock-a-block with the reinforcements and supplies with which General Wilson was strengthening our advance forces, but I was back with my old friends, the New Zealanders, on the evening of Thursday, January the 16th.

Conditions with them were much the same as they had been outside Bardia, but Tobruk appeared to be a much stiffer proposition. It had a fine deep-water harbour and, with the exception of Benghazi, which still lay over two hundred and fifty miles to the west of us, was the most important city in the whole of Eastern

Libya. In addition to its strong fortifications an Italian cruiser and other warships lay in the harbour and were assisting the defence with their big guns.

Such heavies as we had been able to get up were pounding the place while our smaller calibre batteries barked and coughed at the strong points in the outer ring of the defences. All day long the aeroplanes droned overhead, some spotting for our batteries and others swooping to machine-gun columns of Italian lorries or concentrations of troops which were too far distant for us to see. It was grand to know that at least we had the mastery of the air in this campaign as on the rare occasions that Italian 'planes did put in an appearance they were always either shot down or driven off immediately. That made an immense difference, but the Italians here seemed full of fight and they had masses of ammunition. The guns roared day and night; shells whistled and screamed over, and there was hardly a moment during daylight when in one direction or another one could not see an Italian shellburst sending up a great fountain of sand.

Over the week-end we worked like niggers as orders had come through which indicated that the General Staff were now contemplating a direct assault on the city. Many batteries were moved forward almost into the fighting line, and we carried stores and ammunition up by hand during the nights to form dumps as near as we dared to the enemy.

On Tuesday, the 21st of January, the Navy, Army and Air Force attacked simultaneously at dawn. The cruiser in the harbour was shelled until it became a burnt-out skeleton. Five of the perimeter forts were taken, and in several places our troops penetrated the inner defences of the city. On Wednesday the 22nd, the flag on the Italian G.H.Q. was hauled down and Tobruk surrendered with a further 25,000 prisoners.

Once more my friends, overjoyed as they were by their victory, thought that the maximum possible profit had now been reaped from our offensive, and that we should have to sit down to consolidate our gains; but our General Staff in the Middle East seemed to have taken a leaf out of the Germans' book and grasped the great lesson made so tragically apparent in the battles for Norway, Holland, Belgium and France. Defence was no longer superior to attack, except in quite exceptional circumstances and, given speed and imagination, there appeared to be no limit to the gains which might be secured by a victorious army providing that it was properly directed, and that the men composing it were prepared to march and fight until they dropped.

Within an hour of the fall of Tobruk General Sir Henry Maitland Wilson was calling upon his army for new efforts, and he did not call in vain. It was now just on seven weeks since the first assault had been delivered against Sidi Barrani, and during that time there had been no days off for anyone and barely even the time to keep ourselves and our arms reasonably clean. Few of us had a bath and sometimes we were unable even to wash for days at a stretch, but there were no grumblers. Home Forces, Australians, New Zealanders and Indians alike were all so elated by the smashing blows we were dealing the enemy that fatigue, dirt and discomfort were forgotten. All they asked was to be led on to further triumphs.

Once again I was left behind at Tobruk to help cope with the new flood of prisoners so I was one of the few lucky ones who was able to live for some days in a comfortable house where I could actually take my clothes off to sleep in bed each night and get a bath each morning.

By the Sunday following the fall of Tobruk our men were fighting in the neighbourhood of Derna, which was as far again along the coast as Tobruk had been from the frontier. This was much the most spectacular advance that had so far been made during any four days in this remarkable campaign, but it was to be far exceeded before the full triumph was completed.

A week after the capture of Tobruk, the bulk of the prisoners there having been dealt with, I was again ordered to rejoin my battalion, but by the time I reached Derna I found that this fine town, which the Italians had converted in recent years into a fashionable pleasure resort, had already fallen. That was on January the 30th, and it now seemed that the Italians' Libyan Army was cracking up in all directions. From February the 1st onwards it was one wild, tireless drive by tanks, Bren-gun carriers, armoured cars and lorries to catch up with the fleeing Eyeties.

I had lost all trace of my battalion, so I simply went on into the blue, picking up lifts as I could and snatching an hour or two's sleep whenever I felt too utterly worn out to go any further. Except for sandy stretches here and there, we were now mostly free of the desert, having passed into the pleasant fertile region of Western Cyrenaica, where there were grazing herds, fields of crops and groves of date palms.

At every village through which we passed the little groups of Arabs never seemed tired of cheering and thrusting presents of fruit and sticky sweetmeats upon us. We rarely saw an Italian

135

except for strays and small detachments who wished to give themselves up, but for the time being we were too occupied in pressing on without wasting a single moment to bother with them. On February the 3rd the old town of Cyrene, which in Roman times had been the capital of the province, was taken, and three days later there was a great tank battle in which Major-General Martel, having raced right across the inland desert almost to the bottom of the Gulf of Sirte, cut off and smashed the retreating Italians. That night, Thursday, February the 6th, Benghazi surrendered, and the whole of Cyrenaica was in British hands.

From start to finish it had been a magnificent feat of endurance on the part of the troops and a supremely brilliant demonstration by our General Staff of the art of waging war. Only too often in the Boer War, and in the 1914-18 War, our generals had received completely unmerited praise, titles and high decorations for flinging their troops against positions held strongly by an enemy or standing to fight a desperate battle in the most adverse circumstances. It does not need forty years of specialized training, staff courses and experience in command to order men to attack —or fight with their backs to the wall. Any fool can fling troops against a hill or require them to stand and die when he has made a mucker of his job; but it needs real brains, imagination and enormous organizing ability to direct the spearheads of a small force with maximum striking power against the weak spots of a vastly superior enemy, and to do it again and again until his whole army is broken up in confusion and his strong places destroyed. That was what our generals had done; with a force of little more than sixty thousand men they had utterly routed an army a quarter of a million strong and overrun a territory nearly as big as England. We were immensely proud of them and not without pride in ourselves to think that, with our sweat and drive, we had been among those who had contributed to re-establishing the prestige that the British Army had lost in Norway, France and Belgium.

During those exhausting days of questioning prisoners for hour after hour, writing reports for despatch-riders to rush off to Intelligence, and thrusting forward day after day, across territory which a few weeks previously we had never dreamed that we'd be able to reach, I had little time to be anxious, as I otherwise should have been, about Daphnis.

After leaving Fort Capuzzo I had made up my mind that I must not expect to hear from her. In an open warfare offensive of this kind it is utterly impossible for the Army postal service to keep in touch with constantly moving units and sometimes mails get hung up for weeks before, at last, reaching their destination; but actually I fared much better than I expected, as I got a first letter from her while we were still outside Bardia.

In it she told me how utterly shattered she had been when she had learnt that I had been taken prisoner, and of how all her old fears about the prophecy that a sword lay between us and that we were fated never to belong to each other had possessed her mind to the exclusion of all else until her parents had feared that she was going to have a breakdown. Then how Teddy Bannister had arrived one morning and seen her mother, after which they had broken the news to her that I was alive and free.

While I was in Bardia itself I had two more letters from her, all glowing with love and confidence in our future happiness. After that there was an interval of over a fortnight, at the end of which five letters turned up in one bag of mail that reached us at Tobruk. From that point on the postal people lost me, and I certainly can't blame them, as I never slept in the same place twice until I arrived in Benghazi two days after its capture.

All through those weeks I wrote to her, when, how and where I could in ink or pencil, and when I had run out of ordinary paper, on the backs of Army forms or anything I could get hold of. Only once did more than three days elapse without my being able to get a few lines off to let her know that I was still alive, well and unwounded, and whenever I could keep myself awake to do so I scribbled long screeds of adoration.

On my second day in Benghazi the mails caught up, and I received another batch of letters from Daphnis. As I read them through, my fingers trembled so that I could hardly hold the sheets. Every line of them radiated a love that rivalled my own, and I knew, now that a halt had at last been called to our victorious progress, I should be able to get leave and be with her very soon again.

We were once more dealing with prisoners as hard as we could go, and thousands of them had been concentrated in great wire cages just outside the town, near one of which I occupied a hutment. But on the morning of the 11th I chucked work, collared one of the innumerable little Fiat cars that we had captured, and drove over to the New Zealanders.

I had not been with them during the most desperate fighting, and to my distress I learned that my friend Jack Benham had been wounded. A shell-splinter had entered the fleshy part of his

137

leg above the knee, but it was hoped that he would not suffer any permanent disability from the wound.

Reports said that 'Long Willie' had proved the sort of Colonel that every subaltern dreams about. Caked with filth and covered in blood, he had apparently gone without sleep for days at a stretch, while he tirelessly directed his men or actually fought with them at any point where the fleeing enemy turned to offer resistance. But when I found him he was as clean and immaculate as ever, the same tall, rather stooping mild-mannered man with a ready grin that had kept us at it, yet from grumbling without cause or openly quarrelling, when our tempers had been frayed to rags by the blistering heat during those ghastly months at Mersa Matruh.

When I asked him about leave, he said: "I know how anxious you must be to get back to your fiancée, Day, but I'm afraid it's no longer my pigeon. Now that we're consolidating here I could let any of my own boys off in a case like this, but you fall into a different category. There are still such shoals of these Wops to be dealt with, and as long as they have to be sorted out you've been lent to Division. I'll raise no objection, of course, but I'm afraid you'll have to get a chit from someone higher up before you stand much chance of leave to Alex."

I tried to hide my disappointment as well as I could, and after leaving him it occurred to me to go into Benghazi and see the staff captain whose Intelligence work I admired so much.

Having driven into town, I ran him to earth in one of the hotels that had been taken over as a part of the Area Headquarters. When I had put my case to him he said, at once:

"You're quite definitely needed here, but I do sympathize, and if I possibly can I'd like to do something for you. Your own work has been absolutely first-class, and I was speaking to the General about you only the other day. It's over a year now since you received your commission and I suggested that he should put you up for your second pip."

"That's most awfully kind of you, sir," I stammered. I certainly hadn't expected any such bouquet as even in wartime it's generally eighteen months or two years before an officer is promoted to full lieutenant unless he proves specially valuable.

The Captain sat smoking thoughtfully in silence for a moment, then he went on:

"As a matter of fact I've no doubt at all that your promotion will go through, but I'm equally certain that the General wouldn't grant you leave at the moment. Still, I think I see a way round

138

that. As you know, we've sent over a hundred thousand prisoners back to Egypt already. At least two-thirds of them have not been grilled as yet, so there's still a mass of stuff to be picked up as a result of skilful questioning. How would it suit you if, instead of leave, I had you transferred to Alex to carry on the good work there?"

"But that would be absolutely magnificent!" I exclaimed. "I'd be able not only to get married and have a honeymoon, but take a flat and live in it with my wife for a month or two anyway. I'd be most terribly grateful if you could, sir."

"All right," he smiled. "I'll see what I can do. It may take a few days, but if it comes off I shall expect a piece of the wedding-cake to put under my pillow!"

That splendid temporary chief of mine was as good as his word. Three days later orders came through for me to report to the senior commandant, Prisoners of War Camps, Alexandria. I was now more than double the distance from Alex than when I was stationed at Mersa Matruh, and as yet there was no organized transport for casual passengers, but I set off in my captured Fiat, and in spite of the military traffic on the road, and the endless trudging lines of prisoners, I was in Alexandria two afternoons later.

Tired and dusty as I was, I drove straight to the Diamopholi house. There had been no means of letting Daphnis know that I was coming, but I was absolutely bursting with the splendid news I had for her. If I had been granted even a fortnight's leave it would have meant that either there would have been no time at all to prepare for the wedding or we should have had to cut our honeymoon down to a bare week, whereas now that I was to be stationed in Alex I should have no cause to grudge Daphnis a little time to issue fresh invitations and arrange the big reception that she wanted. Graziani's army had been so thoroughly defeated that, so far as one could possibly see, all menace had been removed from Egypt, and it seemed that the glorious prospect of starting our married life in almost peace-time conditions lay before us.

It was about half past five when I arrived at the house. Daphnis and her mother were both at home and Alcis was with them. Daphnis' eyes looked as big and as round as half-crowns when I was shown into the room. She dropped some work that she was doing, but her surprise gave way to a shout of delight. Rushing at me, she flung her arms round my neck and clung to me until I thought that she would never let me go.

139

My own joy and excitement were hardly short of hers as I gathered her to me, quite regardless of the two onlookers, and felt her lovely face once more pressed against mine.

It is said that all the world loves a lover, and our feelings for each other were so obvious that my mother-in-law-to-be could only smile indulgently. When we had recovered ourselves a little, she spoke to me very kindly, saying how exciting our romance had been, and how, since we loved so much, she felt quite certain that I would make her daughter happy. Then she kissed me on the forehead and said that henceforward she would regard me as her son. At such a happy moment I could feel no animosity towards Alcis and I called her 'Cousin' as she held out her hand for my formal kiss of greeting.

The later details of that evening are only vague in my memory. I remember old Nicholas Diamopholus coming home from his office and being kindness itself to me. I remember lots of Diamopholi relatives and friends who had been called up on the telephone coming in for an informal party. Champagne flowed the whole evening; innumerable toasts were drunk and I put away buckets of it; but fortunately there are two states in which it is impossible for any man to get tight. He cannot do so if he is utterly and completely miserable through the loss or betrayal of a woman, and he cannot do so if he is deliriously happy and in the company of one whom he loves wildly, and by whom he knows himself to be beloved. It was very late when I reached the Cecil, where somebody had telephoned during the evening to reserve a room for me. But when I went to bed in the small hours of the morning I sighed with utter contentment, feeling myself to be the luckiest fellow in the whole world.

Next morning I was at the Diamopholi's by ten o'clock to discuss the hundred and one things that needed settling before the wedding. Since Daphnis wanted a large wedding I had not the least objection, providing that fixing it up was not going to take too long, but there seemed no fear of this, as the more lengthy matters, such as her wedding-dress, the bridesmaids, one of whom was to be Barbara Wishart, and their frocks, had all been agreed upon in the previous November.

Madame Diamopholus told me that I was now to consider myself free of the house, come there whenever I wanted to and stay as long as I liked, but I was still very much in the Army, and I knew that most of my days would be occupied with duties. That afternoon I took Daphnis out to see the Wisharts, who had played so large a part in our romance, and the following morning

I reported to the Senior Commandant at the vast prisoners-of-war camp.

In addition to the preparations for the wedding there was now the question of a flat to live in afterwards. We decided, as the war made the length of time we should be allowed to occupy it uncertain, it would be better to take a furnished apartment, and the day after I reported at the camp I got the afternoon off so that I could spend it with Daphnis and her mother looking round likely places.

Those few hectic days had passed like a dream between odd moments snatched whenever possible for love-making, a round of parties for me to be presented to the Diamopholi's innumerable friends, and my new duties. I could hardly keep track of the days of the week, but it was on Wednesday, February the 19th, that having been to see suites of furnished apartments we had chosen a very nice one for our future home; and it was on that night that I parted from Daphnis after our usual lingering farewell, little knowing in what horribly perturbing circumstances I should see her again.

CHAPTER XIV

RED-HOT CONSPIRACY

DURING the Libyan campaign we had had little time or opportunity to follow the progress of the war on other fronts. Days later we learned of the complicated diplomatic moves by which Hitler was systematically strengthening his hand for a great spring offensive. Hungary, Rumania, Yugoslavia and Bulgaria were all played off against each other with consummate skill. Marshall Pétain sacked the arch-traitor Laval, but Admiral Darlan's growing power increased the Nazi grip on France.

The German Army remained sinisterly inactive while Britain and Greece slogged Mussolini until he was punch-drunk. Milan, Genoa, Brindisi, Turin and Naples were all heavily raided by the R.A.F., and there was even a hope that Italy might be forced out of the war, until the Germans began to take over in the peninsula, and by mid-January they had transferred an entire air fleet to the Sicilian bases of Catania and Comiso.

The R.A.F. also consistently hammered the invasion ports and submarine bases at Brest and Lorient, but the Luftwaffe hit back at many English towns and on December the 29th London had a frightful pasting, in which the Guildhall and eight Wren churches were destroyed.

Lord Lothian's sudden death earlier in the month was a sad blow, and it was followed by the loss of General Metaxas and another great servant of the British Crown, Lord Lloyd.

At the end of January a new campaign was launched in Abyssinia. Kassala, on the Sudan frontier, was recaptured, and by a swift advance into Eritrea we took Agordat and Barentu in the first days of February. But these bits of news only trickled through to us.

With the fall of Benghazi, however, we had been able to get more regular news. On the day that I reached the Cyrenaic capital it had come through that the United States Senate had passed the Lease and Lend Bill, and everyone had been immensely cheered by the thought that the Americans were now really as good as in with us; but Hitler was getting very active in the Balkans.

On February the 13th he summoned the Yugoslav Prime Minister to Berchtesgaden. He was pumping German troops into Rumania as hard as he could go and hundreds of German 'tourists' were already infiltrating into Bulgaria. Turkey was still standing firm, but now that her western frontier was directly threatened through Bulgaria it looked doubtful if she would go to Greece's aid if the Nazis decided to pull the Italians out of the mess they had got themselves into in Albania.

It was on the night of the 16th-17th that London suffered one of the worst raids of the war. On the 18th we were all depressed by rumours that a great part of the city had been entirely burnt out, but it happened that on the 19th I had been so busy that I had missed every one of the B.B.C. bulletins. In consequence, on getting back to the Cecil a little after eleven o'clock, instead of going straight up to my room I went into the lounge to see if there was any further news of the damage done to the dear old city.

A man and woman were sitting at a small table near the door. I got a vague impression that he was tall and dark and that she was a peroxided, smart-looking woman, possibly French; but I paid no special attention to them as I passed, and paused at a large table in the centre of the room where a number of newspapers and periodicals were always left for the use of the guests.

There were very few other people in the lounge so it was quiet there, and although I now had my back turned to the couple near the door I heard the man speak quite distinctly. There was nothing in what he said to attract my attention, but I stiffened where I stood. The voice was unmistakable. It was that of the man who had been with Daphnis in the garden.

I knew now why I had felt such instinctive hatred and dread on hearing that voice before. Then, strive as I would I could not recall who its owner might be, but now one glimpse of that dark, sleek head had been enough to give me a cue.

Very cautiously I turned and looked over my shoulder. I could see the man three-quarter face now: his high forehead, his aristocratic Roman nose, and his full-lipped cruel mouth. I was right. It was the Portuguese, Count Emilo de Mondragora, one of the seven devils who had brought about poor Carruthers' suicide and wrecked my own career.

All the seething anger that I had felt at the time of the tragedy, all the bitterness of my wasted years, surged up in me. Those seven men who were responsible for my friend's death and my own downfall had amassed so much money that without ever lifting a finger again they could have lived in affluence for the rest of their lives. It was through sheer greed and a perverted pleasure in sin that they continued to operate their vast criminal organization which, by espionage, dope-running, white-slaving and blackmail, battened upon the follies and miseries of mankind. They were utterly pitiless, and without pity I had sworn to hunt them down.

In the early months of 1939 I had got on their track again and dealt with two of them. O'Kieff, when I had last seen him, had been on foot without transport, water, or supplies, and in the midst of a violent sandstorm somewhere south-east of the oasis of Siwa. I had left him to his fate in the desert a hundred miles or more from the nearest well, and it was outside the bounds of all probability that he had been able to remain alive for more than a matter of hours. Zakri Bey I had no doubts about at all, as I had strangled him with my own hands; but I had never succeeded in getting on the track of the other five, and six months after my first kill I had been absorbed into the war.

Now I had happened upon another of that unholy crew, but the grim satisfaction which I should normally have felt was tinged with fear. This man knew Daphnis. It was he of all people who had been with her that first night in the garden before my arrival.

Those horrible little whispering doubts which I had striven

with such resolution to put away from me, yet which for all that had refused to be smothered ever since my interview with Major Cozelli, became in one moment certainties.

In time of war first place in the activities of these aristocrats of crime would unquestionably go to big-scale espionage. The Portuguese was a neutral, so he could move freely still in any country. Had I come across him in German-occupied territory I should have considered it a possibility that he was spying for us, Britain having proved the highest bidder, but in Alexandria there were no secrets which he could learn other than those which would be useful to the Axis. Then, too, there were Daphnis' Italian sympathies and the fact that at that time she had been engaged to Paolo. Everything was terrifyingly clear now in my shocked and agonized mind; since it was Count Emilo de Mondragora who had been with Daphnis there was but one explanation: he had come there to collect her report. She had been—perhaps was still—spying for Italy.

During the seconds that the full implications of this shattering revelation raced through my brain I made a great effort to control my physical reactions. I felt that, although my back was turned to him, even an abrupt or awkward movement might attract the attention of that saturnine devil, and if he once recognized me any advantage which I might have over him would be gone.

Actually the only time that we had ever come face to face had been at that dinner-party when poor Carruthers and I had met the Big Seven in Brussels. It was quite on the cards that, even if he saw me, he would not know me again, but first-class brains usually have long memories, and I could not be too careful.

Having held the paper in front of my face for the space of about a minute without having absorbed one word that was printed on it, I folded it neatly, laid it down carefully on the top of the others, and walked out of a glass-panelled door at the far end of the lounge.

It wasn't until I was outside that I even dared to breathe freely, and to my surprise I found that I was sweating. Small beads of perspiration had broken out all over my forehead.

As I mopped them up with my handkerchief I realized that I had ample cause for the acute anxiety that I was feeling. A cruel fate had ordained that my adorable Daphnis should be mixed up with this monster whose outward elegance of appearance I knew to conceal the mentality of a rattlesnake combined with that of a carrion crow.

I lit a cigarette and drew heavily upon it as I wondered

agitatedly if Daphnis had given up spying for Italy when she became engaged to me, or if she was still playing that dangerous, and now treacherous, game. Since she had worked for Mondragora, and I now considered that to be as good as an established fact, I feared it was extremely unlikely that she had been able to break away from him, even if she had tried to. Men like the Portuguese are adepts at 'framing' their helpers so that they can hold the threat of blackmail over them should they at any time wish to give up the work.

If he had got something on her it might prove the devil of a job to get her out.

For a moment I thought of going straight back to the house and charging her with being Mondragora's associate, or at least demanding to know what she had been up to that night with him in the garden, and when she had last seen him; but I was quick to realize that any idea of a showdown must wait for the time being.

If I left the hotel I might lose touch with the Portuguese, and one thing stood out a mile—whatever part Daphnis might be playing in this affair, the fact remained that I was his sworn enemy. I had no intention of hanging for his murder if I could possibly avoid it, but, given the chance, I was determined to kill him with as little scruple as I would have crushed a poisonous scorpion under the heel of my boot.

I felt confident, too, that whatever Daphnis might have done in the past, once she became engaged to me she would never willingly have done anything that might harm my country; but if Mondragora had some threat which he could hold over her he might now be compelling her to carry on against her will and she must be suffering the most frightful mental torture from the dread that I might find her out. If that was so I had a double motive for eliminating Mondragora.

Through the glass panel of the door behind which I was now standing I could keep watch upon the Portuguese, but the distance was sufficient to prevent his recognizing me should he chance to glance in my direction. After about ten minutes he and the peroxide blonde got up and went out through the far door of the lounge. I immediately walked back through it and emerged cautiously after them into the hall. He was getting himself into a big overcoat and I waited for a minute until he and the woman went out of the front door.

It was dark outside, but as I followed there was just enough light for me to see that he put the woman into one taxi before getting into another himself. Directly he had driven off I slipped the negro night-porter, who had held the cab doors for them, ten piastres and asked him what address the gentleman had given.

He knew me well enough to recognize me by my shape and voice in the semi-darkness, and he replied without hesitation: "Ambassador Court, sah. Dat's 'em beeg block ob flats along da waterfront, jus' on da corner ob da Sharia Nur-El-Din."

"Thanks," I said. "Maybe I'll go there tomorrow morning and see if he's the fellow I think he is. I didn't like to go up and speak to him while he was with a lady, but he looked just like a man I used to know—a Major Robinson."

"No, sah, youse all wrong 'bout dat," laughed the big negro genially. "Ah dunno da gentleman's name, but he ain't no English gentleman. Ah's as sure ob dat as ma own name's Abdullah."

"Oh," I said in a disappointed tone. "Well, in that case I must have been mistaken." And I turned back into the hotel.

Having nodded good night I went up in the lift to my room, where I pulled a big cabin trunk from under the bed. Most of my pre-war possessions were being stored for me in the baggage room of the Semiramis Hotel in Cairo, but when my battalion had first been ordered to Mersa Matruh I had packed one trunk with things such as flannels, bathing-suits, etc., which I might need on short leave and deposited it with the management of the Cecil in Alex. From the trunk I took a dark-blue lounge suit and the things to go with it, my Mauser pistol, and the rubber goloshes which I had brought ten months before with the idea of surprising Daphnis the night of my first clandestine visit to her garden. Getting out of my uniform I changed into the civilian clothes, put on the goloshes and slipped the loaded gun into my pocket.

Opening the door cautiously, I peered out into the corridor. Nobody was about so I walked swiftly along it and tiptoed down the service stairs. On the ground floor I had to wait for a moment while two sleepy Arab servants grumbled to each other about having been kept at their work so late they would now miss the last bus and have to walk home. They shambled side by side along a passage which led to the back entrance of the hotel. Having given them a moment to get clear, I followed them outside. A quarter of an hour's quick walk along the front brought me to the Sharia Nur-El-Din, and on one corner there was a big block of flats which I knew must be Ambassador Court.

A flight of steps led up to its entrance, and a uniformed porter was standing in the hall. I had to wait there in the shadows for twenty minutes until a taxi drove up and some people went in. The porter took them up in the lift, leaving the hall empty. That was the opportunity for which I had been waiting, and I slipped inside.

I had had to take a chance on Mondragora's having a flat at Ambassador Court and living there under his own name, but I had felt that if I temporarily lost him there was a good chance of my picking up his trail again or finding out if he had rented a flat under some alias by describing him to the porter. One glance at a big board bearing the names of the occupants of the flats in gilt letters showed me that my luck was in. Count Emilo de Mondragora's name appeared opposite Flat 42 on the top floor. Delaying no longer, I started swiftly up the stairs.

As I reached the second landing the lift shot down again, so I knew that I could proceed in safety at a more leisurely pace, and I mounted to the top of the building. So far fortune and cautious planning had proved extraordinarily favourable to my project —and my project was murder.

People have an idea that it is difficult to commit murder without being found out, but I don't think that is necessarily so. Murder in itself is easy enough, but where ninety-nine out of a hundred murderers fall down is that they have an obvious motive for their crime which there is no possible way of concealing. The first rule of police procedure is to go into the history of the family concerned and find out who, among the associates of the victim, would be likely to benefit from the deed or derive satisfaction from it. Then every tiny detail as to the way in which anyone against whom there is the remotest suspicion spent their time during the hours, days or even weeks preceding the murder is checked up.

From such a system it is almost impossible for the murderer to escape, however skilfully he may have plotted the crime and even when he has what appears to be a watertight alibi. To provide himself with an alibi he has to lie and one lie leads to another. Sooner or later the painstaking questioning of the detectives catches him out. In the great majority of cases the police are virtually certain within a few hours as to who did the job, purely on grounds of motive. Their real hard work consists in trapping the murderer into some admission and collecting sufficient evidence against him to convince a jury that he is guilty.

But it is an altogether different matter when a murder is committed by someone of whose existence the friends of the victim are not even aware. Then there is nothing whatever for the police to go upon and, providing the murderer exercises reasonable caution in doing the actual job, the chances are a hundred to one in favour of his getting away.

That, I felt, was my own situation. Even if Mondragora's associates were in Egypt, none of them knew that I had set eyes on him during the past four years, so they certainly would not suspect me of his murder. He had not seen me himself, so there was no risk of his having told anybody else that I was on his track or of his leaving a written message to the effect that he had recognized me that night and was dreading that I might endeavour to take my revenge.

When his death was discovered there would be nothing whatever to connect me with the crime. No one had seen me leave the Cecil or enter Ambassador Court. Even if the porter at the Cecil came forward to state that I had asked him what address Mondragora had given the driver of the taxi when leaving the hotel, which was most unlikely, it would transpire that I had only mistaken him for somebody else and had made no attempt to follow him, but had gone straight up to bed.

I foresaw the danger of being seen if I attempted to re-enter the Cecil in the middle of the night so I had already made up my mind to go for a long walk right out of the city after the job was done, then stroll back into the Cecil at about half past nine. I was never called in the morning, so if I was seen going up to my room it would be assumed that I had slept there all night but already been out, and no one would be able to prove the contrary.

The only real risk that I ran was being caught while still in Ambassador Court just after having committed the crime, and that, too, appeared to be almost negligible. Mondragora's flat was on the top floor, and since the air raids of the previous autumn top-floor flats had not been popular in Alexandria. In addition it was still winter, and Alexandria, apart from its business activities, is a summer town. Between the past air raids and the season of the year it was most improbable that any of the other three flats on the top floor of the building were occupied at the moment, and as the night porter was in the hall, seven storeys below, he certainly would not hear the shot at that distance.

I felt perfectly calm and collected, and it even struck me while I tiptoed past the front door of Number 42, along the broad landing to its solitary window, how very curious it was that I could be thrown into a state of the most appalling jitters by the mere presence of Daphnis, whereas now that I was about deliberately to deprive another human being of his life, I did not seem to be possessed of any nerves at all.

On reaching the landing window I drew on a pair of gloves, slipped back the catch, gently pushed it open and looked out. It was as I had hoped when I first viewed the big block from the street: this modern steel-and-concrete building had a balcony on each floor running for the whole length of its frontage.

I wriggled over the window-sill on to the balcony. The night was fresh and I paused for a moment to take in a deep lungful of the salt air as I thought what a splendid view the front windows of these luxury flats must have over the bay in daytime. The sound of the surf rolling on the beach far below and the faint white line of the creaming breakers were just perceptible through the darkness.

Turning, I made my way stealthily along the balcony until I came to the windows which I knew must belong to Mondragora's flat. Faint chinks of light came from one long row of them, but it was impossible to see anything inside as they had all been carefully blacked out; then I came to a solitary window a little further on which was half-open.

This, too, was curtained, but I gingerly eased the curtain aside until I could see that the room was in darkness. I put my hand in and carefully felt along the sill. It came in contact with a large cut-glass jar, then with some small bottles. As I had suspected from the single window, it was, I now felt sure, the bathroom.

One by one I took the bottles off the ledge and placed them out of the way down on the balcony. Having lifted out the large jar, which proved to contain bath-salts, I opened the window to its full extent, thrust one leg over the sill, levered myself up and felt about cautiously with my foot until it came in contact with a lavatory seat. Placing my foot firmly, I lowered myself into the room without making a sound.

As soon as I was inside I caught the murmur of voices and realized to my intense chagrin that Mondragora was not alone. A light was shining under the bathroom door and through its keyhole. Crawling forward on hands and knees with the utmost caution, I peered through the keyhole and found that I could glimpse a small section of the lighted apartment. I could not see very far from side to side, but by raising my head I could peer down towards the carpet, and by lowering it I could look up as far as the edge of the ceiling, so what it really amounted to was that I could observe a tall narrow slice of the room.

About two yards from the door, on my right, there was a long pair of legs and feet. The legs were crossed, but my view of them was cut short just above the knee. The trousers were of a black material and I felt fairly confident that they belonged to Mondragora, as he had been wearing a dinner jacket when I had seen him at the Cecil.

Opposite to me was seated a man I did not know, although there was something about him which was vaguely familiar. He was a high-caste Arab of about fifty, but he was dressed in European clothes. I could not see any portion of any other human beings, but I was aware that there were others in the room, as a voice was speaking rather monotonously in Arabic, and the man I could see was evidently watching the speaker as his eyes were turned away from the pair of legs.

My first reaction on discovering that Mondragora had company was bitter disappointment. It had been getting on for midnight when he left the Cecil, and as he had sent the woman with whom he was off alone in a taxi it had been reasonable to assume that he was going straight home to bed. I had expected to find him about to settle down for the night, whereas here he was holding some sort of conference with at least two companions. Any idea of murdering him was now entirely out of the question, at least for the time being, but I felt it was quite on the cards that as a consolation I might be rewarded for my efforts by overhearing some piece of dirty business against Britain. With luck I should be able to foil that, and an opportunity for settling my score with the Portuguese might present itself later.

It was then that I began to study more closely the features of the Arab who was seated opposite the keyhole. They were certainly familiar. Suddenly I got it. I had never seen him in the flesh before, but I had seen his photograph often enough in the Egyptian papers. He was the Grand Mufti of Jerusalem.

I was so thrilled with the discovery that I very nearly lost my balance and fell over sideways. The Grand Mufti has for many years been one of Britain's most deadly enemies. Unfortunately his position as one of the heads of the Mohammedan Church gives him considerable influence in the Arab world, and he had used it to cause every sort of trouble for us in Palestine. The Baldwin-Chamberlain Government had not had the guts to arrest this ace trouble-maker when they had the chance, and by the time the decision to do so had virtually been forced upon them by events, he had escaped in disguise to Iraq. Since the outbreak of the war little had been heard of him, but it was quite certain that this intelligent, active and ambitious man was not sitting idle and that by now he was hand in glove with the Nazis.

He had been barred from Egypt as well as Palestine, so only business of the greatest importance, in which go-betweens could not be trusted, could have caused him to risk arrest by this secret visit to Alex. Even as I was thinking what a grand job it would be if I could succeed in getting this unscrupulous intriguer pinched by the police, another voice cut into the conversation.

It was a guttural voice which had a staccato note from the habit of command and, though I might not have recognized it had I heard it in other circumstances, I was instantly certain that it belonged to Mondragora's German colleague, the Baron Feldmar von Hentzen.

My excitement redoubled. In a single night two of my five remaining enemies had again appeared on my horizon. The problem now was how could I best bring about their immediate discomfiture and eventual deaths?

Although I was armed it would have been madness to attempt any form of coup on my own. There were at least four, and possibly more, men in that room, and I felt certain that Count Emilo and the Baron Feldmar would be carrying guns. The presence of the Grand Mufti further complicated the problem as it was clearly my duty to secure his arrest if possible. If I called the police in it was as good as certain that anyone found with him would also be held, at least for questioning. That would prevent my two personal enemies seeking safety in flight, and as von Hentzen was a German officer he would automatically be interned for the duration. Mondragora, as a neutral, would doubtless have to be released unless any special evidence came to light against him; but now that I was stationed in Alex I should probably be able to ascertain what the authorities intended to do with him and take further measures accordingly.

While these thoughts had been flitting through my mind I had been trying to follow the conversation. Practically all the talking was being done by von Hentzen and the Arab that I could not see, but unfortunately the Arab spoke in such a low voice that I could catch very little of what he said. They seemed to be discussing the practicability of invading some place by air, and while von Hentzen maintained that this could be done, providing one had sufficient troop-carriers and dive-bombers, the Arab disagreed with him. The conference had presumably been going on for some time before my arrival, as the Grand Mufti suddenly intervened and I heard him say in a clear cultured voice:

151

"My dear Masry, it is pointless to discuss that angle of it further. If von Hentzen says that the Luftwaffe can do it you may be assured that it will be done. As a soldier you are quite right to anticipate difficulties, but in this case the landings should be absurdly easy. The British Minister is a shrewd and able man, but he has been left entirely unsupported by his Government, and the English are so slow and stupid that they will not even think of sending troops there until it is too late. Therefore where is this opposition of tanks and ground defences of which you speak to come from? You may leave the local forces to me, Pasha; I already have two-thirds of their high officers in my pocket. Let us pass to the matter of money." He looked towards where I knew von Hentzen to be seated and added, "Have you brought it with you?"

"No, Eminence," the Baron replied quickly. "We felt that such a large sum would only embarrass you on your return journey. It is all in English five-pound, French mille and Indian one hundred rupee notes; but even so the bundles are so bulky that they would fill a large suitcase. I therefore gave directions that they should be sent through the Italian legation; on your return you will find that they have already arrived."

"Is it the sum for which I asked?" inquired the Grand Mufti suspiciously.

I could almost hear the smile in von Hentzen's voice as he purred back: "Eminence, I am well aware that bribery is an expensive business, and we Germans believe in getting results, whatever the cost in men or money. Herr Deputy *Fuehrer* Rudolf Hess is the final authority in such matters, and I spoke to him personally. He ordered the equivalent of a further five million marks to be added to the sum that you suggested."

This pretty little speech made it obvious that something really big was on foot. At pre-war rates five million marks would be somewhere in the neighbourhood of four hundred thousand pounds, and Hitler's right-hand man had apparently added that tidy little sum as a bonus to the cash that the Grand Mufti was to receive by way of expenses for organizing some wide-scale revolt. The name Masry Pasha also sounded familiar in a military connection, and after a moment I remembered where I had heard it. Up to a few months ago Aziz Masry Pasha had been the chief of the Egyptian General Staff, but soon after Italy had entered the war he had been sacked on account of his violently pro-Axis leanings. Having held such a key position he must have known innumerable important secrets with regard to Britain's proposed defence of Egypt, and one would imagine that common prudence would have demanded that he should be locked up as a highly dangerous Fifth Columnist.

Doubtless some high official in Whitehall, who was frightfully good at 'cricker' or 'hocker' felt that it wouldn't be quite the decent thing to lock up an ex-Chief of the Egyptian General Staff, because, after all, although the Gyppies hadn't exactly come in with us, we weren't fighting them and they might think it a bit high-hat, don't you know! Yet here was this pro-Nazi General calmly discussing, as far as I could gather, a plan for a German air-borne invasion of Egypt.

"Please convey my thanks to Herr Hess for his wise generosity," said the Mufti, standing up. "The money will be well spent. Have no fear of that. Now, gentlemen, it does not seem that we can proceed further tonight with any profit, and it grows late, so I suggest that we should resume our business tomorrow."

In a sudden panic I realized that I might lose the whole lot of them. There was no charge that I could bring and substantiate against Mondragora. Unless either von Hentzen or the Mufti were staying with him, by the time I had telephoned the police and they had reached the scene the only people they had the power to arrest might have left the building.

Realizing that I now had not a second to lose, I came swiftly to my feet and turned abruptly towards the window. My anxiety to get away quickly was my undoing. In turning, my hand brushed against a glass powder-bowl that was standing near the edge of a small table beside which I had been kneeling. For one frantic second my fingers slithered on its surface in a wild endeavour to grab and save it; but in the darkness it slipped from from my grasp and landed with a loud crash on the floor.

Von Hentzen must have been standing just on the other side of the door. I had not even taken another step forward before it was thrown violently open and light streamed in.

The sudden blaze of light placed me at a fatal disadvantage. I had only been able to put one of my eyes to the keyhole now and then, as it was more important to listen than look, and most of the time I had had my ear glued to it. After the pitchy darkness the light almost blinded me. I instinctively blinked my eyes as von Hentzen came charging into the room.

The Baron was a big, broad-shouldered, bull-necked man but he was extraordinarily agile for his bulk. I had barely time to thrust my hand in my pocket and not enough to drag out my gun before he came at me like a charging rhino. My feet flew from under me and I crashed backwards into the bath.

As I fell my head hit the tiled wall a most frightful crack, and the blow completed what the sudden glare had started. My wits were so paralysed that it didn't even occur to me to bring my knee up into von Hentzen's groin as he threw himself on top of me. I tried to thrust him off instead of taking some really effective action, like jabbing him in the eye with my thumb. Before I had even had the chance to put up an effective resistance I found that I had been rendered powerless.

During the brief struggle I had glimpsed the other three over von Hentzen's shoulder. They had pushed excitedly into the room, and it was Mondragora who eventually relieved me of my gun while von Hentzen, having wrenched me up out of the bath, held me in a gorilla's grip with my arms twisted behind my back.

By the time I could think clearly again I had been thrust into the sitting-room, and while von Hentzen continued to hold me the other three crowded round me, each angrily demanding in a different language who I was and what I had been doing there. Suddenly Mondragora stopped speaking and poked his head forward to peer at me curiously. After a moment he waved the others into silence and exclaimed:

"I know this man! At one time he was a British diplomat and his name was Fernhurst, but he's changed it since to Day. Look at him, Feldmar! Am I not right?"

The Baron was still behind me, but to see my face he had only to look in the mirror over the mantelpiece. As he did so our eyes met. His were hard and blue: they suddenly grew round and he cried:

"*Gott in Himmel!* You're right! This is the young fool that O'Kieff led up the garden path so skilfully in Brussels." He jerked me round and gave me a great push which caused me to flop backwards into an arm-chair.

"Who is he, who is he?" asked Masry Pasha fussily. "What do you say about his being a British diplomat? Surely not! They are so stupid that they do not even allow their Intelligence people to use their Legations. You are either wrong about his being a British diplomat or else he is not a spy. He cannot be both."

"He is not a diplomat any longer," said Mondragora with a cynical little laugh. "I don't think he's a spy either, in the proper sense of the term. It's much more likely that, having heard I had this flat, he came here with the intention of endeavouring

154

to carry out a little personal vendetta against the Baron and myself. He has already been responsible for the death of one of our colleagues."

"Two," I said, with a sudden flare of spirit.

The tall, lean Portuguese shook his head. "No, no! You certainly killed poor Zakri, but O'Kieff got away. After you had stolen his aeroplane it was a thousand to one against his living, but he did. He staggered fifty miles across that desert, and on the third day an aeroplane which chanced to be doing some surveying work from Siwa spotted him. It's a pity that he's not here tonight as he has been hoping for a long time that he might run across you again."

That O'Kieff was still alive when I thought that I had settled his score was certainly a blow, but at the moment I had much more urgent matters to think of. I was wondering what they would do to me. These men were conspirators. The Mufti had a price upon his head for inciting to rebellion. Von Hentzen was in enemy territory. The other two would be arrested if known to be associating with them.

Masry Pasha voiced the thought which I most dreaded, as he said, "If this fellow was in the bathroom all the time he must have heard every word we said."

I had known from the moment I was cornered that there was little chance of their letting me go free, but I had hoped that they might turn me over to the police, believing me to be a burglar. Their discovery of my identity had put an end to any hope of that, and now Masry Pasha had raised the matter that must be occupying all their minds: the question of their own safety. They would stick at nothing to preserve that. But how could they ensure my not talking? What did they mean to do to me?

I stared round at the ring of hostile faces; von Hentzen must have been quite good-looking when he had been younger in a blond beast kind of way, but he had gone prematurely bald and his high-domed forehead above the heavy brutal jowl did not make a pretty picture; Aziz Masry Pasha was regarding me with cruel dark Oriental eyes that had something snake-like about them; Mondragora's aristocratic face had the attractiveness of a Latin Mephistopheles, but his thin lips were firmly pressed together and there was not one iota of pity in his steely look; the Grand Mufti stood a little apart behind the others; his face was calm, almost indifferent.

As my glance swept from face to face I *knew* what they would

155

do to prevent my talking, and the palms of my hands became damp with sudden sickening fear. There was only one thing they *could* do. The Grand Mufti's quiet voice suddenly cut into the silence with a horrible finality.

"If this man overheard even a part of oui conversation it **is** too great a risk for us to permit him to live."

CHAPTER XV

ONE MINUTE TO LIVE

VON HENTZEN'S brutal mouth curved into a smile. "We have no intention of letting him live, Eminence. It is only a question as to how we can most conveniently liquidate him."

I swallowed hard. When I had gone into the building I had been quite prepared to murder Mondragora in cold blood. Now I was to be murdered in cold blood myself. The fact that it was a case of biter bit did not make it any easier. I didn't want to die. I wanted most desperately to live. I simply must not die now that I was to marry Daphnis.

Gripping the chair-arms, I heaved myself to my feet. Before I could lift a finger von Hentzen struck me a thumping blow on the chest which sent me reeling back into the chair again.

The Portuguese spoke conversationally, as though he had not even observed my sudden show of resistance:

"The trouble is to know how to liquidate him without his death proving inconvenient for ourselves. There is no way in which I can dispose of his body here, and there's just a chance that somebody either saw him enter the building or would ask awkward questions if we took him downstairs and out of the place between us."

"Yes, it's of the first importance that we should not attract unwelcome attention to this flat," agreed the German. "It might be difficult to find another where all the other flats on the top floor were empty and the risk of anyone locating the high-power radio concealed in the roof so entirely negligible."

"You could carry him along the balcony to the far end of the block and throw him over," suggested the Grand Mufti quietly.

No one would know from which floor he had fallen, and if all the tenants disclaimed any knowledge of him it would be assumed that he was a cat-burglar who lost his footing."

"An admirable idea, Eminence," purred von Hentzen.

I tried not to show fear as I listened to the plans these charming gentlemen were making for me. The block of flats was one of the highest in Alexandria and from the top floor it must be at least eighty feet to the ground. If I dropped that distance every bone in my body would be smashed as I hit the pavement. In a genuine accident it was just possible that my fall might have been broken by one of the lower balconies, but with these merciless devils, two of whom were professional killers, there was no hope of that. They were far too expert at looking after their own skins to bungle things. It would be death all right, or after the crash I should have so many broken bones in my ruptured body that I should not wish to live, except—yes, except long enough to give the names of the four men who had sent me hurtling to my death. If I jerked my head up and thrust my legs down as they flung me over the balcony so as to strike the pavement feet first, I might possibly survive until someone found me, a bleeding, twisted mess in the gutter.

The Portuguese was speaking again. "To throw him from the far end of the block is an excellent plan, Eminence. The only flaw in it is that, although the drop is considerable, the fall might not kill him. If he could still talk when he was found he might give us away before he died."

Mentally I groaned. These men were clever as fiends, cunning as serpents. They thought of everything. It was the Grand Mufti who again administered the *coup de grâce*, this time to any hopes that I retained of living even long enough after my fall to have a chance of making certain of my revenge. In his cold disinterested voice he said:

"It is quite simple. One of you must knock his brains out so that, before you throw him over, he is already dead."

Count Emilo smiled; his fine white teeth gleaming in his sallow face. "Your Eminence is a positive fount of inspiration. The injuries to his head will be assumed to have been caused by his fall, but will certainly ensure his silence."

"I do not like this," said Masry Pasha suddenly.

It is said that the drowning man clutches at a straw, and in my desperation a sudden surge of hope rose up in me from the idea that Masry Pasha meant to intervene on my behalf. I looked swiftly at him, striving to discern any indication of softening in his face; but it was still hard, ill-humoured and angry, as he went on:

"I will have no hand in it. I am a soldier, and it is not fitting that a soldier should kill people in cold blood."

Von Hentzen swung upon him. "You are old-fashioned, Pasha. I, too, am a soldier, but we Germans have learnt to kill our *Fuehrer's* enemies in any place we may find them, at any hour and in any way."

The Egyptian shrugged, and my hopes vanished.

"As you will, then, but do it quickly so that we are soon done with this unpleasant business."

"We had better take him into the bathroom," said Mondragora. "I don't want this room messed up with his blood. The cleanest way would be for you to hold his head over the basin, Feldmar, while I smash it in with the butt of a gun."

Without a word the German leaned forward to grab me; but I ducked and slid out of the chair under his arm. For a second I was on my feet and clear of them; then the Portuguese thrust out one of his long legs and I stumbled against it. Next moment von Hentzen had sprung upon me from behind and grasped the collar of my coat.

In vain I strove to twist free of his grip. He stood over six feet tall and there was tremendous strength in his bull-like shoulders. While I flailed ineffectively with both fists he thrust me before him at arm's length towards the bathroom. Mondragora grasped the doorknob and pulled the door open.

As I was forced through it I knew that except for a miracle the last moments of my life had come. These men were utterly ruthless. They had decided only too wisely that I was a menace to their safety, and they would not even consider the matter again before the decision they had taken had been carried out. With his huge strength von Hentzen could force my head down over the porcelain basin which was within two yards of me as easily as I could have held the head of a small child there. Then the Portuguese would smash and smash at the back of my cranium until my body went limp and my life's blood was pouring through the broken bone and matted hair of my skull down the waste-pipe.

Even as I began instinctively to shout for help I knew that no one outside the flat was near enough to hear me. Von Hentzen had said only a moment before that all the other flats on the top floor were unoccupied. We were a good eighty feet above the street level, and it was now the middle of the night, so few people would be about.

It was then that I played my last card—a trick that a fellow who was said to be an *apache* had once shown me in a low night haunt in Montparnasse, which I had visited with some of my Oxford undergraduate friends during a trip we had made to Paris. Stepping out so that I planted my left foot firmly on the floor, I threw my head forward and at the same instant brought my right heel up behind me in a cow-kick that had every ounce of force I could put into it.

The trick worked: my heel caught von Hentzen between the legs. He let out a roar of pain and I felt his grip on the collar of my coat loosen. Next second I had torn free of him.

To have reached the window I should have had to turn sideways across his front. Before I could have scrambled out over the lavatory seat one of them would have caught me and dragged me back. In front of me, and only three feet away, there was another door. I had no idea where it led, or if it was locked, but my one and only chance lay in making a dash for it.

The same jerk which had freed my collar from von Hentzen's grip sent me plunging forward. My outstretched hand grasped the knob of the door. Praise be to all the Gods! It was not locked. In one wrench I had it open, and with a choking gasp I flung myself through it into the room beyond.

I should have been caught again even then, if it had not been that von Hentzen was doubled up with agony and momentarily unable to see or hear. He got in Mondragora's way, which gave me just time to slam the door and fling my weight against it.

The room was in darkness, and I could see nothing. My fingers fumbled wildly down the door-edge. Suddenly they came in contact with the key. Once more, at the eleventh hour, the gods seemed to be on my side. Just as someone in the bathroom hurled themselves against the door I turned the key and heard the lock click home.

I drew a deep sobbing breath of relief, but even as I did so I was conscious that I must not let up for a single second if I was to get out of that place alive. The safety of four strong, resolute, unscrupulous men hung upon my dying there, so they would leave nothing untried to get me yet, however much explaining they might have to do afterwards.

My fingers fumbled again, and found the light switch. I clicked it on. The room was a comfortable bedroom. In fact, it was furnished so luxuriously that it was more suited to a woman than a man, although I felt sure that it was Mondragora's because a wardrobe stood partly open, and in it hung several suits of men's

159

clothing. I wasted no time in examining the room, but took these details in as I was racing across it to another door which evidently led direct on to the hallway of the flat.

I reached it only just in time. One of them had already run round there with the intention of taking me in the rear, and I saw the handle turn as I sprang forward to lock it.

From both doors there now came the sound of hammering, and from moment to moment a heavy crash followed by the creaking of the locks, as one or other of my would-be assassins strove to force an entrance. The door out into the passage seemed the stouter so I gave my attention to the bathroom door first. Exerting all my strength I dragged a heavy chest of drawers across it so as to form a barricade and keep the door in position even if the lock were forced.

When I had done, I turned panting to the other door. The top inner corner of it now showed beyond the frame with every thud as someone outside flung their weight against it. Fortunately the dressing-table, although elaborate, was a fairly heavy piece. Sweeping all the pots, bottles and brushes from its top on to the floor, I dragged that over to form a second barricade. My next concern was the windows. These might serve yet for my triumph or undoing as Fate decreed.

If I could get out of one of them before any of my enemies thought of coming along the balcony, I might get clean away through the landing window and down the hall stairs before they knew what had happened to me. On the other hand, if they reached the windows first they could just as easily climb in through them as I could climb out, and they were armed, whereas I was not.

The curtains were all drawn, so while I had been busy barricading the doors it had been impossible to tell if any of them were open. I had been casting swift glances at the long line of curtains in an agony of apprehension, anticipating that at any moment I should see one of them bulge as Mondragora or von Hentzen came tumbling into the room. Now I dashed across, and thrusting two of the curtains apart peered behind them along the line of low windows. Only one was open and that was on the far side of the bed.

Racing round to it, I thrust out my head. To leave my cover for the balcony was a big risk, as my pursuers were so desperate that they were not concerning themselves in the least about the noise that they made in trying to break down the doors. If they saw me out on the balcony they would certainly shoot me. Yet, as there seemed no other way of escape, I made up my mind to risk it. At that moment from further along the balcony there was a shout. The Grand Mufti's voice came clearly:

"Come quickly! He is getting out on to the balcony." Evidently it was below the dignity of his holy office to enter into this fracas, so he had taken on the job of keeping watch from the bathroom window, and had seen my head sticking out.

Instantly I drew in my head, slammed the window to and latched it. As I did so I noticed with a sigh of thankfulness that they were Crittall windows—steel frames enclosing small panes of not more than eighteen inches in width and a foot in depth. Had they been larger, the killers could easily have smashed one of them and got into the room, but even a child would have had difficulty in squeezing his way through one of these many small steel rectangles, a number of which made up each window.

I saw at once, though, that by smashing a central pane one of my enemies would be able to thrust his hand through, and on pulling back the lever catch fling open a window. If I remained on the inner side of the curtains they would be able to do that without even my seeing which window they were attempting to open and so make any effort to prevent them. There was only one thing to do. Black-out regulations must go to the blazes. Only by drawing the curtains could I see the whole row of windows at once.

If I had had even a second to think about it I should have realized that drawing back the curtains was the best move that I could possibly have made. The sudden appearance of a whole row of bright lights shining right across the bay would attract the immediate attention of every policeman who was patrolling the long curve of the waterfront. The arrival of the police was the one thing that my enemies wished to avoid, and now that I was cornered in the bedroom the one hope of my getting out of that flat alive. But the part that showing lights might play never even occurred to me. In my first glance round the room I had seen a telephone beside the bed, and all I had so far lacked was breathing-space to use it.

I was still in the act of pulling back the last pair of curtains when I heard footsteps pounding along the concrete balcony; then Mondragora's satanic countenance was thrust against one of the panes. Ignoring him for a minute, I grabbed the telephone and rang the exchange.

A sleepy voice answered, and I yelled into the transmitter in

Arabic: "Police! Quick! Flat 42, Ambassador Court! An urgent message for Headquarters . . ."

I had only got so far when there was a sharp splintering of glass. Mondragora had seen me snatch up the telephone and was firing at me through the window. Three bullets whizzed past my right ear and thudded into a large satinwood wardrobe.

The instant I heard the first shot I flung myself flat on the floor, dragging the telephone with me. Mondragora must have thought that he had hit me, as for the moment he stopped firing.

Immediately he did so I yelled into the telephone again: "Police Headquarters! This is an urgent message for Major Cozelli! I am speaking from Flat 42, Ambassador Court. The Grand Mufti of Jersusalem is here, and if you surround the block at once you should be able to get him."

I shouted not only through excitement but because I wanted Mondragora to know that I had succeeded in getting through to the police. It was the one thing which might induce him to take to immediate flight instead of firing shot after shot through the window until he succeeded in wounding and finally killing me.

I had already wriggled half under the bed when a bullet thumped into the carpet within an inch of my elbow. A slight cough had preceded the thud, and I knew now why I had not heard any reports when Mondragora had first fired at me. He was using a silencer on the end of his automatic. The sleepy operator had become very much alive and put me through to Police Headquarters. Pulling my head and shoulders under the valance, I repeated my message again in both Arabic and English, then jammed down the receiver and squirmed my way out at the far side of the bed.

Cautiously raising my head I peered over the bed at the window, outside which Mondragora was standing. His hand was just reaching through the smashed pane to undo the catch. Snatching up a bedside lamp made out of a porcelain vase, I jerked the flex from its socket and hurled the lamp at the window. The shot was an oblique one from where I crouched, so with the best aim in the world I could not have sent the vase straight through the broken pane at the Portuguese, but it shattered on the steel frame and he swiftly withdrew his hand.

Suddenly the telephone began to ring, and I felt certain that it must be the police calling me back for further particulars. I could not answer it unless I abandoned keeping an eye on Mondragora and crawled back under the bed; but he had heard my call for help and evidently he thought, as I did, that the ringing of the telephone was the police trying to get on to the flat. His long hand, with its noticeably crooked first finger, had come in again to fumble for the catch, but he withdrew it and began to call urgently to someone further along the balcony.

Between the short intervals of the insistently ringing telephone I could now hear the shrilling of whistles. Evidently the police on the waterfront were becoming agitated about the long row of brightly-lighted windows which at this height could probably be seen a dozen miles out at sea.

For some moments there was no further sign of Mondragora, but I remained crouching where I was, fearing some trap, and that he might be prepared to risk having to make a last moment escape from the police in order to kill me, and thus make certain of my silence first.

The telephone rang and rang; the whistles shrilled. Then I caught a fresh noise. Someone was beating loudly upon a door across the hall. I knew the odds were now on its being the police, but having avoided death in the last half-hour only by a hair's-breadth, I was still taking no chances. I waited where I was while the sounds of splintering wood told me that they were breaking in the front door. Only when they began to bang on the bedroom door, and we had exchanged shouted remarks by which I had ascertained that they really were the police, did I drag aside the ornate dressing-table and open to them.

There was a coffee-coloured sergeant and four *tarbooshed* policemen, ranging in colour from burnt sienna to coal black. They knew nothing of my call to the station for help, but on seeing such a flagrant breach of the black-out regulations they had decided that the occupant of the flat was deliberately guiding enemy aircraft in for an attack on the city, and that bombs might start to fall at any moment, so on getting no reply at the front door they had felt quite justified in breaking in.

While the men quickly drew the curtains again the sergeant answered the telephone. It was Police Headquarters, and they confirmed my story that I had rung them up to report the presence of the Grand Mufti. However, the flat was now empty except for ourselves, and two of the policemen had seen some men run out of the block and drive away in a car just as they had come up, so evidently Mondragora and his friends had escaped.

Five minutes later an inspector arrived from the station with two plain-clothes men and a negro constable. The patrolmen were sent back to their duties and the newcomers from Headquarters took charge. The inspector was a nice-looking, youngish

Levantine with a small black moustache. At first I think he regarded me as either a mental case or a deliberate nuisance-maker, and he obviously did not believe my story that the Grand Mufti of Jerusalem had been there less than half an hour before; but when he began to question me and ask about all sorts of things which had no bearing on the matter, I told him that I was a friend of Essex Pasha and that I would not answer any more questions, except to one of the British commissioned officers of the Egyptian police.

He replied sourly that I would probably soon have that opportunity, as in my original call for help I had mentioned Major Cozelli's name. In consequence the report that the Grand Mufti was in Alexandria had been telephoned to the Major, who was expected to put in an appearance shortly, but having been roused in the middle of the night on my account he would be in no mood to be trifled with.

The Major turned up about quarter of an hour later. At first he did not recognize me, which was hardly surprising as I had only seen him on the one occasion, eight months before. Then he said:

"Why, hallo, Day! So it was you who made this extraordinary statement about the Grand Mufti having been in this flat tonight. Are you quite certain that you weren't mistaken?"

"I'd swear to it, sir," I replied. "I not only saw him with my own eyes, but the other men who were here addressed him as 'Your Eminence'."

"And who were they?"

"One of them was the late chief of the Egyptian General Staff —General Aziz Masry Pasha."

The Major grunted: "So that would-be Quisling was here, too, eh? All right. Let's sit down while you tell me the whole story."

Up to that moment I had hardly given a thought as to what account I should give the police of my night's adventures. The reaction to my extraordinarily narrow escape from death had set in on their arrival and, the frightful strain which I had been suffering having abruptly ceased, I had done little since but breathe prayers of thanksgiving for my release. Now, for the first time, it really came home to me that, having called in the police, I must tell them not only a coherent story but one which they could not easily disprove, otherwise I might get myself into serious trouble. However, I felt that, as I was so obviously on their side, it was unlikely that they would run me in on a charge of housebreaking, and I decided to stick as near the truth as I reasonably could.

I told the Major that Mondragora and I had a long-standing quarrel, the particulars of which I had no intention of disclosing at the moment; but if he thought it necessary he could get them at any time from Essex Pasha, who knew the whole story. That night I had seen Mondragora, after an interval of several years, in the lounge of the Hotel Cecil, and I had followed him home, as I was anxious to have a showdown with him. I admitted to having evaded the porter at Ambassador Court and having made an illicit entry through the bathroom window of the flat for the purpose of taking Mondragora by surprise. Of course, I did not confess that I had gone in with the intention of murdering him, but inferred that I had meant to give him a darn' good hiding.

I then related how I had found that he was not alone, seen the Grand Mufti through the keyhole, listened for some minutes to scraps of conversation, been discovered and been within inches of meeting with a sticky death from being thrown head first over the balcony.

I gave the whole of the latter part of my story exactly as it had occurred, and Cozelli's eyes gleamed in his cadaverous face, as I recounted all that I had overheard relating to an invasion by air-borne troops and the great sum in English, French and Indian currency which was to be used for bribery. He made me repeat the phrases used several times, cross-questioned me on them, and had one of the plain-clothes men, who was a detective-sergeant, take down a verbatim report of that part of my story.

The inspector and sergeant were given the job of finding the secret wireless transmitter which von Hentzen had mentioned as being concealed in the roof. The other plain-clothes man set about taking fingerprints from glasses and door-knobs, while the uniformed policeman was posted in the hall to detain anyone who might enter the flat. Major Cozelli then declared his intention of searching it, and told me that I had better give him a hand.

No crime had been committed there, and how far Cozelli's powers extended I had no idea; but apparently he considered my word good enough that the place was being used by enemy agents. Some counter-espionage officers are naturally hesitant in doing anything which might result in their receiving a rap over the knuckles from some fusty old gentleman who has not yet awakened to the fact that Hitler is the greatest gangster of all time and out to plunder the world, irrespective of all so-called rights, decencies or customs; but Cozelli was evidently of a very different school, and prepared to risk trouble with his superiors, if there was any hope of getting results against the enemy by immediate action.

He picked up a large suit-case, emptied the contents, which were mainly clothes, out on to the bed, and told me to carry it round after him while he set about a systematic inspection. Pulling open every drawer, he ran swiftly through its contents and threw anything he thought might prove of interest into the suit-case, which I held open behind him. Such drawers as were locked he opened with the help of a bunch of skeleton keys, at the manipulation of which he appeared to be an expert.

We did the bedroom first, and in it there were not many items which he selected to take away, apart from a small collection of maps and guide-books to Egypt, and an out-of-date passport. But in the sitting-room he made a much bigger haul.

At one end of the long, low room there was a handsome bureau. The papers in the upper part did not appear of any special interest. They were mostly old bills, unused notepaper, foolscap, a few letters from local tradesmen and a big pack of newspaper clippings. The lower drawers had in them a nice stock of cigars, cigarettes and crystallized fruit. Having flung the letters and the newspaper clippings into the bag, the Major took all the drawers right out of the bureau and kneeling down began to fiddle about inside it.

"I thought as much," he muttered. "The drawers aren't so deep as the bureau, you see, so there's a secret compartment in the back of it."

After a few moments' fiddling he found the spring that released the panel, and as it opened I saw that there were a number of pigeon-holes behind it, nearly all of which were stuffed full of papers.

One by one he passed the bundles out to me. There were several wads of banknotes, in English and Egyptian currency, which one could see at a glance amounted to considerable sums, about half a dozen blueprints, and at least two hundred documents.

The cache was very nearly empty when he turned to hand me a pack of about eight letters held together by a rubber band. As I took them a sudden terrifying apprehension made my heart miss a beat, and I almost dropped the packet. I knew that heavy angular writing, so unlike a young girl's, far too well to be mistaken. They were from Daphnis.

CHAPTER XVI

GRIM MOMENTS

My first impulse was to slip Daphnis' letters into my pocket instead of putting them in the suit-case, but before I had time to do so the Major had turned to hand me the last two bundles of papers from the back of the bureau. We were both kneeling on the floor face to face with the open suit-case between us. I had absolutely no option but to drop the letters into the case with the rest, and he promptly slammed the lid to.

"I'll just have a look round the other rooms," he said, "but I don't think there'll be anything worth taking. It's pretty certain that the cream of the stuff was kept behind this secret panel."

I had a wild hope that he might leave me there so that while he was gone I would be able to open the case again and retrieve that bundle of letters upon which I felt my whole future happiness might hang. But as he rose to his feet he picked up the case, and carried it with him through the door out into the hall.

I followed, still hoping desperately that he might put it down again and there would be a chance for me to get at it while he was not looking. He did put it down in the richly-furnished dining-room, while he took a quick look through the drawers of the sideboard and a cupboard which only contained table glass and drinks; but nothing engaged his attention long enough for me to dare to touch the case.

There was, of course, just a possibility that Daphnis' letters might be completely innocent, but everything pointed to their being highly incriminating. Count Emilo de Mondragora was definitely acting as an agent for the Axis Powers, and Daphnis had strong Italian sympathies. That she had been in the habit of meeting him in secret was clear from the conversation I had overheard between them in which she had regretted the fact that he could not come openly to the house, and he had replied that it was quite impossible because her stepfather hated him so much.

At last I saw a possible explanation for that passage in their talk over which I had so often puzzled in vain. Old Nicholas Diamopholus had evidently known Mondragora at some time or other and discovered, as I had, that he was an international crook of the highest order. But in any case the fact of the letters having been hidden in one of the secret pigeon-holes was an almost certain indication that they were highly confidential and contained incriminating passages.

For the moment Daphnis was still safe, because Major Cozelli had as yet had no time to examine his haul. But once he sat down to go through it, item by item, God alone knew what he might learn about her anti-British activities. Very probably enough to have her tried and imprisoned, perhaps even enough to have her shot. At the thought my brain reeled.

I tried to reassure myself with the accepted belief that the British never shoot women spies, but I was by no means dead certain of that, and we were not now in England but in Egypt. Egyptian law was probably quite different, and the code of penalties in states the bulk of whose population is coloured is usually much harsher than in Anglo-Saxon countries.

While I was still turning these nightmare thoughts over and over in my mind, the negro policeman came in from the hall to say that the inspector had found the secret wireless sending apparatus. It was concealed between the ceiling of the boxroom and the roof.

"Now's my chance," I thought. "Cozelli is certain to go and ook at it, and he'll leave the suit-case here."

But once again my hopes were doomed to disappointment. The Major picked up the suit-case and handed it to the man as he said: "Right, Ahmed, I'll go through and have a look. Hang on to this and carry it down to the car for me when we leave."

Left alone with the policeman, I wondered what the hell to do. He was now gripping the suit-case by its handle with a hand the size of a ham and his shiny, black face, although not radiant with intelligence, was by no means the countenance of a fool. He did not look at all the sort of man whom I could trick into handing the case over to me by any ruse thought up on the spur of the moment.

The desperate impulse to attack him, snatch the suit-case and make off with it came to me. If only I could get clear of Ambassador Court with it and retain it in my possession for five minutes afterwards, that would be enough. Later I could give myself up and plead a brainstorm.

Wild horses would not drag from me the real reason for my act, and what did it matter if I got into trouble with the police about it if only I had managed to get Daphnis' letters out of that case, and either destroy them or dispose of them in some place where they would not be found? I would be court-martialled for assaulting a police officer and obstructing others in their duty, but that would be a small price to pay if only I could once and for all eliminate the evidence which would cause Daphnis to be connected with Mondragora.

It may be thought that, in putting Daphnis before my country, I was acting a traitor's part, but I do not consider that I was. The restrictions with which Daphnis was hedged about by her family made it quite certain that she could be only a static agent, collecting information which happened to come to her in her own home and passing it on. It was most unlikely that she had more than one contact, and that contact had now been unmasked. Everything about the secret cache indicated that there was enough stuff there to put an end to all Mondragora's activities in Alexandria and land him in prison on the gravest charges if he were caught. If that happened, all the better. I hoped that they'd shoot the swine. But if he succeeded in evading the police and smuggling himself out of Egypt, the effect as far as Daphnis was concerned would be just the same. With her contact gone there would be no one else to whom she could pass on her information, so she would automatically be rendered incapable of doing any further harm.

But that was allowing for the very worst possibilities of the case. Daphnis' passion for Italy had suffered a severe setback when Mussolini's Fascists had attacked Greece, and I felt certain that it had been further neutralized by our engagement. In justice to her, whatever she might have done in the past, unless it was proved or she admitted it herself, I refused to accept the suggestion that she had been communicating with the enemies of Britain since she had become engaged to me.

Major Cozelli would have plenty to employ him in rounding up the really dangerous gang who had been conspiring in the flat that night, and following other leads that his haul of documents had given him, without chivvying a young girl who, possibly months before, had contributed a few pieces of gossip to a spy's budget out of a romantic passion for what, after all, was her father's country.

Those were my views on the ethics of the thing and, whatever Daphnis had done, I was determined to protect her in any conceivable way that I could. What man would not have felt the same in such circumstances?

The ghastly problem was—*how* to set about it? The negro-policeman stood there actually looking at me. He was a huge six-footer, with a deep chest, and shoulders almost as broad as von Hentzen's. If I suddenly went for him he would drop the bag to defend himself, and taking advantage of his surprise there might be just time for me to snatch it up; but even if I rushed him I felt that there was little chance of my being able to knock him down and none at all of getting away with the bag before his shouts had attracted his officers across the hall. As they came running to see what was the matter they would inevitably cut me off from the front door.

It was the man himself who unconsciously put me on the track of the opportunity that I had been seeking. Having stared at him in silence for a moment I closed my eyes and passed my hand over them. It was no more than an automatic reaction, due to the strain which events of the night had placed upon me, and I was just about to pull myself together when I heard him ask with concern if I were ill.

Instantly I realized the possibilities that such an opening offered. I took a hesitant step forward and staggered to a chair. Then letting my head fall between my hands, as though I were trying to prevent myself from fainting, I murmured: "I'm about all in. Water! Get me a glass of water."

The good-natured negro immediately put down the bag and left the room. He was hardly across the hall before I was kneeling by it. I could still hear the bathroom tap running when I already had Daphnis' letters in my pocket and the case shut again. By the time the negro returned I was sitting on the chair where he had left me.

He had only just given me the water when Major Cozelli came back into the room.

"Hullo! You feeling ill, Day?" he asked.

I raised a sickly smile. "It's the reaction, I'm afraid, sir. It's not a very jolly experience to be told that in a few minutes time you're to be thrown over a high balcony so that you'll be dashed to pieces on the pavement."

"No, I should have thought of that before," he said very decently. "I shall want to see you in the morning, of course, to take a more detailed statement, so you'd better report to Police Headquarters at ten o'clock; but you can get off now. We've finished here in any case."

Having thanked him, I drank the rest of the water and made a show of pulling myself together. The detective-sergeant was left in charge of the flat and the rest of us went out on to the landing together.

As we went down in the lift I was smiling inwardly at the thought of my unexpected triumph. The evidence that Daphnis

170

had been a Fascist agent was now in my pocket, so it would be impossible for Cozelli to bring any charge against her. Yet we had hardly reached the entrance-hall of the block when a new thought came, like an ice-cold douche, to quell my smug self-satisfaction. What if among the mass of papers that Cozelli still had in the case there was a list of agents and Daphnis' name appeared upon it? Or references to her occurred in letters from some of Mondragora's other correspondents?

Directly he got back to Headquarters, Cozelli and half a dozen of his assistants would begin a frantic sorting out of the captured documents. Speed of action was absolutely vital if the maximum results were to be obtained from the haul, and Cozelli was nothing if not efficient. Within an hour or so he would have given instructions for the arrest of perhaps half a hundred people. Only by not losing a second could he hope to catch Mondragora's principal associates before the Portuguese had a chance to warn them that, the police having raided his own flat, their whole organization must now be considered in danger.

If there was anything in the case to connect Daphnis with the Fascist Secret Service, her name would be on that list. She would be roused from her sleep and questioned before she had any chance to collect her wits and her room would be searched by the police in the hope of finding incriminating documents before she had any opportunity to remove or destroy them.

I saw now that by having stolen the letters I had won only half the battle. I must go straight to Daphnis, have a showdown with her, and warn her that the police might be arriving with a warrant at any moment.

On the steps of the block Cozelli told me that, although technically I had committed a criminal act by breaking into Mondragora's flat, I need not worry myself on that account, as it had resulted in throwing a really big spanner into the works of such an exceptionally dangerous gang.

I said perfunctorily that I was glad to know that, and impatiently watched him and his men get into their car. It was now close on two in the morning and too late for any taxicabs to be about in this section of the town, which was some way from the principal night-clubs, so immediately the police car had disappeared I began to run. Ten minutes later I was dashing up the broad marble steps of the Diamopholi mansion. My breath was coming in painful gasps, but I knew that every moment might be of the utmost importance as Cozelli must by now have arrived at Police Headquarters.

171

Jamming my finger upon the electric bell, I kept it there. The bell pealed shrilly through the house, but at least five minutes went by before a faint line of light appeared under the great frosted-glass double doorway which was protected by a decorative iron grille. The door swung open and I saw young Tweifik, one of the Arab footmen, staring sleepily at me.

As I thrust my way inside and slammed the door to the portly figure of old Mohammed Abu, the Diamopholi's head manservant, appeared upon the scene. Half-clad, and with his scant hair fluffed up at the back of his bald head, the old boy was far from his usual dignified self, and he asked with ill-concealed annoyance what had happened to cause me to rouse the house at this unusual hour.

I told him that I did not wish to see Monsieur or Madame Diamopholus, but he was to go straight upstairs and bring Mademoiselle Daphnis down to me.

As he waddled off I was immensely tempted to kick his vast stern in order to stir him into greater activity, but I knew that I must restrain myself, and I stood champing in the hall while he slowly heaved his great bulk up the broad shallow stairs.

He was actually away for over a quarter of an hour by my watch, although it seemed very much longer to me. Eventually I grew so frantic with impatience that I had just decided upon the extraordinarily drastic measure in such a household of invading Daphnis' bedroom myself, when Mohammed Abu reappeared. But with him, instead of Daphnis, was her mother.

"My dear boy!" she exclaimed in Greek, as she hurried down the stairs in front of him. "What is it? Are you ill? Have you been ordered back to the Front? Why do you look so pale and worried?"

"Forgive me," I said. "I must see Daphnis at once."

"But, at this hour!" she protested.

"Yes," I insisted. "It's most important. I'm sorry that I can't tell you why; the affair is purely personal."

"But—but . . ." She spread out her hands and I noticed that, even to come downstairs in the middle of the night, she had put on her magnificent rings as well as dressing almost entirely. "I know that you are engaged, yes, but even for engaged couples it is not done for them to have private interviews at such an hour."

"I'm sorry," I reiterated, "but I've simply got to see Daphnis —and, if you must know . . . this is a police matter."

"The police!" she exclaimed, her eyes going round. "It is not

172

true! How can my little Daphnis have done anything which would cause her to become mixed up in the affairs of the police?"

"For the moment it doesn't matter what she's done. The point is that I must see her before they get here."

"What! The police come to this house!" My future mother-in-law threw her hands up in alarm and distress. "Oh! But this is awful! How I wish that Nicholas was not away!"

It was only then I remembered that old Diamopholus was spending that night in Port Said on some urgent shipping business —which was unfortunate because I felt that he would have been easier to deal with than Daphnis' mother.

Time was flying. Well over half an hour had gone since I left Mondragora's flat.

"Listen!" I said in desperation. "I'm terribly sorry about all this, but you know that I love Daphnis. I'm trying to save her from what might turn out to be very serious trouble. Either you must go up and bring her down to me without any more delay or, sorry as I should be to offend your susceptibilities, I'm going upstairs and I'll rout her out of bed myself."

"Dear God, dear God! All right, then, wait here." Puzzled, anxious, but evidently feeling herself no longer capable of thwarting me, the portly lady shrugged her shoulders with an eloquent gesture which suggested that I, like all other English-men, was mad. Then gathering her ample skirts in front of her, she went as quickly as she could upstairs.

Another ten minutes dragged by, and either Daphnis was beautifying herself quite unnecessarily for my edification or else her mamma was anxiously cross-questioning her in an effort to find out what she had done to attract the attention of the police.

At last they appeared. Daphnis, dewy-eyed and flushed, in a flowing dressing-gown of heavy silk, looked like something straight out of a dream.

"Julian, whatever is the matter?" she cried, as she ran downstairs. "Something awful must have happened for you to get us all out of bed like this."

Even at that anxious moment I could not bring myself to be abrupt with her. Going forward I took her hand and kissed it, as I said: "I must see you alone for a few minutes. I've already told your mother that, so I'm sure she won't object. Let's go into the library."

Without further reference to Madame I took Daphnis by the arm and led her into the room at the back of the house, where

173

months before Paolo had shamed me in front of her. Closing the door, I said quickly:

"Daphnis, for your own sake as well as mine I want you to answer my questions truthfully. If I know the full facts it may enable me to save you from being sent to prison."

The colour drained from her face as she stammered, "What —whatever do you mean, darling?"

"I mean that the police may be here at any moment, and once they come on the scene I'll no longer be able to advise you about the best line to take with them. If we're going to talk we've got to talk fast and there'll be no time to spare with half-answers and evasions. Are you an Italian agent?"

"No," she replied without hesitation.

I pulled the bundle of letters from my pocket and held them up for her to see. "That's your writing, isn't it?"

"Yes."

"Those letters were found tonight in the apartment of a certain Count Emilo de Mondragora. Do you know the Count?"

"Yes."

"Did you know that he was an Italian agent?"

"Yes, I knew that."

"Yet you deny that you are one yourself?"

"I do."

"Daphnis, these letters were hidden with other obviously confidential papers behind a secret panel in an old bureau in the Count's sitting-room. I take it that you did write them to him and that you remember what's in them?"

"Yes."

"I haven't read them, but if you can assure me that they contain no information which might have been detrimental to the interests of my country you'll be taking an enormous load off my mind."

She shook her head. "I'm sorry, Julian, I can't tell you that. They contain particulars about shipping, things I learnt from my stepfather and passed on to Count Mondragora."

"Yet you maintain that you are not working in secret for Italy against Britain?"

"I do, but I never said that I had not done so in the past. Those are old letters, written last summer and autumn."

"When did you stop giving information to the Italians?" I asked, and my voice had gone a little husky.

"I thought I ought to stop when they went into Greece. As I'm half-Greek it seemed to me that, much as I love Italy, I

174

ought to become neutral. I was still undecided when you came on leave early in November, but our getting engaged settled the matter without my having to think about it any further. How could I possibly even think of working against the country of the man to whom I had plighted my troth?"

A great wave of relief surged through me. Whatever Daphnis might have done in the past, she had acted with complete honesty towards me. I needed no proof of that. Her voice was calm, her clear eyes steady and untroubled.

"Bless you, darling," I murmured. "From the beginning I had an idea that you might be mixed up with Italian espionage, but I felt certain that you would never continue to do such work once it was settled that we two were to marry. The devil of it is, though, that the Anglo-Egyptian authorities here won't recognize that dividing line of the day that we became engaged. It was the police who found these letters tonight and they might still bring a charge against you for something that you did last summer."

"What's happened to the Count?" she asked quickly.

"I don't know. He got away before the police raided his apartment."

"What were you doing there with the police, Julian? Are you—are you really in the Secret Service?"

I shook my head. "No. I'm nothing to do with the police. I only happened to be there by chance."

"You just said that it was the police who found the letters. If you're not connected with the police, how did you get hold of them?"

I smiled a little ruefully. "To tell you the truth, darling, I stole them. They were packed into a suit-case with a whole lot of other confidential documents which came out of the bureau, and as they were put into it I recognized your writing. When the police chief wasn't looking I opened the case and got them out again."

"Wasn't that running an awful risk?" she whispered.

"It might have been a bit awkward if I'd been caught," I agreed. "But I felt that if only I could get hold of the evidence and destroy it, they would never be able to bring a charge against you."

She smiled up into my eyes and laid a hand on my shoulder. "Darling, how wonderful of you! And you did that, knowing all the time that I might have been working against your country."

"I felt pretty certain that the letters were old ones. But even if I had seen that they were dated last week, I should have done what I did just the same."

"I'm glad this has happened," she said suddenly. "It's proved us to each other—proved our love. I put you before my country when I agreed to marry you and now you've put me before your country by stealing those letters without knowing what they contained."

I nodded. "Yes, I'm glad it's happened, too, because now we have no more secrets from each other and nothing can possibly ever come between us again. But we must get things sorted out as far as the police are concerned; otherwise you may find yourself in serious trouble yet."

"How do you mean?" she asked.

"As I told you: the police have got all Mondragora's papers. Among them there may be a list of the people who have worked for him. If your name appears on that or is mentioned in any of the other documents the police will certainly come and question you."

She shrugged. "Let them come. Since you have retrieved my letters what can they do? The only times that I ever saw Count Emilo were when he used to come secretly by night to the bottom of the garden to tell me what he particularly wished me to find out. If I say that I have never met him they cannot possibly prove that I have."

"Is he the only Italian agent that you ever had any dealings with?"

"Yes."

Again I sighed with relief. "That's all right, then. You'd better say that you've never even heard of him and stick to that through thick and thin. There's only one other thing and it's the reason why I insisted on seeing you tonight. If the police do come across your name among Mondragora's papers they'll not only come here to question you but they'll search your rooms to see if they can find anything which will incriminate you there. Have you anything of that kind—a diary, with notes about what you put in the letters—an address-book, with his name in it—or a list of the things that he asked you to find out? If so it's vitally important that you should destroy it at once."

She shook her head. "No, I've nothing—nothing at all which could connect me with him as an Italian agent. I'm absolutely certain of that."

"Thank goodness!" I said, more cheerfully. "Then if there's nothing at all which can be used as evidence against you except those letters it only remains to destroy them, and you're safe."

I still had the letters in my hand and I held them out, but

she gently pushed them away. "No, you take them, darling. Read them if you like, then destroy them."

"All right," I agreed, thrusting the packet back into my pocket. "Now everything's settled we'd better face your mother; but what we're going to tell her Lord in heaven knows!"

Daphnis stood silent for a moment, then she said: "Mother's always known about my love for Italy, so she wouldn't be at all surprised if I confessed now that I was rather indiscreet last summer about the family shipping business to a friend of Paolo's. I can say that the friend has just been arrested as a spy and that when you got back to your hotel tonight you became involved in a late party, where you were tipped off by someone that this spy had mentioned my name and that the police intended to question me about him. Naturally you felt that you must find out at once what I had been up to and let me know that the police might be coming to see me. Does that sound all right?"

"It's a marvellous explanation," I smiled; "and you're an absolute wonder to have thought it out so quickly." Upon which I gathered her warm, soft little body to me and pressed my mouth on hers.

We were in the middle of a second long kiss when, in the silence of the night, both of us distinctly heard an electric bell ring.

"It's the front door!" exclaimed Daphnis, as we started apart. "Do you think it can be the police already?"

Only a moment before I had noticed that it was a quarter past three by the clock on the mantelpiece, so Cozelli had already had over an hour to examine the contents of the suit-case—ample time to compile a list of names and despatch a score of agents to different addresses.

"It must be," I answered swiftly. "And if they find me here they'll guess that I got you out of bed to prepare you for their visit."

"That would never do if I'm to plead innocence. You must go out the back way." As she spoke Daphnis ran across to a big table desk, pulled out a drawer and, snatching up a key, thrust it into my hand.

The bell shrilled again. "Quick!" I cried. "Get along to your mother and warn her not to give the game away by letting the police know that I've been here."

Daphnis already had the library door open. As she turned towards the front of the house she pointed in the opposite direction. "The garden door's just along there and it's only bolted on the inside. The key belongs to the gate in the wall. Bless you, darling!"

"Bless you, my sweet," I called back, then she ran one way and I the other.

When I had drawn the heavy bolts of the back door of the house it opened almost silently. Closing it carefully behind me, I tiptoed down the steps, past the fountain and the stone bench, and between the three palm trees of that well-remembered garden.

The moon was just entering its last quarter, and without being brilliant gave enough light to see by. The heavy key turned easily in the lock of the postern door, and I swung it open. As a stepped through it into the street two men who had been lurking there in the shadows of the wall closed in on either side of me.

I started back, but one of them seized my arm, and by the pale light I recognized him as he said, "Mr. Day, I must ask you to come with us."

It was the Levantine police inspector who had been at Ambassador Court. With an awful sinking feeling in the pit of my stomach I realized that I still had Daphnis' letters in my pocket.

"You're not going to give us any trouble, are you?" the Inspector purred, and I knew that now he actually had hold of me it was useless for me to endeavour to break away from two of them. Yet I was most hideously anxious to unload that incriminating packet.

"You have no right to detain me unless you produce a warrant," I said firmly.

"Do you refuse to come to Headquarters at our request?" asked the Levantine.

That was a nasty one, but I faced it boldly.

"Yes, I've had one hell of a night, and I'm tired out. I'll answer any questions Major Cozelli wishes to put to me in the morning."

"It'd be a pity if we had to use force," said the Inspector. "The Major wants to see you at once so, warrant or no warrant, I'm going to take you to him. Come on, now."

He pulled sharply at the arm he was holding, and the burly native policeman who was with him laid a great paw on my other elbow.

"All right," I conceded, seeing that resistance was hopeless, and they led me between them to a waiting car which had a third policeman at its wheel. The three of us got into the back, and the car moved off.

The ride was not a long one, and during it my thoughts were

racing. Like a squirrel in a cage they went round and round the same awful question. Should I retain those incriminating letters or make some effort to get rid of them? Even seated between the two policemen as I was I could probably get them out of my pocket unobserved, but if I stuffed them down the back of the seat it was almost certain that they would be found there sooner or later by one of the police chauffeurs. Again, if I suddenly leant forward I could throw the fat packet a good way out of the window, but the chances of being able to dispose of it permanently that way seemed to me very slender. The car would be pulled up and the local patrolmen summoned by whistles. They would then be set to the task of hunting for the thing that I had thrown out of the car, and the odds were a hundred to one that by daylight, if not before, they would find it. On the other hand, if I took no such crazy risks, but kept my head and retained the papers in my pocket, I thought it unlikely that things had got to the point where I might be forcibly searched, so I would probably have an opportunity of disposing of them later.

That was my decision, and looking back on it I think that it was justified by the situation in which I found myself, but I was proved entirely wrong in my optimistic belief that they would not search me.

Immediately we arrived at Police Headquarters I was taken to a room where there was an elderly Scottish chief warder. He greeted me politely and said at once: "I'm very sorry, sir, but I have orders to search your person. Do you mind turning out the contents of your pockets, and making it as easy for us as possible?"

Now that I was inside my chance to fight had gone. As casually as I could I produced the packet of letters about half-way through the process of emptying my pockets, then at the warder's request I stripped while he and his assistants went carefully through every article of my clothing.

When I had dressed again I was taken along to a cell and locked up in it. I knew now that, for the time being, it was quite useless to protest. I would have to reserve anything of that kind until Major Cozelli had done with me. About twenty minutes later my cell was unlocked, and I was taken up to Cozelli's room. At a glance I saw that the bundle of Daphnis' letters had been untied and several of them lay spread out before him. He did not ask me to sit down, but just sat there staring at me, his dark eyes burning in his cadaverous, olive-complexioned face.

A good two minutes passed without his uttering a single word and his bright eyes never left mine.

"Well?" I said sarcastically at last. "What do you find so interesting about my appearance?"

His answer came slowly and each word cut as though he had slashed me across the face with a whip.

"I'm interested in criminal types, and I was studying your physiognomy. It is not often that one has the opportunity of encountering a British officer who is actively engaged in assisting his country's enemies."

"What the hell do you mean?" I roared. "You may be my senior officer but I'm damned if I'm going to stand here and let you insult me. You had no right to have me arrested without a warrant. You had no right to have me stripped and searched. Who the hell do you think you are?"

He remained entirely unperturbed, and said with a little shrug of his lean shoulders: "Take it easy now, young man. I haven't even started on you yet, and with luck I shall end up by producing evidence upon which you will be shot. You see I happen to know your past record . . . Mr. Fernhurst."

CHAPTER XVII

IN COZELLI'S TOILS

"But this is fantastic!" I burst out. "The fact that I changed my name is not a crime. Besides, in that old business there was not one atom of proof against me."

"Indeed!" he said coldly. "On the other hand there was not one atom of proof to show that you were not in league with your country's enemies at that time. The verdict of the Foreign Office was 'Not Proven'. You were given the benefit of the doubt because there was not sufficient evidence to bring you to trial, but they dismissed you with ignominy from the Diplomatic Service."

"So it's simply a case of 'give a dog a bad name and hang him'," I cried bitterly.

"And hang him," the saturnine Major repeated softly. "I congratulate you upon your apt choice of phrase."

"You can't use anything that happened in the past against

me," I blustered. "And you've no right to let it influence you. It's not fair. It's not just."

"I don't need to," he shrugged. "I have all the proof I require in the present instance to frame charges against you which you'll find it extremely difficult to answer."

I tried to control my temper and my growing apprehension as I said: "Now look here, sir. It really is utterly absurd to suggest that I'm an enemy agent. After all, it was I who telephoned the police tonight to tell them that the Grand Mufti was at that flat and to try to get those other crooks arrested."

"True. I suppose they refused to give you what you considered a large enough cut for some piece of dirty work, so you ratted on them."

Even as a hot retort rose to my lips I checked it, realizing that he was deliberately endeavouring to make me lose my temper in the hope that I would give something away.

"That's sheer nonsense," I said after a moment. "If I'd been trying to sell the others out is it likely that I should have telephoned from the flat while they were still in it and given them the chance to try and shoot me?"

"Why not? Perhaps the shooting started first and you telephoned only when you found yourself trapped there and knew that the one chance you stood of escaping from the place alive was to get the police in."

"But, hang it!" I cried in desperation. "That's sheer irresponsible guesswork, without the least foundation of fact and not a tittle of evidence to support it."

"I don't agree. My theory that tonight's little party arose out of a quarrel among thieves is a perfectly sound one. We know that you had been associated with Mondragora and his crew before. If you weren't in this thing with him up to the neck, what were you doing with him in his flat in the middle of the night in the company of a German Intelligence officer, a traitor Egyptian General and that anti-British firebrand, the Grand Mufti of Jerusalem, all of whom were there according to your own statement?"

"I broke into the place and found them there, as I've already told you. I hadn't seen Mondragora since that old business years ago—until tonight. I followed him back from the Cecil. If you want the truth I've sworn to be revenged on that swine and I meant to murder him."

"So you're a killer, eh? Or that's what you'd have us believe. For something which happened in the distant past you were quite prepared to run the risk of sacrificing the present. You have made a new identity for yourself, and under it acquired a circle of friends who know nothing of your past; you have received the King's Commission, and are, so I'm told, engaged to a good-looking young woman with whom you're very much in love, and that young woman is the step-daughter of a millionaire. Yet you were ready to let all that go west and swing for murder, if need be, in order to get even with someone who had done you an injury years before the war. No, I don't believe one word of it, and neither would any jury."

I saw then that I had blundered in admitting what my real intention had been when I left the Cecil that night. No jury *would* believe that a young man of twenty-six who was just about to marry a rich and beautiful girl would be crazy enough to jeopardize everything that the future held for him to settle an old grudge, however bitter.

A telephone rang on the Major's desk, and he muttered a few monosyllables into the mouthpiece. Then he hung up, pressed a buzzer on his desk and turned back to me.

"I have other matters to attend to now, so we'll continue this conversation tomorrow, or rather later today. In the meantime let me tell you, Fernhurst, Day, or whatever you call yourself, that you're in a very sticky position. Your one chance of being dealt with lightly is to tell the truth, the whole truth and nothing but the truth, when you're brought before me tomorrow."

An orderly had appeared in response to the buzzer, and with my brain whirling I was taken down to a cell on the ground floor. It was quite a fair size, spotlessly clean, and its sparse furniture included a narrow iron bed, which was already made up.

Once I was alone I tried to sort things out in my mind and get them into proper perspective. After a little I decided that much of the time the Major had been simply bluffing and that his threats were only thrown out to scare me. As I had never committed any act of espionage or communicated with any enemy agent, I did not see how they could possibly bring me to trial as an enemy agent myself; yet on second thoughts I had reluctantly to admit that, although I did not regard Daphnis as an enemy agent, Major Cozelli very definitely did, and I had certainly been in communication with her. The events of the latter part of that night were certainly going to take a lot of explaining, and the most unfortunate thing of all was that Cozelli had dug up my past association with Mondragora, as that

182

naturally contributed in a most marked degree to blacken the suspicion against me.

I am quite certain that there could have been no more worried a man in Alexandria than myself when, about five in the morning, I climbed into the narrow bed. But nevertheless, owing perhaps to the strain I had been through, I dropped off to sleep almost at once.

It was about half past ten before Cozelli sent for me. Once more he did not offer me a seat, so I stood in front of his desk, but I had made one firm resolution before entering the room. This time, whatever he said, I would not lose my temper, and not once did I raise my voice during the whole interview.

He favoured me again with that beastly stare of his for quite two minutes without speaking. Then he said:

"I hope you've made up your mind that only the truth is going to save you from having to face a firing-party. Now forget everything you've told me before and give me again the full story of what you did last night from the time you left your fiancée's house, round about eleven o'clock, after having dined there. We've checked up on that, so we know that it's right."

I told him then clearly and concisely about my having recognized Mondragora in the lounge of the Cecil and all that had followed. I did not retract my previous statement that I meant to kill him because I knew that if I did I would probably be led into telling other lies, and it was very important that I should tell as few as possible in order to minimize the likelihood of my being found out. Some lies I should have to tell, but those were necessary to protect Daphnis.

When I got to his own arrival at Mondragora's flat I wound up the story with a cheerful shrug. "There you are! That's the whole truth and you know the rest."

"Oh no, I don't!" he said. "What happened after you pretended to be ill, and I said you might go home?"

"I didn't pretend. I was ill," I insisted. "And I thought the fresh air would probably do me good, so I decided that I'd have a short walk. I suppose instinctively I walked in the direction of my fiancée's house. When I got there I was feeling so awful that I really feared that I'd collapse. As there was no taxi about which could have taken me back to my hotel I decided to knock them up, knowing that they would look after me until I was better."

"And did you knock them up?"

"Yes."

"And whom did you see when you were let in?"

I went cold all over as I saw the trap into which he had very nearly drawn me. When the police had questioned Daphnis and her mother they could not possibly have known that I had just been arrested on leaving their garden, so they would have maintained, as I had arranged with Daphnis, that I had not been to the house. If I were to say that I had, either they or I would obviously be lying, yet I had had to say that I went there because I'd actually been caught coming out of the garden.

"I didn't get into the house," I said quickly. "I rang the bell two or three times, but there was no reply and it occurred to me that it was really rather a drastic step for me to drag them all out of bed at that hour of the morning; so I stopped ringing, went through the tradesmen's entrance at the side of the house, across the garden and out through the door in the wall, where your people arrested me."

"Why did you go out through the back garden? That was a somewhat abnormal procedure, wasn't it?"

"Very abnormal," I replied, being ready for him this time. "But it happens that I knew that there was a fountain in the garden, and I was feeling so feverish that I felt I must get some water."

"You must have the stomach of an ox, then," he remarked sarcastically, "otherwise you'd be in the infirmary with dysentery this morning."

"Not at all, as I only sluiced my face at the fountain."

"Indeed?"

"Yes. I've been quite long enough in Egypt to know that one shouldn't drink unsterilized water."

He took Daphnis' letters out of a drawer and held them up. "Now, where did you get these?"

"I stole them," I said, "from Mondragora's flat."

"Why did you do that?"

"Because they are in my fiancée's writing."

"Do you consider that's a sufficient reason for stealing other people's letters?"

"Yes, if I happen to know that the other person is a blackmailer."

"Do you know what's in the letters?"

"No, sir."

"How did you get hold of them?"

"I found them in the drawer of the dressing-table in the bedroom when I was looking round during the few minutes that elapsed between Mondragora and his friends getting out and the police coming in."

"Your last statement is a lie. You stole those letters in Mondragora's flat last night, but you took them out of the suit-case into which we had collected all the articles that I intended to take to Headquarters."

"That's not true. I got them from the dressing-table, I tell you."

"You did not. You took them from the suit-case, and I'll tell you how I know. Mademoiselle Diamopholus' writing is very unusual. I've got a good memory, and I distinctly recall handing you that packet to put in the case. It was, I think, the second or third from the last. Anyhow, when I got back to Headquarters and began to go through the stuff I missed it at once. I guessed what had happened, guessed who had written them, guessed where you'd gone to and why, and sent my people off at once to pull you in or get you as you came out of the back of the Diamopholi house."

"You're mistaken," I insisted. "Those letters were never in the suit-case. I had them in my pocket the whole time."

"Oh no, you didn't." He leant forward and thumped his desk. "And I can prove it. Directly they came into my possession I had them examined for fingerprints. My own fingerprints *were already on those letters*, which proves conclusively that I handed them to you. How do you like that, you rat?"

He had me and I knew it. How I had got hold of the letters could not affect their contents, and nothing I could do or say would protect Daphnis from any measures which the police chose to take against her for having written them; but the point did make an immense difference to the mental attitude with which they would regard her.

If I could have maintained that I knew nothing of the contents of the letters and had taken them only because I thought that Mondragora might be blackmailing her, and if she swore that she had renounced all connection with him since becoming engaged to me, they might take a lenient view. But if they could prove that I knew or suspected what she had been up to the whole time, that I was aware that the letters were not due to some private indiscretion but conveyed information to the enemy, and that I had deliberately stolen them after the police had obtained possession of them, it would at once be assumed that Daphnis and I had conspired to defeat the ends of justice. Quite apart from anything that might happen to me, a much graver view would be taken of her part in the affair, and it might even be believed that the two of us had been concerned right up to the previous night in communicating to the enemy. The saturnine Major stood up and his black eyes bored into mine as he said harshly:

"Now I'll give you a reconstruction of what really happened. You were warned by Essex Pasha and myself not to involve yourself with this young woman. I indicated to you clearly, months ago, that I had reason to suppose that she was furnishing the enemy with particulars of our convoys. You ignored our advice, and her attraction proved too much for you. She's a good-looking piece and she got you into her rotten game. She reintroduced you to Mondragora, with whom you had had the most dubious dealings in the past. Her letters only run up to October, but when we've sifted things out we shall probably find that you've been acting as go-between for her since. Last night you had business to transact with the Portuguese, and that you were anxious not to be easily identified as having visited Ambassador Court is proved by the fact that, although you are not on leave, you changed into civilian clothes. When you got there you quarrelled with the rest of the gang. They tried to shoot you up and you locked yourself in the bedroom.

"The only way you could save your neck was to call in the police. When I arrived you helped me search the place. While we were emptying the contents of the pigeon-holes behind the secret panel you recognized your young woman's writing on one of the packets I handed to you. You had to put it in the case with the others, but you made up your mind at once to prevent any evidence against her which might be in it falling into our hands if you possibly could. Ten minutes later, when I left you alone with the native policeman, you feigned illness in order to get him out of the room. Directly his back was turned you retrieved the packet. As soon as you could get away you went straight to the Diamopholi house, got your girl out of bed, told her what had happened and tipped her off to destroy any other incriminating evidence which she might have before the police arrived to search the premises."

He pressed the buzzer on his desk. "A charge will be brought against you for aiding and abetting an enemy agent, and I've got quite enough to prove my case."

My miserable state of mind can be imagined as I was led back to my cell. On thinking things over it seemed that I had got myself into a hopeless mess, and so far had been quite unable to protect

Daphnis. I asked permission to be allowed to write a line to her just to tell her where I was and not to worry about me, but I was told that, under the section of the Defence Regulations by which I was held prisoner, I was not to be allowed to communicate with anybody.

On February the 21st, the day after my interview with Cozelli, a junior officer and a shorthand writer visited me in my cell and took down in detail a long disposition with regard to the length of time that I had known Daphnis, the dates of our meetings, and many other matters, most of which did not seem to have any bearing upon the case at all. After that I was left in peace for some days.

I was treated quite well. The food was passable, and newspapers were brought to me when I asked for them. To keep my thoughts off my wretched situation I tried to interest myself in what was going on.

Hitler was getting very active in the Balkans. On the 13th he had summoned the Yugoslav Prime Minister to Berchtesgaden. He was pumping German troops into Rumania as hard as he could go, and hundreds of German 'tourists' were already infiltrating into Bulgaria.

On the 17th one of the worst air-raids of the war so far had been carried out on London, and a few days later we learnt that a good part of the City had been burnt out.

But to balance that there came the good news that on the 19th strong reinforcements had arrived in Singapore, and that on the 20th South African Forces, having invaded Italian Somaliland from Kenya, had crossed the Juba River. By the 25th, Mogadishu, the capital, had fallen to a lightning thrust, and it was after having read of this new offensive which had started so brilliantly in the morning paper on the 26th that I was taken up again to Cozelli.

He was in a different mood from that in which I had seen him at the two earlier interviews. Having said good morning quite politely, he told me to sit down.

As I did so I wondered if I could take this as a good omen, or if his gentle manner indicated that he meant to try to lead me into some trap.

"Now that I've had a few days to go into things," he began, "I'm taking rather a different view of this case, Day. Please don't imagine that you're going to get away with it. Whether you were actively assisting the enemy or not, the fact remains that you committed the very serious crime of stealing that packet of letters

187

after they had passed into the possession of the police. I've also excellent grounds for believing that, even if you hadn't read them, you had a very shrewd idea of their contents. It'll interest you to know, too, that I've got you on another point. Madame Diamopholus and her daughter denied that you got them out of bed on the night of this affair, but we've now checked up with the footman who let you in, and the old butler whom, with no trace of illness but in a great state of agitation, you sent upstairs to waken the women. There's no doubt in my mind at all that you went there to tell the girl what had happened and to warn her to destroy any incriminating papers which she might have in her possession.'

He paused for a moment, then went on, "The thing that I'm undecided about at the moment is whether to press the case against Mademoiselle Diamopholus or not, and that depends very largely on yourself."

"What do you mean?" I asked guardedly.

"There are some grounds for believing that, upon becoming engaged to you, she severed her connection with Mondragora, and that since the end of October last she has been running straight. The stuff she sent in was to do with the making up of our convoys in Alex and Port Said last summer and autumn; but at that time Hitler had not brought any considerable proportion of his Air Force down into the Mediterranean, and the Italian Navy was skulking in its ports; so I don't think her reports resulted in any very serious damage having been done."

"Thank God for that!" I sighed.

"Mark you, it's not her fault that hundreds of British and Greek seamen did not lose their lives, but since she's half Italian one can't altogether blame her for wanting to help what she evidently considered as her country at that time. However, upon becoming engaged to an Englishman she seems to have transferred her allegiance to Britain, and she's very young so I don't want to be unduly hard on her. Still, as I said just now, that depends to a considerable extent upon yourself."

"Naturally I will do anything I can to save her from having to pay for what she did before we became engaged," I said.

"Well, this is the situation. Normally we should not hold you for longer than a week without preferring a definite charge against you. Once that is done there can be no jobbing backwards—the whole thing will have to come to light, and your fiancée, as well as yourself, will have to take the knock. On the other hand I have an idea at the back of my mind that if you two are kept apart

188

for a bit, Mademoiselle Diamopholus may see her way to giving me a little more information about her contacts in the past than she's inclined to do at present."

"You—you've got her under arrest, then?"

"Oh no. She's still at liberty, but of course we're keeping a careful eye on her."

"I'm sure there's nothing more that she *can* tell you," I said quickly, and next moment I could have bitten off my tongue.

"So you *did* know what she was up to." A slow smile lit up his sombre face.

"No," I countered, trying to bridge my stupid slip. "I only meant that I'm sure she couldn't have been very deep in this thing because she lives in a pro-British household and is very strictly looked after."

He shrugged. "Just as you like; but there's no sense in your denying further that you had a pretty shrewd idea that she was mixed up with Mondragora before you ever went to his apartment. Anyhow, we'll let that pass. The point is that if I once charge you I'll no longer have a lever to get what I can out of Mademoiselle Diamopholus, so if you wish to press for trial the whole balloon will go up. On the other hand if you're prepared to remain quietly in prison for a week or two, there's just a chance that I might be inclined to overlook the whole affair."

There was no trap in this, as far as I could see. Daphnis had assured me that she had not been in touch with any other agents except Mondragora, so there was nothing at all which she could give away on her own detriment in consideration of a promise that if she talked I should be set free; so I replied:

"It's very good of you, sir, to take a lenient view of the affair, and I'll willingly remain in prison for a month or more, if there's a decent chance that at the end of that time you won't prosecute Mademoiselle Diamopholus."

"Right!" he said. "That's very sensible of you. Some days ago I informed your C.O. at the prisoners-of-war camp that you had temporarily been seconded to Intelligence for special duties, so that you shouldn't be posted absent without leave, and no one, except your fiancée, knows that we've got you inside here. She's been warned not to talk, so if my further discussions with her are fruitful you'll be able to reappear without a stain upon your character and free of any apprehension that she'll be tried and sentenced in the way many people might consider she deserves." He pressed the buzzer and the interview was over.

The days that followed were boring but not altogether

unhappy ones. My hopes were high now that both Daphnis and I were going to escape the consequences of this wretched business, and that sometime in March we might be happily married after all.

Three days after my last interview with Cozelli, Bulgaria definitely joined the Axis. Anthony Eden and Sir John Dill were much in the news as they had flown out to the Near East and were holding many conferences: first in Ankara, then in Athens, and lastly in Cairo. It was clear that they were making a stupendous effort to prevent the remaining Balkan countries falling into Hitler's hands without a blow.

The Greeks were still putting up a magnificent fight against the Italians and were fiercely attacking Tepeleni, but a dark shadow was falling upon their prospects of continued victory. They had stood up to the Italians in a way that was beyond all praise, but the Germans were a very different proposition, and it seemed certain now that the Nazis meant to attack Greece through Yugoslavia and Bulgaria. It was only wishful thinking to imagine for one moment that the gallant little nation could stand up against the full weight of a Nazi blitzkrieg. On the 3rd of March it was reported that German troops had crossed Bulgaria and reached the Greek frontier.

The following day the papers splashed a British landing in Norway. Our naval forces had raided the Lofoten Islands and destroyed the valuable fish-oil plants there, taking a number of Germans and Norwegian Quislings prisoner. It was a fine exploit, but such gallant actions could not possibly affect the main strategy of the war or act as a bar to the armoured giant that was steadily rolling down into the Balkans.

A proposal was put up by the Nazis that the Yugoslavs should sign a pact with them, and for a couple of days it looked as though Yugoslavia, too, was to fall a victim to von Ribbentrop's machinations; but the leaders of the Yugoslav Opposition put up the strongest protests against any pact with Germany, and from all quarters the Yugoslav Government was being urged to stand firm.

The best news for a long time came on March the 8th. The United States Senate had passed the Lease and Lend Bill, and it was immensely cheering to think that the Americans were now really as good as in with us. It was on the morning of the 11th that Major Cozelli sent for me again.

This time he greeted me very pleasantly and said, "Well, Day, you'll be glad to hear that this business isn't going too badly, so I've decided to let you out on parole."

"Thank you, sir," I said. "Am I to take it that my fiancée has

190

helped you with further information, or that you've satisfied yourself that she can't tell you any more than she has already?"

He smiled. "She hasn't told me any more and I don't think that she could if she wanted to; but she has proved amenable to reason."

"What do you mean by that?" I asked, with sudden apprehension.

"I mean that she agreed to my suggestion that she should accompany her stepfather on a visit to Greece."

"Good God!" I exclaimed. "Whatever for? Besides, if the Germans invade Greece she might get caught there."

"I don't think so. We should have plenty of time to evacuate important people like Diamopholus, and of course his step-daughter would be brought back with him."

"But why have you sent her there?" I asked anxiously.

His smile broadened. "Germany has not yet declared war on Greece, so the German Legation is still functioning in Athens, and of course it's crammed full of their agents. Amongst others, as I happen to know, the Baron Feldmar von Hentzen is there, and it's quite on the cards that the Portuguese won't be far away from his colleague."

"But—but . . ." I stammered, a horrible fear gripping my heart. "What's that got to do with Daphnis?"

He shrugged. "Surely you realize that Mademoiselle Diamopholus must pay a price for her liberty and yours. She has agreed to get in touch with Mondragora again through von Hentzen; but this time she will be working for us."

"You swine!" I cried, springing to my feet.

"Control yourself!" he snapped. "This girl can be extremely useful to me, and I have no intention of allowing you to interfere with my plans."

I was positively seething with rage and fear as I cried: "I see your rotten game now. You've blackmailed her—probably told her that I'd be shot, played on her love for me in order to induce her to go into this dangerous game as the price of my life. Don't you realize that a young girl like that would not have a hope in hell of double-crossing men like von Hentzen and Mondragora? You've as good as sent her to her death!"

"I sincerely trust not," he said calmly; "and I simply made her a fair offer—your freedom and hers as the price of one piece of really useful authentic information. When she gets that she will have paid up for you both, but not before."

191

"But this is despicable!" I cried desperately. "It's the sort of thing that you'd expect of the *Gestapo*, not of a British officer."

He stood up and stared straight into my eyes. "Listen to me, Day, you'd better get this straight. Our people at home seem to think that we can fight this war with kid gloves on. Half of them are like ostriches with their heads buried in the sand. The bishops play Hitler's game in urging that war work should not be carried on on the Sabbath. I wonder what the fools would say if our R.A.F. pilots refused to go up on Sundays. The Service Chiefs still have the mentality of the bayonet instead of the tommy-gun. The Foreign Office is so frightened of offending Catholic opinion that it still refuses to make any serious attempt to get Germany's greatest natural enemy, Soviet Russia, with her 8,000 tanks and 20,000 aircraft, in on our side. The Propaganda people waste their breath dithering about the poor dear French, instead of working up a proper hate spirit against the Nazis; and they're days behind the enemy with every piece of news that breaks. The Government panders to the Trade Unions and lets them play their own hand for after the war, instead of conscripting absentee labour that takes days off in the week because it gets double pay on Sundays. But I don't use Whitehall methods and I'm not bound by Camberley rules. This is Total War, and if we mean to save the British Empire from annihilation we've got to use every weapon which comes to our hand and which our imagination can suggest."

I knew that he was dead right, yet I shouted: "You're wrong! Utterly and horribly wrong. Churchill has said that we must win this fight with clean hands, and it's against everything that we've ever believed in to blackmail a woman into doing our dirty work for us."

He simply shrugged. "Your fiancée is a valuable weapon and I intend to use her."

"In that case I'll go straight to Essex Pasha," I threatened. "I'm certain he'll support me and force you to change your tune."

"You can't. He's with a mission in Turkey. Besides, the girl is in Athens now, and by the time you could get my decision overruled by a higher authority she'll either have been caught out or on her way home."

"All right! The moment I get out of this building I'm going to wire her that I've decided to face my trial and that she's to stop any work that she's engaged upon at once. I'd rather do that a thousand times than have her imperil her life."

"Oh no, you won't! I've already informed the postal authorities that no telegrams or letters addressed to the Diamopholuses are to be despatched without having been censored by myself."

He paused for a moment, then went on: "It only remains for you to say if you prefer to remain in prison or to be released on parole, having first given me your word that you will not endeavour to get in touch with Mademoiselle Diamopholus. I bluffed you about not being able to keep you inside without making a formal charge in order to get a little time to deal with her while you were out of the way. I have ample powers to detain you without trial for as long as I like. Now take your choice."

CHAPTER XVIII

THE GREAT DECISION

"IF you have powers to keep me in prison without trial for as long as you like, why are you offering to let me out now on parole?" I asked suspiciously.

"Because I promised Mademoiselle Diamopholus that I would if you proved sensible," he replied calmly. "And it so happens that whenever I make promises I endeavour to keep them."

My brain was racing furiously. I didn't believe that Cozelli was the sort of man who would trust anybody on parole in a case like this unless he had to. He might have promised Daphnis that he would give me my freedom on these terms as soon as she reached Athens; but if he had the chances were that it was because he was lying about his powers to keep me in prison indefinitely without trial. If I could have been certain of that I should have told him that he could send me back to my cell—but I was not certain. Instead of being kept there for a day or two longer and then regaining my complete freedom, it was just on the cards that this clever devil could use some clause in the Emergency Laws to keep me confined for several weeks more without formulating definite charges against me.

And time was precious. As long as I remained in prison I could not make any attempt at all to get in touch with Daphnis and beg her to abandon instantly the dangerous business upon which she was employed; and even a day might make the difference between life and death to her.

"All right," I said. "I'll give you my parole."

"Good," he nodded. "Your C.O. believes that you were sent away from Alex at a moment's notice on special work. You will report back to him tomorrow morning and resume your normal duties. It is understood between us that you will neither leave Alexandria without my permission nor seek in any way to communicate with Mademoiselle Diamopholus. I have your word as to that?"

"Yes," I replied abruptly.

"Very well, then." He pressed the buzzer on his desk, signed a form authorizing my release, and when the orderly appeared said that I was to be let out of the side door of the Police Headquarters.

As I walked back to my cell I was still seething with anger. I could cheerfully have killed Cozelli. My adorable Daphnis was now in Athens, where she had been set the impossible task of trapping some of the cleverest criminals in the world. As well send a bird of Paradise into an iron cage and expect it to get the better of two vultures. I had not the faintest intention of keeping my parole. Cozelli had deliberately placed my future wife in a situation where at any moment of the day or night she might be caught, and once caught would probably die a violent, horrible and painful death. Daphnis meant more to me even than my word of honour, and Cozelli's wildly optimistic idea that she might secure some important piece of information which would help Britain win the war seemed to me so fantastic that I did not allow it to weigh with me for a second.

By the time I was outside the prison I had already considered and dismissed most of the means of getting in touch with her. Those not barred by Cozelli's special censorship were subject to either insupportable delays or grave danger of total miscarriage owing to war conditions. There was only one thing to do. By hook or by crook I must join her as speedily as possible in Athens.

I had no sooner reached this decision than I turned my steps towards the docks with the idea of finding out what ships would be leaving for Greece in the next few days and arranging for myself an unauthorized passage in one of them. The commandant at the prisoners-of-war camp had now been deprived of my services, through no fault of mine, for just on three weeks, so he could remain deprived of them for a bit longer.

As a British officer it might have been exceedingly difficult to get a passage, but I was still wearing the civilian clothes in which I had been arrested; and the lack of a passport did not particularly bother me. The world pays its merchant seamen scandalously badly, so it has little right to grumble if the less scrupulous among them do not resist the temptation to accommodate stowaways as a regular means of making a bit of extra cash. Money, thank goodness, was my strong suit, and ever since the outbreak of war I had carried a considerable sum on me, so I felt as confident of being able to buy an unofficial passage to Greece as I was that I meant to order myself a gin fizz at the nearest decent-looking bar as soon as I had found out what ships in the harbour were sailing for Athens.

I was not half-way there when a sudden shout roused me from my black day-dreams and brought my vacant gaze back into focus upon the people along the pavement. Bearing straight down on me, his face wreathed in smiles, was Toby Spiers.

"Julian!" he cried the moment our eyes met. "I felt certain it must be you. But what the devil are you doing out of uniform?"

"It's a long story," I smiled, coming to a halt. "But what are you doing here in Alex? Managed to wangle some leave, I suppose!"

"Good lord, no! It's been almost as good, though." He looked anxiously round at the passing crowd and lowered his voice. "The Battalion's been down here for the best part of a fortnight, refitting for a big show. But come on, let's find a place where we can have one."

The Morocco Bar was just across the street, so we disappeared into its cool depths and were soon seated on two high stools with frothing gin fizzes before us.

The place was almost empty, and as the barman moved away Toby said: "Come on now, spill the beans! What're you up to in that blue lounge suit, and where the devil have you been all this time? Directly I got here, after having visited Jack in hospital——"

"How is the old boy?" I interrupted.

"Going splendidly. It was a nasty flesh wound on the inside of the thigh, but not high enough up to be dangerous. It's cleaning up now, and he'll be out in about a week, but of course he won't be fit enough to come with us on this new party. As I was saying, directly I'd seen him I went along to the prisoners-of-war camp to dig you out, but they told me that you'd been seconded for some special duty."

"Hush!" I whispered with a meaning wink.

He whistled and his boyish face took on a half-incredulous, half-serious look as he murmured: "My hat! Secret Service, eh! How frightfully thrilling!"

"What's all this about the Battalion re-equipping and going on a new show?" I asked, before he could say anything further.

"D'you mean to say that in your job you don't know?" he asked incredulously.

I shook my head. "I've been too darn' busy for the last few weeks to think of anything except my own work."

Toby lowered his voice again. "It's so secret that I only know because I've been taken on to do Assistant Adjutant while we're down here. For God's sake don't even whisper it to anyone whom you wouldn't trust with your life; but we're going to Greece!"

With a great effort I suppressed a start of surprise and managed to mutter, "When are you off?"

"Word hasn't come through yet, but the re-equipping was completed two days ago and permission to leave camp is not being granted to officers or men for more than three hours at a stretch and never after sundown; so we may embark any night. Isn't it thrilling? We'll be able to get a crack at those blasted Nazis at last, and that'll be much more fun than chivvying these spineless macaroni-eaters."

"Rather!" I agreed, with a heartiness that I did not feel, and I went on earnestly, "Listen, Toby, I'd give my eyes to go with you and the rest of the crowd in this new show, and I think I can fix it."

"Splendid!" he beamed. "But how?"

"As an interpreter, of course."

"Arabic won't be any good there, or Italian, unless we pick up some Italian prisoners."

"Perhaps not; but I speak German and quite enough Greek to arrange about billets and that sort of thing. The point is—have you yet had a Greek interpreter attached to you?"

"No. You've got a clear field there and it would be absolutely grand if you could come. But what about your other work? This hush-hush stuff you're on?"

"I'll have to see what can be done," I replied cautiously; "and there's one way in which you can help me. Directly you hear definitely that the Battalion's got its marching orders, ring me up at the Cecil so that I can make a last eleventh-hour effort to get permission, should I have failed in the meantime. Naturally you'll have to be careful what you say over the telephone. You'd better ask me out to dinner, and if you know the hour at which the embarkation is due to start you can give it to me by saying that you've got two or four or ten other people coming to the party."

"Right, I'll do that," he agreed at once. "Let's have another drink to the success of your efforts."

We talked on, mainly about other things, for the best part of half an hour, and before we parted I impressed upon Toby that, for reasons which at the moment I could not disclose, it would be very much better if he did not tell 'Long Willie' or any of the others that he had seen me or that I had any intention of trying to come to Greece with them.

There was no point now in going down to the docks, so after leaving Toby I went straight to the Cecil, where I saw the manager, who by this time was an old friend of mine, and explained my sudden disappearance. I told him that on the night of February the 19th, without receiving any warning at all, I had been despatched on a special mission which had taken me right through Palestine into Syria; hence, as I had just returned from a neutral country, the fact that I was wearing civilian clothes. He had had my things packed up after I had been absent for two days, and now he had them sent up to another room, upon which I went upstairs and got back into uniform.

After lunch I called upon my prospective mother-in-law, who appeared anxious to see me, although she was obviously worried and anxious about the turn events had taken and the second postponement of her daughter's marriage.

The interview was a difficult one, as I had no means of knowing how much she knew as to the true state of affairs, and I did not wish to alarm her unduly. She quite obviously connected my sudden disappearance with the visit of the police to question Daphnis on the night that I had roused them out of bed, but had accepted the explanation given her that I had been sent away from Alex without warning.

I soon found that she believed that Daphnis and I had had a quarrel, which was not sufficiently serious for us to decide on breaking off our engagement but quite enough for us to agree on my sudden enforced absence being an adequate excuse to postpone our wedding indefinitely. Daphnis had suddenly declared her intention of going to Greece as a nurse, and made everybody's life a misery until her stepfather had agreed to take her with him to Athens. Nobody appeared to have suggested that my own absence from Alexandria would be indefinite, whereas, once Daphnis was launched upon nursing the Greek wounded, it might be months, or even years, before she returned to Egypt, so the deduction that we had had a serious difference was quite a reasonable one.

I tacitly implied that her assumption was correct but that I was still desperately in love with Daphnis, which God knows was the truth, and that I hoped to induce her to return to Egypt so that we could get married in the not-far-distant future. I then obtained the address of the Diamopholi shipping offices in Athens, and after a little polite conversation took my leave.

There was nothing further that I could do until I heard from Toby, so I decided that I'd better sit tight at the Cecil. After listening to the news that night, March the 11th, which was mainly about an attempt to assassinate our Minister to Bulgaria, of an emergency meeting of the Yugoslav Crown Council, which had been called by the Regent, Prince Paul, and of British attacks on the Eritrean stronghold of Keren, I went up to my room. I was almost sick with worry about Daphnis, but I knew that it must be many days before I could get news of her, and that if I was not to become a nervous wreck I must occupy my mind somehow; so I got out my war maps.

I had said nothing to Toby that morning when he had thrown his bombshell about the decision to send Imperial troops into Greece. I'm no defeatist, and the last thing that I would willingly do is to damp the ardour of a keen young subaltern like Toby. But my training for the Diplomatic had necessitated my taking a high degree in history at Oxford, and it is impossible to have absorbed all the main facts about past wars without learning something of the art of strategy.

As long as the French had been with us it had looked as though the Allies would, in time, be able to put into the field approximately the same number of 'planes, tanks and men as the Germans.

But once France had been put out of the game and Italy had come into it, the future presented a very different picture. Any really considerable increase in our Indian Army would create a special problem, and failing that the British Empire simply has not got the numbers ever to be able to put into the field an army of the same size as the combined armies of the Germans and Italians. Their united populations total a hundred and twenty-five millions. The white population of the Empire is seventy millions, including the Irish, and it is doubtful if the fact that they are not fighting with us can be balanced, as far as numbers are concerned, by the oddments of Poles, French, Czechs and other Free Forces who are.

In consequence the major strategy of the war must be governed by this simple arithmetic. Nobody but a lunatic would suggest pitting the armies of a 70-million population against the armies of a 125-million population, *as long as the larger is united under its leaders, has eight years' start in the armaments race, and air superiority*.

Nevertheless, while it is stupid to underrate the Germans' strength, initiative and drive, it is equally stupid to allow oneself to be scared into thinking that they can do the impossible.

One thing which is fundamentally impossible is to transport, supply and munition a major army by air. A division or so of air-borne troops may certainly be used with success to establish a first foothold; but their final defeat is absolutely inevitable unless they can be reinforced within a very limited period with heavy equipment, approximately equal in weight to that of the army that they are opposing.

The only way to do this is obviously by sea, and as long as the British Navy remains paramount in the Mediterranean it must continue to be a most hazardous undertaking for the Axis to endeavour to supply any main army across the water.

From this very simple reasoning it is perfectly clear that we might meet a German Army in favourable, or at worst equal, terms, and have a good hope of defeating it in North Africa, or the Middle East; solely because there are definite limits to the numbers of men and the weight of material that the Germans could bring over. On the other hand, no such handicap applies to the Axis Forces anywhere upon the mainland of the European Continent.

The Italians are good enough and numerous enough to be used as garrison troops to hold down the defeated and disarmed peoples of the conquered countries, so this leaves the Nazis free to launch the whole weight of their own vast war machine in any direction that they choose. Clearly, therefore, it would only be asking for the most grievous trouble to attempt to stop Hitler if he decided to march eastward *until he got to the Dardanelles*, or southward *until he got the Straits of Gibraltar*.

It was going to be difficult enough in all conscience to stop him then; but if the Turks stood firm there seemed a really good chance that we might check any attempt by Hitler to break out to the east.

The south was much more tricky, as however well the fortress of Gibraltar might be defended that alone could not stop Axis Forces by-passing it and crossing the narrow waters. But there was the Moroccan International Zone over which the Spanish had arbitrarily reassumed control, and one hoped that we might feel strong enough to send an Expeditionary Force there immediately the Nazis crossed the Pyrenees, which could contest the landing of Axis Forces in Africa.

Libya was the third possible, but more difficult, road for the Axis, but General Wavell's magnificent sweep between December and February had carried the outposts of the Army of the Nile nearly six hundred miles further to the west, so all that territory would have to be re-won before Egypt was again threatened.

The fourth and only remaining way out of his cage for Hitler lay through Russia, and if he was desperate enough to take that, whether we liked the Bolsheviks or not, we would have every excuse for cheering our heads off. Any attempt to assess the rear fighting strength of the huge Soviet Army and Air Force could only be sheer guesswork, but it was as plain as the nose on one's face that even Hitler could not take on 200 million new enemies without crippling himself so severely that it would shorten the war by years, and leave Germany at the mercy of our rapidly-growing Air Force.

In considering the prospect of our success in this Greek campaign one remembered that Hitler was said to have over 180 divisions at his disposal. That meant that if one wrote off 80 divisions for guarding the German eastern frontier against any surprise attack from Russia, and wrote off the whole of the Italian Army as good for nothing more than garrisoning conquered territories, Hitler still had 100 divisions of the finest and best-equipped troops in the world which, within a few weeks, he could concentrate upon any front on the Continent from the Baltic to the Mediterranean and from the Atlantic to the Black Sea.

How many divisions were we in a position to send against this armoured spearhead of the mightiest army that history has ever known? Six, eight, ten, twenty? As a serving officer of very junior rank I was in no position to know, but I was prepared to bet my bottom dollar that we couldn't put more than a dozen divisions into Greece, and to do that would mean denuding Libya, Egypt and Palestine to a wickedly dangerous degree.

I was prepared to make another bet—that this crazy piece of gallantry was not being undertaken without opposition on the part of Generals Wavell and Wilson, who had proved themselves so brilliant in the Libyan campaign. My third bet was that Mr. Churchill did not like it either, because he is not only an idealist but also a trained strategist and a realist.

Perhaps the answer to this riddle lay in Mr. Churchill's well-known loyalty to his colleagues. Certain of them were known from their past actions to be men of great ideals; but in Total War it must at least be questioned as to if idealists who have not proved themselves also to be realists make the wisest leaders. On grounds of principle alone it was clearly our duty to support those splendidly heroic Greeks. The idealists in or near the War Cabinet would naturally make a highly impassioned plea that we should do so; but had they paused to count the possible cost? Or was it that some of them had pledged us prematurely?

Looking at the map again it seemed so transparently clear what our strategy should be. To land another Expeditionary Force on the mainland of Europe *before we had air superiority* was to invite certain defeat. But if Hitler attempted to break out of his cage, either into Asia or Africa, we should fight like tigers with everything we had. If we could only keep him in the cage, the blockade would do its work and the R.A.F. would grow until by constant and terrific bombings we could destroy German morale, and cause the captive peoples to revolt. Then, and then only, should we be justified in again landing an army on the Continent, since it would have a decent prospect of waging a victorious campaign and speedily finishing the war.

Therefore, we ought to have said frankly and honestly to the Greeks: "If we send you six divisions, which is about all that we can possibly spare, there can be no hope whatsoever of this support being sufficient to enable you to hold any part of the Greek mainland against the main German Army.

"You have all our sympathy, but we are pitted against a remorseless enemy who for the moment is still more powerful than ourselves. You will recall that less than a year ago we lost all our first-line tanks and equipment by so rashly going to the aid of Belgium. We cannot possibly afford to lose a second mass of invaluable war material. The sole hope of restoring world freedom lies in us, therefore we dare not squander a single 'plane, tank, gun or man in any but a vital issue.

"In the main strategy of the world war the mainland of Greece has no significance. But Crete and the Greek islands of the Aegean which lie on the very doorstep of Asia are of real importance. Don't ask us to sacrifice our tanks and men in Greece to no purpose, but let us put everything we can possibly spare into Crete and the other big islands, because by so doing, with our Navy to help us, we can bar the road to the East."

Even for the sake of the Greeks themselves that was the policy that should have been urged; because if we lost our tanks and guns on the mainland, how could we hope to defend the islands successfully afterwards? With Crete, Mytilene, Lemnos, Samos, Khios and Samothrace in our keeping, the Greeks at least stood to retain some of their country, and could have evacuated their Government, and all of their Army and leading men that we could take off, to these bases. Whereas now, because of the irresponsible chivalry of some of our idealists, they looked in a fair way to lose everything they had.

This was no case of being wise after the event, and it required no special knowledge of military education to see the course which events were bound to take. All I could hope now was that the God who so very obviously watches over our interests would once again enable us to come out of this party better than we deserved; but I was heavy-hearted as I put away the maps and began to undress.

I had hardly got into bed when the telephone rang. It was Toby and he said: "We're having a little supper-party tonight, old boy. There'll be about a dozen of us and it's frightfully short notice, but I was wondering if you could come along."

"Thanks," I said. "I'd love to." And next minute I was out of bed again, pulling on my clothes as quickly as I could.

It was only a little after ten so I really had ample time, and having packed my things I went along to see the manager to pay my bill to date and tell him that I had been ordered away at short notice on special duties again. Then with my service kit I took a taxi down to the docks.

As the battalion had been standing by for several days it was a bit of real luck for me that embarkation orders should reach them on the very day of my leaving prison. It saved me any complications through having to report the following day at the prisoners-of-war camp and return to duty there, which might have proved a nasty snag if Toby had telephoned the Cecil urgently while I was at my job.

Down at the docks there was considerable activity. Tanks, Bren-gun carriers, lorries, A.A. batteries, searchlight units, and the mass of paraphernalia without which a modern army cannot function in the field were trundling slowly along the streets and through the dock-gates. Such embarkations have to be kept as hush-hush as possible, for which reason they are always carried out at night, when most of the inhabitants of the ports are asleep; but there was little chance of keeping this big-scale embarkation secret, particularly as the moon was only two days short of full and it was nearly as bright as day.

After considerable trouble I found the wharf from which the New Zealand brigade was to sail. One of the sister battalions of that to which I was attached was already engaged in loading their equipment. Soon after midnight the wharfside had been nearly cleared, and the advance parties of my battalion were able to place their markers for the approaching vehicles to drive up.

Within a few minutes I caught sight of 'Long Willie's' tall figure as, accompanied by his adjutant and Toby, he arrived to supervise the embarkation. Leaving my baggage in the shadow of a shed, I walked straight up to him and saluted smartly.

"Why, hallo, Julian," he said in his kind voice. "What are you doing here? Come to see us off and wish us luck on our travels?"

"I certainly wish you luck, sir," I smiled. "But I'm happy to say that I'm going with you. I had to wangle things a bit, and I couldn't get away until the last moment, but I now have the honour to report."

"Do you speak Greek, then?" he asked.

"A certain amount, sir. Enough to get you most things that you're likely to want. You may remember that my fiancée is a Greek."

"Of course," he nodded. "Well, I'm delighted to have you with us. It'll be quite like old times, except that it may be a little more exciting. For the present you'd better just stand by in case the Arab dockers need a word of mild encouragement in their work."

As I went back to collect my kit and park it near him, I felt a great relief. 'Long Willie' had taken the whole thing as perfectly natural and not asked a single question. But actually there was nothing very extraordinary in his old battalion interpreter reporting to him for duty without his receiving any official notification of it at such a busy time. Yet one never knew what unforeseen snags might arise in such a case, and I was heartily glad when, at about three o'clock in the morning, I went on board with 'Long Willie' and the rest of the Headquarter staff.

Toby and I managed to get a cabin together. I could no longer make myself useful by cursing or encouraging the Arab porters in their own tongue, so I went straight to bed, as I was anxious to be seen by as few people as possible before the ship sailed. When I awoke it was bright sunlight and we were already standing some distance out to sea. I had given Major Cozelli the slip.

Our ship was just a unit in a considerable convoy, and

naturally the pace of a convoy is the pace of its slowest member, so although our large, rather old-fashioned liner could probably have done eighteen knots comfortably, she rarely made more than ten. In addition, from time to time the course of the whole convoy was altered on orders from its Naval escort, so although I fretted uselessly at the irritating slowness of our voyage on account of Daphnis, it was March the 15th and we had been three days at sea before we even sighted the Greek mainland.

Except for the fact that we had to sleep and practically live in our cork life-saving jackets, from fear of our striking a mine or being torpedoed without warning, and my personal worries, the voyage was rather a pleasant one, as it was a wonderful change to get these few days of winter cruise in the Mediterranean after all those many months of sand and dust and flies and heat in Egypt.

There was never a moment when destroyers were not to be seen making great circles round the convoy and the 'planes droned overhead; but the Navy and the Air Force took such splendid care of us that during the whole three days I saw only one incident. A single 'plane—Italian, presumably, although it was much too far off for us to identify from the deck—suddenly appeared out of a patch of cloud to northward. Instantly half a dozen of our airmen were swooping towards him, and before the enemy pilot could have even had a chance to press a wireless key his reconnaissance aircraft had been shot to smithereens.

As soon as we sighted the mainland my anxieties as to at which port we were to be landed increased. Naturally the plan for the coming campaign was a closed book to us. We had no idea at all if we should be expected to hold Thrace, so as to keep Turkey's communications with Greece open in the event of an attack by the Germans through Bulgaria, or if we should be sent to some more central position up on the Yugoslav frontier.

In either case, Salonika seemed the most likely port of disembarkation, and I wondered how the devil I was going to manage to get down to Athens from there. It was most unlikely that I should be able to get leave; yet every hour was of importance, if I was to stop Daphnis jeopardizing her life before she had been caught out by Mondragora. On the other hand, in general conversation the more experienced officers on board pointed out that when a modern army is shipped from one country to another the number of vehicles is so great that even the largest port cannot comfortably accommodate them all. Unless days are to be wasted every crane in every available port in the country concerned is needed to hoist the hundreds of tanks, Bren-gun carriers and lorries out of the holds, and that therefore whatever our final destination might be we might arrive at *any* port.

This comforted me a lot, as Piraeus, the port of Athens, has the finest harbour in Greece, so it would certainly take a large share of the traffic, and as it happened my luck was in; on the afternoon of March the 16th we docked there.

At least we anchored and lay off the port until sundown. The officers were then assembled and addressed by the Brigadier, who informed us that it was desired to maintain the greatest possible secrecy regarding the landing of Imperial Forces in Greece, as Greece was still officially at peace with Germany. Therefore the disembarkation would take place as usual at night, but in addition we were to be sent up-country in trains with drawn blinds, and in no circumstances was any officer or man to leave the dock or railway siding at Piraeus until their respective units were entrained.

For me this was a shattering blow, as Piraeus is only eight miles from Athens, and having got so near I was certainly not going to be carried away again without having seen Daphnis, and assured myself that she would immediately drop the dangerous game that she had been playing for my sake. There was only one thing for it. I must take a few hours' French leave and risk any trouble which might come to me from my C.O. in consequence.

Having told my batman not to worry if he couldn't find me on the train but to take good care of my baggage and try to get me a corner seat, directly we landed on the quay I slipped away from the rest of the Headquarter staff.

As I thought it likely that the guards on the dock-gates had orders not to let anyone through without a special pass, I made my way to the extremity of the enclosure and walked along the wall for some distance. The moon, which was just getting up, enabled me to see quite well, and I soon found a big coal-dump which had been stacked against the inside of the wall, by mounting which it was easy to slip over and lower myself into the street on the other side.

Walking back towards the dock-gates again I managed to pick up a taxi and half an hour later it set me down in the Kolokotroni, a broad thoroughfare in central Athens, where the offices of the Diamopholi company were situated.

It was now nearly eleven o'clock, so the offices were naturally closed, but after some little difficulty I got it out of the janitor, who was in charge of the big block, that Monsieur Nicholas Diamopholus had a suite at the Hotel Grande Bretagne.

Jumping back into the taxi, I ordered the man to drive me there. It was not far away, only just round the corner in Constitution Square. Having paid the man off, I marched into the hotel. Neither the taxi-man, the janitor, nor the hall-porter had shown any surprise at the sight of a British officer in uniform walking about their city; only charming smiles and an obvious desire to be of every assistance, and on entering the hallway of the Grande Bretagne I saw, as I had expected, that a number of British officers were in the Greek capital already.

Naturally many arrangements had to be made, and their presence was probably considered to be no more than that of an unusually large military mission, whereas had every shipload of soldiers which was arriving been allowed to roam about the cradle of modern civilization at will, the cat would soon have been out of the bag. In any case, I felt that the presence of one additional officer like myself for the space of an hour or two at night would not do the British cause any material damage, and my own business was of the most deadly urgency.

Upon my inquiring at the desk for Nicholas Diamopholus, the frockcoated clerk told me that he was in the hotel, and rang through to his suite. A moment later a message came back to say that I was to be taken straight up.

A page led me past the great restaurant, on the oval floor of which many pretty girls and a number of officers, the great majority of whom were Greeks, were dancing. As I went up in the lift my heart was high. Daphnis would almost certainly be living in the suite with her stepfather, even if she was working as a nurse during the daytime. The odds were a good three to one that within the next few minutes I would be holding her loveliness to me once again.

Upstairs the page led me down a long corridor. Old Nicholas was standing at the door of his suite waiting to greet me.

"Where's Daphnis?" I asked. "I must see her and I'm terribly pressed for time."

The old fellow regarded me sadly with his kind dark eyes. "She is not here," he said. "She ran away from me two days after we landed."

CHAPTER XIX

THE STAGE IS SET

THE disappointment was like a physical blow. "Oh God!" I muttered. "Haven't you any idea where she is at all?"

He drew me inside. "I had a postcard from her three days ago. It only said that I was not to worry about her. It was posted in Sofia but it gave no address."

I groaned. Sofia was now in the hands of the Germans, so even if I could have got leave there was no longer any possibility of my going there in search of her.

"Why should she run away?" the old man went on unhappily, as he led me into his sitting-room. "I cannot understand it, but when I heard you were here I thought that you might know."

Evidently Daphnis' stepfather could not help me, and there was no point in increasing his anxiety by telling him that she had run away in the hope of saving my neck and was now risking her own by spying for the Allies in the Bulgarian capital. He asked me a great many questions and was evidently under the impression, like his wife, that the original reason for Daphnis' insisting upon coming to Greece as a nurse was because she had quarrelled with me. I assured him that was not so and that my own absence from Alexandria had been caused by a Service matter.

He wanted to give me supper, but I had to explain that I had come to Athens from the Piraeus without permission and must get back as soon as possible. He then insisted that I should at least drink a glass of wine, and gave me some lovely stuff, which, unfortunately, I was in no mood to appreciate. It was very rich and luscious, having something of the qualities of a heavy sherry, a Château Y'Quem and a Muscatel, all blended together. I happened to notice the label on the bottle, and it was called Daphni, so I asked if it was from some special vineyard of his own which he had called after his stepdaughter, but he told me that it came from a little village of that name just outside Athens, on the road to Eleusis.

We discussed the possibilities of tracing Daphnis, and as Bulgaria and Greece were still officially at peace, old Nicholas said that he would willingly have gone there, despite the risk of his being caught by a sudden declaration of war, if there had been any reasonable hope of tracing his stepdaughter; but the postcard which he showed me gave no clue whatever to her whereabouts, and it was quite possible that by this time she was no longer in Sofia.

After half an hour we parted with mutua assurances that, if either of us heard anything of her, he would take all possible steps to let the other know.

Outside, in front of the Syntagmatos, I managed to pick up a taxi, and just before one in the morning I was back outside the dock-gates at the Piraeus. I had some difficulty in getting into the dock, but I swore that I had come out of the gate earlier that night and had, unfortunately, lost the special pass I had been given. The fact that I was in the uniform of a British officer was more than half the battle, and being able to speak enough Greek to reason with the officials was a help, so eventually they let me through.

On reaching the ship's side I found that the first battalion had already disembarked and entrained, and that my own was now in the process of doing so. When the Colonel saw me he asked me where the hell I had been and what was the good of having a interpreter if when you wanted him he wasn't there to interpret.

I had never seen 'Long Willie' angry before, but of course he had every reason, and I felt very guilty indeed about having taken French leave at such a time. The only course was to offer the most plausible excuse and show contrition; so I said that a couple of hours before I had run into a Greek naval officer whom I had known in Athens before the war and that he had insisted on taking me along to the Naval mess for a drink. Once there I had found it absolutely impossible to get away again, and I could only offer my sincerest apologies.

I felt an awful swine at deceiving 'Long Willie', but I knew that if I told him that I had been into Athens in flagrant disobedience to the direct orders of the Brigadier, he would obviously have to put me under arrest, and that would not really have done either of us any good or helped to defeat the Nazis.

He took my excuse well, murmuring something about its being difficult not to fraternize with our new Allies, but that I'd find myself in hot water if I disappeared like that again.

The Bren-gun carriers were being hoisted out of the hold and lowered direct on to long flat railway trucks. As each carrier was received by its crew they checked it up then covered it with a great tarpaulin so that when daylight broke anyone observing the train on its journey up-country would see just a goods train which gave no indication of being loaded with military vehicles.

Soon after three the job was completed. The train was shunted out and the men marched to a long, low customs warehouse, where a cooked meal had been prepared for them. Everything was excellently organized, and in spite of my personal worry I ate as heartily as I could, since I knew that once we were in the train it might be many hours, or even days, before we saw hot food again.

By four o'clock we had been ed by Greek guides from the customs sheds along the best part of a mile of criss-crossed railway tracks to a siding where our train stood. Half an hour later it chugged slowly away towards the north-east; but after only twenty-five minutes' run it stopped again, and for hours it remained without moving another yard.

The blinds of every coach were drawn, and the order was that in no circumstances should any officer or man pull them up or show himself by leaving the train; so we had to sit there, hour after hour, in the semi-darkness. I came to the conclusion that we were one of the many trains which had been loaded that night with portions of the British Expeditionary Force disembarking at Piraeus, all of which had been moved up to the main marshalling-yard of Athens, and that we were now having to wait our turn until, one by one, the trains could go up the line from Athens to the north.

In addition to our iron rations we had been issued with biscuits, fruit and chocolate at the dock; so we had no cause to fear hunger; but the twelve hours which followed our leaving Piraeus were boring in the extreme, and everyone was heartily glad when, at about five o'clock in the afternoon, the train gave a sudden jerk and began slowly to move again.

However, as I believe has always been the way with troop trains, this one appeared to be in no hurry to reach its destination. While we dozed through the night it stopped and started, stopped and started, jolting us back into wakefulness with every alteration of its pace and never at any time making more than twenty miles an hour.

Next morning the glimpses we could see by peering round the drawn blinds showed us that we were travelling through wild mountainous country right in the heart of Greece. The sky was much the same blue as we had become so accustomed to on the southern side of the Mediterranean; but the snow-capped peaks and the rugged gorges which often dropped sheer for many hundred feet to stream-washed rocks below were a great tonic after the dead flatness of Egypt. We all wished that we could have seen more of it by pushing up those wretched blinds, but although most of the day was spent in passing through desolate country, inhabited only by occasional shepherds and herdsmen, we were absolutely forbidden to do so.

During the afternoon the train began to wind down from the mountains and entered a fertile plain, through which we were still slowly making our way as night fell, depriving us of any further glimpses of the landscape. It was soon after midnight and we were trying to doze again when, after one of the innumerable stops, the door of the compartment was flung open and a British railway transport officer got in to inquire for the Colonel. Five minutes later we were ordered to detrain, and a Greek captain reported to 'Long Willie' as guide and interpreter.

I suppose I should have foreseen that when the Battalion arrived in a foreign country it would naturally have one of the officers of that country's army attached to it for liaison purposes; yet in my anxiety about Daphnis and my excitement at having managed to get out of Egypt in spite of Major Cozelli it had never occurred to me. Now I was considerably perturbed that the fact that I had no right to be in Greece at all would soon be discovered; but I knew that for the moment I had no need to worry as everybody was far too busy to concern themselves with the question of my superfluity.

I learnt from the Greek captain that the town we had reached was Larissa, and I saw from the map with which I had been issued that it was an important junction where the main line from Athens was joined by a line from Volo, a port on the east coast of Greece, at which he told me Imperial Forces were also disembarking.

As soon as the detraining had been completed we rattled away through the streets of the town. Normally its inhabitants would have been sleeping, but there was no disguising from the people here that British troops were now arriving in large numbers to assist in the defence of Greece, and in spite of their police, who were trying to keep them from showing lights, they could not be restrained from leaning out of their windows and lining the streets to give us a tremendous welcome.

We trekked west across the plain for about twelve miles then turned north towards Tyrnavos; until, on the left side of the road, the cornfields ended, and the ground became more broken as we approached the foothills of a range of mountains. Our guide led us into a shallow valley in which chunky outcrops of grey rock showed here and there through the green of the sloping pastures,

210

and in the lower levels trees became quite numerous. He then indicated a fairly level stretch which he told us had been chosen for us to camp in.

There was a brief conference of company commanders, after which the officers set about choosing sites under trees for each individual vehicle, and selecting positions for the company field-cookers, anti-aircraft guns, latrines, officers' messes, and so on. By ten o'clock things were beginning to take shape, and by mid-day we had fully settled in. 'Long Willie' gave notice that he intended to carry out an inspection the following morning, so the afternoon was spent in a thorough overhaul of all equipment; then we turned in early and got our first really good night's sleep since we had landed in Greece.

There followed ten days of exceptional quiet and rest. We had occupied our camp in the wooded foothills, some miles to the north-west of Larissa on March the 19th, and we did not leave it until March the 28th.

During that time we did practically nothing except sleep and amuse ourselves, as we were not allowed to carry out any military exercises or hold parades in which a group of more than six men could be seen from the air in any formation. We were also forbidden to use the roads or go into the neighbouring villages. The whole idea being to keep both vehicles and men under cover. Our lads played up splendidly, and although we knew that in the neighbouring valleys many other units of the Imperial Expeditionary Force had taken up positions, I doubt very much if a traveller, motoring through that part of the country, would have had any idea that a considerable army lay concealed there.

Actually there is very little motor traffic in Greece. I remembered one spring day three years before, driving along the main road from Athens to the west to put in a night at Delphi and pay a visit to the ruins of the famous temple there. The distance is well over a hundred miles, yet in the whole journey, once I had left the environs of Athens behind, I met only one other car and two motor lorries.

It was then that I had been so impressed with the friendliness and the courtesy of the Greeks. Most continental peoples seem to regard travellers as a natural prey. Every sight of special beauty or interest is converted into a racket in which the local inhabitants get up to all sorts of dodges in order to make the enjoyment of them more expensive to foreigners; but not so the Greeks. Perhaps it is their mountains that have protected them from the modern Philistine licensed-bandit spirit; but they are the one

211

people in Europe that I have ever met who give visitors to their country a really generous deal.

In Greece, instead of taking you to the most expensive shops to make your purchases, so that he can get a double commission on them, your guide will bring you a gift of a bunch of flowers, or a bottle of wine each morning when he calls for you at your hotel; and the most astonishing experience of all for a foreigner is to motor about the country. In order to keep up its stretch of road, every town and village levies a small tax on each vehicle that passes through it; but if the car contains a foreigner the chauffeur simply calls out, *"Touristiko, touristiko!"* and the toll collector waves the car on with a friendly smile. The Greeks are so proud of their beautiful country and its unique place in the history of civilization that they would think it quite wrong to charge travellers anything for the privilege of going about freely in it.

In those ten days of inactivity and later we had innumerable examples of the kindness and hospitality of the Greek peasants. Although we were not allowed to go into their villages they sought out our camps not only to stare at us and ask for souvenirs, but to bring us gifts of cheese, vegetables, honey, meat and wine. One often thinks of the Balkan peasant as poorer than his Western counterpart, but I believe that idea only originated in the heads of the economists, who have never travelled outside the great cities.

Perhaps it is because the labourers of the West have to pay away an undue proportion of their earnings for such benefits as electricity, insurance, and houses, motor-cycles and radios, bought on the hire-purchase system, that they have lost the natural gaiety and assumed the appearance of perpetual hard-upness; but the Balkan peasants, who have not yet been affected by modern progress, have retained their boisterous gaiety and a limited but real wealth. The Greek peasants were much better clothed than our men had expected to find them, and if much of the food that they brought, such as goat's flesh and resin-flavoured wine, appeared strange, there was certainly abundance of it.

Just as in the Western Desert there were no newspapers, and we had to rely entirely on the wireless bulletins for news. On the 16th of March, the Sunday that we had arrived at the Piraeus, Berbera, the capital of British Somaliland, had been recaptured and our columns invading Abyssinia seemed to be making the most remarkable progress.

In Tangier the Mendub, the representative of the Sultan of

212

Morocco, had been ejected by the Spaniards and his residence handed over to the German consul. That indicated pretty clearly that although General Franco was obviously doing his best to keep Spain from being forced into the war on the side of the Axis, he was having to give way to Nazi pressure in this area, which might become of such vital importance to Britain.

As long as the Mendub had remained in Tangier, that important zone at least had the semblance of neutrality which we, taking a leaf out of Hitler's book if necessary, could have gone in to 'protect' had the Germans crossed the Pyrenees. Given proper advance planning there would have been ample time for us to do so before the Nazis reached the Straits of Gibraltar in force. But now that the Mendub had been kicked out, Hitler would be able to go full speed ahead with one of his undeclared wars, and would pump it full of German 'tourists', so that if the British ever found it necessary to land there they would be slaughtered by the hundreds before they managed to secure the town, even if they were not ignominiously driven out again.

It made one wonder how many years the war would have to go on before it occurred to the British Government to send a few 'tourists' somewhere—as even a few thousand stout-hearted Britons sitting pretty under orders in the ports of North Africa and Syria might make an immense difference to the whole future course of the war.

Our principal interest was, however, much nearer home. We were all on tenterhooks to know if the Yugoslavs would fight or go over to the Axis. On March the 20th four Serbian ministers resigned from the Cabinet as a protest against the suggested pact with the Nazis; but in spite of that on the following Sunday the Yugoslav Government was reported to have sanctioned the passage of Axis troops through the country in sealed trains. On the Tuesday Yugoslav representatives actually signed a pact with Germany in Vienna, and it looked as though yet another country had surrendered to Hitler.

The following day there were patriotic demonstrations in Yugoslavia against the Government's betrayal. Then on Thursday the 27th there came the startling news of the revolution. In the middle of the night General Simovitch and his trusted corps of Air Force officers had taken over the broadcasting station, the War Office, and a number of other key strategic points in Belgrade. The Regent, Prince Paul, was quietly arrested as he stepped out of a railway train, and his nephew, Peter II, assumed full powers as King, issuing a proclamation which had been accepted by the nation with the greatest possible enthusiasm.

This extraordinary last-minute defeat of Axis machinations in Yugoslavia would, we all knew, mean war. It was not in the bill drawn up by the megalomaniac of Berchtesgaden that any nation should keep its freedom and choose its own rulers. The fact that the pact had already been signed and that another fourteen million slaves were as good as in the bag and had suddenly slipped out of it again as free men must have made him livid with rage. One could well imagine him tearing down the curtains in his fury and grovelling in an epileptic fit upon the floor after the news was brought to him; but when he recovered enough to think coherently he would see to it that the Yugoslavs paid for their temerity. It could only be a matter of days now before the great Balkan blitz started, and we were not surprised when next morning we received orders to break camp and take the road further into Northern Greece.

From our old camp we had been able to see the snow-capped peak of Mount Olympus towering into the blue sky some thirty miles to the north of us. For the next five days we trekked by short stages slowly round it, first up through the desolate mountains to the north-west, then down into the valley of the Aliakamon, where we followed the course of the river to the north-east until Olympus was behind us, and we came out of the foothills in the north to the lower ground, where a great plain with an eight-mile-long lake in its middle forms the basin of the Varda.

Here we halted and learnt with considerable relief that it was not the intention of the Allied High Command that British Forces should hold the narrow strip of Thrace with their backs to the sea against any attack which the Germans might launch from Bulgaria. We were to remain where we were and fight with our backs to Mount Olympus.

During the trek we learnt of the Battle of Cape Matapan, in which the Royal Navy and Fleet Air Arm had once more so signally distinguished themselves by sinking three Italian cruisers and two destroyers. The news from Abyssinia was also good. On April the 1st, Asmara, the capital of Eritrea, Italy's oldest African colony, fell, and to cheer us still further the Air Ministry had disclosed the fact that we were now using a new type of bomb for our air-raids on Germany which had more than four times the explosive power of those previously used.

In the Balkans the game of lies and bluff still went on. Germany was not yet at war with Greece or Yugoslavia but became more threatening every day. Every sort of dirty trick was being used in Yugoslavia to ferment trouble. The Nazis had demanded that the new Government of General Simovitch should ratify the pact already signed and, having played their old game of using Fifth Columnists to provoke riots among the Croat minority, was now warning the Yugoslavs that action would be taken if they could not restore order in their own country.

It was now just on three weeks since I had left Egypt, so for some time past I had been wondering with increasing anxiety how long it would be before someone tumbled to the fact that I had not the least right to be with my old friends, the New Zealanders, or Major Cozelli, having discovered that I had broken my parole, succeeded in tracing me and set the machinery in motion for having me brought back to Egypt.

Only two factors, I felt, had enabled me to remain out of trouble for so long. Firstly that as I had spent so many months with the battalion in the Western Desert no one dreamed of now questioning my presence with them. Secondly although I had been officially posted from Benghazi to the Prisoners of War Control Staff in Alex in the latter part of February, I had done only two days' duty there. After that I had been arrested, and I had served for such a little time in that command that even if anyone there knew that I ought to have reported back on the 12th of March, but had failed to do so, it was quite on the cards that they had forgotten all about me.

On the other hand, sooner or later the fact that I should be there but was not would emerge in the returns of strength sent into the A.G.'s Department in Alex, even if Cozelli did not trouble to check up on me and find out that I had disappeared.

That I should get into exceedingly hot water before very long seemed an absolute certainty, but I was much too worried about Daphnis to care about myself. Old Diamopholus had promised to use his considerable influence with the British authorities to get a priority telegram through to me should he receive any news of her, and as I had not heard from him I felt certain that it was because he had no fresh news to send.

I thought of her constantly, but since she was in enemy territory there was nothing—absolutely nothing—I could do to trace her. She might still be in Bulgaria or possibly by now she had followed Mondragora's trail into Hungary, Italy, or Germany. The awful haunting knowledge that wherever she might be she now went in peril of her life made me so wretched that I began to lose weight; but as an additional officer on the Battalion H.Q.

staff I was able to make myself useful in all sorts of ways to 'Long Willie'; so once more to tire my mind and secure sleep through bodily fatigue I took on every sort of job that offered.

During those days when we were preparing our positions opposite Janitsa the news was far from good. While the Navy had been occupied in performing another miracle and escorting the whole of the Imperial Expeditionary Force from Egypt to Greece without the loss of a single man or gun, the Germans had taken the opportunity to pump stuff across the Sicilian Channel for all they were worth in ships which, with the connivance of the treacherous French, then ran down the territorial waters off Tunisia to Libya. By means of their extraordinary determination and organizing ability the Nazis had succeeded in landing a really formidable force, consisting of Hitler's personal friend, General Eric Rommel, and the African *Korps*, which was fully mechanized and comprised panzer units specially trained and equipped for fighting in hot countries.

On March the 26th El Agila, on the Gulf of Sirte, the furthest point to which the British had penetrated in Libya, was taken. A withdrawal was immediately ordered, but the Germans surprised us both with the speed of their advance and their strength. Benghazi, with its valuable airfields, had to be evacuated on April the 3rd, and soon afterwards 2,000 of our men, including three very able Generals, were taken captive by the enemy.

This calamity, arising from the overstraining of our Navy and the weakening of our Libyan Army and Air Force, was the direct result of our sending an Expeditionary Force to Greece. It was the first fruits of placing chivalry before strategy in Total War, and many of us wondered how much more it was going to cost us without anything equivalent to show in the weeks to come.

Of course the apologists in Whitehall would say afterwards that we had gone into Greece in order to induce the Yugoslavs to fight; conveniently forgetting that the Yugoslavs had refused even to have staff talks with us, and that their Government had actually signed a pact with the Nazis *after* the British had landed in Greece. And if the Yugoslavs did fight, as it now seemed likely that they would, what then? For how long did our stainless knights imagine that the poor fellows would be able to stand up against the Nazis' Luftwaffe and panzer divisions? Every enemy we could make for Hitler was something to the good, but if the French Army was not powerful enough to prevent our limited forces being driven out of Belgium, the Yugoslav Army was certainly not strong enough to prevent our being driven out of Greece.

Another nasty smack was the revolt, on April the 3rd, of Sayid Rashid Ali, a dirty little Iraqi lawyer, who had been a former Premier of Iraq and a source of trouble to the British for years. Quite obviously he had been got at by the Nazis and was a Quisling of the first water. After a day or two there was talk of the Nazis landing specialists by 'plane *via* Syria to assist Rashid Ali against the British, and it seemed quite clear that most of the Iraqi Army had gone over to him. I then remembered that when the Grand Mufti of Jerusalem had been kicked out of Palestine he had sought refuge in Iraq, which some wiseacre in the Foreign Office had considered quite fitted for self-government, although our vital pipeline, by which the Mediterranean Fleet was supplied at Haifa, ran through the country. Putting two and two together I came to the conclusion that it had been a revolt assisted by German air-borne troops in Iraq and not Egypt which had been under discussion that night when I had so nearly lost my life in Mondragora's flat.

Another ominous item was the death, soon after admitted to be suicide, of Count Teleki, the Prime Minister of Hungary. Germany had been putting pressure on Hungary to make war on Yugoslavia in spite of the friendship pact which existed between the two countries, and there could be little doubt from the fine record of this upright statesman that, at the last, he had preferred to take his life rather than be a party to such a betrayal.

By April the 4th seven German divisions were reported on the Bulgarian frontier in the neighbourhood of the Struma Valley. It was a foregone conclusion that certain of them would drive down through Thrace, cutting the whole of Eastern Greece off from the main body of the country; but the general opinion was that the Yugoslavs would be able to hold the Germans in the mountains to the west of the Struma.

Personally I doubted that. It was no particular prescience on my part but common sense applied to knowledge that had already become history. In the Norwegian campaign the Germans had amazed everybody by doing the apparently impossible when they had crossed the great mountain range which separates the Osterdal from the Gudbrandsdal Valley to descend upon the all-important railway junction of Dombas, where the British were taken entirely by surprise and completely routed. Those Norwegian mountain roads, still covered in ice and snow at the end of April, had appeared absolutely impassable to tanks, but nevertheless the Nazis, with their incredible determination and endurance, had thrown their panzer divisions across them to our complete discomfiture, and I saw no reason whatsoever why, if the Germans could do that sort of thing in Norway, they should not do the same in Yugoslavia.

It seemed obvious that unless the miserable Italians were to be entirely squeezed out of Albania and the whole country have to be reconquered later by the Axis Forces, the Germans must direct their main stroke to joining up with their Allies in the neighbourhood of Lake Ochrida, at the south-eastern corner of Albania. Such a thrust would also separate the Greeks from the Yugoslavs and was thus of such enormous value that it was inconceivable that the German General Staff should neglect to undertake it, whatever the cost in men and materials. However, it seemed from the very little that I as a second lieutenant could gather that the Allied Command was banking on the Serbs, who had neither tanks nor war 'planes in any quantity, to hold their mountains against the most powerful military striking force which had ever been created in all history.

On April the 5th all Yugoslav frontiers except that with Greece were closed, and we were given the order to stand to for all emergencies. On Sunday, April the 6th, the open town of Belgrade was blasted and reduced to flaming ruins by the blond beasts of Goering's Air Force. With that news the tidings reached us that at dawn that morning the Germans' advance units had crossed the Bulgarian frontier into Thrace. We had sown the wind, and now must real the whirlwind. The Battle for Greece was on.

CHAPTER XX

THE HURRICANE BREAKS

WITH growing tenseness we waited hour by hour until we should be called upon to face the tidal wave of steel and flame which we now knew to be advancing inexorably upon us; but that was not to be for some days yet.

At first, as always seems to be the case when the Germans start a new blitzkrieg, the news was better than we had expected. During that fateful Sunday and Monday the Greeks fought with indomitable spirit, and a terrible toll was taken of the Nazi shock troops all along the Bulgarian border; but by the Tuesday it had been forced in at least four places. After that any hope there had been of holding Thrace was gone.

On Wednesday morning the Germans reached the sea at Maritzan on the Turkish frontier, cutting the Greeks off from their potential Allies, and that night they also entered Salonika; but that was by no means the worst of the picture. At last news was beginning to come through from Yugoslavia, and it was exceedingly perturbing. The most weighty of all the German thrusts had been delivered against the Yugoslavs' southern army, almost before it had taken up its positions. The panzer divisions had gone through the much-talked-of Serbian mountains like butter, and were already at Skoplje, which was two-thirds of the way to the Albanian border.

The destruction of the Yugoslavs in the south had left the Greek flank uncovered, so they were now forced to abandon Eastern Macedonia and make fresh dispositions. It was then that we blessed Generals Wavell and Wilson, who must have insisted that the Imperial Forces should not be exposed to the possibility of complete annihilation by being sent up to the Bulgarian border, but had arranged for them to hold a zone to the north of Mount Olympus. For us there was no question of having to change front at the last moment, and we knew that we would at least have the benefit of fighting on ground deliberately chosen for us by Generals who had already proved themselves to be great commanders.

On Thursday the 10th the Germans broke the Metaxas line and occupied Xanthe, which virtually put an end to all organized resistance in Thrace. By this, the first day of the battle, they had also penetrated into Southern Yugoslavia in sufficient numbers to divide into two spearheads, one of which was racing forward to join the Italians in Albania, while the other had turned south-east to come crashing down the Valley of the Varda. Meanwhile dozens more German divisions, with Hungarians as auxiliaries, had overrun the Banat and all the low-lying country to the north-east of Belgrade, so that about a third of Yugoslavia was already in German hands and the armies of our new ally thrown into the utmost confusion.

On the sixth day Zagreb, the Croatian capital, fell in the north, and the Nazis reached Monastir in the south, thereby cutting the last communications by road or rail between Greece and Yugoslavia. On that day, too, we saw the first signs of the fighting.

Salonika is only twenty miles along the coast from the mouth of the Aliakamon, and our sappers had done great work in the big port by dynamiting harbour facilities and war plants before the Germans got there. They had also helped to evacuate considerable numbers of the civil population. In the meantime our modern cavalry, the tanks, had been ranging the low-lying campana in front of us through which ran the several rivers' mouths forming the delta of the Varda. On the Friday dusty Greek troops with many wounded began to retire through our lines from the north and north-east to re-form under the shelter of the mountains, and during the afternoon our tank units were in contact with the enemy. By evening the town of Janitza, which lay to the north of us, was burning and a great pall of reddish smoke hung above us.

That night we had our first clashes with the enemy, and by the light of a full moon, which was from time to time obscured by dark scudding clouds, we participated in a dozen different engagements; but none of the separate actions took place after midnight. Having felt out the position and ascertained that it was held in force, the Germans withdrew to wait until daylight. Our chaps had destroyed three enemy tanks, and we felt very pleased with ourselves that we had not given an inch of ground anywhere, but we then had little conception of what we should be called on to face in a few hours time.

Soon after dawn there came a distant hum, which almost instantly increased to a terrific roar. The sky to the north-east seemed to be speckled all over with German 'planes. Every anti-aircraft gun we had went into action. Here and there a Nazi 'plane was hit and spiralled down with smoke streaming from it; but the remainder never swerved from their course, and flight after flight of them dived straight down at us.

I shall never forget the twenty minutes that followed. We were all crouching in specially-prepared pits, but whenever we raised our heads to get a quick glimpse of the ground ahead, the whole earth seemed to be going up in spurts of smoke and flame. The noise was so terrific and so continuous that one could not make oneself heard, and it was only by pointing that one could draw the men's attention to something one wished them to do or see. In that short time the Germans must have rained down at least a thousand bombs on us, but considering the weight of the attack the damage done was amazingly slight. We lost only one officer and twelve men killed and wounded, and half of those were the result of one bomb which made a direct hit on an anti-aircraft gun's crew.

WHITEMAN

The moment the dive-bombers had ceased, the tanks, which had crept up in the meantime, came at us; but our anti-tank weapons had been well placed and our artillery immediately opened fire from the far side of the river, so between us we gave the first wave of German tanks an exceedingly hot reception. Seven of them were knocked out, and a number of others seemed to be in difficulties, as the bulk of them withdrew.

They had hardly retired when fresh flights of dive-bombers took up the game, and once more the earth shuddered as the bombs rained down. Immediately they ceased, the tanks returned to the attack. We laid out more of them, but they took their toll of us, and so the game continued hour after hour during the whole of the morning. The Germans never let up for a single moment, and one by one our positions were either destroyed by bombs or by tanks when they managed to penetrate deep enough into our defensive zone to enfilade them.

Later in the day we got some respite. Several flights of R.A.F. fighters, which had doubtless been operating on some other sector during the morning, came up and sailed into the Jerries. Dive-bombers are easy game for fighter aircraft, and the Germans had to call the attack off until they could rectify the air situation. There were a lot of dog-fights between Hurricanes and Messerschmitts, in which our men seemed to be keeping up their extraordinary average, and every time a German was shot down we cheered like hell. But the time that a fighter can stay in the air is extremely limited, and again and again our people had to break off the battle and return to refuel, whereas it seemed that the Nazis had so many squadrons that these could relieve each other in an endless chain. Nevertheless, the R.A.F. protected us from the worst during the greater part of the afternoon.

At last darkness came, bringing us relief from the dive-bombers and the chance to move our wounded without being machine-gunned from the air. During the night there was sporadic fighting, but it was a picnic to the daytime, and as soon as the light was good enough on the Sunday morning the dive-bombers came at us again.

That Sunday was sheer hell, and how we managed to hang on to our positions I have no idea. The R.A.F. gave us what little cover they could, but they were hopelessly outnumbered. The sky was never free of droning aircraft, and nine-tenths of them were Nazis. The tanks, too, were much more numerous than they had been on the preceding day, and the earth all about us had been churned into a pitted sea of mould from the thousands of explosions. By the late afternoon our ghastly plight was made even worse as the Germans had had time to bring up considerable quantities of artillery with which they now opened a heavy bombardment. To us, caked with the dirt and sweat and blood of battle, it seemed that twilight would never come, but come at last it did, and with it the order to retire.

I never thought that I would be glad to participate in one of those famous 'withdrawals to fresh positions' which in this war we have read of so often, but I honestly don't believe that any troops ever born could have stuck it out for another day now that the dive-bombers and artillery were both getting to know every detail of our positions and systematically blasting point after point.

Our withdrawal during the night was to a zone facing east, where our backs were to the Agosto Mountains. The retreat was successfully accomplished without the Nazis tumbling to what was on, so on the Monday they spent quite a time dive-bombing and bombarding our old positions before, in a great tank attack, they found that we had already left them. By this time we had at least succeeded in instilling into the enemy a wholesome respect for us, so when his tanks came on they nosed their way towards our new positions with considerable caution. Being further into the mountains the ground was much rougher here, so more difficult for tanks and better cover for our anti-tank guns. The fighting was stiff all day, but not as bad as it had been on the Sunday. Yet that night we had to withdraw again.

This time the retreat was not caused by the impossibility of hanging on any longer, but by the fact that the Nazis had swung round the northern end of the short Agosto range and were now advancing towards Florina, which was immediately behind us, through the Monastir Gap. We were outflanked and liable to be surrounded during the night. In consequence we crossed the Aliakamon near Velvendo and this time faced almost due north with our backs to Mount Olympus.

The river took a sharp bend in front of us, and from the sides of the wide valley we could see it wind away for some distance. The Germans were now advancing down both sides of it, but another battalion of Imperial troops had the nasty job of holding the right bank, whereas we had the comparatively easy task of preventing them crossing the bend immediately in front of it and enfilading them if they endeavoured to thrust down the far bank. As things had gone so far Tuesday was an easy day for us, but some of the Home regiments further to the west had the devil's own pasting, and that night a further withdrawal was ordered.

This time we were moved a few miles further up the valley of the Aliakamon. The river here makes a huge V down which runs the open country from the Monastir Gap, leading right into the heart of Greece. The left-hand stroke of the V was being held by the Greeks, who had swung back from the Albanian border. Its right-hand stroke was to be held by the Imperial Forces and mine was amongst the units given the task.

The position was a good one, but so furious were the Nazis' onslaughts that on the Wednesday they succeeded in forcing the passage of the river. Our own tanks and 'planes had fought splendidly, but a certain toll had been taken of them with each day's fighting, and they could not be everywhere at once; whereas the Nazis had enough of both to use them with the greatest prodigality in all sectors. By Wednesday afternoon we had been forced back into the lower defiles to the west of Mount Olympus, and since the ground there was impossible for tanks, the Germans sent hordes of infantry at us.

From excellent cover in the scrub and behind great boulders we mowed down the oncoming Huns until in some places their bodies were piled in heaps, yet still they came on. We fired at them until the barrel of our Brens and rifles were almost red-hot, and for a short while we ran out of ammunition so were reduced to fighting with the bayonet in order to hold the Nazis off from streaming up the pass until further supplies arrived. At last in falling back we met our ammunition parties coming up, and the fact of being able to use our weapons with real effect again gave us a new lease of life.

That night orders came through for us to retire to a shorter line, south of Mount Olympus. To carry out such a lengthy retreat in darkness along roads that were little more than tracks was a ghastly business. We had suffered heavily that day, and it had been impossible to get any but the walking wounded away, so most of the others now had to be abandoned to become prisoners in the isolated farms and barns which were the only buildings available in that wild country for casualty clearing-stations. The less seriously wounded made the journey with us in such of our Bren carriers as had survived; but these could only move at a walking pace for fear of going over the precipices in the dark.

Somehow we made it, and got back the twenty-odd miles to a new zone that had been allotted to us, which was no great distance from the sparsely wooded slopes where we had spent ten days in a peace that now seemed utterly unbelievable.

The Australians had been left to hold the main pass at the side of Mount Olympus, so while they were suffering the hell that we had had the day before we were able to get a few hours badly-needed sleep and afterwards a chance to give ourselves a bit of a clean-up. During our five days and nights of fighting, none of us had been able to snatch more than an odd hour's rest while fully dressed each night, and shaving or proper washing had been entirely out of the question. There was little enough that we could do now but it was a blessed relief to be able to sleep even for a few hours without being bombed or machine-gunned, and to be able to get the worst of the caked dirt off our hands and faces.

That night the Australians, having done their job, fell back through us, and in the morning we had once more to face the full fury of the German onslaught. Whether all the British fighter 'planes had by this time been overcome through the hopeless odds against them, or if those that survived had been withdrawn from the unequal contest I do not know; but from that point on the sky was not disputed with the Germans. I saw one of our New Zealand sergeants bring three 'planes down with his Lewis gun that Friday morning, but it didn't seem to matter how many of the dive-bombers crashed in flames. Others took their places and wave after wave of them launched their bombs upon any temporary strong point or gun-position that they could see.

The news trickled through that on the previous day all organized resistance had come to an end in Yugoslavia. The million-strong army of the Yugoslavs had lasted exactly eleven days. But of course not a twentieth part of it had been armed with modern weapons, so why, when their country was already four-fifths encircled, anyone should have imagined the poor fellows capable of standing up to Hitler's fire-belching, petrol-driven robots, heaven alone knows.

The past successful resistance of the Greeks, although also poorly armed, had been in very different circumstances. They had defeated not Germans but Italians. They had been attacked on only 100 miles of their 500-mile frontier, and whereas they had had direct communications with their main bases, the Italians had had to bring every man, loaf and bullet over by air or water into Albania.

That was the plain outstanding fact. Ill-armed nations, of which by comparison the British Empire was still one, could defy

224

well-armed nations *only when a belt of water lay between their forces*. Even channels like the Bosphorus or the Straits of Gibraltar could make an immense difference; because the sloping away of their promontories on either side narrowed the zone of attack, enabling the weaker power to concentrate its forces and, given naval units, protect its flanks. Further, Hitler's best weapon was the lightning speed with which he struck. *Any piece of water too wide to be bridged* robbed him at one stroke of his greatest innovation in modern warfare. Every bit of his heavy material and the bulk of his men, munitions and food would have to be unloaded from its trains and lorries, taken over in ships or barges, and loaded up again the other side. The time lost would be an incalculable gain to us and more than double our powers of resistance.

To see that needed no high knowledge of the art of war; it was kindergarten stuff. Yet here we were involved in a hopeless battle on the mainland of Europe. Of course those of us who got out alive would be told that we couldn't have let the Greeks down and that we'd killed a lot of Germans. But one could not escape the fact that there had never been the least conceivable hope of our turning the scales of battle for the Greeks with such limited forces as we could send, and that killing a few thousands of Hitler's millions was not bringing us any nearer winning the war. The truth was that Hitler could afford to lose trained men, 'planes and tanks infinitely better than we could, so all we had done was seriously to jeopardize our future chances of victory when we had to defend the gateways out of Europe which were the real keys to the strategy of the war.

History would doubtless disclose the personalities of those who, on chivalrous grounds alone, had urged this enterprise at the awful risk of later enabling Hitler to break out into Asia and thus perhaps transform what should have proved a three- or four-year war into one which dragged on for eight or ten.

I was far too busily occupied in trying to kill my share of Germans, preventing them from killing me and directing parties of men whose own officers had been killed earlier in the battle to sit about and make a morbid analysis of the doctrine of personal responsibility; but it did get under my skin pretty badly to see one good chap after another, whom I had known for months in Egypt, either killed or whimpering with pain from some ghastly gash where a shell or bomb splinter had torn his flesh and tendons. One cannot make an omelette without breaking eggs and one cannot fight a war without killing men, but the eggs should be

225

broken into the frying-pan, not on the kitchen floor, and it hurts like hell to see good troops slain in a battle which cannot possibly contribute to final victory. And that Friday afternoon I lost one of my best friends—Toby Spiers.

Throughout the whole of the week's fighting he had performed innumerable gallant actions, but he wasn't doing anything spectacular when he was killed, which somehow seemed to make it worse. For a quarter of an hour there had been a bit of a lull in the fighting, and he had just filled his pipe. He was about to light it when a Nazi sniper got him. His face showed blank surprise for a second, then he dropped the pipe and quite slowly slumped over sideways. It was only when they saw the blood run down his cheek that the men who were near him realized that he had been shot clean through the side of the head.

The week-end that followed was one long nightmare. On the Saturday we were driven across the river Tampe, about half-way between Larissa and Trikkala, and on the Sunday we endeavoured to hold some high ground between the two plains on the river's south bank; but the Germans had thrown their pontoons across during the night, and scores of their tanks came at us again in the intervals when the accursed dive-bombers were not harassing us with all their might. I'll swear that no men could have been gamer than those splendid New Zealanders, and from what I had seen of them in the Libyan battles I had no doubt at all that the Australians and our own Home Forces were putting up just as good a show in their own sectors; but you can't pit men against metal, and we simply had to continue our retreat. By evening we were staggering back along the railway-line, and on the Monday morning it was a weary battered crew which halted for a scratch meal on the south shore of Lake Xynias.

I have said the nights were dark, and except for an occasional spell of moonlight when we were blundering through woods or gorges they were as black as pitch, but during our grim argosy we had never reached higher ground without seeing some poor village in flames, or a burning farmstead. Night and day, in addition to the dive-bombers whose job was army co-operation, there were hundreds of the big machines of the Luftwaffe coming over to disrupt our communications and wreak havoc among the humblest dwellings of that once fair and lovely land. Wherever we passed we had left a trail of burnt-out ruins behind us, yet the Greek people were accepting their martyrdom with indomitable bravery.

I had been told that when our troops retreated through

226

France great numbers of the villagers not only impeded them by their panic, but hissed at them and threw stones. There was nothing of that kind about the Greeks. Even in their dire extremity they came to our temporary resting-places, often under the fire of Nazi machine-guns, to bring us gifts of food and drink, while their women did what they could for our wounded.

That was the one thing which made us feel that there had been some possible justification for this crazy expedition; yet in cold, sober sense no one could deny that we would have served the Greeks better as well as ourselves by following the first principle of war and saving our strength to strike the enemy at our own chosen time and place. We had not saved Greece from defeat and devastation, and were witnessing the piecemeal destruction of the entire modern equipment of another British Army.

On Monday, the 20th, the nightmare retreat went on. We staggered back to Lamia, which was already in flames, and south of it towards the famous Pass of Thermopylae. It was clear now that we could do no more and, although our units were holding together with splendid discipline, the great battle had now dissolved into a series of local actions over which the High Command could no longer exercise any great control. It would only be a matter of days before the British Army was smashed to pieces. The Royal Army Service Corps performed miracles in supplying us with munitions and food, but the men were almost sleeping on their feet from lack of rest, and the unceasing din had made most of us half-deaf. Dirty stubble covered our chins and our eyes were sunken in our heads. I knew that, except for a miracle, the end must be very near.

We were still covering the railway-line some miles west of Thermopylae on the Tuesday and had taken up our position in a wood, mostly composed of dwarf oak trees, not very close together, so that one could see some distance down the mossy glades where crocuses, anemones and asphodel were in blossom. It was just the sort of place where one expected to see a hama-dryad or satyr peep out at any moment, and the setting alone was enough to make one believe in the old Greek legends, of those half-human, half-divine denizens of the woods.

But as the day wore on the scene changed. The turf was torn up in great craters, the trees blasted and the flowers wilting on their stalks from the acid fumes of the high-explosive. Towards evening a runner came to tell me that the Colonel wanted to see me, and I accompanied him back through the woods for half a mile to a shallow cave in a rock face which was temporarily being used as Battalion Headquarters.

'Long Willie' was lying there with his back propped against a boulder. His left hand was tied up in a blood-soaked bandage and there was another bandage about his right leg just above the knee; but he flatly refused to be sent down with the other wounded, although he could no longer walk, and for the last two days he had had himself carried from place to place on a stretcher.

"Hallo, Julian," he said, with a tired smile. "Queer how the old clock continues to tick at a time like this, isn't it; but I've just had a packet of routine orders which have found their way here somehow. Most of the stuff's a week old and none of it has the least bearing on the present situation, but two of the orders in it concern you. I'd better sugar the pill by telling you the good news first, because I'm afraid there is bad to follow. Your promotion's come through. As from the 20th of March you have been a full lieutenant and are entitled to pay and allowances of that rank. Heartiest congratulations! You deserve it.'"

"Thank you, sir," I said. "And now, what's the bad news?" Although I already had a pretty shrewd idea of more or less the form that it might take.

He sighed. "It's an order for me to place you under close arrest and send you under escort immediately to the Provost Marshal's office in Athens. No reason is given, but I suppose you must have an idea why it's been issued. What the hell have you been up to?"

"It's a long story, sir," I said sadly. "The main fact of the matter is that I had no right to leave Egypt. I had no authority at all to report to you for duty as an interpreter on the night we embarked, but I had private reasons for wanting to come to Greece and I'm afraid I took advantage of the possibility that you might accept my coming with the battalion as quite natural."

"I see. Is that why you did a bolt for two or three hours the night we landed at the Piraeus?"

"Yes, sir. I'm afraid I lied to you about meeting a friend who took me into a Naval mess. There was somebody I wanted desperately badly to see in Athens."

"So that's how it was, eh? Well, I can only say that you've more than pulled your weight, and I'm sorry to lose you now; but I don't see how I can ignore an order like this, even in the middle of a battle. One thing I'm not going to do is to deprive our boys of another officer to act as your escort. You must find your own way down to Athens."

As he finished speaking he began to write in his field-message book, and when he had done he tore the sheet out and handed it to me with a murmured: "Take that. It may help you out of this scrape you're in."

I read the note, which ran:

I wish to record that Lieutenent Julian Day of the Interpreters Corps has carried out his duties satisfactorily in every way since his arrival with this battalion in Greece. Since we have been in contact with the enemy he has also voluntarily carried out all the ordinary duties of an infantry subaltern and has fought with the greatest gallantry. On one occasion his quick grasp of the situation saved an entire company from being surrounded and wiped out. On another, while commanding a platoon, he fought a rearguard action which enabled the remainder of his company to get across open country without loss and rejoined with the majority of his men after darkness had fallen. On a third he rescued a wounded sergeant under fire at great risk of his own life.

This officer has been attached to my command, apart from one short break, for fifteen months. I consider him of the highest character and most strongly recommend that his services in the present campaign should be taken into consideration in the event of any disciplinary charge being made against him.

I was rather surprised that he even knew of the acts to which he referred in his memo, and I am quite certain that I had not put up half as good a show as some of the other officers, but I was most touched by his kindness.

"That's all right," he smiled as I thanked him. "There's only one thing. As I can't possibly spare an officer to act as your escort I must ask you to give me your word that you will report to the P.M.'s Department in Athens as soon as you reasonably can and not play any monkey tricks."

I hesitated only a second, then I promised, knowing that having promised I could not possibly break my word to him as I had to Cozelli. The two cases were entirely different, and whatever happened afterwards I would have to report as directed.

"Right, then you'd better draw some extra iron rations from the Quartermaster, and get off at once. Further down the line you may be able to pick up a train or, if not, you can lorry-hop." He held out his hand and I grasped it warmly, wishing him the best of luck.

Twenty minutes later I'd said good-bye to those of my friends who were near enough for me to get at without undue risk of exposing myself to the Nazis' machine-gun fire, and set off south-east down the railway-track. After half an hour's walking I reached a village halt and at it left the track for the road, where I waited for a while to try to pick up a lift; but no lorries were going my way and German bombers came over to strafe the village, so I got out of it again as quickly as I could. Darkness had come when I entered a second village, and here I had better luck. A line of British R.A.S.C. lorries was drawn up just outside it facing south. The place had been used as a temporary headquarters and it was now being evacuated; so I got a lift on one of our lorries, and with the guns and bombs still roaring in our rear we trundled down the road until we reached a small town called Dadio.

The lorries were going no further for the time being, but the railway was still working between Dadio and Athens, and at two o'clock in the morning I managed to get on board a train into which people, mainly Greek civilians, were jammed like sardines.

The train was little faster than the one in which I had made the journey north, and it did not get into Athens until midday the following day, having twice been bombed and once machine-gunned that morning. At the station I had myself shaved and cleaned up as well as I could, then I took a taxi to the Diamopholi shipping office. It was just possible that the old man had had news of Daphnis since the battle for Greece had started, and if so it was quite on the cards that any attempt on his part to communicate with me had failed, as no mails or personal telegrams had reached us at all since we had come to grips with the enemy. I felt quite certain that 'Long Willie' would not grudge me an hour or two's freedom before I reported, as once I did so it was highly probable that I should be formally arrested and so not able to make this call at all.

Diamopholus was there, but, as I feared, he had no news of Daphnis. She had vanished into the blue. In an attempt to cheer me up the dear old chap took me to lunch at Costi's in Korai Street. The cold lobster and champagne tasted unbelievably good after the rough fare, snatched in the intervals of fighting, on which I had been living. He told me that, although Churchill had protected Athens from air raids by a threat to carry out reprisals on Rome, the Piraeus was being bombed almost hourly; but if one of his ships that was due in that day escaped he meant to leave for Egypt the following night. Having wished him a safe journey, and much comforted in my inner man, I walked round to the building in which the P.M. had taken up his quarters.

I was kept waiting for about half an hour, then a staff captain saw me. At first he was extremely brusque and evidently regarded me as a bad hat who was wasting valuable time at a critical period of the war; but when I gave him 'Long Willie's' chit his attitude changed entirely.

"This rather alters things," he said. "Normally I should send you back to Egypt on the first ship under escort, but everything's at such sixes and sevens now that it seems rather stupid to waste a competent and experienced fighting officer because some disciplinary question is pending against him. I think you'd better go to the Officers' Club. They'll fix you up with a room, or anyway a bed, until you hear from me. I'll try to get a decision by tomorrow from higher up that you can return to your unit."

He seemed a most sensible fellow, and having thanked him for the way in which he had treated the matter I went off to the Club, where I revelled in the luxury of a bath, was able to get my hair cut, and reappear, except for some stains which only a professional cleaner could have got out of my clothes, like a civilized individual again.

Most of the base-wallahs who made up the Club's occupants that evening regarded my sadly-faded battle-dress with obvious distaste. The war in Greece had not been on long enough for them to have become used to fighting soldiers returning from the front to disturb the serenity of their days spent filling up forms and their peaceful evening in their nice new Club. But some of the more human ones had congregated in the bar, and after a few rounds of drinks for the first time in days I got a fairly clear picture of what was going on.

Having broken through the Serbian mountains, thus outflanking the Greek Eastern Front, the Germans had penetrated Central Greece in overwhelming numbers, forcing the British back from their position in front of Mount Olympus on the one side and the Greeks back from their positions round Kastoria on the other. The retreat of the Greeks from the Albanian territory, which they had conquered so gallantly in the autumn, had not been quick enough, and great numbers of them had been pinned down in North-Western Greece without 'planes or guns, and with very little ammunition. On the previous day, April the 22nd, this Army of the Epirus, numbering 250,000 men, after having fought one of the greatest campaigns in history, had been compelled to surrender.

The position of the British was almost equally desperate as the port of Volo, which was their principal base of supply, had been captured on the previous Monday. But it was thought that, if the Pass of Thermopylae could be held, the British might establish a short line from the Gulf of Lamia to the Gulf of Amphissa across a neck of land which was only about thirty miles in width. Thus, according to the base-wallahs, Athens might yet be saved and the whole of the Peloponnesus retained in Greek hands.

It seemed to me that they were sheer wishful thinkers who had not, even after the lessons of Norway, Holland, Belgium and France and the *débâcle* that was even then taking place to the north of us, realized the terrible speed, ingenuity and determination which animates a Nazi blitzkreig. And a few moments later I got a nasty shock.

I learned that, within twenty-four hours of their having reached the Mediterranean on the coast of Thrace, the Germans had flung air-borne troops into Samothrace and Lemnos; since, they had also made landings by speedboat and 'plane in the islands of Mytilene, Khios, Nikaria and Samos. It was said that some of the Greek police in these islands had put up a stout resistance, but of course they had soon been overpowered; and nobody in the bar seemed to think that these sparsely-populated islands were of any great importance. To me it seemed utterly incredible that they had not been garrisoned weeks before with the best armoured units which were available in the whole of the Near East.

The Dodecanese, which lay a little further south, had comparatively little significance so long as they were five hundred miles from the nearest Axis base on the mainland; but with the Germans in Athens, as I knew they soon must be, those Italian-owned islands could be reinforced with ease. Now that the Germans had occupied all the principal Greek-owned islands further north it meant that, with their forces in Bulgaria as well, the Axis Powers had encircled the whole of Western Turkey; yet apparently not a blow had been struck to prevent them.

Surely we should have gone into Samothrace, Lemnos, Mytilene and Khios at the same time as we had gone into Crete. To do so was so clearly all part of the same operation, and an essential precaution if the Nazis were to be prevented from breaking out of their European cage into Asia.

With air and submarine bases in every one of those islands the Germans could render the Aegean Sea untenable to us. If Turkey were attacked and called on us to assist her, the best immediate help which we could give was to send a powerful

232

squadron from the Mediterranean Fleet through the Dardanelles and the Bosphorus to help defend Turkey's long and vulnerable northern coast against a Nazi invasion from the Rumanian and Bulgarian ports across the Black Sea. It was obvious, too, that we ought to land every man that we could spare in North-Western Turkey as this was one of the great gates to the outer world in which, if necessary, the men of the British Empire must be called upon to fight and die. The holding of it was not just another battle but one of the keys to winning the war.

Again, even if the Turks did not ask us to support them with troops, they would badly need munitions and supplies. By throwing Lemnos and Samothrace away we had made all these ways of helping them impossible. No convoy of troops or supply ships would ever reach the Dardanelles now, and even the sending of a squadron of the British Navy to reinforce the Turks in the Sea of Marmara and the Black Sea would be hazardous in the extreme.

But worst of all it seemed to me unlikely now that Turkey would resist German demands to send troops across the Bosphorus and through her possessions. It was unreasonable to expect her to do so when we were no longer in a position to reinforce her properly, and by leaving those all-important islands undefended had virtually handed the Nazis the key of her front door.

Of course the reason for leaving the islands undefended was not far to seek. Only tanks and anti-aircraft guns could break up concentrations of Nazi air-borne troops. Evidently our numbers of these were still so limited that we could not afford to garrison the islands with them *and send them into Greece*. Once more we were paying up for that chivalrous gesture of ours which had been allowed to overrule the really vital question of winning the war while we were still strong enough to enforce a lasting peace. There seemed no end to the grim possibilities for which we had been let in by this Greek adventure.

I went to bed very depressed, but what a joy it was to slip between clean sheets again! I had hardly sensed the first pleasure of it before I was asleep.

In the morning, as I had nothing to do, I had meant to have a good lie in bed; but about half past eight a sapper, who was occupying the room next to mine in the Club, thrust his head through the door and said: "Heard the news? We're evacuating!"

I sat up in bed and lit a cigarette as I replied: "Thank God for that! I had an idea that they'd be trying to take off as many of us as they could pretty soon. When did it start?"

"The Air Force people have been at it for some days. They've

233

been flying ground staffs out in big seaplanes, but the Army only started last night. I've got to rush. So long!"

I saw no particular reason to hurry as the news having only just come through it was certain that several days would be occupied by the operation, and in Athens I was within a few miles of the biggest port in Greece. Parodying Sir Francis Drake, I felt that there was plenty of time to have breakfast first and run from the Germans afterwards. With the help of the Navy, the Army was going to perform another 'miracle'. How sick the Navy must be of those stupid 'miracles' by now, which cost them precious ships and lives of highly-trained officers and men who were absolutely irreplaceable!

After bathing and dressing I contemplated going to see the A.P.M. captain instead of waiting for a message from him, but I thought that he was probably incredibly busy with more important matters, and that it would be unfair to bother him at such a time; so leaving a message with the English-speaking porter that if I were wanted I should be at the Grande Bretagne, I went along to see Nicholas Diamopholus.

The old boy was just off to his office to make final arrangements pending the occupation of Athens by the Germans.

I urged him most strongly to leave Greece immediately, because he could be so much more useful to the Allied cause as a free man; and he told me that his ship was in, so he hoped to sail that afternoon.

Nicholas knew all about the evacuation and had helped for some days past in making arrangements for it. He was optimistic enough to think that the ships would be able to get the best part of our men away, owing to the very indented coastline of Greece, which would help to conceal them from the German aircraft; but it meant abandoning all our tanks, guns and stores. He said that the King of Greece was going to Crete and our people had pledged themselves to hold that to the last man in order to maintain a Greek Government on Greek soil. I prayed that we could, as otherwise we'd lose our naval base at Suda Bay and the power of the Fleet to prevent the Nazis from sending strong reinforcements into Libya would be immensely crippled.

The old boy was pro-British to his fingertips and I found his confidence in our ability to hold Crete rather touching. Naturally the last thing I should have dreamt of doing would have been to sow doubts in his mind, but once more I was miserably puzzled and bitterly angry. Of course we could have held Crete, and Mytilene, and Lemnos, too, if we had put the flower of our troops

234

into them in the beginning and used these wasted weeks to fortify them with every anti-aircraft gun that could be spared, or even that could not be spared, from Egypt and Palestine.

Britain's element was the water; those sea-girt islands should have been our chosen battleground, and from them we could have barred the path of the wild beast eastward. Malta was in a far more exposed position than any of these islands, yet we had hung on to that in spite of the most devastating air attacks. We could have hung on to the Greek islands if we had spent our substance on them, and even if the Nazis decided to sacrifice thousands of their air-borne troops by making crash landings, we could still have overcome those landings and broken up their concentrations, if we had tanks.

We had tanks, but where were they now: scattered over the length and breadth of the Greek mainland, and those which had escaped destruction in the frightful battles of the past eleven days were to be thrown away, abandoned on the beaches in these coming nights. By our decision to fight on the wrong ground the first round in the Battle for Asia had been lost before it had even started.

I told Nicholas that I should get back to Egypt as soon as my duties permitted and that, should Daphnis reappear in the meantime, I wanted him to tell her that she was never out of my thoughts and that I was half-crazy from worry about her. Then wishing each other luck we parted.

Athens now knew the bad news that very soon it was to be abandoned to the enemy; yet there was no panic and the people showed the greatest fortitude. There were no longer cheers for the little groups of British troops that passed, but the people still smiled at them sympathetically and understandingly. They realized that, like their own soldiers, we had put up a good fight, and it was only that our enemies had proved too many for us.

There was no reliable news, but it was said that the Germans had forced the Pass at Thermopylae, and from the roads to the north there were now considerable numbers of British vehicles making their way towards the Piraeus.

I lunched at the Club and at about half past two a chit arrived for me from the A.P.M. It simply said: "You are hereby temporarily released from arrest and instructed to rejoin your unit forthwith." So having collected my few belongings I set off to walk to the station in the hope of finding a train which would take me part of the way up to the Front.

It was a lovely afternoon and the sun was still shining upon that miracle of loveliness, the Acropolis, which can be seen from almost any part of the city. As I looked at it, away there in the distance, it revived in me a comforting sense of proportion. The Germans would not be the first invaders to enter Athens. Romans, Venetians, and Turks had all overcome her in their day, but in the end she had overcome them and risen again to resume her rightful place as the first free city of the world. The same thing would happen once again, only this time her people would have earned a new glory and a new respect from all other peoples.

As I looked up to the Acropolis I thought again of Daphnis. She was one of the millions who, through nearly a hundred generations, had gazed upon it. That beauty was the common property of us both, especially as she must have seen it so recently. I had only missed her in Athens by a few days but, I reflected bitterly, a miss was as good as a mile. She must, I felt sure, have got on Mondragora's track through von Hentzen, as according to Cozelli the Baron had been in Athens when she first arrived there. If only I could have traced Mondragora I felt absolutely certain that I should have found Daphnis; but there was not a single clue for me to start on.

At that moment a car crawled by me; its driver was the Portuguese.

CHAPTER XXI

STRONG MEASURES

MONDRAGORA was driving a long, low, dust-covered car. As it passed me I saw that the metal coachwork at the back of it was holed and torn in several places, evidently by bomb or shell splinters; so it looked as if he had come from the battle zone. The streets were not particularly full, but he was driving at an easy pace, perhaps from being tired after a long journey. The moment the car had passed me I began to run.

It was checked at the crossing by traffic lights, which gave me a chance almost to catch up with it before it turned right opposite the Stavrou; but obviously I could not possibly keep up with even a slowly-driven car on foot and no taxis were in sight.

As I ran I looked wildly round for any means of keeping on

bring your basket back if I can, but if I have to leave in a hurry I'll pay you for it."

When she had taken the things I picked up the big basket and, holding it in front of me chest-high, I propped it against the wooden gates while I rang the bell.

There was a sound of footsteps on the gravel and the gateway was opened a crack.

"Washing," I announced, in as casual and throaty a voice as I could manage.

A pair of blue eyes peered at me suspiciously from a fair-skinned shiny face, which was topped off by a typically German shaven skull.

"Vare is der vooman who usually der vashing brings?" said the servant in Greek with a heavy German accent.

"Sick," I replied laconically. "I'm her nephew."

Apparently satisfied, he opened the gate to let me through, and closed it again carefully after me. A quick glance round showed me that the long garden was empty, then I followed him down a narrow semi-dark open-air passage, which lay between the high garden wall and the blank side-wall of the little house.

He was about half-way along this passage when I called after him and he turned.

"Here," I said, thrusting out the basket. "Hold this a minute, will you? I've just trodden on a nail."

Grudgingly he took the basket from me, thereby rendering himself temporarily powerless to use his hands in his own defence. Immediately he was supporting the full weight of it I drew back my right fist and gave him a terrific swipe under the jaw.

That is not a nice thing to do to an inoffensive person, but this fellow was a German and we should both have attempted to do much worse things to each other if we had happened to meet that evening a few miles outside Athens with half a dozen Mills bombs in our pockets and a tommy-gun apiece.

His look of surprise as he saw the blow coming was almost comical, but he had no time to dodge it, and although he let go of the basket he was much too late to protect his face. My fist contacted good and hard with the side of his jaw, and he went flying backwards so that his head smacked against the old brick wall.

My first blow hadn't knocked him right out, so, as he swayed there dazed for a second, I had to hit him hard again. Immediately he'd slid to the ground I took his belt off and used it to strap his ankles together, then, pulling the cover off the basket of washing,

I used a thin towel to tie his hands behind his back and stuffed a couple of handkerchiefs into his mouth so that when he came to he would not be able to cry out.

The short passage was a *cul-de-sac*, which gave access only to the back door of the garden house. The door stood open and outside it there was a dustbin, a pig-tub and a pile of empty cases. Grabbing my victim by the collar, I dragged him behind them, where he would not be seen by anyone coming through the gate. Having drawn my gun and slipped off the safety-catch, I entered the back door. It gave on to a scullery and beyond was a small but well-furnished kitchen, where the manservant had evidently been at work cleaning the table silver.

Tiptoeing into it I paused there, listening intently. On coming through the gate I had one quick glimpse of the house, and I felt sure that in a small one-storey affair of this kind there could not be more than three, or at the outside four, rooms, probably just kitchen, sitting-room, dining-room and bedroom.

Almost at once I caught the murmur of voices. A door that evidently led from the service quarters to the rest of the house was shut, and I decided that the sound was coming through a service hatch in the kitchen's inner wall.

For a few moments I walked round the room, deliberately making a certain amount of noise, knowing that whoever was on the other side of the hatch would think that it was the man-servant. I shifted some of the pots and pans, jingled the forks on the kitchen table, and turned on one of the taps in the scullery. I then shut it off, marched back into the kitchen, pulled open the service hatch and shut it again, but in doing so I had been careful not to close it quite completely; so that if I remained quiet myself I'd be able to hear much better what was going on in the next room.

The first result of my manœuvre verified a guess I had made when I had heard that this was the back lodge of the German Archaeological Institute. This nice little hide-out belonged to the Baron Feldmar von Hentzen. I could now hear his arrogant guttural tones distinctly.

Standing near the hatch, I continued to fiddle with the silver; not sufficiently loudly to disturb my enemies or to prevent myself catching the main gist of what they were talking about, but just enough to create the impression that the servant was there, busy at his work. The fellow had looked just the sort of human robot that von Hentzen would employ in a place where he had to keep a servant at such close quarters. No doubt he was completely satisfied that the man was both too scared of what might happen to him if he was caught listening to his master's conversations and too stupid to make use of anything that he might overhear if he did.

Mondragora and von Hentzen were talking about the war. It was evidently some time since they had met, but the Portuguese was taking advantage of his position as a neutral to go backwards and forwards through the war zone with the latest intelligence that the German agents could collect behind the Greek lines to the General Field Headquarters of the German Army, as it moved southward after the advancing troops. Baron Feldmar was grunting and chuckling over the fact that everything in the Balkan campaign had gone like clockwork and entirely according to plan; while Count Emilo, who was evidently very tired and had had a nerve-racking journey, said how thankful he was that when he went north again it would be his last trip and that next time he entered Athens it would be on the heels of the German Army.

There was a gurgling noise as drinks were poured from a bottle, and after toasting the speedy conclusion of Hitler's latest victory the German declared that nothing would prevent his being in at the death himself, and that he meant to go out of Athens at the last moment in order to enter it again with the High Command of the triumphant army in his uniform as a Colonel of the Prussian Guard.

They talked for some time, then Mondragora said: "You'd better give me the packet now as I'm absolutely dead beat, and I must get along to the hotel so that I can put in a few hours sleep. I shall probably leave again at about three o'clock in the morning, and if anything fresh breaks before that you can always telephone me."

Just as he was on the point of going, von Hentzen remarked, "By the by, have you still got that girl with you?"

As I listened my pulses raced, for I felt sure that he must be referring to Daphnis. The reply came at once.

"Yes. As I am a civilian no objection has been raised to my having her with me at Headquarters, and she gets through quite a lot of work when I'm not there. She picked up typing very quickly and no ordinary clerk could be trusted with the job, so she makes a most suitable little secretary."

"*Mein Gott!*" exclaimed the German.

"What's the matter?" asked the Count.

"Has she had any chance to communicate with anyone on the other side?" inquired the other anxiously.

"No, how could she, since all normal communications have been cut for the best part of three weeks? But what makes you think that she might wish to do so?"

The Baron's deep voice came again: "Because I have reason to believe that she is trying to double-cross you. A report from one of our agents in Alexandria reached me only yesterday. He managed to obtain access to some of Cozelli's files. Did you know that she was engaged to be married to that interfering young fool who now calls himself Julian Day?"

"What's that?" exclaimed Mondragora.

"It is just as I say," the German replied; "and if you remember I was vaguely uneasy about her *bona fides* when she turned up here in Athens early in March and offered to work for us; but you were so certain that she was all right that you vouched for her."

"Of course. I had good reason to. She did splendidly for us in Alex until Italy attacked Greece; and you know what these amateurs are—they will never work against their own country."

"How, then, do you account for her change of heart?"

"She told me she was quite convinced that peace could have been restored after the Greek successes against the Italians had it not been for the British, who were manipulating the small nations quite unscrupulously for their own ends, and wanted to use Greece as a continental jumping-off ground against Hitler. Of course she saw, as we all did, that the British would be flung out neck and crop, but she felt so strongly about the utterly unnecessary and great additional suffering which would be inflicted on Greece, owing to British intervention, that she wanted to lend a hand in defeating them as swiftly as possible; so that although Greece might lose her freedom for a time, the actual devastation caused by active warfare in the country would be limited."

"Not bad," the German grunted. "But unfortunately that's not the case. You'll recall that it was through Julian Day that your flat in Alex was raided. Why, I can't quite understand, but Cozelli seems to think that Day is mixed up with us. Anyhow, he put him behind the bars for about three weeks and in the meantime got hold of the girl who, as my agent has quite definitely verified, is engaged to Day. The invitations were actually issued for the wedding. Apparently Cozelli, who's a clever devil if ever there was one, made the girl believe that he had much more on Day than was actually the case. He had her taped, too, it seems, on some letters of hers that they found in your flat. Knowing of this old hook-up of hers with you, he was able to blackmail her into going to Greece to get in touch with you again and to double-cross you as the price of her lover's freedom."

There was silence for a moment, then Mondragora spoke thoughtfully. "If this is true it explains quite a lot of things. She's been damnably difficult these last few weeks. She suddenly made the discovery just about the beginning of this month that she was not suited to the work, and she's pleaded with me several times since to let her go home to Egypt, *via* Turkey."

"In view if what we now know, the explanation is clear," said von Hentzen. "She had evidently been with you long enough to get on to something good, and ever since has been trying to get away so that she can turn her information in to Cozelli. Thank God she did not succeed and has no way of communicating; but are you sure of that?"

"Certain. She would not know how to use a wireless if I put her in a room with one. Her correspondence has been practically nil—a postcard to the old man to relieve his anxiety after she first ran away from him—and later two letters to her mother, both of which were carefully censored. In these last weeks she has been travelling with me as I moved with Marshal List's Field Head-quarters, so she could not send letters or get in touch with a neutral consulate however hard she tried."

"Then no harm has been done, but if she has been acting as your secretary she knows too much. You must deal with her, Emilo. We cannot afford to have love-sick young women who are attempting to betray us in our midst, and you can take it that my information is absolutely accurate."

"Very well," Mondragora agreed, with a tired sigh. "I'll see to it the moment that I get back, but I shall drop asleep where I sit if I don't get some sleep soon."

There came the sound of footsteps and a door opening. Von Hentzen called out: *"Gute Nacht!"* and the Count called back: *"Auf Wiedersehen!"* Then von Hentzen's heavy tramp returned to the room.

I caught a glimpse of Mondragora as he passed the kitchen window, and my first impulse was to run after him with the idea of waylaying him and settling my account with him there and then; but I had hardly moved away from the hatch before I realized that now, if ever in my life, everything depended upon my keeping a cool head, and that to murder Mondragora in the streets of Athens would be the very worst way to go to work. The washerwoman was outside and I did not think she would stand for murder. Within a few moments of his having driven off in his car he would either have outdistanced me or else be back in a crowded thoroughfare where, if I attempted to assassinate him, I should immediately be seized by the crowd; and that would not save my adorable Daphnis.

Count Emilo had stated clearly that he was going to bed, and would not set off up to the Front again until round about three o'clock in the morning, so he would be out of the game for the best part of twelve hours. It was my job to utilize every second of that precious lead. My intense relief at learning that Daphnis was still alive and undetected in her role of British secret agent, and my pride in her cleverness at having picked up work so entirely strange to her quickly enough to get taken on as Mondragora's secretary, was offset by the awful knowledge that she had now been found out. My job was to discover the whereabouts of German Field Headquarters, then by hook or by crook get there before Mondragora, as, now that von Hentzen had informed him of her intended treachery, her life would not be worth a moment's purchase once the Portuguese rejoined her.

The only way in which I could get the name of the town or village in which Marshal List and his staff were at present was from either Mondragora or von Hentzen. Neither would tell me willingly, and even if I could catch up with the Portuguese I saw little chance of being able to force him to give away such information in the street, whereas I felt that if I played my cards properly in this quiet little box of a house I might get the German entirely at my mercy.

There was not a moment to lose, as now that Mondragora had gone at any time von Hentzen might come into the kitchen to give his servant some order. Getting out my gun again I walked quietly over to the door and eased it open. It gave on to a short passage, and I crept silently along it until I reached the sitting-room. Luck was with me as the door was standing ajar, and, peering in with my gun held ready before me, I saw the Baron was sitting working at a desk in the window with his back turned towards me. Covering him with the gun, I opened the door another few inches and said sharply:

"I've got you covered! Drop your hands beside you or I'll blow your head in."

Von Hentzen was no coward. If we had been face to face I little doubt that in that small room he would have chanced being shot and attempted to rush me; but he must have known that since he would have had to jump up and fling the chair back

244

before he could even turn round to face me, he would have no chance at all of getting to grips before I could shoot him.

"In case you don't recognize my voice, I'm Julian Day," I went on; "so you know that I'm not bluffing when I say that I'll make you dead as mutton if you attempt to lift a finger."

From the moment I had first spoken he had gone stiff and rigid in his chair. Now with a rumbling curse he slowly let his hands fall beside him.

I knew that my own life would hang in the balance for the next few moments. It is no easy matter to keep a strong man covered and tie him up at the same time. If I made a single slip the great hulking brute would turn the tables in a second, and I knew that I should be as good as dead if I once allowed him to get his hands on me.

Swiftly I looked round for the means of trussing him and my eye fell upon a standard lamp which had a long electric flex attached to it. Keeping a wary eye upon the German, I jerked the plug out of the socket and made a running noose. As his back was towards me he could not see that, while making the knot, I had at times to point the gun a little away from him; but while I was doing it I kept on talking to him so as to occupy his mind.

"That's right," I purred. "I'm so glad to see that you're prepared to be sensible. It's just as well for you that you didn't take a chance on looking round, otherwise one glimpse of me would be the last thing that you would ever have seen on earth. As you probably know, it would be a great pleasure to me to kill you where you sit, and I certainly hope to kill you some time. In fact I shall be terribly distressed if I hear that you have been killed by a stray British bullet or bomb if you go up to the Front for the triumphant entry into Athens, as you told Mondragora that you meant to just now; but unfortunately I must deny myself the pleasure of killing you this evening. The Fates ordain that I can do no more than have a little talk with you. However, as you may be angry at what I have to say, I think it would be wisest if I tie you up first. Then there won't be any risk of your being tempted to act rashly and compelling me to kill you prematurely after all. Remain quite still, please, while I throw this wire over your head. You can take my word for it that I have no intention of strangling you."

As I finished speaking I advanced to within two feet of him and threw the wide noose of electric flex over his bald head. The moment I had done so I had an awful thought: I was still wearing Mondragora's raincoat.

If he missed it when he reached his car he might come back for it; then I should be caught between the two of them. As I had acted immediately upon Mondragora's leaving the house barely two minutes could have elapsed since he went out of it; but even that was time for him to have reached his car. Fortunately the raincoat had been lying on the back seat, so there seemed a good chance that he might not notice that it was gone.

The possibility that he might reappear at any moment was damnably unnerving, but if he once drove off in his car, owing to his extreme tiredness, I doubted very much if he would trouble to come back again; so I tried to put the matter out of my mind by assuring myself that two or three minutes having elapsed the worst risk of his returning was already over.

With a none-too-gentle jerk I drew the noose of wire tight about von Hentzen's neck, and once that was done I felt a little more certain of myself. No man can fight his best with a heavy standard lamp attached by a piece of wire to a tight noose round his neck.

Carrying the lamp several feet nearer to him, I transferred the gun to my left hand and made a loop out of the slack of the wire with my right. I then ordered von Hentzen to hold his right hand behind him.

As he demurred I thrust the cold steel of the gun-barrel into the soft puffy ridge of fat at the back of his head, and that caused him to comply at once. Slipping the loop over his wrist, I pulled the slack up again, made him put his other hand behind the chair and looped that also, so that his two hands were now caught behind his back and attached to the loop of wire that went round his neck. Placing my foot on the base of the standard lamp, I gave the wire a sudden pull and wrenched it from its terminal. Then, as von Hentzen could still not see what I was up to, I felt that I now might risk putting the gun down for a minute.

Having placed it on the floor within easy reach, I secured his hands more thoroughly, and by reaching between the chair-legs took the wire first round one ankle, then round the other, so that as the result of a little hard work and twenty feet of electric flex I had him securely tied to his own chair.

As he was sitting opposite the window, I had had to work fast in case anyone came into the garden, but the job was done under two minutes. With a sigh of relief I picked up my gun, drew the curtains, switched on the light and went round in front of him.

"Well," he said calmly, "this is quite clearly your round. What do you want to know?"

246

"The present whereabouts of the German Field Head-quarters," I replied.

His large mouth twisted into a grin. "So you are anxious to save that young woman of yours? Well, she's no good to us, and if you care to risk your own neck by trying to get through the German lines to reach her, good luck to you! As far as I know, Marshal List is at present at Koziani."

"Thanks," I said. "I'm very glad that you appear to be behaving so sensibly; but I shall want a little proof of that. Have you some document which will bear out what you say?"

"*Gott in Himmel, nein!*" he exclaimed. "Is it likely that I should have a list of the places provisionally selected as German Field Headquarters?"

"Yes," I replied, "it is. Otherwise you would not be able to get such information as you can collect through to them with any rapidity." I let an ominous note creep into my voice as I went on: "There seems good reason to suppose that you've been established here ever since you escaped from Egypt; so I expect you've got quite a lot of interesting documents hidden in this place somewhere. Are you going to talk or must I make things uncomfortable for you?"

"Go to hell!" he snapped, and his hard, blue eyes flashed defiantly.

I took another look round the comfortable little sitting-room, and my eye fell on some long wooden spills for cigar- or pipe-lighting, which were stuck in a vase on a small table beside the sofa. Taking one of them, I lit it, and walking up to von Hentzen from behind I placed the lighted spill without warning under the lobe of his left ear.

He let out a bellow of pain and tried to spring out of his chair. Of course he could not because he was lashed to it; but he managed to get on his feet with the chair attached to his back and almost bent double, which gave him something of the appearance of a tortoise endeavouring to walk on its hind legs.

"Now, now! Sit down again or it will be the worse for you," I threatened, and as he swung round towards me I jabbed the lighted taper under his nose. The instantaneous result was that, with another yowl of pain, he flung his head back, overbalanced and was promptly sitting down again.

"Why waste time?" I asked. "You know well enough that I've no cause to love you, and I'm not going to let up if I have to burn your flesh inch by inch off your body. Sooner or later you'll have to tell me where your papers are, so why not do it now?"

247

As he maintained his stubbornness I held his nose until he was forced to open his mouth and stuffed his handkerchief into it. I told him that he could nod his head when he was ready to talk, then I set to work on him in earnest.

I don't think I should make a very good professional torturer as, although I was applying persuasion to one of the men who had done me an irreparable evil and whom I regarded as my most deadly enemies, I did not enjoy the next ten minutes. I was damned nearly sick from the smell of burnt hair and faintly singeing flesh. How the German managed to stick it for so long I cannot think, and I'm certain that I should never have been able to hold out for half that time. At last he nodded, so I removed the gag. He gave a gasp, then whimpered:

"All right damn you! That board on the right-hand side of the bookcase, the second one from the wall—it's loose. Pull it up and you'll find some maps there which will give you what you want to know."

I found the maps with a mass of other papers. Having spread them out I saw that the third I opened had a number of cryptic signs marked on it in ink against which there were certain dates, and one lot of signs, all of the same character, ran in a chain from Sofia through Southern Yugoslavia right down to Athens.

Koziani, although in the centre of Greece and practically on the line, was not one of the places marked; but fifteen miles south-south-west of it Ventsa was, and against it was the date, 23–26.4.41. It was no good asking von Hentzen if my assumption was correct about these markings as there was no guarantee whatever that he would reply truthfully; but I felt pretty confident that I had found out what I wanted to know, and of course he had given me the wrong town in the first instance, because although he had said that Daphnis was no longer of any use to them, he had purposely glossed over the fact that she could be extremely useful to his enemies. If only I could get her back she might have information of the most vital nature which she could pass on to us.

There was a large attaché-case beside the desk, and after a quick glance through its contents I threw most of them out, then proceeded to fill it instead with all the papers that were in the cache under the loose floorboard.

Von Hentzen fumed and swore, but there was nothing that he could do about it. I next went through his pockets. He tried to bite me, but I held his nose with one hand while searching him with the other, and I acquired a fine collection of passes, among which was one issued by the German General Staff and signed by von Keitel, which I reckoned would get me into most places between Narvik and Tripoli.

When I had done I said to him: "I hope this won't be our last meeting. In fact I'm sure it won't, because I mean to get you sooner or later even if I have to swing for it. That goes for Mondragora, too, as you might tell him from me next time you see him."

He regarded me with a curious stare for a moment and said with considerable bravery, "If you feel like that about it why don't you kill me now?"

"Because," I replied, "I told you soon after I first entered this room that I did not mean to kill you tonight. I had to do that otherwise you would never have allowed me to tie you up without a struggle, and I might have had to kill you before I had a chance to get the information that I wanted. Subconsciously, at least, you must have trusted me, though why you should God only knows! Still, you were right about that."

Seizing his nose again, I stuffed the handkerchief back in his mouth, as I added, "I can't afford to have you rousing the neighbours with your shouts, so you'll have to stay here until someone finds you." I then pocketed my gun, picked up the attaché-case, and, switching out the light, left him.

Out in the alleyway I spent a couple of minutes bundling the trussed and gagged servant into the scullery. Having shut the back door upon him, I let myself out through the wooden gate. The washerwoman was still outside, and she asked me with considerable curiosity if I had succeeded in doing whatever it was that I went in to do.

I told her that I had given the two Germans an exceedingly tough time and that I had left them tied up in there because I did not want them to follow me. The good soul was delighted, but wanted to know what I had done with her laundry basket.

I said that I would go in and get it for her if she wished, but I thought that it was much better to leave it there, as when the man who had let me in had asked why she hadn't brought it, I had said that I was her nephew. To retrieve it now would only lead any inquirers to suppose that she had been my accomplice, so she had best say that the basket of linen had been stolen from her; but I added that in case she did not get the basket back I would like to pay for it, and I produced a thousand-drachma note, which is something under £2.

However, she flatly refused to take it and said that the basket was well lost to her if it had helped an English soldier to give a bad half-hour to two of those dirty Nazis.

Having retrieved my cap, tin hat and gas mask from her, I took off Mondragora's mackintosh and laid it down on the pavement where any passers-by, who thought they might find it useful, could pick it up. Then I parted from the washerwoman with a good hearty handshake and set off towards the centre of Athens.

Already my mind was working desperately fast on the steps it would be necessary to take in order to get to Ventsa and find Daphnis. A car was one thing I must have and ample Greek money another. If Diamopholus had not yet left the Grande Bretagne to join his ship in the Piraeus I felt sure that he would provide me with both, and I hurried forward as fast as my legs would carry me.

I then realized that not only was I going back into the battle area, but that I would have to pass right through the German lines and that I could not possibly do so in the uniform of a British officer.

As I was thinking of the immense difficulties of the journey that lay ahead of me, I put my hand in my pocket to make certain that I'd got the passes and it came in contact with a flimsy piece of paper. I did not need to take it out to see what it was. I knew, and my heart sank like lead to my boots at the thought of it. That paper was the order that I had been sent only an hour earlier to rejoin my regiment at the earliest possible moment. If I failed to do so—if instead I endeavoured to save Daphnis—if I changed into a civilian suit . . . I should be a deserter.

CHAPTER XXII

DARK JOURNEY

THE thought appalled me. It had been decided that I should go into the Diplomatic because as a child I had shown such an unusual flair for languages; but I came from a family of soldiers. From my earliest days I had heard the stories of courage and endurance by which older, or dead-and-gone, members of the Du

Crow-Fernhurst clan had achieved high rank and coveted decorations. It had become with me an accepted article of faith that desertion at any time is cowardly, criminal and absolutely without justification, however great the extenuating circumstances may appear to be.

Yet Daphnis' life almost certainly hung upon my speed of action and an immediate decision to throw all that overboard. I continued my way, but thinking more furiously than ever as I went.

From conversations with other officers over lunch at the Club I knew that the British Front was now rapidly dissolving; certain units were being embarked at night, wherever a favourable opportunity offered to get them off, while others were gallantly covering their retreat in a series of desperate rearguard actions. If I made my way up towards Thermopylae I might run into the New Zealanders some time during the next forty-eight hours; but there was quite a possibility that I would fail to locate them or that they had already been evacuated.

I asked myself then what help I could give if I did find them. A spare officer could always make himself useful, either in directing some small local operation or holding the men together during a retreat; but in a day or two at most the party must be over now, and I felt that I was playing absolutely fair in regarding it as only a fifty-fifty chance of my being able to get back to them at all before they were out of Greece.

It seemed then that this was not a question of my deserting a post or a command that had been entrusted to me and abandoning my duty in a crisis on account of my private affairs, but rather as if I was to occupy the next few days before it became imperative that I should leave Greece, if I was to avoid capture, by looking for the New Zealanders or endeavouring to save Daphnis. There was also the indisputable fact that I should not technically be a deserter unless I was absent without leave for more than seven days.

Finally I decided that what really mattered was one's intentions. Desertion in the ordinary sense is an endeavour to escape further military service; but in my case there was no intention of that kind at all. Far from running away, I was about to take on about as desperate a job as one could imagine. No less than an attempt to penetrate to the Field Headquarters of the German General Staff, and if I got away with my life I did not intend to lose a moment in reporting back for routine duties just as soon as I could reach any British military authority.

While facing up to this harassing dilemma I had been hastening along as fast as my legs could carry me towards the Grande Bretagne. When I entered it I felt now what a ghastly blow it would be if old Diamopholus had already left; but the hall-porter relieved my fears by telling me that the shipping magnate was still upstairs in his suite, and after a telephone inquiry I was asked to go up at once.

As I had never told him anything about Daphnis' relations with Mondragora I did not think there was any point in going into that now, particularly as time was so precious.

He was packing when I arrived, and he told me that, although the ship in which he intended to sail had been twice hit by bombs during the day, she was still considered seaworthy. Owing to the constant air raids on the Piraeus, intending passengers had been asked to remain in Athens until ten o'clock, but the evacuation authorities hoped to have them on board and the ship under way by midnight.

I thought that the easiest line to take was that I had learned, purely by chance, from a friend in the British Intelligence Service, that a girl answering Daphnis' description had been living at German Field Headquarters for the past three weeks and moving with it every time Marshal List advanced. I said that the description tallied so well that I had made up my mind to go there and find out, and if it was Daphnis persuade her to come away with me; but that for the purpose I should need a car, a good sum in Greek money in case it was necessary to bribe people, and an outfit of civilian clothes.

Nicholas raised his eyebrows and shook his white head with amazement at my story; but it tied up to some extent with Daphnis' old pro-Italian feelings which were known to him and the fact that on running away she had gone to Sofia, which was in Axis hands.

He said that I was a brave fellow to take such a risk, and he would willingly help me in every way possible. It would be easy for him to go down to the Piraeus in a taxi so I could have his car, and although he feared it would fit very badly I was welcome to a suit of his clothes and any other things of that kind that I required. As for money—he pulled out a fat pocket-book and insisted on giving me notes to the value of a hundred thousand drachma, which is roughly about a hundred and eighty English pounds.

I gave him the attaché-case containing the papers I had taken from von Hentzen, and without saying what they were I impressed upon him that they were important, and asked him to undertake their personal delivery to the duty officer at the British G.H.Q. in Athens. He promised to hand them in before going down to the Piraeus, and the thought that there must be the clues to at least some valuable enemy secrets amongst them made me feel that on account of this *coup* alone I had more than earned the 'French' leave that I was about to take.

Among Nicholas' things I found a plus-four suit of a heather mixture which reeked of Scotland, and I decided on that as, owing to its natural looseness, the disparity between his figure and mine would not be so apparent as if I had worn one of his lounge suits.

While I was packing it with a shirt, shoes, socks, tie, etc., in a spare handbag that he gave me for the purpose, he telephoned the hotel garage giving orders that his car was to be made ready for a long journey, then brought round as soon as possible.

In two stiff whiskies we drank a solemn toast to the downfall of the Axis and the resurrection of Greek independence. Then he accompanied me downstairs. His car proved to be an open six-litre Bentley, and the chauffeur obligingly showed me where the maps, tools, etc., were kept before handing it over. I said good-bye to them, thanked old Nicholas for his help and promised I would do my utmost to let him have news as soon as I possibly could if I succeeded in finding Daphnis.

I had returned to Athens by the railway which runs round Mount Parnes and enters the city from the north-east. The road that follows that route would, I knew, be one of the main lines of retreat used by the British Army. The road to the north-west was much more mountainous and would doubtless also be crowded with retreating troops, but it was the more direct route to Central Greece, so I decided to take it.

Leaving the city by the famous Sacred Way, which is now a broad well-kept motor road passing between rich olive groves, I ran up the hill to Daphni, the little village from which Nicholas' luscious wine had come. As I passed through I remembered it now from my peacetime travels in Greece. To the left of the road there was an ancient ruined monastery with a round-domed church. It was famous for its mosaics of strange wide-eyed Byzantine saints; those thin-lipped emaciated successors of the handsome Apollo and the beautiful Aphrodite who, centuries earlier, had been worshipped in that self-same grove. The tall cypresses beyond the wall of the monastery garden still threw long shadows in the bright late-afternoon light.

Another few miles, down the hill now, and I reached the Bay of Salamis, where the greatest naval battle in ancient history had been fought in 480 B.C., and the Greeks had saved their civilization for countless generations of men by smashing the Persian armada from the East.

The road now ran north along the seashore and it was black with cars. Nine-tenths of the traffic was military, but as it was nearly all coming towards me and the road was broad, I was able to make fairly good going until I reached Eleusis, where to my fury I got stuck for over an hour in a bad traffic jam.

The little town and harbour had been mercilessly bombed, so that many of its modern buildings were hardly to be distinguished from the great area of ancient ruins spread out on the slope of the hill, where once the celebrated Greek mysteries had been performed.

Eleusis was only fourteen miles from Athens, but on entering it I found myself right back in the war zone. Ships of all sizes were in the bay, from quite large liners to the old sailing *caiques* of the Greek fishermen, and nearly all were in constant motion, zig-zagging about to avoid the bombs of the German 'planes, flight after flight of which came roaring overhead. On shore in the fields and gardens, British and Greek troops were taking cover as well as they could during the long wait for the darkness which would conceal them from their enemies while they carried out the tricky business of embarking.

At last I got through the jam of cars and lorries, and turning inland drove on up into the wooded hills. It was Spring and those woods of Attica were indescribably lovely. Their variety seemed endless, and they were sufficiently broken up for vistas of one mossy glade after another to be visible with every twist and turn of the road; but I had no leisure to dwell upon their loveliness now.

After leaving Eleusis the wide way narrows until at times there is barely room on it for two lorries abreast. As it corkscrews higher and higher up into the mountains the precipices become ever more terrifying, for the road has not even a stone kerb at its edge to keep a carelessly driven vehicle from hurtling over to certain destruction many hundreds of feet below.

In normal times there is so little traffic that the road serves its purpose quite adequately; but now it was jammed by the retreating army.

I must say that the drivers behaved splendidly. There was no sign of panic, and as soon as they could they drew in to let me pass; but at every bend I came face to face with more tractors and

254

lorries, so the going was slow and nerve-racking. It did not help matters either that from time to time formations of German aircraft flew over for the specific purpose of harrying the retreat. The bombs they dropped were more frightening than dangerous, as owing to the steep slope of the mountain-side and the continual twisting of the road it was almost impossible to hit it; nine-tenths of the bombs burst a hundred or more feet above or below us. Few casualties were caused by lateral bomb-splinters, but the machine-gunning was about the severest nerve test that any motor-driver could ever be called upon to endure.

Even if the column had halted each time a Nazi 'plane hurtled down spitting fire and lead there was nowhere on the more mountainous stretches for the men to take cover; and if they took their eyes off the road, even for a moment, through ducking as the aircraft roared down, there was a good chance of their running headlong over the precipice. In an hour I saw at least ten Army vehicles go whirling over and over in space; but in most of the cases I think it was due to the fact that the driver had been shot and his companions had not had time to grab the wheel before it was too late.

At last I was through the Pass on the eastern end of Mount Cithaeron and slowly descending the winding road towards Thebes, but, long before I reached the plain darkness had fallen.

There was no moon now, which was a big blessing, as that made it impossible for the Germans to bomb road junctions and the embarking troops with any accuracy during the night hours; but on the other hand it made it infinitely more difficult for the retreating British to keep in touch with each other and find their way along dangerous roads in this, to them, unknown country.

I reached Thebes at about three in the morning, and there I got badly held up again. It, too, had been bombed and was still in flames; a lurid beacon in the dark night. Thebes was on the main-line railway, and it was also the principal junction of the two arterial roads, one to Chalkis in the north-east, and the other running to the north-west, which served the whole of Central Greece. In consequence a great portion of the Imperial Forces was jammed on the far side of the flaming town.

The narrow high street was a raging furnace into which the German aircraft sailing low overhead hurled more and more loads of bombs. It was now utterly impossible for anything to get through. The tanks, caterpillar tractors and walking troops were by-passing the town, but the ditches to be crossed were too steep for cars and lorries, and I knew that if I once got my car stuck that would be the end of any hope of my being able to reach Daphnis. I simply dared not chance taking it off the main road. The only course was to wait until the fire had died down.

For company I had a detachment of British military police who were directing the one-way caterpillar traffic which was coming round the town and shepherding the unfortunate civilians who were fleeing from it. The police were mostly Londoners and splendid fellows. Unshaven, hollow-eyed, weary from days of orderly retreat under hellish fire, they still had not lost their sense of humour and the kindliness that is such a strong feature of the Cockney. Although the Theban townsfolk could not understand a word of English the soldiers talked to them with cheerful unconcern all the same.

"Come on, Mother! I'll take your bag, while you climb on the cart. Steady there, son; what's your hurry? You'll all get to the seaside in time for August Bank Holiday without shoving! Now, miss, it's no good crying. What's your little brother done? Burnt himself? Just stand aside a minute and I'll fix that with my first-aid kit."

Yet somehow the Greeks seemed to sense the meaning, and instead of rioting took their turn calmly for a place in the procession along the crowded road.

I soon realized that it would be several hours before I could get through the town, so having asked one of the police to rouse me when the fire had died down, I curled up on the back seat of the car to snatch a little sleep. He woke me about seven with a welcome mug of strong scalding tea. By daylight I could see that great clouds of black smoke were still billowing up from the houses, but I decided to make an attempt to get through. Having put on my gas-mask and turned on the headlamps of the car, I drove into the pall of spark-filled smoke.

It was one of the most terrifying experiences that I have ever had. I could hardly see more than a yard in front of the headlamps. The air was as hot as the inside of an oven, and I feared that at any moment my clothes might ignite. The street was littered with debris, and I was never quite sure if I was on the road or running into a byway where I should find myself hopelessly lost.

Without the gas-mask it would have been utterly impossible; but that enabled me to breathe without discomfort, which is two-thirds of the battle in facing any fire, and although I was in constant apprehension that the car might be wrecked by a falling girder or the tyres blow up from the heat, I at last bumped my way into clearer air on the far side of the town.

I had hardly congratulated myself on my success when a group of Tommies started yelling at me, and on turning I found that the back seat of the Bentley was on fire. A piece of burning rafter had fallen on it; but the men gave me a hand and we soon had the flames out.

The road now ran north-west again through flattish country, but the way was even more crowded with troops than it had been the night before. All through the morning I was compelled to crawl along it, leaving first Mount Cithaeron and then the splendid Mount Helicon on my right.

By midday I reached Lavadia. The little market town was not on the railway, and although it had been repeatedly bombed it had not yet been burnt out. I had had no breakfast and no dinner the previous night, so it was now nearly twenty-four hours since I had eaten. With the idea of getting a meal I pulled up the car in the open square in front of the one hotel. As I got out the dark sturdy-looking proprietor, who was standing in front of it, shook his head and waved me back, the obvious inference being that the soldiers had already eaten and drunk him out of everything. Nevertheless when I spoke to him in Greek and begged him to tell me where I might stand a chance of getting any sort of meal, he came forward, courteously removing his hat, and said that if I could make do on goat's milk cheese and black olives he would furnish me with them; but that I must come down to his cellar. Otherwise, if I were seen eating at one of the tables in the restaurant which faced on to the open street, he would be invaded, and as it was he had barely enough food left to keep himself and his family alive for a week. After that . . . He shrugged eloquently.

I accompanied him down to a cool cellar where with thick slices of home-made bread I ate some of the cheese and washed it down with a pint of dark yellow, incredibly harsh, resin-flavoured wine. Naturally I wanted to pay for my meal, but the proprietor would not allow me to. He was pleased to come across an Englishman who spoke Greek well enough to explain to him a little of what was going on, and like all the other Greeks with whom I had talked, he showed a complete conviction that in due course the cause of freedom must triumph.

From Lavadia I had a choice of two roads, and decided to take the more southern as, although it was slightly more hilly, it was likely to be less congested. All through the Friday afternoon I climbed steadily up into the mountains again, ever higher and higher, winding my way through rugged desolate gorges of fantastic grandeur, until at last, at about five o'clock, I saw ahead on my right a grassy shelf in the mountain-side covered with tumbled ruins. Among them, facing the valley, was a semi-circular open theatre with seats of stone, and the still standing portico of a temple. I knew then that I had reached Delphi, at one time regarded as the centre of the ancient world, and from which the priestesses of the Pythaeon Apollo used to act as the Voice of an Oracle that often governed the fate of kings and nations.

Half a mile further on I entered the town, which consists of little more than one long street straggling along the mountain face. To the left, far, far below, I could now see the little port of Itea, and I noticed that this also was being used for the embarkation. Khaki-clad figures were straggling down through the myrtle on the cliff-side and ships waited on that wine-dark sea, where once the argosies of Jason and Odysseus had proudly sailed.

Turning inland now and north again, I went up and up still further, until I reached the little town of Amphissa, then on, as darkness fell, along the never-ending valley. It must have been about half past ten when, on rounding a bend of the road, I saw a bright beam of light sweep to and fro for a moment, apparently some distance ahead; but it proved to be less than half a mile away. I reached it much sooner than I expected and found that it was caused by a man waving a torch slowly backwards and forwards over a wide arc.

It was hours now since I had seen any British troops except for a few stragglers, so I felt certain that this must be a Greek Fifth Columnist signalling to the advancing Germans. Stopping the car as I drew level, I pulled out my gun and called in Greek: "Hi, you! Come here!"

As the figure approached I saw that it wore British battledress, so I said sharply in English: "What the hell are you doing with that light? You'll have a Nazi night-hawk machine-gunning you if you wave it about like that."

A quiet voice answered me. "Oh yes, they do. About every quarter of an hour; but fortunately one man doesn't present much of a target in the dark."

"But, good God, man!" I exclaimed, staring at the white blob which in the darkness was all that I could see of the face of this apparent maniac. "What's the idea? Surely you don't want to get yourself killed. Yet you're certainly going the right way about it."

258

"Perhaps," he said mildly. "But, you see, from this point the light can be seen for many miles, and four tracks meet here. By turning myself into a lighthouse I'm able to guide some of our stragglers in."

"I see," I said a little weakly. "Who—who are you?"

He chuckled. "Oh, just one of the 'Gilded Staff'. Once Operations ceased to function I was left with time on my hands. As I had no men to look after I thought I'd stay behind and collect a few. But who are you? And where are you off to in that fine Bentley?"

"I'm an Intelligence merchant," I said, "and I've got a job to do." As I spoke I let in the clutch and roared away. I had no intention of being ordered back by a senior officer, and I should have hated to have had to enter into a fracas with such a splendid fellow.

It has been suggested, in view of events in Norway and France, that some of our General Staff are not overburdened with brains; and quite definitely the one thing they hate most in all the world is any form of 'advertising'. That is unfortunate, because that word, more than any other, embodies the qualities of imagination, modernity, originality, speed and drive; but when it comes to a real showdown they are absolutely unbeatable for their calm, unassuming courage and refusal to be stampeded.

As I drove on into the night it made me just a little bit prouder of my own race to think of that gallant English gentleman standing there on the northern slope of Mount Parnassus making himself a target for enemy bombs and machine-gun bullets in the hope of guiding a few stray soldiers that he did not even know, but who for all that were 'his men', whatever country or Dominion they had come from, on to the road which might lead them to safety and to home.

I was tired now, damnably tired. Apart from my spell of sleep in the car outside Thebes I had been on the go ever since I got out of bed at the Officers' Club on Thursday morning, and it was now nearly midnight on Friday; but I knew that I had a long way to go yet and that there could be no letting up.

For the next ten miles I may have passed a few stragglers in the dark, but I saw no one, although from time to time 'planes droned overhead and from the mountain bends I could sometimes catch glimpses of burning villages. Soon after midnight I decided that I must be nearing the German advance units, so I pulled the car in on a grassy space beside the road, where it widened slightly, got out my borrowed suit of plus-fours, changed into it and hid my uniform under the back seat of the Bentley. Then I drove on again.

It was about two in the morning and I was approaching Velukhi when I heard the sound of rifle- and machine-gun fire. Proceeding at a more cautious speed, I reached the outskirts of the town and was challenged in English. As I pulled up, two figures in battledress loomed up out of the darkness and asked me who I was and where I was going. It was a sergeant who questioned me and he had a broad Scots accent. I told him that I was a British Intelligence Officer and that I was going straight through into the German-occupied territory on a special mission. Of course I did not expect him to believe that, so I tipped up the back of the car and showed him my uniform. That satisfied him of my *bona fides* all right, and we had a cigarette together while I asked him what prospects there were of my getting through the town.

He said that he thought I had better wait a bit as the Highland Battalion to which he belonged was fighting a rearguard action there; but that when the Jerries had been beaten off his unit would be retreating again and I would have a fair chance then to push on without being shot.

I waited on the roadside for about half an hour, then the firing died down, and a little later the remnants of that gallant Scots battalion passed me in the darkness, making their way back to put up another stand in the next village or mountain gorge which offered a good chance for a delaying action.

In a casual conversational way the sergeant had told me a little of what they had been through since they had been thrown in to cover the retreat, and I wondered if they would get a line in the English papers. I didn't think it likely because I had followed the news of our other campaigns in Libya and Abyssinia too closely. Just as in the last war, the people who handle our propaganda seem to think that the Dominions won't play unless they are given all the praise for every action in which Empire troops participate.

There were many more Home troops than Overseas troops both in Libya and Greece, and in both cases there was nothing to choose between the severity of the fighting which each was called upon to face; yet to read the newspaper accounts one might have imagined that all the men from Scotland and Wales, Devon and Yorkshire, Liverpool and London, the Home Counties, the Midlands and the North were just sitting sunning themselves in Cairo and Jerusalem, which was wickedly and criminally wrong.

Quite apart from any question of unfairness it gave the whole world outside Britain the impression that we were prepared to fight only to the last Australian, New Zealander, or South African; and that, although Britain might be standing up to the air raids all right, her men were too effete to have any real offensive spirit, so they were just doing garrison duty while the Dominion troops were left to do the dirty work. It was difficult to conceive a policy calculated to do more damage to our cause in wavering neutral countries, in the United States, and above all in the Dominions themselves.

I gave the Highlanders ten minutes to get away, then I drove slowly on into the village, hooting my Klaxon as I went.

"Wer ist denn dort?" rang out a challenge, and as I pulled up a little group of Germans armed with tommy-guns ran towards me. I greeted them with a *"Heil Hitler"* and produced von Hentzen's special pass. An officer was sent for, and for a few minutes I waited in the acutest possible anxiety to know if they would let me through or if they would search the car, find the uniform and have me shot; but to my intense relief the pass acted as a magic wand. The moment the officer saw it he handed it back to me, saluted politely and waved to his men to let me through.

I was stopped four more times within the next two miles, but each time directly someone in authority had seen the pass I was allowed to proceed and even treated with deference. As usual the German organization was so good that all junior officers evidently had detailed instructions with regard to these special passes, so that there should not be a moment's unnecessary delay in their agents or important fifth columnists who had such passes carrying on their work of bringing in vital ingelligence.

In the early hours of the morning I made much better going, and just as dawn was breaking I arrived outside the considerable town of Trikkala. It had been badly blitzed, but many houses were still intact, and there seemed to be a great deal of activity going on there. Some of the Greek townsfolk had been formed into labour gangs by the Germans and were at work on repairing roofs and clearing up. German troops swarmed everywhere and numerous Staff cars were constantly running in and out of the town while patrolling aeroplanes kept watch overhead; so it was evidently an important headquarters. I was challenged twice, but the magic pass still worked, and on clearing the town I settled down to do my last fifty miles to Ventsa.

In the country through which I was now passing there was

ample evidence of the desperate battle which had been fought across it and the terrific punishment that our men had inflicted on the enemy. Hardly a farmstead was left standing and round their shells there were almost always more German than British corpses. In one gorge the bridge had been blown up and the river was spanned by a temporary structure made by the German pioneers, and the enemy dead were lying in heaps where our machine-guns must have swathed them down just before the bridge was blasted; and in a wood on the south side of the Aliakamon I came upon a most extraordinary sight. It was the aftermath of a great tank battle. At least fifty wrecked German tanks were lying there, and as far as I could see only six of ours; so it looked as though our fellows had led the Nazis into a trap, luring them towards a spot where, concealed among the trees, we had had a number of carefully planted anti-tank guns.

During that last stretch I was very, very weary; not so much from many hours' consistent driving, as I had had to pull up many times, often for considerable periods, since leaving Athens, but from cumulative lack of sleep during the past three weeks; yet I was buoyed up by the fact that, if my luck held, within an hour or two now I would have found Daphnis. At eight o'clock on the Saturday morning I re-crossed the river Aliakamon, which we had defended with so much blood and sweat, and by half past I was running into Ventsa.

As I did so my heart sank. It was not on account of the fact that the town had been blitzed, because nearly every town in Northern Greece had suffered that fate, but the place was practically deserted; except for five truckloads of German soldiers there was no one there and not a sign of a headquarters.

Halting the car I called a *Feldwebel* from one of the trucks over to me, showed him the pass and asked him the whereabouts of Marshal List's headquarters. He told me at once that they had moved the preceding night and that he and his men were the rear party who had been left to clear up. Field G.H.Q. was now at Trikkala.

I was almost too tired to curse myself for a fool, but curse I did. Common sense should have told me that, now British resistance had virtually ceased, the German G.H.Q. would be moved forward more quickly than was allowed for in their original plans; and if I had had my wits about me I should have realized that all the cars and activity in the town through which I had passed just after dawn could hardly be anything else but Marshal List's headquarters. Now I had to go all the way back there, and through my stupidity in coming on to Ventsa without bothering to make any inquiry I had added many hours to my journey.

Having thanked the sergeant I turned the car round and pulled it up at the side of the street while I considered what to do. I would have given a great deal to be able to sleep again, but I knew that I dared not.

I had left Athens at five o'clock in the afternoon, whereas Mondragora had declared his intention of leaving it at about three o'clock the following morning. That should have given me ten hours' clear start. But apart from shorter halts I had been caught in the traffic jam at Eleusis for an hour, stopped by the fire at Thebes for five, and had lost another two by coming on to Ventsa unnecessarily. That was eight hours of my lead lost already. True it was pretty certain that Mondragora would not get through the battle zone without meeting serious checks here and there; but I now had only two hours' clear lead over him, and it was going to take me all of that to get back to Trikkala.

With sudden apprehension I realized that in the unlikely event of his getting a clear run he might arrive there before me, and that in any case it was going to be a neck-to-neck race. Flinging aside the cigarette, I let in the clutch and settled down to drive like hell.

As I sped south back across the battlefield I made better time than I had on my northward journey. All night long and through the early hours of the morning one-half of the road had been an almost unbroken column of German troop formations moving into Greece; but although there was little danger to them now from aerial attack, as a matter of routine the great majority of them had pulled off the road into the woods and narrower gorges to feed and sleep during the daylight hours. Shortly after ten o'clock I was back in Trikkala.

I parked the car with a number of others in a small orchard just outside the town, showed my pass at a police post which had been established at its entrance, and walked down the main street. I knew that I was now entering upon the really dangerous part of my undertaking. It was most unlikely that more than one in several thousand officers and men in the German Army happened to know the Baron Feldmar von Hentzen personally; but here, at Field Headquarters, it was a very different matter. Although comparatively few of the ordinary military police might know him, a good proportion of the Intelligence officers and German General Staff definitely would. Therefore to pose as him here meant taking my life in my hands.

Yet how else could I hope to find Daphnis but by making inquiries for Mondragora, and it was quite certain that no German officer or man was going to give a civilian any information unless he produced some form of pass. Another matter for acute uneasiness was that, although I spoke German fluently, I was extremely doubtful if my accent was good enough for me to pass as a German in any conversation which consisted of more than a few formal sentences.

On second thoughts I decided that I could do neither Daphnis nor myself any good by risking being shot to start off with, so I had better see how far I could get by pretending to be a Greek fifth columnist before burning my boats by impersonating the Baron.

Considering that the soldiers and N.C.O.s were less likely to be inquisitive and dangerous than the officers, I spoke to several until I found one who could direct me to the quarters of the Intelligence section, with which Mondragora would undoubtedly be working. It was located in a large private house on the northern outskirts of the town and no great distance from the place in which I had parked my car.

On arriving there I tackled the sentry on the gate, but he had never heard of Count Emilo de Mondragora, and he called up his N.C.O. The *unter-offizier* knew Mondragora by sight but said that he had not seen him for the best part of a week, and had no idea where he was or if he would return. He then demanded my papers.

I told him that I was a Greek who had been working with Mondragora and that I had arrived with information which I was prepared to give only to him; but that I had no papers as the filthy British had arrested me in their lines and taken my papers from me, after which I had only just managed to escape with my life.

I was led through the garden into the house, and put in a guardroom for half an hour, then taken out and led before a fat bespectacled captain, to whom I repeated my story.

"Mondragora left us on Tuesday," he said at once, "and we're expecting him back some time today. In the meantime you had better give me your information."

This I refused to do, saying that only Mondragora and the Baron von Hentzen were in a position to assess the value of the information that I had brought, as this hinged entirely upon other data already in their possession.

The name von Hentzen evidently impressed the captain, as his eyes lifted quickly on my mention of it, and I thanked my stars that I had not been rash enough to pose as the Baron.

Before the captain had time to reply I added, apparently as an afterthought, that one other person who had the data was the young woman who had been acting as the Count's secretary. If I might be taken to her I was willing to talk at once.

With a beating heart I waited for the reply, but the captain shook his head. "I know the young woman you mean. Mondragora got a special permit for her to accompany him on the campaign. But she is not here, and I have not seen her for some time—not since we left Monastir."

I felt sick with disappointment; but I realized that my only chance of finding Daphnis lay in sticking to Mondragora's trail, so I said that I would wait for him. I added that I was very hungry and desperately tired, so I would be grateful if he would give me a chit enabling me to buy some food at the nearest canteen and let me spend the time waiting for Mondragora in some place where I could get a sleep.

My mention of von Hentzen and Daphnis had evidently established my *bona fides* in the captain's eyes, as, summoning an orderly, he told the man to take me to the Intelligence section canteen, where I was to have anything I wanted and that afterwards I was to be given a shakedown in the orderly's sleeping-quarters.

In the canteen I made a passable meal and half an hour later, when the orderly returned for me, I told him that it was of the utmost importance that I should see the Count the moment that he arrived back. I then gave the man a handsome present out of Diamopholus' money to be personally responsible for coming along to rouse me without delay.

That the captain had not seen Daphnis since the Headquarters had moved from Monastir was horribly disquieting, but Mondragora had said quite definitely in Athens that she was still working with him, so I could only hope that the captain was wrong and that she was perhaps actually quartered in one of the houses only a few hundred yards from me.

My own position was now extremely precarious, as if Mondragora arrived while I was sleeping and the captain sent him straight along to see me, or if I could find no way of evading being taken up to him, the moment we came face to face he would recognize me, and the fat would then be in the fire. I was a British officer who had penetrated into the German Headquarters by disguising himself in civilian clothes and posing as a Greek fifth columnist, so it would be a brick wall and a shooting-party for me without even the formality of a trial.

In spite of my new grounds for anxiety about Daphnis and my now considerable perturbation on my own account, I was so tired after my long journey that I soon fell asleep and I got in the best part of six hours. It was after six o'clock in the evening when the orderly came to rouse me with the news that Mondragora had just arrived and was now with the captain.

I said that as soon as he had finished with the captain I must see him, but in the meantime I'd be glad if I could have a wash to freshen myself up; so the man led me out of the back of the house to the stables, where some canvas troughs had been fixed up for the ordinary soldiers to wash in.

I was wondering agitatedly now if, in order to get free of the man, I would have to knock him out, but fortunately he saved me the trouble by saying: "When you've done you know the way up. You'll find me in the passage, and I expect they'll send for you when they want you."

Immediately his back was turned I began to dry my hands, and the moment he had disappeared into the house I slipped out of the stable. Walking swiftly down a short path that was screened with bushes, I climbed out over the garden wall.

As he was a civilian and had a woman secretary travelling with him, I thought it unlikely that Mondragora would have quarters with the officers and more probable that a billet would have been allotted to him in one of the houses near by. There was at least a chance that Daphnis was already there, waiting for his return; so clearly my next move was to keep an unremitting watch on the big villa, where the Intelligence staff was quartered, and follow Mondragora wherever he went when he came out of it.

I found a good place among some bushes in the next-door garden from which I could just see over the wall without much risk of being spotted myself, and I settled down to wait there with such patience as I could muster.

My wait proved so long that although I had kept my eyes riveted on the front door of the house, I began to feel a rising sense of panic from imagining that somehow or other I must have taken them off it for just a moment while the Count walked out, or else that he had gone out of the back entrance and that I'd lost him. But I could only hang on there; and thank God I did, as at a little after eight he appeared on the porch, walked swiftly down the stone steps, across the front garden and out of the gate.

Cautiously emerging from my hiding-place I was about to follow when I saw him cross a small open space towards his car, which was parked under some trees. My own car was in the orchard, not very far off, so giving the sentry on the gate of the Intelligence H.Q. a wide berth I made my way as quickly as I could to the orchard. By the time I reached my car, Mondragora was already in his and just driving it on to the main road. He did not turn towards the town, but north towards the open country, and slipping in my clutch I followed.

Very soon we had left all the houses of Trikkala behind and were covering the same ground that I had crossed early that morning. A sudden conviction seized me that I was on the right track at last. Mondragora had made his report, but the captain was right and Daphnis was not in Trikkala. She had been left in some town further back, and Mondragora was now going either to rejoin or collect her. I felt absolutely certain of it.

Although twilight had fallen there were nothing like as many troops on the road this Saturday night as there had been on the preceding night, but I imagine the Germans must have realized by now that their victory was complete, so there was no point in their bringing additional formations further south into the peninsula. Darkness fell, the stars came out and by half past ten we were just approaching Ventsa.

It had been an anxious business keeping on Mondragora's tail, in case he turned off up some side-road, but I had never lost him for more than a few minutes, and now I put on speed to close up with him in case he left the main road somewhere in the town. As he entered it I was not fifty yards behind him and could make out his car quite clearly in spite of the uncertain light. He slowed up, then halted in front of an unblitzed building in the main street. I passed him and pulled up a hundred yards further on. When I turned to look back he was on the pavement and just going into the house. I got out of my car and walked back along the street.

The place was strangely and sinisterly silent. It is true that nine-tenths of the buildings in the little town had been either blown down or burnt out; but one would have thought that the owners of those still standing would have remained and the homeless among the townsfolk have sought shelter with them; but not a soul was to be seen and not a light showed anywhere. Perhaps the Greek civilians here had put up a resistance and fired upon the Germans. If so the Nazis had probably machine-gunned the whole population—men, women and children—as a reprisal, and that would account for the 'city of the dead' effect which the place had upon me.

I was within about forty yards of the doorway into which Mondragora had disappeared when I saw a small figure come out of it and turn in my direction. Swiftly I stepped back into the shadows of a great semi-circular arch, which led to the courtyard of a burnt-out house. My one glimpse had been enough to tell me that the child was a boy, and from his height I judged him to be only about eleven years old. Waiting there in the darkness I held my breath until he passed, then with one swift movement I grabbed him and muffled his startled cry by clapping my thick driving-glove over his mouth.

"Listen, sonny," I said in Greek in a low voice. "There's nothing to be frightened about. I promise I won't hurt you but there are one or two things that I want you to tell me about that house that you've just come out of. Is there a lady there—a young lady with dark hair who's very lovely?"

I eased my hand off the child's mouth so that he could reply, and he said in a deeper voice than I had expected: "Who are you? Why should I tell you anything?"

"Now look here, I don't want to hurt you," I said in a stern voice. "But I'm in a hurry and I may have to unless you tell me what I want to know."

"I won't tell you beastly Germans anything," cried the child, wriggling like a worm in his efforts to get away.

This defiance from such a mite struck me as so strange that grasping him firmly by the scruff of the neck with one hand I got out my lighter with the other and flicked it on to have a look at him. I saw then that he was older than I had thought—possibly about fourteen or fifteen—but he was a hunchback. The poor little fellow's head was twisted on one side and his face was not that of a child. Although young it was wizened like an old woman's, but it was relieved by a pair of remarkably beautiful and intelligent brown eyes. Those eyes had something fine and strong and compelling about them, so that quite instinctively I altered my manner towards their owner.

"What's your name?" I asked gently.

"Tino."

"Then listen, Tino, I'm a great friend of the lovely lady whom I believe to be in that house. She's a Greek. I'm not a Greek, as you guessed, but on the other hand I'm not a German nor an Italian, and I've come all the way from Athens to try to rescue her from your country's enemies."

"What are you if you're not a German?" he asked suspiciously.

"I'm English," I replied quietly.

But he was not satisfied and said: "The English soldiers were here for some time, and I know how they swear. If you're English you must prove yourself by swearing to me as they swear."

I let him have a choice selection of English swear words, and the grin spread over his funny tilted little face.

"All right," he said. "I'll tell you now. The lady's in the cellar. She's been here for a week. She was kind to me, so I stayed to look after her."

"Well done, Tino," I murmured, giving his arm a little friendly shake. "I'll see you don't lose by that; but is she well—quite well?"

He nodded. "She's very well, but she's worried. She wants to get back to her own people, but these devils won't let her go, and there's no way that a lovely lady like that could get through the battle zone all on her own."

"Never mind, Tino." I was laughing now. "We'll fix that somehow. Is there anyone else in the house except the tall thin man who's just arrived?"

"No," he said. "No one. He's sent me out to see if I can find a chicken remaining in one of the hen-houses, because he's hungry and wants a meal."

"Right-o," I said. "Try to get your chicken. Then you and I and the lady will eat it. I don't think the man will be there if you come back in about half an hour."

He flashed me a smile and was gone—a small crooked shadow —into the darkness. Immediately he had disappeared I got out my gun, made quite certain that it was fully loaded and slipped back the safety-catch. I knew all I wanted to know, and as far as I was concerned there wasn't going to be any argument. Tiptoeing down the street, I gently lifted the latch of the front door and entered the house.

CHAPTER XXIII

DEATH FOR TWO

THE house had a small hallway. It was in darkness, but a faint streak of light came from under a door on my right a little way down the passage. No light had shown from the street, so the window of the room must, I knew, be carefully blacked out. I paused for a moment to listen. No sound broke the stillness. I tiptoed forward and felt about very carefully until I found the knob of the door. Very gently I turned it, then holding my gun in front of me I jerked it open. The room was empty.

It was the sort of sitting-room that might have belonged to a small landowner in a provincial town, and had now been converted into an office. There were a few nice bits of old furniture, but most of the stuff was indifferent and well worn. In one corner there was a pile of broken glass and china. The fragments of the ornaments had been swept up there, after having been flung from their places and broken by the concussion of the bombs. On the table stood a typewriter, some baskets with letters in them and several files. The room was lit by an oil-lamp which dangled from the ceiling.

I gently drew the door to and eased my way down the passage. Round a corner another streak of light showed under a second door, and as I listened again I could hear movements.

Again I found the door-handle, turned it gingerly, then flung the door open. It was a roomy kitchen and Mondragora was there, standing near the big old-fashioned range. He had evidently been stoking it up as a preliminary to cooking himself a meal.

I saw the fear spring into his dark eyes as he recognized me and realized that he was trapped; but I did not give him time to speak. Poor Carruthers' suicide, the fact that he was an Axis spy, and a hundred other crimes, in addition to his being my personal enemy, made this no matter for gloating triumph or a trial, but only for an execution. I squeezed the trigger of my pistol and gave him three bullets in the stomach. As he collapsed with a single wailing cry I put a fourth through his head. He lay twitching for a moment on the kitchen floor, then it was all over.

I left him lying there and found the entrance to the cellar. It was through a heavy wooden door at the far end of the hall. As I opened the door and looked down the curving stone steps I saw that it was already faintly lit by an old beaten copper oil-lamp, which stood upon a rough table. Beside it in a corner on a pile of rugs Daphnis was lying sound asleep.

My heart brimming over with joy, I tiptoed down the worn stone stairs towards her. She was sleeping quite soundly, and it was hardly surprising that she had not been roused by my shots. As she had accompanied Mondragora on the road south through Yugoslavia with German Field Headquarters, for several weeks past she must have been both night and day within the sound of exploding bombs and the crash of guns.

I knelt down beside her, anxious to prolong this perfect moment of achievement in finding her at last before I woke her and relished the full joy of our reunion. It was then, while I was kneeling there, that I heard a sound above me and turned to find von Hentzen standing in the doorway with his automatic pistol trained on her.

Next second the pistol spurted flame; the whole cellar seemed to rock with the deafening thunder of its repeated explosions. Before I could draw my pistol the bullets thudded into the pile of rugs where Daphnis lay.

As she jerked up, her eyes staring, her mouth open, I sprang to my feet, and wrenching my gun from my pocket dashed up the stairs. But von Hentzen was too quick for me. I heard his pistol, which was now levelled at me, click once, then realizing it was empty he stepped back and flung the heavy door to.

I hurled my weight against it, but I heard him ram the thick wooden staple through its socket and knew that I was caught; yet that mattered nothing. My movements had been impelled only by the instinct to endeavour to exact instant vengeance. In any case, I should not have followed him further than the hallway; my whole mind was distraught with fear for Daphnis. Turning, I plunged down the cellar stairs again towards her.

She was lying still now, but groaning slightly. As I knelt beside her she opened her eyes and murmured: "Darling, it can't be you. I'm dreaming."

"It is," I choked. "I came to Greece weeks ago praying that I'd find you, and I've come to take you back. But, oh God, you're wounded!"

As I lifted back the soft wrap of white angora wool which covered her, my feelings were beyond description. My beautiful beloved was already lying in a pool of blood. Steeling my nerves, as gently as I could I made a swift examination. In the upper part of her thighs she had five bullet-wounds, and I felt sure that there must be others in her pelvis. Von Hentzen had emptied the whole contents of his automatic into her, which meant eight or nine shots.

"We must get a doctor," I gasped; but even as I spoke I remembered that we were bolted in. Covering Daphnis again, I dashed back up the stairs and hammered on the door with my clenched fists, calling upon von Hentzen—yes, and even pleading

271

with him—to let me out so that I could get a doctor and save my love from death.

There was no reply. My own shouts and thumpings echoed back through the empty house. He had gone. With heavy feet I slumped downstairs again. What could I do? No tourniquet could serve to staunch the bleeding of such wounds. What *could* I do?

In her first convulsion Daphnis had heaved herself up so that she was lying half-twisted on her side. Taking her gently in my arms I sought to lay her down again flat on her back so that she would be more comfortable, and she clung to me, moaning out my name.

When I got her straight I thought the best thing was to raise her legs in order that the blood should not flow down into them so easily. Making a great bolster of some spare rugs, I slid my hand under her knees and lifted them to push it in. As I did so she screamed with pain and suddenly went limp.

For a second I thought that she was dead, but she had only fainted, and I took the opportunity while she was unconscious to arrange the bolster to the best advantage. At the far end of the cellar I noticed a cabin trunk. Rummaging into it, I selected two light dresses. One of them I tore into wide strips and tied tightly round her upper thighs; the other I afterwards bound round the whole middle of her body.

When she came to she asked me who it was that had shot her. She had seen nothing but the flashes of the pistol.

I told her, and for the first time had a moment to wonder at von Hentzen's sudden appearance there. But I recalled his declared intention of leaving Athens to enter it again in triumph, dressed in his uniform, with the German General Staff. Directly he had got free he must have set out for Trikkala. On reaching there he had probably seen the Intelligence captain and learnt from him of the Greek fifth columnist who had inquired so urgently that morning for Mondragora, then disappeared. Von Hentzen would have put two and two together in a flash, realized that the fifth columnist had been myself, and Mondragora's danger; and followed hard on our heels in an attempt to save his friend and prevent my obtaining any information from Daphnis.

"But why—why should he shoot me?" she asked faintly.

"Because his agents in Alex found you out, darling. They knew that you were trying to double-cross them for my sake."

"So—so you knew—that?"

I nodded. "That swine Cozelli told me. Oh, bless you for your bravery! But the moment I knew what he'd done I realized that you'd never have a chance."

"But I succeeded," she murmured. "I've been trying—trying to get back for weeks. I did get the information which would let us both out." She paused for a moment, then went on: "It was in the middle of March, soon after—after I got to Sofia. They'd planned an insurrection in Iraq. Rashid Ali was to lead it and the Grand Mufti was to play a big part."

I groaned. In mid-March that information would have been invaluable to us, but the revolt had taken place on the 3rd of April—over three weeks ago. All her courage and her skill had proved useless after all, and Cozelli's plan to use her had only ended in this soul-shattering nightmare. The irony and utter futility of it were enough to drive one crazy.

There was a noise up at the door. Somebody was pulling back the wooden staple. Springing to my feet, I drew my gun, thinking it was von Hentzen coming back; but as the door opened I saw that it was the little hunchback. I had forgotten all about him.

He came crabwise down the stairs, carrying a dead chicken by the neck. His eyes were wide but not frightened as he saw the great splash of blood that had seeped up through the white wool covering, and I knew that unless von Hentzen had removed it the boy must also have seen Mondragora's body upstairs.

Suddenly my heart flamed with new hope. Unexpectedly he had freed us. "A doctor!" I cried. "We must get a doctor at once! D'you know where one lives?"

"No, master," he said in a voice which I now realized was low and musical. He looked sadly towards the corner where Daphnis lay. "The town is empty. Everyone is either killed or gone."

"I've got the car," I said swiftly. "You must stay here while I drive off and find one." My thoughts were racing again. I might have to drive some distance, but sooner or later I should meet German troops and they would be certain to have army doctors with them. Even if I had to tell the truth and surrender myself as a prisoner, what did that matter if only I could save Daphnis' life? All through these past agonizing minutes I had known that, unless I could secure professional help, she would certainly be dead from loss of blood before morning.

But as I started towards the stairs she called to me, and her voice was stronger than it had been.

"Julian—don't go—don't leave me! You may be away for hours—and by the time you get back . . ."

I turned and stared at her in miserable hesitation. She nodded

273

slowly. "It's no good, darling. He got me through the middle—as well as through the legs. A doctor couldn't save me. I haven't very long to live."

Desperately I tried to persuade myself that she was wrong, but I knew that she was right. Still worse, I had the horrible suspicion that she also had bullets in her lower stomach, which meant that she would have a very painful death; but there was one way in which I could make things easier for her. With my uniform, under the seat of the car, I had my first-aid pack, and in it I had always carried triple the ordinary issue of morphia.

The little hunchback had knelt down beside her and was holding her hand.

"This is Tino," she said slowly. "He—he's been very good to me and he's very, very brave. He wouldn't go when they—when they evacuated the other children; and—and when the people who had survived the blitz ran off into the woods he came back —to help the wounded. That's how we found him."

"Stay there a moment, Tino," I said. "I'm going to get something from the car." Running upstairs and out of the house, I collected my first-aid kit, then before returning to the cellar I got a bowl of water and some towels from the kitchen.

When I got back, Daphnis was lying silent with her eyes closed and Tino was still kneeling beside her.

There was always a chance that a German unit, arriving by night, might take over the remaining houses in the town for billets, so I told Tino to go upstairs, put all the lights out in the house, and remain on watch in the hall so that he could warn me if anyone was approaching. Without a word he shuffled quickly sideways up the steps and I took his place.

Daphnis opened her eyes again and said, "How did you manage to—find me, Julian?"

I gave her an outline of all that had happened since I had learned from Cozelli that he had sent her to Greece, and afterwards she said with a little smile:

"Poor darling, I—I'm so sorry I've got to die. It's—it's so hard on you."

I had to turn my face away because the tears were streaming down my cheeks.

For a little time she was silent, then she began to groan and I gave her some of the morphia. I knew now that the time to say good-bye was very near. To save her from her agony I must dope her into unconsciousness, and once the drug had taken full effect she would never be able to speak to me any more.

After the morphia had eased her pain, she rallied a little and said quite suddenly:

"I hate the half of me that is Italian now. I've seen—seen the things that the Axis have done to Greece. It—it's been simply terrible, Julian. They've no mercy—none at all. You were right. Some—somehow you must finish the Dictators—otherwise there'll never be free people, or—or laughter, in the world any more."

Soon her poor mouth was twisting again, and great beads of sweat were standing out on her broad forehead. The black curls were damp with it and clung to her temples. As I wiped away the sweat and laid a towel soaked in cold water across her head I swore that I'd devote my life not only to seeking vengeance against von Hentzen for the frightful thing he had done, but to killing or breaking the brutal spirit of his countrymen wherever I might find them.

Daphnis' groans grew louder, and at last she moaned, "Can —can I have some more of the morphia?"

Without replying I gave her some. Her breathing gradually grew less laboured, and with an effort she spoke again. "You never told me what happened to the Count—after you traced him."

I gave a mirthless laugh and said: "He's upstairs in the kitchen. I've filled the swine full of lead."

The grip of her damp hand suddenly tightened on mine. She opened her eyes and stared at me as she whispered, "You—you killed him?"

I nodded. "Yes. For the past hour he's been stone-dead."

"The fortune-teller was right," she murmured. "A sword—the Sword of Fate—lay between us. We—were never meant to marry. Even if—if von Hentzen hadn't shot me we couldn't have, after that."

"Why?" I asked in a puzzled voice.

"Perhaps—perhaps I should have told you. Count Emilo was —my father."

"But, darling!" I exclaimed, aghast. "He wasn't an Italian— but a Portuguese."

She shook her head very slowly. "He took—took Portuguese nationality ten—years—ago; at—at Mussolini's orders. So that in the event of—of a war he could serve Italy better as—as a neutral."

Fate had indeed dealt harshly with us. I knew that Daphnis could only be one of the thousands of men and women who must be dying in Greece that night; yet that did not make the death of

275

this young and lovely girl who was on the threshold of life one whit less tragic; and for me it was the irony of ironies that this, the one woman I had ever really loved, should be the daughter of my mortal enemy. The Sword of Fate *had* lain between us.

The second dose of morphia had still proved insufficient to more than temporarily dull her pain. After another ten minutes had passed I had to steel myself to give her a third and larger dose, which I knew must prove fatal.

Her pitiful whimpering gradually died away and I could see that she was getting drowsy. The heavy lids were drooping over her eyes, though she strove to keep them open. A few more precious minutes went by in silence; then she rallied for the last time.

"Darling," she muttered with a great effort. "I was ready to betray my father—to save you from prison. And—and—you risked disgrace to come and find me. We must have loved each other—very dearly."

There was a little pause before she whispered, "Kiss me, darling."

I kissed her very gently on the mouth. Then she fell asleep.

How long I remained crouched there on the ground beside her I've no idea, but eventually the hunchback boy roused me by coming to the door at the top of the stairs to ask if there was anything that he could get for us. I found then that the clasp of Daphnis' fingers was already stiffening round my own. I felt her heart for a long moment, and there was not a flutter beneath my hand. She was quite dead.

I crossed her hands upon her breast and drew the coverlet up over them; but I did not cover her lovely face, which now had a calm serene beauty. Kissing her for the last time, I picked up the lamp from the table and followed the hunchback upstairs.

After routing round in the kitchen for a bit, where Mondragora's dead body still lay, I found a hammer and some nails. With them I nailed up the cellar door. I had no means of securing Daphnis' proper burial and nothing would have induced me to consign her to the bare earth; but I knew that now the Germans had completed the conquest of Greece some form of order would soon be restored. Nailing up the door would prevent any casual looters from disturbing Daphnis' body to see if she had any jewels concealed on her. In due course the townsfolk would return and I felt certain that they would find a priest to bury her in the churchyard.

Tino asked me if there was anything that he could do for me, but I told him 'No', and that he had better go upstairs to get some sleep. Going into the front room, I left the door open so that I should hear anyone who might approach along the street, and sitting down there I tried to think.

Four years before Fate had dealt me one blow, wrecking my career and making me an outcast on account of what was no more than an excess of zeal to serve my country and youthful lack of judgment. Now Fate had hit me again by robbing me of the one woman for whom I had ever really cared. It was just over a year since I had met Daphnis, and during all that time there had not been a day or a night that I had not thought of her with love and longing, and in these latter months with pride and joy and thanksgiving. When we had at last become engaged I had considered the old business more than made good by the gods, and myself the most fortunate fellow in the whole world. Now it was all dust and ashes. I had nothing—nothing—nothing left to live for.

I must have sat there for about half an hour slowly but logically making up my mind. I no longer wanted vengeance on von Hentzen, and the death of a million Germans could not compensate me for what I had lost. I knew that now. There was only one thing that I wanted. That was to be done with it all—to get out.

I took out my pistol and looked at it. There were still four bullets in the magazine. I clicked one up into the chamber and raised the gun until it pointed at my right temple.

Suddenly something came at me through the half-open door like a whirlwind, dashing the pistol from my hand. It was the hunchback boy. He must have been crouching there watching me. He now stood beside me, panting slightly and gripping my arm with all his strength.

"What the hell!" I exclaimed, coming to my feet.

He twisted his little puckered face up towards me as he cried: "You can't do that! You can't do that, master! You're an Englishman—you told me so. You must go on fighting the Germans—killing them and killing them and killing them, until you drive them out of Greece."

I shook my head. "I'm sorry, Tino, but I don't suppose you know. It hasn't been altogether our fault, and we've done our best—but we British aren't quite as strong as your statesmen told you we were; so it's the Germans who've driven us out of Greece. We killed a lot of the enemy, but they killed a lot of our men, and for the last few nights the rest have been leaving Greece in the ships sent to fetch them."

277

For a moment he stared up at me quite stupefied; then he said, "But you haven't given in, have you?"

"No," I said. "We haven't given in and we never shall give in. We'll beat the Germans one day, but maybe not for quite a long time yet."

"Then you can't kill yourself," he argued. "If the fighting's still going on it doesn't matter where it is. It's a pity that your soldiers have had to leave Greece, but that's all the more reason you should go and help them, because they must need every man they can get."

"There's something in that," I agreed doubtfully. "But getting here took me much longer than I expected, so I should think that nearly all our men who could manage to get away have gone by now. Before I could get back to the coast they certainly will have, and I'd probably find it impossible to get off. I've got nothing to live for now in any case; and I'd rather be dead than a prisoner of the Germans."

"You got here through the Germans, so why can't you get back again?" he demanded. "If you could get us to Keramidi in your car I could find you a boat to take you off."

"Could you?" I said in surprise.

"Yes. My father was a fisherman until he married a farmer's daughter; but he used to take me to Keramidi to see Grandpa once a year, and I've often been sailing with the fishermen in their boats."

"Where is Keramidi?" I asked.

"Do you know Volo?"

"Yes," I said.

"Well, it's near the coast, about twenty-five kilos north of Volo."

All this time he had been staring at me with those strange compelling lustrous eyes, and there is no doubt about it that they did something to me. Of course he was right—right every time —about its being my duty to get back somehow, if I possibly could, and fight on until Britain had broken the Nazis. It was too early for me to see my private grief in due proportion to the agony that was afflicting the world; but I did realize now that it would have been a frightful act of cowardice to take my own life. How I don't quite know, but I raised a smile for this extraordinary little fellow who seemed to have powers out of all proportion to his size, his age and his poor twisted little body.

"All right, Tino," I said. "Let's go to Keramidi."

It wasn't far off dawn when, having provisioned the car from

278

a secret store that Tino had accumulated during the past week, we set off. We drove east through the mountains by such side-roads as I could find on my map for most of the Sunday until the late afternoon, when I pulled up in a quiet spot and roused Tino, who had been asleep. I told him that it was my turn to sleep now, and, giving him my watch, asked him to wake me again at midnight. Then I settled down to get a little badly-needed rest.

At midnight we had a snack, then drove on and got ourselves hopelessly lost. I no longer had any fear of the Germans from having found that, whenever we were stopped, von Hentzen's pass always aroused in them immediate respect. The next lot we happened on went to quite a lot of trouble to put us right.

At about three o'clock on the Monday morning we reached Keramidi; but only to find the village a burnt-out wreck. The little harbour, too, which lay a mile or so below it on the coast, was a blasted ruin, from the waters of which the masts of a dozen fishing smacks protruded where they had been sunk. Poor Tino wept a bit to think that his grandfather and most of his friends among the fishermen must be dead. It was my turn to try to forget my own agony in order to comfort him.

After a little I decided to take the coast road to the south on the chance that we might sight a vessel, as many of our men who had been driven through the low country to the east of Mount Olympus along the seashore must have been taken off in that neighbourhood.

Driving slowly along the ribbon of road I kept a sharp lookout, and about half an hour later, on rounding a headland into a low bay, I saw a light flashing out to sea. We drove on until we were opposite to it, then abandoned the car and walked down to the beach. The signalling had stopped, but I could just make out the dark hulk of a small ship about half a mile out. As we reached the water's edge I caught the sound of voices and saw that some men, who had just waded out, were being hauled into a boat.

I gave them a hail, not too loud but loud enough for them to hear, and an English voice called back:

"Who are you?"

"A British officer," I cried.

"Right-oh, come along!" called back the voice. "The Navy's here!"

I took out my wallet, which still contained most of the big sum that Diamopholus had given me. Stuffing it into Tino's pocket, I said:

"Take care of that, Tino. It's enough to buy you a little

cottage and a garden when things settle down. You've been a good friend and I wish you all the luck in the world."

He didn't reply for a moment, then he gulped out: "Thank you, master. Good luck." And we solemnly shook hands before I waded out into the water.

I had gone perhaps fifty yards and was up to my waist before a new thought struck me, and turning I raced back. The men in the boat were now shouting at me to make haste, but I took no notice of them. Tino was still standing where I had left him.

"Look here," I said, "what happened to your father and mother?"

"They're both—both dead," he said in a whisper.

"What's to become of you, then?" I asked.

He shook his head and twisted it again to look up at me. "I don't know, master. The Germans will rule us now, won't they, until the British bring us back our freedom? They taught us in school that the Nazis hate cripples, so things may be—may be difficult for anyone like me."

Something stirred in me then. He was a grand little man—this hunchback. Fate had been savagely cruel to both of us. It had striken him at birth and worse than it had me. Perhaps I could help to make that up to him by giving him a good education, a chance in life to make the best use of his quick brain and the affection that every child must crave.

"Come on, old chap," I said. "You're coming with me." And picking him up in my arms, I waded back into the water. In Greece I had lost something that could never be replaced. My heart had died with Daphnis; but I was not leaving Greece empty-handed. I was carrying out of it a spirit that was brave and kind and free.

*This book
designed by William B. Taylor
is a production of
Heron Books, London*

*Printed in England by
Hazell Watson and Viney Limited
Aylesbury, Bucks*